Mishpocha
Marcia Zuckermann
Translated by Michelle Standley

Originally published under the title, *Mischpoke*
by Frankfurter Verlagsanstalt, in Germany in 2016.

Published in the United States in 2024 by

Clevo Books
1026 Euclid Avenue
Cleveland, Oh 44115
www.clevobooks.com

Library of Congress Control Number: 2024947794

ISBN: 978-1-68577-017-4
Paperback: 978-1-68577-018-1
E-book ISBN: 978-1-68577-019-8

Printed in the USA

Cover design and interior layout: Ron Kretsch

First American Edition

MIS
HPO
CHA!

THE CHARGES AGAINST ME

IN THE AMBULANCE FROM THE BERLIN TEGEL AIRPORT TO the mental hospital, I was diagnosed with “acute syncope with partial amnesia.” Truth is, I can’t remember anything since the port of Istanbul. Lights out, sound off, a long, blank nothing. Blackout.

I didn’t wake up until I was already in a hospital room in Spandau. Apparently, no one knew where to go with me. Nurses built like prize fighters rolled me from one place to the next.

“I can walk,” I offered timidly, “Why are you taking me all over the place?”

“For technical reasons related to legal and insurance-related matters,” explained the bald head with menacing eyes, hovering at the foot of my bed.

Afraid, I clutched my bag even closer against myself. Not that there was any point. I could tell that it had been searched, probably more than once. Someone had even cut open the lining! First, they took me for some senile, old woman and then for a criminal. The Federal Republic of Germany accused me of suspicion of violating The Resident Act, Section 96, Paragraph 1, “assisting with smuggling,” and pursuant to Paragraph 2, suspicion of “the commercial smuggling of foreigners.” That’s exactly how it’s stated in the official charges.

In accordance with Paragraph 1, they threatened me with three months to five years. In accordance with Paragraph 2, they threatened me with twice that: from six months to ten years! Now I’ve ended up in the psych ward. The police officer stationed outside my door has disappeared.

Is this a prison cell or a hospital room? Don't think about Kafka! Maybe it's good that I can't remember anything?! Something must have gone terribly wrong. But what?

There's a fly caught between the panes in the double window of my hospital room; it's pushing up against the glass. For two hours now, I've been sitting here listening to it, annoyed.

Like the idiotic fly shoving with all its might against the outside pane, I take aim at Dr. Vogelsang who is trying figure out what led to my memory loss. On the edge of losing my patience, I finally snarl, "Maybe my whole life has been one long post-traumatic stress disorder?!"

Dr. Vogelsang's left eyebrow shoots upward, forming a black gothic arch. Her lips follow suit, making a sour pucker.

"You are no doubt aware of the seriousness of the situation? Is there perhaps something you would like to share with me?" I notice Vogelsang's eyes. In the dark recesses beneath the gothic arches reside two mouse eyes. Pupils only. Dim in vision, but sharp in reproof, the mouse eyes glare at me.

What I said wasn't all that rude, was it? I mutter to myself, fidgeting nervously at the thought. I bet she's interpreting my body language as impulsive or defensive. But what do I care?!

Dr. Vogelsang scribbles furiously in her notes. Then like an analyst with a job to do, she begins to study me. From the way she's looking me over I can tell that she thinks if a patient makes light of her and her serious work, they must be either idiots or neurotics. She's not yet sure to which category I belong. Neither am I.

Maybe it's not an either/or question?

She's writing madly on an old, blue clipboard with a scratched-up backside. I strain my neck to see. From upside down, I can make out the word "manic"; at least it has a question mark after it. It jumps out at me. The rage with which she's been attacking the paper has loosened a strand from her carefully pinned-up hair. What was once an elegant coiffure is starting to look like a complete hairdo disaster.

At what point does cheerful cross over into manic? I wonder.

The freewheeling lock of hair has curled itself into a "six" across her forehead. It strikes a humorously dissonant chord against her fatigued expression. It's distracting.

Where have I seen just such an image before? Garbo in Camille! Were this a game show, I'd have just earned 100 points!

Laughter is building up in my belly, rolling around like glass marbles. Dr. Vogelsang has about as much in common with Garbo as a cow with a nightingale. Everything about her is slightly askew. When she speaks, her mouth pulls a bit to the left, as if she were trying to emphasize what she was saying. Or is that a facial tic?

A dozen jokes about psychiatrists come to mind. I resist them all.

It's not only Dr. Vogelsang's mouth that skews left, but the tip of her nose does too. Her left eye is smaller than her right. And now this errant strand of hair! I can't stop staring at this dark blond, hairy "six."

To avoid embarrassing myself, I look out the barred window. Crows are again gathering on the edge of the roof. It's curious how they always perch next to the forensics department. Over two hundred birds ready and waiting. They stay busy preening their black-and-gray feathers. The way they constantly bob their heads from left to right while on the lookout, makes them appear like hired lookouts with poor eyesight, wearing glasses that keep slipping from their nose as they anxiously keep watch. "Hitchcock!" whispers my other self.

The sky above the forensics department, where the birds have assembled, reminds me of very dirty bedsheets. The very thought of dirty laundry sets off my cleaning compulsion. Clorox, cleanser, and elbow grease are not what's needed right now, I chide my compulsion. I need to concentrate on my conversation with Vogelsang. Any fantasies I may want to entertain about spotlessly clean skies are forbidden because I have to admit: I am in serious trouble.

Half curious, half annoyed, Dr. Vogelsang regards me and leans forward, as if expecting something. I surely have something to say, she says. Instead of saying something, though, I grin and turn toward the barred windows. I look at the birds and think of the word bread the way that actors do when they're supposed to look worried or serious.

It works.

I'm not really interested in the "before" part of my life that Dr. Vogelsang is trying to help me recover, which I realize is rather odd under the circumstances.

Dr. Vogelsang shrugs her shoulders and suppresses a sigh.

She masks her exasperation behind a façade of professionalism. "All right, why don't you tell me what you do remember." As she says this the left side of her mouth again takes on a curious life of its own. She steals a glance at her watch. Some secret pact dictates that all therapists engage in the ritual of removing their watch at the beginning of a session and setting it in front of them with a bit of flourish. Since there's no table here, Dr. Vogelsang resorts to clamping her watch to her clipboard, subtly demonstrating that her time is both measurable and valuable: I am not supposed to waste it.

"I suggest that we start making our way toward the traumatic event with as few jokes as possible," she begins slowly. "As we get closer to the point where you can no longer remember everything, I will try to help you protect yourself by telling you once again: you have nothing to fear!"

Nothing to fear?! The words reverberate, as if mocking me; my skull's starting to feel like its stuffed with cotton candy.

Dr. Vogelsang takes a deep breath.

"Do you want to explain your statement 'my whole life has been one long post-traumatic stress disorder'? Or should we start with your observation from yesterday that 'when we fall, we fall hard!'? Who do you mean by we and who exactly is doing the falling?"

It's too sensitive for me to go over the details of my "post-traumatic" life. That would involve talking about the fact that I narrowly escaped death at birth. Umbilical cord prolapse. The umbilical cord had wrapped itself around my neck seven times. Strangled in the womb. That was winter 1947, in a poorly insulated shack in the north of Berlin. And no doctor within miles. Without a caesarean section it was either my mother or me. The life of the mother comes first. Only Catholics have it the other way around. It has something to do with the innocence of the unborn child, my mother later told me. With the help of some home-distilled schnapps—from a brown medicine-bottle labeled "96 percent medicinal alcohol"—the midwife had plucked up her courage to aid my exit from the womb. Then, giving me one last chance, she pronounced: "it's now or never!" I owe my life to the skilled hands of this woman who finally succeeded in pulling over my head the umbilical cord that had tightened around my neck, not once, but seven times. To think, I don't even know her name! With a blue, deformed head I barely escaped from "the jaws of death," as my mother liked to boast. What she didn't mention is the fact that at the time they all assumed that I would be no better than an idiot the rest of my life. To this epic tale of my dramatic birth, I always like to add, "the world welcomed my arrival with the stench of alcohol."

Despising death, we laugh at it. As a matter of principle! We refuse to believe the tears. That's why we find drama and suffering cause for laughter. It's only fitting then that the drama of my birth was succeeded by the chaos of my paternal lineage. I had two fathers, and three surnames in quick succession, and three certificates of birth. My first surname belonged to my mother's first husband who had died in the war; my second was my mother's maiden name; lastly, somewhat later, I took the surname of my real father, who on the day I was born was also battling to escape the "jaws of death," lying in an intensive care unit in Potsdam. A motorcycle accident involving black ice on the autobahn. My father had already escaped death more than once. So have I. My birth was my first victory over death.

I didn't tell Vogelsang any of that. I don't trust her. She's not a real therapist. She works for the public prosecutor. Maybe she's even an appointed "expert"? If you're lying in a locked-down psych ward, aren't you already halfway to prison, in a sort of medical custody? I decided not to reveal anything about myself.

Nothing at all!

In my family we've mastered the art of silence.

It's best to start with something innocuous: with eloquent silence or with a banal account of the events that led up to now.

KADDISH FOR A CROWN PRINCE

The decline of the Kohanims began sometime around noon on March 10, 1902. Not that anyone would have suspected such a thing. No soft click; no hairline crack; no icy breeze; no dramatic silence; no flock of ravens taking flight; no clock stopped at noon exactly; no black cat crossing from left to right; no picture falling from a wall; no scattered broken glass; no curse muttered aloud; and no symbolic black line like in Thomas Mann's Buddenbrooks. No, nothing at all to inspire a premonition of what was to come. The sky itself, beyond a feeble sun struggling to make the icicles weep, portended nothing but more of the same.

For as far as anyone could tell, March 10th was shaping up to be a typical unhappy day in the family, as inevitable as it was common among the better-off Jewish families in rural West Prussia[1] in the mid-19th century. Like most such families, they reacted with appropriate calm to ordinary sources of unhappiness, of which in their small town of Sauermühle, not far from the county seat of Schwetz in Brandenburg, were not in short supply. The only thing unusual about this, otherwise ordinary, unhappy day was the sound of a Yiddish lullaby.

Amol iz geven a mayse,
Di mayse iz gornit freylekh,
Di mayse heybt zikh onet
Mit a yidishn meylekh.

Once upon a time, there was a tale.
The tale is not a happy one.
The tale began
With a Jewish king.

Lyulinke mayn feygele!
Lyulinke mayn kind!
Kh'hob ongevoyrn aza libe,
Vey iz mir un vind!

Hush, my little bird!
Hush, my child!
I have lost such a love,
Oh, woe is me!

Der meylekh hot gehat a malke
Di malke hot gehat a vayngortn
Im vayngorten hot gehat a boym
Wey iz mir un vint!

The king had a queen,
The queen had a vineyard,
In the vineyard was a tree.
Oh, woe is me!

Der boym hot gehat a tsvayg
Der tsvayg hot gehat a nestele
In nestele iz gevén a feygele
Wey iz mir un vint!

On the tree was a branch,
On the branch was a little nest,
In the nest was a little bird.
Oh, woe is me!

Der meylekh iz opgestorben
Di malke iz gevorn fardorben
Der tsvayg iz opgebrochen
Di fegele vun nest antlofen.

The king died,
The queen pined away,
The branch broke,
The bird flew from the nest.

Vu nemt men aza chochem
Er zol kennen de shtern zeylen
Vu nemt men aza dokter
Er zol kennen mayn horts heylen?

Where can we find a learned man
Who can count the stars?
Where can we find a doctor
Who can heal my heart?

Lyulinke mayn feygele!
Lyulinke mayn kind!
Kh'hob ongevoyrn aza libe,
Vey iz mir un vind!

Hush, my little bird!
Hush, my child!
I have lost such a love,
Oh, woe is me!

To non-Jewish ears, this sounded rather strange for a lullaby. A mother sings to her children about a queen who lost her king. The branch from the queen's tree breaks. The bird who had nested there flies away. Death, loss, and mourning.

Is that really how Jewish families wanted to lull their children to sleep? What so disturbed Christian ears as rather morose, sounded quite normal to Jewish ones, however. Accustomed to misfortune, in the not-so-distant past Jewish people were not so squeamish; they were pragmatic. If their singing and prayers could not prevent tragedy, then they wanted to at least prepare their children for a life of hardship, beginning in the cradle. The earlier, the better! Even if you were well off, or maybe precisely because you were. A reminder that fortunes could always change and that everyone always had to be ready to start from scratch to conquer life's twists and turns.

But the Kohanim family had lived free from such material worries for some time; wealthy for generations, they were almost messianically obsessed with the belief in progress. In the community and district of Schwetz, my great-grandfather, Samuel Kohanim, was regarded as a liberal maverick. He was a modernizer. He always wanted to be the first to introduce the latest machines and methods. He was passionate about overthrowing everything that he deemed traditional, backward, and outdated. My great-grandmother called this the "Kohanim streak." My great-grandfather regularly studied a dozen technical and scientific journals. He was also the only liberal republican and free spirit among all the monarchists and subjects loyal to the emperor. This meant that within the family all medieval Jewish traditions were rigorously despised. The Kohanims found Yiddish so embarrassing that they even pretended not to understand it. Whenever they heard anyone so much as utter a word, they reacted with furrowed brows and made a show of how they could not possibly understand. This Yiddish song was therefore unheard of in the Kohanim house in two senses. Mindel Kohanim, my great-grandmother, was no less stubborn than my great-grandfather Samuel. She only half-heartedly disapproved of Jewish traditions and on March 10th she indulged a relapse "into the era before the flood." Just this once, in light of the circumstances.

Wasn't Mindel just as unhappy a mother as the mouse mother in the ancient Yiddish lullaby? Her seven daughters, my six great-aunts, and my then-young grandmother had no desire to hear such a gloomy song and quickly grew tired of its many verses, none of which they understood, apart from “wey, wey, wey,” which was close enough to the German weh, meaning “woe,” that it didn’t have to be translated. They impatiently waited for a transition to more familiar tunes, songs that talked about little stars and sheep, the sort of which were always illustrated with cute pictures in their schoolbooks. Fat, naked cherubs fluttering around, with eyes rolled upward, all of them looking rather idiotic and incapable of flight.

Even “Frére Jacques” would have been okay for my young grandmother and her teenage sisters. The seven sisters all agreed on one thing: their little brother lying in the cradle would have much preferred songs about little stars to ones about breaking branches and birds abandoning their nests.

On top of the usual jealously, bickering, and complaining between the sisters, was also boredom. Lots of boredom.

The melancholy strains failed to penetrate the hearts of these modern, Jewish girls. With no place to go, the one or two-stroke As, Ds, and Bs lingered helplessly in mid-air in the overheated parlor. Only the fringes on the lamp responded, letting loose a shiver as the song came to an end. Laden with gloom, the notes slowly sank to the floor, and like the singer’s tears, they disappeared beneath the floorboards.

The detested lullaby was meant for Mindel’s youngest, the only one of my great uncles still alive. Yet, little Benjamin was the only one who couldn’t hear it. He lay buried deep in his white, tomb-like pillow, over which lace stretched like cobwebs across a rooftop, engaged in a battle between life and death. When he heaved a sigh of relief, life had just won a round. If he gasped or took raspy breaths, then death appeared to be turning the match around. The duel went on for three days and nights.

Little Benjamin was supposed to inherit the throne, to be the family’s crown prince. But after just twenty months of life, the prince was threatening to abdicate even before assuming the throne. Just as the five crown princes before him had.

Nothing worked. No lullaby, no doctor, no miracle-making rabbi from Sadagora, whom my mother had secretly brought into the house in exchange for her pearls. The ones she wore on holidays were now fake. Her tears, however, were undeniably real.

Meanwhile the cradle carved from walnut swayed like a boat on the high seas. A colossal green coal-burning stove, so tall that it nearly grazed the ceiling, loomed dangerously above. The behemoth had been shored up with green tiles, like a fortress with ramparts, to protect the home from the Siberian cold. The cradle made a curious grinding sound as it rocked against the scrubbed-white floorboards. Accompanied by the ponderous ticking of the grandfather clock, the ticking and the rocking combined to form a duet of transience, provided you were attuned to the metaphysical. The seven sisters, however, lacked such sensitivities.

Elli was thinking about how she had missed the last ice-skating of the season. Flora was silently reciting all twenty-three verses of Schiller's "The Cranes of Ibykus." Martha was pondering whether the lovers in the novel she was reading would ultimately unite. Fanny was thinking about the housework that had been left undone. Jenny was hungry and fretting over the late lunch, which by now was smoldering in the oven. Franziska was wondering who she could put in charge of the hated task of splicing the goose feathers. Selma, my great-aunt with a religious streak, was reciting prayers and rituals prescribed for infant deaths. Not long before, Selma had taken a sudden interest in the ritualistic subtleties of the various branches of the Jewish faith.

Wrapped in thought, the seven Kohanim daughters stood frozen stiff with boredom in the overheated bedroom. Fighting the urge to yawn, they longed to be able to sleep standing up, like the liveried servants in the count's castle who knew how to do it without falling over.

The boudoir, as my great-grandparents referred to the bedroom, was full of massive, dark furniture, besieged by carpets that had been worn to exhaustion. Fearing a deadly draught, my great-grandmother had had a servant nail up the narrow double window. The roofing nails stuck out from the white window frame: long, rusty, wild, and almost accusatory. Only the glowing red door of the green-tiled mountain offered a modicum of comfort. Now and again the seven sisters let their eyes wander to watch the fringes of the lampshade as they waltzed in place. Then they would turn back to the cradle, staring as intently as if there were an insect lying there. "He won't last much longer!"

"The human-thing," as the girls called the dwarfish, yellow old man in the cradle, had been the center of the family's life for far too long, they thought.

For nearly two years, they, the Kohanim princesses, had been as invisible as air as far as their parents were concerned. To add insult to injury, they were supposed to be especially loving to their little brother. Loving toward a creature who had up and usurped the throne overnight? For such impertinence, they truly wished him the worst from the bottom of their hearts. They took it as a sign from God that his demise was actually taking place before their very eyes. In gratitude for their answered prayers, they vowed piety until the end of their days.

Stout Elli, the third child, and Franziska, peered into the cradle, examining the situation. Enough is enough, they thought. Sometimes you just have to give fate a helping hand!

"Corrigez la fortune!" was the line they liked best in Lessing's play, Minna von Barnhelm. They winked mischievously at each other and crossed the index fingers of their right and left hands behind their backs, smiling gently like angels. Little Benjamin, lying in the cradle, turned blue.

"Mama!" Martha shrieked, "Elli and Fränze made the sign of the cross! I saw it very clearly!" The cross! The heretic sign! The sign of death!

"That's not true! She's lying through her teeth!" Franziska barked back. "Like she always does!" Elli replied grumpily.

Mindel wasn't paying attention to the girls, however, she was staring tearfully into the cradle. Elli seized her chance. Quick as a cat, she grabbed Martha's red mop of hair, and then elbowed her in the stomach. Franziska joined the fracas, kicking Martha in the shin. "You ugly little witch! There you go, you tattletale!"

Martha wailed like a ship's siren.

Heretical signs and brawling would normally have resulted in at least a day of house arrest with dry bread and pork potatoes. One day for each offense. But on a day like this one, nothing was normal. So instead of meting out the usual punishment, my great-grandmother, weary from the bickering, resorted to merely proscribing feeble "God protect us" prayers for everyone.

Selma, the second eldest, who surpassed all her sisters in Jewish piety—not that any of them were even interested in competing for such an honor—spat on the floor suggestively. Such a thing was usually only done by Hasidic Jews when talking about apostates, heretics, goys, impurity, or sin. Hypocritically, Selma then tilted her head. To the left. She had picked up this gesture from Catholic votive images and figures of saints in Catholic churches. "What a bigot!" hissed Flora.

The other sisters rolled their eyes. Enduring Selma's piety was trial enough, and now they were subject to Flora's latest fancy new word bigot. Flora was the youngest and for some time had been annoying everyone with her foreign words and pretentious manner of speech. She was constantly poring over her father's volumes of the encyclopedia in search of unusual words, which she then speared and displayed like a collector of rare butterflies.

They had inherited none of the tastes and traits of their eleven deceased siblings, except for one thing. According to legend, the one characteristic that the eighteen children born to my great-grandmother Mindel shared was that none of them were born with flat feet. Mindel was very proud of this. Whether babies could actually have flat feet or not has been the subject of debate ever since. The five girls who had died, were not counted in the family's flatfoot statistics.

Benjamin, the eighth and youngest, was the only surviving male child. And since no female heir could carry the family name, Benjamin was responsible for continuing the great line of the Kohanims in West Prussia. But he was now wasting away, heading towards a premature end to his young life.

A mother who had buried eleven of her children, including every single boy, had grown accustomed to mourning. Back then it was simply a matter of course for half of the children to die. But the death of all of the boys left my great-grandmother no peace. What possible divine explanations might there have been to explain why the male seed in the Kohanim line no longer flourished? What was the reason? Who was to blame?

My great-grandfather, Samuel, sought out scriptures and the rabbi for answers: "Had the Almighty decreed it, for reasons we cannot yet comprehend? Well, what were they?!" Mindel Kohanim searched her family's line for anything like it. But she found nothing. "There has never been anything like this in our family!" she exclaimed. There was no doubt about it, the Kohanims, whose line she had joined by marriage, were to blame. The explanation was as plain as day: the tribe was simply too old. After a good four to five thousand years, this branch of the Kohanim or Cohn priesthood was no longer strong enough to give birth to strong sons. "That's the way it is! You only have to look at nature!"

Mindel was thinking of the ancient cherry tree in the courtyard. It was old, its broad canopy spread across the slate roof of the stocky manor house. Every May, thousands and thousands of tiny white blossoms fell like snow onto the brown cobblestones. Beautiful but barren: it didn't produce a single piece of fruit.

Mindel Kohanim, daughter of Juda Beinesch, from the Russian-Polish town of Inowrazlaw, drew her own conclusions from this. Apart from the usual arbitrary nature of the divine order, she identified the source of their misfortunes as the sustained inbreeding of Aaron's sons. As every Jew knew, the Kohans, Kohns, or Kohanims were the Jews' priestly lineage, all direct descendants of Moses' brother, Aaron. Aaron was to blame; he had neglected his duty as a guardian of the faith, proposing the golden calf, and thereby causing mankind's subsequent fall from grace. They say it was Aaron's pagan wife or concubine who had put him up to it. She wanted to use the golden calf to reestablish the Baal cult with its sacred bull. As punishment for his sacrilegious neglect of duty, Moses forbade Aaron and his descendants from marrying a converted woman from another nation or a divorced or widowed Jewess.

It was for that reason that the Cohns or Kohanims in West Prussia and Poland had never had a sizeable selection of suitable brides. If the matchmaker was unable to find a suitable bride from far away, then they married their sons to someone close at hand: a young girl in the family. The fabled "cousin." This was the easiest thing to do. But Mindel was not such a bride.

What did it matter, though? "Moses' curse on Aaron's line or God's plan, nature doesn't read the Torah. It rules according to its own laws!" Mindel Kohanim decided to keep this insight to herself. She didn't expect others to understand what she could; she was after all a well-educated Jew from the Grand Duchy of Warsaw, descended from the famous Katzenellenbogen[2] family. On her mother's side, she was even a true descendant of the legendary Jewish "king for a day": August 15, 1587. Saul Wahl Katzenellenbogen, the famous tax collector, had ascended to the throne of the Kingdom of Poland, as part of the machinations of the Polish electors who were desperate for the nobility to quit dithering and make up their minds about who they wanted as king. The trick worked. Saul Wahl was thus removed from office as swiftly as he had assumed it, within a few hours. A Jew like Mindel, with such a legendary, semi-aristocratic background, knew when to speak and, above all, when to hold her tongue. Brusque and taciturn by nature, Mindel appeared to be wrapped in a cocoon of brooding. She nurtured a boundless contempt for the world. Put another way: Mindel Kohanim, née Beinesch, the descendant of the Polish "king for a day" was terribly cranky, absent-minded, and good, if in a sinister sort of way. To ensure that she was left in peace, she showed everyone an arrogant, hard, and forbidding face. With few exceptions, she ruled over the house and estate with a perpetually cold, stone-gray gaze and a seemingly inexhaustible repertoire of silent questions, complaints, condemnations, and curses. When she wasn't kvetching, she refused to even open her mouth, and not just during the new moon when all devout

Jewish women were silent. She often chose not to speak for a whole fortnight. Not to anyone.

Inside the Kohanim home, life and death continued their battle. Outside the contest between winter and spring was no less fierce. On the other side of the boarded-up window was the Tucheler Heide, as flat and lifeless as an ironing board. In the parts where the sun had melted away the wintry mantle of snow, the heath lay exposed and dirty like a naked body wrapped in rotting rags. The forests belonging to the Bishop of Kujawy and those to Count Solkowsky, filled by leprously pale and shimmering birch trunks, were an otherwise black and barren void, stretching all the way to the horizon. A land as wide as the sea, covered by a sky as massive as the ocean. The desolate expanse reminded its inhabitants of their nothingness, spreading paralyzing despondency. The sun could be shining brightly and the blackbirds chirping, and even the most cheerful soul would succumb to melancholy. The only known elixir was a glass of something high proof. Especially in March.

With a chirrup, the last spark of life abandoned my great-uncle that afternoon. Mindel wiped her eyes. She felt ancient and dead tired. With a hunched over back and a groan, she draped all the mirrors with black cloth, and shuffled through the house in her well-worn camel hair slippers, closing all the shutters and pulling the curtains shut. In accordance with Jewish tradition, she ripped the girls' skirt hems and collars on the right, and hers, as mother, on the left. She then tousled their hair and her own, and lit candles to the right and left of the cradle for the duration of the shiva, the Jewish mourning ceremony. Last, but not least, she solemnly stopped the pendulum in the grandfather clock. For a few days, time was to stand still, or almost.

For the first time, something resembling an emotion stirred among the seven sisters as well. They found the whole gloomy scene unsettling: the dull glow of the candles next to the black-draped cradle. At any moment, they thought, the unhappy soul of their brother might appear as a ghost. "If he has even an ounce of character…" they whispered.

Much to their disappointment, not once did he pop out to frighten them. "What a schmuck!" they agreed.

For a child under two years old, one day and one night should have sufficed, as opposed to the seven days and nights of mourning for adults. Such rules had been decided by Jews in the region long before. After all, children dropped like flies every day. Not to mention that Jewish children died more frequently than Christian ones, owing to the bad water in their wells. What good would it do to waste a whole week for every little worm that passed away and allowing the living to go hungry for the sake of the dead?

The seven remaining sisters did as they were told, uttering their prayers with droning voices. Flora was the only one who acted as if she was truly mourning from the depths of her soul. She sobbed theatrically and tore at her hair and clothes.

"Oh, come off it! What a phony!" they said.

Wrapped in dark woolen shawls, the women who were part of the funeral party, crouched like a flock of frozen crows. Sitting on tree stumps, they rode on the last wooden cart, taking the bumpy path across the Schwarzwasser River to the Kohanim estate.

In the bluish light of the setting winter afternoon, they could have been mistaken for a battalion of witches, riding not on witches' brooms but on thick pine and spruce trunks. Having beaten the cold out of their blackish shawls, rags, and clammy limbs, the mourning witches fluttered busily through the house, spreading a smell of old armpit sweat and spruce resin. Four professional mourners from "the sect," Hasids, were also present, either by mistake, or because of the new customs of the new majority among the Jews in Schwetz. Or they may have simply showed up from out of nowhere to mooch. Apparently, apart from Yiddish, they only understood Persian.

When they first entered the house of mourning, they were intimidated by its rich, bourgeois splendor. Both timid and curious, they paused and eyed the interior. But then they quickly recovered their wits and with a zeal worthy of professionals, set to work in the mourning room. Their faces smeared with ashes and hair disheveled, they thus began their wild wailing, throwing their arms into the air, tousling their hair, beating their chests plaintively, and tearing at their clothes. The Kohanims' Kashubian servants crossed themselves repeatedly.

With superstitious shudders and hands folded in silent prayer, they watched as the women of the burial party, the chevra kadisha, washed the child's skinny yellow body with kosher water. It resembled a naked yellow baby chick that had fallen out of the nest. After the washing, the women of the burial society wrapped the child in a small, white linen cloth. They placed a bag of earth from the Mount of Olives in Jerusalem between the little body's hands.

If the Messiah were to come one day and call out his name, little Benjamin would not miss his resurrection.

Up to then, the seven girls had only vaguely heard of wailing women and usually only with a shudder. Unlike the children of the other families, who were permitted to wander around, the daughters of the most progressive Jew in the district were under strict orders to stay in the shtetl. Under penalty of punishment, they were not to show their faces in the Litvak or Hasidic part of Schwetz. The Jewish quarter was located directly below the banks of the Vistula and was flooded every spring. For days, if you wanted to visit each other or reach the market, you could only drift from house to house on barges. Rabbi Menachem Streisand, Samuel Kohanim's "born enemy," ruled there. If that weren't bad enough, the Jewish quarter was also the realm of rats, fleas, lice, bedbugs, and scabies. Even cholera and dysentery were common now and again. Not to mention the indigenous smallpox, typhus, diphtheria, polio, and the epidemic consumption that was spreading like wildfire. "Unless it's for charity, this is no place for us to visit!" warned my great-grandmother. "For reasons of hygiene alone!"

To make her point, she frequently reminded them of the last cholera epidemic, which had started in the shtetl of Schwetz. The danger was all too real. When the floodwaters receded every spring, the water in the kosher wells used by the Jews who had recently moved from Russia and Galicia became contaminated. The result was the Hasids suffered from ulcers and boils. The addition of pus-filled boils on their heads and limbs to their peculiar clothing and hairstyles, gave them a frightful and pitiful appearance.

The Jews who had already lived in the region for a long time, "the necktie Jews" who spoke German, shaved, and smelled of eau de cologne, wanted nothing to do with the dark and grimy, Yiddish-speaking, kaftan Jews from the banks of the Vistula, who stank of garlic, dirt, and poverty. They shunned them like lepers. The aversion was mutual. The highly educated Litvaks who considered themselves to be the only true Orthodox, and the more, spiritually ecstatic Hasids, regarded the assimilated German-speaking brothers in faith as apostate Jews who were even more contemptible than the pure goyim.

My grandmother and her six sisters were excited by the exotic spectacle. At last, something to spice up their otherwise dull day! At last, they could see these strange creatures up close. With bated breath and open mouths, they watched the wailing women perform as if they were watching acrobats in the circus. One of the wailing women, whose wailing was even more bizarre than the others, aroused particular interest. Under the woman's headscarf, they could see long blonde braids! There were plenty of redheads among the Hasids from the Near East, but blondes? The girls' eyes widened.

The way the woman with the blond braids moved was too youthful for a middle-aged woman. The sisters winked at each other. A minor scandal was brewing.

"Hey, that's Oda!" whispered Fanny to her younger sister Martha.

"Nebbich! Martha snapped back defensively, because Oda was Martha's best friend.

"It really is!" Fanny insisted. "Look carefully. That's none other than your darling Oda."

Now the other sisters recognized her too. They all burst out laughing. All of a sudden, the suspicious-looking wailing woman stopped her theatrical gesticulations. Her wailing began to tremble strangely, ending in a chuckle. She took off running. The other wailing women and members of the burial society gawked at her in amazement. The seven Kohanim sisters took off after her, laughing as their wooden clogs skidded and slipped across the glassy snow.

Outside, near the icy blackberry bushes behind the bard, the fleeing wailing woman snatched off her headscarf triumphantly.

"Well, I got ya, didn't I?"

Oda!

"That was epic!" bawled Elli, punching Oda appreciatively in the arm. "This young woman's got some spirit! Look what we've got here!"

The girls doubled over in laughter. The worldwide ban on laughter during mourning be damned. What glorious, blasphemous fun! Each girl took a turn imitating the exalted gestures of the wailing woman. It struck them as odd that Protestant Oda's Yiddish was better than all the rest of theirs. Howling with laughter, they pointed in Oda's direction and convulsed with laughter. Tears streamed down their faces until Martha wet her underwear, which she announced, giving them a new reason for whooping laughter. Then suddenly, as if shot out of the ground, a grim-looking ghost stood in front of them in the snowy slush: Father!

Franziska was the first to get herself under control. With eyes reddened from laughing and holding her side because of the stitches in it, she curtseyed and declared as innocently as possible, "Pardon, Papa! But these wailing women! We simply couldn't take it anymore. And instead of…" A fit of laughter shook her once again. "…instead of laughhhh… instead of laaaaughhhhing in front of the dead body…" Like water from a fountain, tears of laughter sprang from her eyes and her face flushed a deep red as a fresh cramp from laughter practically forced her to her knees.

Without so much as uttering a single word, he ordered his wayward daughters to return to the house. To get the point across, he needed to merely show them his tight-lipped, angry expression and point his finger toward the house, his arm held imperiously aloft. The girls responded in kind, scampering off like a flock of geese being chased by a fox. Fränze was the last to stagger after them. Still weak from laughter, she held her sides, panting for air. That left only Oda standing there. With her head bowed in shame, she stepped sheepishly from one foot to the other, wishing she were far away. Suddenly overcome with the cold, she stood alone, half shivering, in front of the tall man, whom she both feared and secretly admired. Compared to her cowardly guardian at home, her friend Martha's dad looked very distinguished with his Sephardic, narrow skull, a trait referred to as "noble" in her dime novels.

Like a helmet with a raised visor, his hair and beard framed his skeptical amber eyes and pale face. Only his left eyebrow fluttered. A family tic, as Oda knew from her stepfather. Samuel Kohanim meant to sound in control and authoritative when he spoke to her. But he was too hurt for that and what came out instead sounded rough and angry. Fifteen-year-old Oda was now deeply ashamed of herself. Kohanim was a benefactor of the poor and patron of the arts! Her family, by contrast, was obsessed with money; they knew nothing about art or charity.

At her house, everything revolved around business deals, bankruptcies, disputes over bills and inheritances, marriages for money, lawsuits over property, and all manner of intrigues, and discussions about how to make or lose a profit. "Goodness! How dull!" Oda would groan. She found her family embarrassingly ignorant, narrow minded, and greedy. A conglomerate of Russian Orthodox, Protestants, and Lutherans, they all hated each other. Oda and her brother Rudolf were not personally privy to the details of their infighting over religion and money. What they did know, however, was that when their father died, a Russian Orthodox priest had denied their father a Russian Orthodox burial, since Oda and Rudolf had not been baptized into the faith. Not until they were already standing in front of the church with the coffin, did the funeral procession receive the news, forcing them to turn around and find a spot for his burial with the Lutherans instead. From then on, the von Güldners considered themselves Lutherans and denounced as traitors all remaining Russian Orthodox members of the family.

When their mother, a baroness, later married Gustav von Steinfeld, he viewed Oda and Rudolf as mere wards and stepchildren, and thus of lesser importance. Oda and Rudolf therefore had to take their meals apart from the family, at either a side table or in the kitchen with the servants. They soon came to prefer the latter, if only as a way to avoid the teasing of their privileged siblings, who, whenever the adults were looking away, liked to bombard the side table with wads of bread and bones. For such insults, Oda and Rudolf found ways to take their revenge. At Christmas, when the relatives had gathered for the holiday ball in a festive mood, Oda and Rudolf didn't appear at the banquet table. When they did appear, after being sent for, they weren't wearing the festive attire sent to them from their relatives in Bromberg; they strutted around in their usual shabby clothes, a sorry hodgepodge of the family's threadbare, hand-me-downs, suitable for servants or as a charity for children of their tenants. "To celebrate, we're wearing our really good clothes!" they announced cheerfully.

Her stepfather and mother were disgraced in front of the whole family and throughout the county. Oda and Rudolf received such a beating that not until New Year's Day could they either sit or lie down in the festive attire they were forced to wear. They, nevertheless, felt like winners. "Beatings end, but our asses endure!" was their slogan.

So it was that on New Year's morning, Oda woke up with both a blistered bottom and an idea. She tossed aside her meticulously kept record of beatings and abuse in favor of furiously drawing up one war plan after another. She secretly recorded every possible plot for revenge. Only her friend, Martha Kohanim, was allowed to know about it. "Oda, I am afraid of you!" Martha had said, even as she also enjoyed it. The prank to join in the Kohanims' lamentation rites was one part of the plan. Not a very good one, she now realized.

"Are you making a mockery of our religion or what could you possibly have been thinking? I will have to speak to your guardian," Samuel said.

Shaking his head, he grabbed Oda's chin, turned her head from left to right, studying the ashes on her face and then her bizarre disguise, which looked doubly strange on the stepdaughter of the German-Russian, liquor-and-sugar czar from next door. Tears of remorse came to Oda's eyes. If only the ground would open up, she prayed silently. How was she to explain to Martha's father that it wasn't only the desire for revenge against her parents that led her to carry out such a thing? Some children, she would have liked to have said, couldn't resist the temptation to be a beggar, a market woman, a Jewish mourner, or any other person, for five minutes. It was a chance to try out someone else's life. Why couldn't adults understand that?

Martha, the fifth Kohanim daughter, was the only one who understood her because she shared the same desire, albeit in her own way.

The friendship between the two girls had blossomed in secret.

In the district of Schwetz, the need for harmony dictated that although Germans, Poles, Kashubians, and Jews lived side by side in the town and villages, in reality, they formed three or four strictly separate worlds, all of which detested each other. Added to the ethnic boundaries were the class ones. The Polish count's lowliest kitchen maid counted herself superior to the keeper of the kitchen sink at the German-Russian factory owner's family, the von Steinfelds, and better than the servants of the even-lower ranking, Jewish timber-king's family, the Kohanims.

"I will talk to you later!" threatened Samuel Kohanim, his eyebrow fluttering, adding a visual tremolo. Oda concluded that there was no way he would follow through on his threat and denounce her to her stepfather. The two families may have been neighbors, but etiquette forbade them from interacting. The Jewish Kohanims had lived in Schwetz and Prussia for a long time but were nonetheless regarded as parvenus. Like the nouveau riche, von Steinfelds, who had acquired their noble title for twenty thousand rubles in Moscow, they were considered "unsatisfactory." Duels, swords, and pistols had been outlawed some time ago, but the glorified old order, which distinguished between above and below, refined and unrefined, was still intact. My ancestors were, by all counts, among the unrefined!

In order to report on the misdeeds of the sugar czar's stepdaughter, Samuel Kohanim would have had to write a letter and send it with a servant from his household to hers. Oda assumed that the punishment for inspiring such a double breech of taboos, would involve a double or triple lashing with her stepfather's favorite tool for disciplining his animals, servants, wife, and children: a seven-corded leather whip with iron bits on each end. Oda doubted, however, that Kohanim would dare to write such a letter in the first place; it would be beneath him. She thus sighed in relief and skipped away.

She nonetheless took the incident to heart, deciding to learn a lesson from it. From now on, she would plan her pranks with a bit more maturity. "Lucky you!" she thought, gathering up her faded black skirt around her waist, and whistling a light-hearted tune, as she skipped home through the freezing slush. She couldn't wait to see Rudolf's astonished reaction when she told him everything that had happened. Her heart raced at the very thought of it.

THE DEFENSE ATTORNEY

My first therapy session was supposed to have ended a long time ago. Dr. Vogelsang makes a show of rustling her papers. The six on her forehead has gone limp. It's now a hook, dangling wearily in front of her right eye. It doesn't seem to bother her. She removes her watch from the clipboard and struggles to reattach it. Just as she is beginning to gather her papers with a bit of dramatic flourish and a loud crack, there's a knock at the door. It's a mere formality, however, because without waiting for an invitation, Dr. Lauer, the supervising physician of the closed ward, marches in, the rubber soles of his shoes squeaking loudly against the honey-yellow linoleum. He gives me a quick nod.

"It's a good thing you're both here!" he says happily. "The patient is being transferred to Ward Four, General Neurology!"

"How nice that I'm no longer considered dangerous! How did I earn this unexpected honor?" I pipe up in amusement.

"You obviously have a very, very capable lawyer!"

Dr. Lauer says this with a scowl. Tourette's syndrome? A psychiatrist's tic? Before I can ask or say anything else, the head nurse storms into the room with two assistant nurses, obviously trying to impress their boss with how good they are at their jobs.

With record-breaking speed and efficiency, they pull open all the cupboard doors and open all the drawers. In my pink-pill induced haze, everything seems to happen in a flash. Before I know it, they have packed all of my belongings onto my bed and are pushing me and my things into the deserted corridor and into the bed elevator.

"Take care!" Dr. Lauer calls after me cheerfully. His gray complexion and the deep circles under his eyes contrast starkly with his upbeat demeanor; he seems to suffer from a high dose of Ritalin combined with mood enhancers. That's how people survive this place.

"You have the new room all to yourself," the young nurse announces, beaming with joy, "and you already have a visitor!"

"My son or my daughter?" I ask hopefully.

She laughs, "No, someone who's actually looking out for you: your lawyer! Haha!"

She thinks this is a good joke and so do I.

We roll through an endless row of corridors, some dark, some bright; and pass through countless doors; some are quietly unlocked and locked; others squeak and screech, as if opened by some invisible force. Finally, I am pushed into a room that is so bright that I have to squint.

"You're in luck! This is the private ward."

Before I can even take it in, Ms. Seraphina Kühnel, my lawyer, approaches my bed with a smile, extending her cold right hand for a handshake.

"You're a regular patient now," she announces, pleased with herself. "And you don't have to be worried about pre-trial detention anymore."

I must have reacted with a rather confused expression. Pre-trial detention? The thought had not even occurred to me. To reassure me, she puts her hand on my arm. I notice her expensive ring.

"Fortunately, I was able to convince the public prosecutor that you couldn't have done something criminal as part of a gang or for money! That's why the charges have been reduced to mere human trafficking. Since you don't have any previous convictions, you can now move about freely. However, you're not allowed to leave the country and your passport has been confiscated until further notice."

Before I can thank her properly, she puts her finger over her mouth and points to the walls and ceiling with her other hand, gesturing conspiratorially in the direction of the bathroom. Then she quickly opens the small refrigerator in my room and puts her cell phone inside and switches on the television. It all seems very odd, but you can forgive a famous defense lawyer for such eccentricities. I can't afford such a star lawyer. But what I can't pay, some foundation will, to support a case of such significant societal precedence.

Once we're in the bathroom, Ms. Kühnel turns on all the taps. I suddenly feel like I'm in some American crime show, a reaction that reads like neon letters flashing across my forehead.

"Please don't think I'm being paranoid. It's just that recently I've experienced some setbacks that can only be explained by wiretapping and sifting through electronic media. When it comes to human trafficking, the investigating authorities pull out all the stops. So let's be careful! To make a long story short: if things go badly, I will plead diminished capacity by way of insanity or, with reference to your traumatic experiences, mitigating circumstances. That would get your sentence reduced to three months in prison. But our aim is to have the charges dropped all together for lack of evidence. Worst case scenario, this will result in a suspended sentence because you have no previous convictions and a permanent residence. If prison looks unavoidable, then we'll have to negotiate for a suspended sentence by reason of a serious mental illness.

"That's the way the wind's blowing!" Ms. Kühnel says as she sits down on the wobbly shower stool beneath the shower head in her elegant gray designer suit and crosses her legs. She exudes professional confidence. Meanwhile, I squat on the toilet seat in my mousy gray jogging suit and look at the white pompoms on my gray plush slippers.

"If you say so," I mutter indecisively into the sound of the water running from the faucets. She pulls a notebook out of her large shoulder bag. She leafs through it.

"What about your electronic media? What could the prosecution find there?"

"I think I've thought of everything," I mumble under my breath, uncertain. Then I snap out of it and crawl out of my shell. She's my lawyer after all. "As far as I remember..." we smile at each other in agreement, "...I destroyed the cell phone, along with the SIM card, and threw it in the water. I replaced the hard disks from the laptop and copied harmless stuff onto the new hard disks. I gave up my Facebook account a long time ago. Apart from that, I've only been in internet cafés. There's nothing you can pin on me from the internet."

She gives me a nod of approval.

"I'm glad you remember that," she grins. "Are there any other confidants, possible witnesses or anyone else who might have seen anything?"

"None! Of course not!"

I make a gesture that could express a great deal or nothing at all, shrugging my shoulders and turning my palms upwards. My defense lawyer looks at me skeptically, "All clients lie," is written on her face.

"I'll take care of the co-defendant, the woman who entered the country with your ID. Ms… Ms. Nasi."

"Nasi Gohari!" I interject.

"That's right. Do you remember how to spell that?" she laughs. "So, let's not delude ourselves. The only thing that really worries me is your previous profession and that it's possible that you could set up and pull off something like this."

I'm a bit confused. "What's so bad about being a former journalist? Can't journalists steal handbags?"

Ms. Kühnel rolls her eyes. "Well, now you're disappointing me! Anything that even suggests a hint of intelligence or intrigue will only hurt you in these proceedings. I have to make it plausible that you've been duped and that you can't hold your tongue. Whether the judge will buy that is another question, especially if Judge Dörfler is presiding. He can't stand smart women. Knowing that, we're gonna have to buckle up and get ready for a possibly very rough ride. To smooth things along, I plan to play down my intelligence and act sweet.

Up to now I've only been vaguely worried. Now I'm alarmed.

"There, there," she comforts me. "Don't panic. They have to be able to prove it first."

I gulp.

THE BIBLICAL PLAGUES

The death of the last son and end to the Kohanim line turned the entire household into a madhouse. While the women from the mourning society carried out their duty, attending to the body of the deceased, the Christian servants milled about either distraught or a bit too curious about Jewish mourning rituals. The girls meanwhile were supposed to be in their room praying and asking for forgiveness for their behavior. But they were doing no such thing. Instead, they were struggling nervously between the urge to giggle and sneak out down the hallway to peer over the balustrade and fear of provoking their father's wrath.

The attendants disapproved of their irreverence. The deceased may have been a mere infant, but death nonetheless deserves more dignity.

Mindel, having fulfilled her duty, disappeared from sight, declaring "Death is for men to deal with!"

Without uttering a word, Samuel Kohanim pressed a coin into the hands of each mourning woman. The women quickly took the coins, and slipped out the door, thanking him as they went. The women of the burial society then departed with words of consolation and blessings, leaving Samuel alone with his dead son. He gazed tearfully at the tiny body with its little eyes hidden beneath large pieces of broken clay. "So that's the end of the Kohanims!" he sighed, standing in front of the window in his prayer shawl and involuntarily tapping his toes. As a matter of course, he began to reminisce about the Kohanim line. He viewed the cult of memory as a disease that appeared as you grew older, and then spread ever more violently, in prolonged bursts, until it devoured you completely. He didn't trust the stories passed down about his family. Like stalagmites and stalactites in caves, each generation deposited sediments of its own fantasies. Even if you went back a mere two generations, it was nearly impossible to separate truth from fiction.

He could only shake his head when he thought about the patriarch of the Kohanims in West Prussia, Baruch Kohanim, and about his disagreeable sister, Zippora Orenstein, both of whom were spoken of as saints. In truth of fact, the Kohanims were not pious; they were outsiders and rebels who rejected tradition. And they had in fact always earned approval for their brazen behavior, something that the more hypocritical members of the family were loath to admit.

"Could that possibly be the secret of holiness?" he reflected. "You identify an honorable pursuit, flout all the rules to achieve it, and then you succeed."

He stared at the painting of Baruch, commissioned a hundred years ago by the Kohanims. A product of pure fantasy. From under a mane of black-and-gray curls with a velvet yarmulke on his head, a rather sinister-looking Baruch Kohanim looked down sternly at his descendants. He was resting his chin resolutely on his chest, so that his beard covered his neck like a canopy and stood in peculiar contrast to the white-silk jabot hanging from his neck. A lot of water had flowed down the Vistula since those days in the 17th century. It was also true, however, that some evil had been eating away at the Kohanim line for some time. Wasn't it misfortune enough that all of his sons had died? Weren't the daughters with which he'd been burdened an even greater misfortune?

People in the village of Osche, three kilometers away, secretly called his daughters the "Seven Biblical Plagues." They added the word "biblical" to refer to the plagues as something Jewish, distinguishing them from the usual plagues in the village: the annual flood, unruly youth, superstition, and so on and so forth.

If you believed in ghosts, you would have sworn that someone had unleashed a horde of devils, *dybbukim*, on the souls of his daughters. Fanny, the eldest, had a face that had been disfigured by measles. The disease had left her face paralyzed on one side, hanging down like a piece of limp dough. The other daughters were monstrous of their own accord, he thought.

Elli, his third child, seemed to be a goyish farmhand. Instead of walking, she ran, jumping over every wall, and even over the roof on occasion. She had also secretly learned to swim in the black water that flowed past the servants' quarters. Instead of embroidering monograms on her trousseau, like other girls her age did, she would tear up her clothes from getting into fistfights with the worst Polish street boys. When she wasn't playing tennis in scandalously short, calf-length skirts, which she would then hike up even further, even more outrageously, she would mount horses without a side saddle. Just like a man, she'd ride the horse between her legs, so that she could shoot at bottles and pigeons. The Polish and German children in the village were so afraid of Elli that they no longer threw stones, mud, and bits of grass containing stones at the Jewish children or teased them. But Elli was a walking scandal, nonetheless. Were she a boy, she would have been feared and respected as an anomaly among the otherwise passive Jews, someone that you didn't dare mess with, and someone who at least did his parents proud. But where would you find a respectable Jew who would take such a mannish woman like Elli as his wife?

At the thought of Selma, Samuel heaved another sigh. Selma, his second oldest, had already at the age of sixteen inherited her mother's double chin and closely set, unpleasantly piercing eyes and had the unshakeable stubbornness of a senile mule combined with the hot temper and compelling eloquence of a Levantine. Selma had not only become addicted to learning but had done so in rebellion against her father. The Hasid dybbuk had thus taken possession of her soul, leading her to cultivate an ultra-Orthodox fervor.

Then there was Jenny, his second youngest, who was a witless coquette. But among all these misfortunes was there any greater than being stricken with a daughter like Martha?

The fifth child, Martha, was ugly, stupid as a chicken, as mendacious as Munchausen and constantly sick. Sometimes it was her nerves, at others her skin, then asthma. Her mewling voice alone could send him into a rage. Of course, he didn't let it show, because he treated all of his daughters with equal indifference and thought it was the right thing to do.

With another prayer he thought of Franziska, the middle one, called Fränze, who was actually his favorite. But he was even more convinced that his beautiful, cool Franziska, who was as thoughtless and heartless as a nihilist, would convert at some point, or something even worse. She was capable of anything.

As for Flora, his youngest? Good God, she was already as hypocritical and untrustworthy as a Catholic!

In short, with the exception of Fanny, Kohanim thought that all his daughters were completely wayward, rebellious, and ungovernable for good or evil. With sons, he could have easily accepted such qualities as suggestive of character. But with daughters, character of this kind was as useful as a boil on your backside and brought only trouble. What was this new era doing to Jewish women? Everything was falling apart and appeared to be heading for a calamity. It was the irony of fate, however, that Kohanim of all people, who had always preached optimism and believed in progress, was now becoming increasingly confused, feeling like the sorcerer's apprentice who could no longer get rid of the spirits he had summoned. "…and that's why God punished him!"

This malediction from Rabbi Streisand, his arch enemy, was the last thing Samuel wanted to be reminded of as he confronted the death of his heirs. Yet, he couldn't escape the question: When had the curse built its nest among the male Kohanims, hatching disaster upon disaster like a snake its eggs? Had it started *before* or *after* the school war? he asked himself, with a touch of superstition that annoyed him.

Back then, it was merely about the introduction of compulsory education in Prussia. Seeing it as progress for Jews and non-Jews, boys and girls, he stood fully behind it, engendering the ire of all the Orthodox Jews. "A Jew belongs in the Talmud school, the *heder*, where they can study the Talmud, the Torah, and the scriptures. What can a Jew learn from unbelievers except unbelief? How to eat pork and commit all manner of blasphemy? It would mean the end of Jewry and thus the end of the world!" prophesied his nemesis Rabbi Streisand, the highest-ranking Hasid in the county. After the school mandate was implemented, Rabbi Streisand had proclaimed: "The only way a God-fearing Jewish child can counteract this sin that has been forced upon him is to spit upon the ground and utter 'Be damned and be erased!' whenever the name of the Jewish traitor, Jesus Christ, is uttered, in the school of unbelievers."

Jewish children who followed Rabbi Streisand's dictate to the letter would have had to fear the ire of their Christian classmates, who would give them a thrashing. Not that they couldn't handle it. Like generations of Jews before them, Jewish kids in Schwetz were used to such things and had proudly endured them as a sign that they were God's chosen ones. However, the Jews in Schwetz feared ignorance, and its companion poverty, even more than physical abuse, and so they sent their children to public school, whether the rabbi approved or not. In so doing, they also avoided troubles with the Prussian authorities.

Soon Jewish children in Schwetz were only thinking of the curse, "Be damned and be erased!" whenever someone mentioned "the Savior" and instead of spitting, they merely gave an innocuous "tja!" or hissed a "tzh."

Even these small acts of revolt decreased over time, until at some point they disappeared all together.

Samuel Kohanim had thus won the school wars. But victory came at a price; thereafter Rabbi Streisand hated the Kohanims even more. Samuel's initial reaction was to try to set an example of true godliness and exercise humility. Sensitive to the injured ego of his defeated rival, he even refrained from the typical mudslinging for which he was notorious. But that wasn't enough! Rabbi Streisand continued to slander him; Samuel continued to respond with generosity. He donated enough money to cover a "proper salary" for the suffering Hasidic population's rabbi, inspiring Rabbi Streisand to revile him all the more. To prove that his religious convictions were not for sale, he railed against Kohanim, even threatening to ban him. It was at this point that Kohanim's patience reached its breaking point. He halted his charitable payments to the poor, Hasidic brethren. "I might be a schmuck, but am I also supposed to pay for the privilege of being insulted? Let him watch and see who pays him now!"

God was punishing him for that!? Nebbich!

Samuel's God was wise and generous, not some petty accounting clerk who besieged humans with ill-tempered old men and their small-minded jealousies. As he looked over at the little bundle in which he had placed all his hopes, he knew that with his last son went his last remnant of faith. God had withdrawn his grace from the Kohanims. Why had Samuel bought the sawmill from the count if there was no male heir to continue his work? With the purchase, Kohanim had once again proven his loyalty to the Polish count's family. He had done a good deed on behalf of the Solkowskys as well as a favor to himself, when he had purchased the sawmill at an exorbitant price, thus helping his former lord come out from under the burden of his oppressive debts. One last time and then never again. It was a shame. In just a few nights in Baden-Baden, the Polish nobles had gambled away all that the generations of Polish farmers had created, and that the generations of Kohanims had earned as managers for the Solkowskys.

Samuel wasn't going to buy the count's vodka distillery that had just gone on the auction block. He had also strongly advised all the other Jews to refuse to buy it. "Do we want people to say that the Jews tempted the farmers to drink in order to drive them to ruin?" Anything that could lead to pogroms had to be avoided at all costs. He was firmly convinced that peace had to be tended to tirelessly, just as one tended a vineyard. Many Jews rejected such worries, believing that real pogroms were out of the question in Prussia. "Never say never!" Samuel warned these die-hard optimists. "A Jew without vigilance is a dead Jew!" The attacks against Jews that had taken place a few years prior in Prussia had been warning enough for him. "No, these Germans have hard hearts which harbor a cold hatred. They promise peace with a piety that cannot be trusted." He wouldn't fall for it!

He liked the Poles best. Unlike the pogroms in Russia, which meant murder, death, and robbery, Poles had outbursts against Jews that were more like fits of rage from a troubled husband. Whenever he was particularly unhappy or had had too much to drink, he would beat his wife. But afterwards he would feel bad, and order would be restored. For a time. It was always like that here and no one would have claimed otherwise. He was so suspicious of Russians, that Samuel Kohanim didn't even trust the Russian-German next door whom he had brought to Osche to run the distillery. "He's got the mug of a crocodile," he would joke about his new neighbor, the sugar-and-schnapps Baron von Steinfeld. Through Izrael Poznansky, the largest cloth manufacturer in Lodz, a pious Jew who had prayer rooms set up in his cloth weaving mills for his Jewish factory workers, Samuel had learned that a certain Baron von Steinfeld, a German-Russian merchant who was interested in a schnapps distillery and similar businesses "out west." Von Steinfeld was desperate to move from Russian-Polish Lodz to Prussia. Drawn by the milder climate, the family had harbored hopes of moving further west for some time, despite the fact that the czar had granted them a noble title and that they owned magnificent estates in Russia.

When Kohanim proposed to old Solkowsky the idea of selling the distillery to Baron von Steinfeld, it must have been around Christmas because the large Christmas tree still stood in the castle hall, which the Solkowskys had decorated patriotically with white-and-red tissue paper flags, as they always would, "as long as Poland lives in servitude."

"Merchant nobility!" sneered Count Solkowsky at the "von" appendage to "Steinfeld." For him, true nobility only counted from seven noble ancestors onwards. And that was the absolute minimum! It was the way of the world that the patent of nobility was sometimes acquired from the Polish king, sometimes from the Russian czar, and after 1806 sometimes from the Prussian king in return for the promise of loyalty and good behavior. But no creature under the sun seemed as contemptible to old Count Zygmund Solkowsky as a snobbish upstart who bought himself a title and even denied his faith to this end, converted from the Protestant to the Russian Orthodox faith, and then back again, as suited his purposes. "Dishonorable German pack, lacking courage, character, and backbone, and at the service of anyone who intimidates them or waves a sausage in their direction!"

That's why the Polish count did not believe for a moment that the so-called "von" Steinfelds only came to West Prussia for its mild winters. No, the "so-called," as the Solkowksys christened the German-Russian merchant baron, wanted to get his flock to dry land. "Things are gonna go south soon in Russia," Solkowsky told Kohanim, who imagined tens of thousands of Jews fleeing to Prussia and himself and the Jews who had been there a long time having to endure increasing difficulties as a result. The Polish count was amused by the horrified reaction of "his Jew" to the potential arrival of an influx of Jews from the East. Kohanim had long since ceased to be the Solkowskys' steward and the Solkowskys had long been dependent on the Kohanims and not vice versa. Yet, he sometimes adopted the humble attitude of a servant, reverting to a musty old habit that had been practiced for generations. Count Zygmund Solkowsky demanded a grotesquely high price from the "so-called" for his distillery, which, to everyone's surprise, the ennobled German-Russian paid without so much as batting an eye. Three weeks later, the schnapps baron bought the count's sugar refinery and the Solkowskys' small country estate near Laskowitz on similarly insane terms.

Less than two kilometers from the Kohanims' Sauermühle estate, the "so-called" moved in with his family. Thus, the Kohanims and the von Steinfelds became neighbors who politely ignored each other and only greeted each other in public when it was absolutely necessary, and even then with a mere nod.

After this transaction, the Polish counts were able to let the balls roll a little longer in the casinos and hang real jewels on their fake French mistresses.

From then on, the people in the district worked either for the "German Sugar Czar" or for the "Jewish Timber King" in the sawmill and adjoining furniture factory, which Samuel Kohanim had been running with his cousin Zacharias Segall since the birth of the crown prince.

Samuel's plan at the time was to build his son a kingdom of planks, tables, chairs, and solid oak cabinets. He had even considered taking a share in the modern paper mill of his successful brother-in-law, Artur Bukofzker in Schwetz, and thus get involved in the production of newsprint for nearby

Danzig, Bromberg, Breslau, and Berlin—a possibility made all the more real by the factory's location directly on the Vistula and Berlin-Königsberg railroad line. What possibilities had lied ahead!

Now, however, he had become indifferent to all projects. "There's no point in striving and aspiring!" With a groan he stripped off his prayer shawl and fringes, tore his shirt as a sign of mourning, and paced up and down the room with heavy steps until he came to a stop in front of the wall of books in the gloomy study. The Book of Job! With a golden pince-nez on his nose, he began to read. Unable to concentrate, he put the book back in its place. Job! "You at least have a duty to live the life God has prepared for you."

He tried to return to his previous state, devout and secure in his faith, but he was no longer able to do so. In his heart, he felt a void that was even heavier to carry than the grief for his son. His God was denying him grace and blessings; he was therefore grieving twice over. In his despair, he almost envied his nemesis Rabbi Streisand who had never experienced doubt. His narrow world always seemed to be in order.

THE GOOD PLACE AND THE BOY WITH TWELVE FINGERS

The funeral for the deceased little one took place shortly before sunset. The evening sky in the east was already glowing cobalt blue and the earth was frozen solid. The Kohanims' extended family had hastily arrived from Zempelburg, Tuchel, Lianno, Bukowitz Krupoczin, Wiersch, and Jeschewo, some by train to Laskowitz, some on horse-drawn carriages and coaches. They now joined the mourning party composed of family and neighbors. For devout Jews in Schwetz death and funerals were the exclusive affairs of men. It was thus only the male members of the mourning party who stumbled through the Jewish cemetery in Schwetz at dusk, making their way to the Kohanims' family grave, which was situated in the honorary section of the cemetery. The women meanwhile were mourning at home, cowering barefoot on the floor, with ashes on their heads.

The men gathered in the section known as "the good place" at the Jewish cemetery, wore prayer shawls, pomaded coal-black beards in the imperial style, some with fashionable black Homburger hats on their heads, but most with shiny, ceremonial top hats. In the last reddish twilight over the Vistula, which could still be seen to the west from the cemetery hill, they surrounded the stone-lined children's grave in silent prayer. Samuel wore a prayer shawl and recited the *kaddish* for his crown prince:

Exalted and sanctified be his great name,
in the world which will be renewed and
where he will give life to the dead and
raise them to eternal life and
rebuild the city of Jerusalem and
complete his temple there and
uproot foreign worship from the earth and
restore Heavenly worship to its position.
And may the Holy One, praised be his name,
establish his kingdom and his salvation blossom
in your lifetime and during the lifetime and
during your days and during the lifetimes
of the whole house of Israel, speedily and very soon.
And say: Amen!

You could almost read the men's thoughts in the night-blue air: Kohanim would no longer have a son to say the kaddish at his grave. They felt sorry for Kohanim. That's why so many men showed up. And those who weren't moved with compassion, came out of curiosity; they wanted to see how Kohanim would hold up when confronted with the fact of the end of his male heirs.

Soon after the funeral for little Benjamin, life went back to normal. The seven daughters resumed their tyranny over the house and estate nearly undisturbed. To help reign them in, a governess had been hired, Madame Bertha from Hanover with a spindly body and a big, Roman nose. Madame Bertha was supposed to teach the girls proper manners and dialect-free German and French. But under her care, the seven sisters stayed more out of line than in and the only evidence of her tenure in their household was the word *merde*, French for "shit." Legend has it that the word escaped from the mouth of General Cambronne when faced with losing the battle of Waterloo. In Francophone regions, girls from better households used the phrase *le mot de Cambronne*, just as in German ones they used the *Swabian salute*. Bedazzled by its gentile origins, the Kohanims preferred le mot de Cambronne to the baser Swabian salute. The expression served three generations as a dainty swear word. In its short forms, appearing as: *Le mot!* or simply *Cambronne!*

When Madame Bertha was fished out of the sawmill's canal one morning, everyone thought that despair over her charges had led her to the water. A victim of the seven biblical plagues! However, the autopsy revealed a more common motive. Madame Bertha was with child. Everyone had their own theory about who had brought her to this state.

After Madame Bertha disappeared into the afterlife, Mindel appeared to be merely simulating a life on earth. Like a ghost whose time here would soon pass, she flitted through the house. Despite her rejection of the world, however, she kept a watchful gaze of iron on the family property, protecting it against all servants and staff, the "natural born enemies of the family."

From her emaciated hips jangled three huge bunches of keys to pantries, cellars, cupboards, and storage rooms. Every napkin, teaspoon, coal briquette, and empty sack, and bottle were counted and noted down. The joke went that since the death of the heir, Mindel's thriftiness had reached such heights of insanity that she had even taken to counting every pea, bean, and grain of rice.

Mindel was so miserly that she would surely have starved or frozen to death surrounded by total darkness. The only things preventing such a fate were the loud protests from Samuel and the seven sisters who refused to spend their evenings in damp rooms, illuminated by only one, dimly lit, flickering kerosene lamp while Samuel read to them from the newspaper and various books he had selected. Even when the candles in the menorah were lit for Shabbat and everyone at the table was supposed to be solemn and in good spirits, Mindel would constantly interrupt the mood by warning of the dangers of waste and gluttony. "You'll ruin your stomach," she would mumble whenever someone would take another bite. "It's bad to rest on a full stomach," she would warn. "Gluttony is a mortal sin, not only among Catholics!"

The family soon got used to Mindel's behavioral quirk, as if it were a natural phenomenon, beyond any one's control. They simply overlooked and ignored it. Only when guests were present did they shoot her glances. Oda often joined them at the table at Samuel's invitation; he wanted her healthy appetite to set an example for his "picky" daughters. The sugar baron's stepdaughter always had the appetite of a ten-headed hydra, gorging on its prey.

Mindel would then spend the entire evening looking offended, as if she were being robbed. The Kohanims did not, however, need to pinch pennies. Business was going well, in fact. And it almost seemed as if business thrived in direct relation to his disinterest in it. Whereas Mindel numbed her pain with absurd miserliness and pointless stinginess, her husband lost himself in acts of charity.

And it wasn't abstract charitable deeds like contributions or participation in charities that helped alleviate the plight of the Jews in Tuchel and Zempelburg districts. Samuel was interested in specific cases: Ruth Lewinski, for example, an elegant, red-headed widow with six small children. He gave Ruth Lewinski a small pension and regularly inquired about the children's progress at school. The local gossips found this unusual interest in the fate of a beautiful widow and her offspring disconcerting enough to make a big fuss over it. After the apothecary in far off Zempelburg made some insinuating comments, Kohanim thereafter carried about any communication related to charity via writing, or after dark, said some who were eager to connect Samuel Kohanim with Madame Bertha's misfortune. Mostly, however, Samuel Kohanim's urge to do good centered on Max, or Maxim Gulkowitsch, the son of Russian Jews from the village of Wiersch.

When the boy was seven years old, he developed polio, which left him with a severe limp. He was also born with six fingers on each hand. For superstitious people, there was no contesting the fact that someone with six or twelve fingers had been marked by the devil. For this reason, someone was always trying to cast out the devil by setting fire to his family's house. Max and his family thus had to leave the village as fast as they could. Max knew how to make the most of his stigma, not by allowing himself to be paraded at fairs but by using his excessive of fingers to play music. He wanted to become a pianist, only he needed a piano. After finding one at the village inn, the Black Ox, he promptly began banging away at the keys of its pianoforte until the owner threw him out. Max didn't help his cause by refusing to play more popular tunes like polkas, marches, or waltzes.

Max always managed to unearth music scores somewhere, which he would then transcribe onto wrapping paper or rolls of wallpaper or memorize. Then when he found a piano, he would play the score with the unrestraint of a madman, using all the pedals and hammering out complete concertos that he had memorized. Max's passion made a deep impression on Samuel. One day he insisted that Max climb into his carriage with him; he planned to introduce Max to old Count Zygmund.

"He is a genius," Samuel explained to the baffled Count Zygmund, who was about to join some guests from Warsaw for a game of cards. He confirmed, however, that a concert piano was still sitting in the castle, an actual French Érard grand piano that nobody ever played. "It hasn't been tuned for a-a-a-ages," Countess Valeska warned with a frown. "Nobody can repair instruments like those these days anyway," her husband replied. "We would have to send for a specialist from Paris."

"Brahms played on an Érard like that," Max whispered excitedly when he heard about it. He begged and pleaded that everything possible be done to save this valuable instrument, until even Samuel found himself supporting the idea.

Countess Valeska wanted to nip in the bud any act of assertiveness from *their* Jew. Kohanim made her uncomfortable and she was determined to "put him in his place." She suggested that if the count were to allow the boy to stay at the castle and play the piano, Samuel Kohanim would have to pay to have the piano tuned, provide a good teacher, and cover his room and board. "On occasion we could organize small gatherings and musical evenings at the castle," he added. Zygmund Solkowsky was unable to refuse Kohanim anything. It was also an opportunity to show off his "grandeur de coeur" and to play the part of a patron of the arts. The idea appealed to him all the more, since it wouldn't cost him a dime. After a great deal of back and forth, the wunderkind was finally brought to the castle.

Max was an unattractive, chubby boy, between eleven and twelve years old. Beneath a mop of wild black hair that stuck out from his head like bristles on a broom, was a pimply face, and a sullen, thick mouth that hung from his face like a sausage from a potato pancake. With small black, beady eyes and the mild contempt of the anointed, Max looked down upon his potential benefactors as if they were no more than a couple of useful toads.

The count, for his part, was as delighted as he was terrified. "Just look at him!" he crowed, "What a specimen! Haha! And he is talented, you say?" He looked at Max through his monocle, as if inspecting an undiscovered species. "Doje! What would he like to play for us?"

"Chopin! Piano Concerto Number One!" Max said haughtily, ignoring the amused laughter of his audience as he limped over to the grand piano, lifted the lid, sat down awkwardly, and then solemnly spread his hands with the twelve fingers above the keyboard, hovering above the keys. Like a magician about to perform a trick, he held them there, without stirring, and then dropped his hands, and struck the keys forcefully.

The count and his guests flinched in shock. The countess crossed herself. The grand piano sounded like a pile of broken glass rattling in an old zinc tub. But this was soon forgotten as Max freely transposed the entire concerto into a more bearable, less out-of-tune pitch. A spontaneous feat of abstraction that filled Samuel first with enthusiasm and then devotion. A true genius!

Maxim's playing alternated between cheerful, delicate, and light as a fairy spell, and dramatic and thundering, a furious maelstrom of sounds. The audience listened, enraptured; the shards of glass in the zinc tub had quieted to a mere occasional rattling. What they were hearing, even for untrained ears, was quite different from the usual piano-playing of daughters from wealthier families. This was no anxious strumming and tinkling of keys by shaky, pale, sweaty fingers. A force of nature was being unleashed. Despite the occasional discordant note and dissonant, whirring, almost ethereal sounds emanating from the piano, Max's playing captivated the audience, or at least compelled them to stand completely still, almost against their will.

As the final notes faded away, Max slammed the lid down over the keys with a bang, leapt to his feet, and hurried away without paying the least bit of attention to the applause. Count Zygmund was "très enthousiasmé." The countess just stood there with her mouth agape, either from shock or amazement. It was clear that she couldn't make her mind up about how to deal with the prodigy in their midst. Darkly, she suspected that any resistance to this course wunderkind would be futile. She decided to give a bitter smile.

The count informed Kohanim that Max could play at the castle whenever he wanted, and that he should now consider the count one of his patrons. They thus called "the genius" back into the drawing room to tell him the good news in person. Max smiled wanly. With the same equanimity with which Jews had endured misdeeds for centuries, Max now accepted this goyish generosity. It was only the prospect of gaining access to such a magnificent instrument, a real Érard, and a genuine desire to avoid offending Kohanim, his benefactor, that led Max to thank the rulers. But he did so as one thanks someone who is merely fulfilling his duty and obligation to God, in other words, as a mere matter of course, and hardly worth mentioning.

Soon the Seven Biblical Plagues were also following the musical progress of the twelve-fingered boy, who did not even so much as deign to greet them, the seven princesses.

"Who do you think you are?!" Fränze got upset and put her fists on her hips. Max apologized, saying that he was suffering from a voice change, and that, after all, the sisters had a certain reputation.

In return for his reference to a "certain reputation," Elli accosted Max by the lilac bushes and punched him until he swore that from then on he would say exactly the opposite about them. Before long, Jenny and Franziska were pestering their father, telling him that they too wanted to learn to play the piano "like proper ladies." Soon a shiny, black piano with gleaming gold-colored brass candlesticks was being lifted up the hill on wide leather straps by four piano movers. Strong as plow horses, they hoisted the piano up the hill and into the parlor. Mindel could not be convinced that there was not the slightest thing to be saved or spared by keeping the good new piano under lock and key. The girls thus always found it locked up and had to beg and explain why they needed to play it right then. Fränze, however, came to the rescue with an idea.

"Let's see if this will work!" she said before putting the key in the keyhole that kept the piano lid locked. Then she ceremoniously lifted the lid. The piano grinned broadly with its black-and-white teeth. Fränze now boldly grabbed the nutcracker from the Bohemian crystal bowl on the piano, placed the head of the key in the nutcracker, as if it were a pair of pliers, and turned it with a sharp tug. "Crack!" The end of the key broke off. With no working key with which to lock the piano, they would now have free access to the instrument.

According to the unspoken division of labor in the Kohanim household, Samuel Kohanim was responsible for acquiring the piano, whereas Mindel was charged with arranging for piano lessons. Mindel thought that paying a piano teacher was a waste of money. Fränze and Jenny were only looking to have something to do that would get them out of housework. Mindel was right about that, of course. But if her husband wanted it, then Maxim Gulkowitsch should work for his benefactor by giving Fränze and Jenny lessons for free. And because she was in charge of the household, that's how it was done. Jenny was heartbroken. She was serious about music. Fränze, by contrast, found piano playing more amusing than crocheting hemstitches, and likewise preferred a teacher that was almost her same age, instead of a gray, old man, who smelled like old age, dirty suits, and cheap cigar butts. Franziska decided that she would give this Max Gulkowitsch a thorough inspection.

Not long after they had commenced their lessons, Max found himself looking forward to the lessons for Jenny. For her part, Jenny surprised everyone with her sudden enthusiasm for music. With a measure of arrogance, Max informed Kohanim that she was indeed making good progress "for a girl." Max dreaded the lessons with Fränze, however. First of all, because she was always coming up with some new sort of mischief and secondly because he always felt so anxious and powerless around her. Fränze, Max thought, had the eyes of an expensive horse. When she looked directly at him, he felt paralyzed. Fränze, sensing his weakness, responded by lowering her velvet gaze into his eyes. Even back then, she had an almost animalistic instinct for sniffing out weakness, fear, and insecurity, and quickly found a perverse pleasure in using this gift to her advantage.

"There's a dybbuk in Fränze!" Max declared, turning so red that his ears glowed like two horseshoes under a blacksmith's hammer. Samuel Kohanim saw this as a welcome opportunity to turn the conversation at the table to the girls' future, more specifically, to the question of which marriage candidates could be considered and which worthy parents they should perhaps talk to, in the not-too-distant future.

"I only want a man I love!" exclaimed Martha. Mindel and Samuel exchanged worried glances. What they had long feared, appeared to be coming to pass.

"What's with these goyish fashions?" Mindel snapped. According to Mindel, romantic love was synonymous with fornication and a general decline in morality. "That kind of thing only ends up in the gutter or in the morgue." She was ready with countless examples, from Hanni who ended it by drowning herself to merely exclaiming, "Think of Bertha!" to an unnamed "person," who following her heart, ended up in a horrible household, and so on and so forth. If none of this helped, there was the cautionary tale of Romeo and Juliet or just one word: "Berlin!"

Faced with a united front of seven sulking daughters, Samuel Kohanim sought to appease them. He had a vague suspicion that he was standing on the same losing side as all other Jewish parents of his generation: against the march of time. You could resist assimilation for another two or three generations, but there was simply no cure for the sweet poison of romanticism to which all girls were now falling victim: German, Polish, Russian, and Jewish. Rearguard actions were the only possible recourse! Samuel Kohanim nonetheless felt that he should try to appeal to his daughters' common sense: "You don't think your parents are villains who want to harm you, do you?" What was meant to be a rhetorical question was met with pouts, sulks, pursed lips, glowering stares, and defiant frowns. All seven shook their heads meekly. Jenny, who didn't quite understand what the fuss was about, focused her attention on creating a pattern in the white tablecloth by pressing the tines of her fork into it.

"Love!"

Long pause.

"Think about it. Young, inexperienced people are sure that it's forever. But the truth is, love is an extremely fleeting emotion. The human heart is fickle. Today one thing, tomorrow another, and the day after tomorrow something else, and then forgotten all together! You can't build a life for yourself on such a foundation. That would be really foolish, wouldn't it?"

The girls were not convinced. For reasons their parents could not fathom, be it evolution or that they, like all young girls, firmly believed in "the great love" that they had read about in novels, where love was until death. However, they offered no counterarguments both because their father had superior rhetorical powers and because they also believed that feelings are not accessible to the mind and thus could not possibly be communicated to their parents who would never understand anyway. So they remained obstinately silent, wearing expressions that said, "We don't believe a word of it!"

"I don't even want to get married. I want to study," Selma spoke up.

"But you're a girl!" Samuel Kohanim smiled at her indulgently.

"So what? Why shouldn't a girl study? I read in the newspaper that girls are now studying too, even at universities! Aren't I just as smart as a boy?"

Shocked, Mindel looked at Selma and began to fiddle nervously with her lace collar.

"That's just it!" Samuel replied good-naturedly, explaining with a laugh, "Only the boys have to learn everything they'll need in life. Girls already know it all. Just look at your mother!" They looked at their mother and agreed that they certainly didn't want such a life, even if they didn't know exactly what they might want instead.

TRUTH AND CREDIBILITY

It's grown quiet in Seraphina Kühnel's office. The paralegal and administrative assistant went home for the day at half past seven. It was around then that I slipped out of the hospital without anyone noticing.

"We're not going to be able to have much of a conversation if we're sitting on a toilet with the water running and a cell phone in the fridge," I had said to Ms. Kühnel before requesting that we meet in the more secure environment of her law firm. Now that the office staff has gone home, all phone calls go directly to voicemail. Emergencies go to the red cell phone, which she has set next to my files on a massive antique wooden desk. A green banker's lamp casts a soft glow over the scene.

Ms. Kühnel is feeling good today. She won a major case that everyone was sure she would lose. It's big news; it will be splashed all over the news tonight and appear in the papers tomorrow. An enormous, extravagantly expensive flower arrangement with thank-you cards and a wooden crate of Heidsieck champagne bear witness to the depth of her absolved client's gratitude. Apart from these recent flourishes, the office appears as if everything was directly imported from an old English manor, a style that apparently impresses people with money and crooks alike. Golf trophies and cups fill the shelves, reminding visitors that Seraphina Kühnel excels not only in the courtroom but on the golf course as well.

Ms. Kühnel looks through my file, explaining that she wants to prepare me for questioning by the police and the public prosecutor's office in court. She had managed to have all requests for my interrogation rejected on the grounds of incompetence. I begin to mumble, "thanks" but before the words can even leave my mouth, she brushes them away with a wave of her hand. She doesn't need such acknowledgements: she knows she's good. She then puts the file aside with an almost affectionate gesture. Collecting herself, she clasps her hands together and sets them on the desk, so that she can concentrate better, and then looks at me the way a doctor does a patient, "Was there a specific reason why you traveled to Istanbul?"

Embarrassed, I study the state of my fingernails. "I went as a tourist, to do some sightseeing, shopping, and so on," I babble.

"Were you traveling alone or with a group, with friends or as part of an organized tour?"

"It's all in the files," I grumble reluctantly.

She's not used to resistance, so she immediately pivots her head in my direction in an aggressive way. "So listen, you're going to be asked all of this a hundred times. I want to hear the whole thing from you, as it is. It's not about truth; it's about credibility! Do you understand what I mean by that? I have to build a strategy with different variables, all of which depend on your level of credibility. I'm assuming that you can remember the journey itself despite some gaps in your memory, right?" She gives me a defense-attorney look, one that conveys infinite understanding. My resistance melts.

"Well," I concede without any momentum. "I flew to Istanbul all by myself and stayed at the Topkapi Palace Inn for four nights."

She peers at me over her elegant reading glasses. Only now do I notice her deep green eyes. "So you didn't book either your flight or hotel with anyone else?"

I shake my head.

"Did you meet anyone at the hotel, such as the co-defendant, Ms. Golani, whom they accuse you of helping to escape?"

"Gohari, Nasi Gohari!" whose full name I helpfully provide. "No! I always travel alone. I prefer it that way."

"Aha!" Ms. Kühnel shakes her head disapprovingly, as if I've confessed to some eccentricity that she is incapable of understanding.

"Is it possible that you and your co-defendant may have been seen together somewhere? Or even worse, might there be footage of you caught on a surveillance camera? Think hard! Surveillance cameras are everywhere these days, especially in Istanbul."

Her question about cameras throws me for a loop, "Why? Is that what the public prosecutor's office is claiming? Then they're bluffing!"

With her lawyer's x-ray vision, Ms. Kühnel looks straight through me, "So we can rule that out?"

"Completely!"

"You're absolutely sure?"

"Absolutely."

"But you're not allowed to answer that question like that at the trial. It could be seen as an indirect admission that you took extra care not to be seen with the co-defendant. Do you understand?"

I nod and grin. She responds with a tight smile. To show her that I've taken the hint, I say, "It's hard to imagine. Istanbul is huge, a totally chaotic, overcrowded monstrosity. There's no way anyone could know whether someone was coming or going at any given moment. I mean, it is possible that the co-defendant and I were on the way to visit the same sights without either of us suspecting such a thing… and, uh…."

My defense lawyer chastises me. "When you testify in court, you have to leave out explanations like that."

I stare at her, totally perplexed.

"My dear Ms. Kohanim-Rubin, the lie always betrays itself through a particularly rich use of words and overly extensive statements on the subject of the lie. The truth does not have to explain itself. It is simply there, standing for itself. As a former journalist, you should be familiar with that."

I'm starting to panic. What if I betrayed myself to Vogelsang by being too chatty? My lawyer seems to read my mind.

"Has anyone questioned you about the case?"

"No, not really," I reply, stalling for time as I think it over.

"What do you mean by 'not really'?" she asks back.

"Well, I don't trust this therapist at the clinic, this Dr. Vogelsang. Because she doesn't seem to be part of the normal medical team. She doesn't even work there regularly. I find that rather troubling. I'd be grateful if you could take a closer look at Vogelsang."

Ms. Kühnel is looking at me now with a mixture of pity and skepticism. "A therapist is bound by confidentiality. But if it would make you feel better, I can look into it. What have you already told Dr. Vogelsang about the case?"

"Nothing at all. I've just been telling her about my family's history."

DISASTER WAITING TO HAPPEN

"God is good to the wicked so that they learn to become good!"

Rabbi Menasseh Caro had a reputation for using bat mitzvah celebrations held by prominent families as an occasion for introducing such theological contortions. But even the modernists among the Reformed Jews thought this one was really taking it way too far. "Is that supposed to be a joke, or what? Has he gone completely meshuga?"

Assembled before the rabbi, on the main floor of the synagogue were the male Kohanims, most of whom wore serious, spade-shaped beards. Upon hearing his words, they arched their brows beneath their top hats or yarmulkes, exchanging puzzled glances with each other. Then turning their gazes toward the balcony, they sought further confirmation of their own indignant responses in the faces of their better halves. They were to be disappointed, however, for the assembled Jewish ladies leaning against the balustrade were barely listening, most were dozing under hats the size of wagons. With their ample, old-fashioned bustles and equally voluminous derrieres, they had to squeeze in the pews at awkward angles, making their feet fall asleep as well. Before the rabbi had uttered this outrageous notion, the only thing that had caused a stir was the stale air as it rose above, causing their fans to tremble slightly. Majestic feathers and flowers waved to the left and right, then up and down, accompanied by whispers, murmurs, and giggles, which the men of faith down below immediately shushed. Eyebrows continued to be raised, concerned over the thought that the Almighty might be making an exception for the young woman whose passage into womanhood they had gathered to witness: Franziska Kohanim. Had God capriciously chosen to respond to evil with good, instead of an eye for an eye, and a tooth for a tooth? Such logic went way over the heads of the giant hats and yarmulke strings of most members of the congregation.

"Does this house of worship belong to God or Kohanim? Is he now buying the blessing, the berakah, for his brood?"

Amidst all the commotion in the temple, stood Fränze before the rabbi, more beautiful than ever and a full head taller than the three adolescent boys with broken voices on either side of her. In her black rep and taffeta, she looked like a young woman participating in a Protestant confirmation ceremony, not a Jewish bat mitzvah. What made Fränze stand out even more than her evident femininity and stature, was that at the age of fifteen she already possessed something that most people would never develop their whole lives: a nimbus.

Just as her mother Mindel was good in a bad way, Franziska was bad in a good way. When her mother engaged in acts of charity, she inspired not joy but fear, because she lacked the traits one associated with true kindness, like warmth and cordiality. So too, Franziska lacked the characteristics inherent to true wickedness; she derived no pleasure from the suffering of others, nor did she desire to cause undue harm. This was for the simple reason that she wasn't interested in her fellow human beings, and by extension, felt no compassion for them either. Thus, the wickedness of which she was accused, had no end in and of itself. Franziska either played the devil or schemed because the situation called for someone to enliven the action or to punctuate her own boredom. The truly wicked revel in malice and thus persevere in the face of obstacles, the way a hunter doggedly pursues its prey. Franziska, by contrast, would quickly lose interest should anything prevent her from carrying out her schemes. Indeed, out of sheer weariness with evil, she could often be conciliatory, even benevolent, much to everyone's surprise. For Franziska, pleasure and amusement were all that mattered; meanness was a mere side effect of that pursuit.

No one really understood this, except for her father. Everyone else interpreted her mood swings as capricious and assumed that if she were not so lazy and careless, she would be able to carry out her diabolical plans more effectively. Or well-meaning observers, like her mother, saw Fränze as a sheep in wolf's clothing, which was, of course, just as patently false as those who attributed to her pure meanness.

To add insult to injury, when the Almighty created Franziska Kohanim he was obviously in a generous mood, scraping together all traces of beauty and grace that resided in her entire mishpocha[3] gene pool since the time of Moses, to give the world a masterpiece of loveliness and charm. Added to her fine limbs and height, she had a delicate skull covered in full, chestnut-brown hair; from the Beineschs, she had inherited dramatically arched eyebrows; from the Halevis, a high forehead and classic nose; from the von Katzenellenbogens, a full, heart-shaped mouth; and from the Rosenbergs, large, dark cherry eyes. As she grew older, her graceful appearance and voluptuous feminine curves, caused a sensation in the world of men. Between her inconstance and beauty, she inspired resentment, just as anything did that stood beyond the provincial and mediocre. Like many naturally beautiful people, she was completely devoid of vanity and preening. She strode about freely, without troubling herself over her appearance, which further embittered and angered other women who spent hours in front of the mirror.

However, Fränze was accustomed to it. Like a seagull against a stiff breeze, she sailed effortlessly above the jealousy and resentment, not allowing it to ruffle her feathers. If the constant hostility and attacks were to cease, she would have nonetheless noted their absence; for her detractors, whom she derided as "the rotten bunch," had become part of her existence. As such, she simply had to stand up to them. So that is precisely what she did on the day marking her entrance into her adult existence. She stood tall, with rosy cheeks and a brave face.

The two croaky-voiced boys offered their Hebrew stammerings, including high-octave "amens." Then to celebrate the bat mitzvah, Max Gulkowitsch fell upon the organ.

"Good Lord, like pearls to swine! These country bumpkins consider 'Little Mary Weeping in in the Garden' great art," Fränze thought. She had to concede, however, that her father's protégé, who was up there banging away, was well worth the money.

Neither the Polish Catholics nor German Protestants could boast of such an organist. They were, therefore, only too glad to borrow Max from the Reformed synagogue to perform at their church festivals and sacred music concerts despite their otherwise strong reservations against "God killers," as Christians sometimes referred to Jews, and a twelve-fingered one at that. Thus, their initial shame-faced tolerance for the assistance of the Jewish Maxim Gulkowitsch for Holy Mass or the Protestant service, soon gave way to appreciation for his artistry, for which they printed special flyers with the name "Max Gulkowitsch" in large, bold letters. In return for packing the churches, Max was made a whole three marks richer.

Hardly anyone suspected that the young man playing the organ was crippled and spent his days working as an apprentice piano tuner, handling tuning keys and hammers of felt and leather, repairing broken piano strings and ailing soundboards. Nor could anyone imagine that this budding piano tuner was also secretly composing operas at night.

The idea for an apprenticeship as a piano tuner came from Mindel, who was always on the lookout for mishaps, "What if the pianist's career doesn't work out? Well, what then? Who would even want to see a crippled, ugly Jew with twelve fingers on a concert stage?" Although his wife's sober judgment offended Samuel Kohanim, the self-appointed patron, he essentially had to agree with her. Mindel chalked it up as a partial victory. In one elegant move, she had offloaded an annoying boarder onto someone else.

Samuel Kohanim nonetheless still liked to prophesy, "You'll see, one day Max will prove that he was a good investment!"

"Yes, perhaps on Judgement Day, when money and property become superfluous anyway!" Mindel countered bitterly, ready to put down Samuel's bold predictions.

A celebration in the Schwetz ballroom followed the bat mitzvah. Fränze watched the subtle choreography unfold before her eyes, one which only those initiated in the Kohanim family secrets would appreciate. A few members of the family had set their sights on a certain middle-aged fellow, who bore a striking resemblance to a heap of angularly chopped chunks of meat, and who just then was busy standing at the periphery of the hall testing out his oratory skills on a group of distinguished guests. The crafty Kohanims were employing all manner of maneuvers to guide him toward the center of their table, directly next to the crooked-mouth Fanny. The "Segal with one *l*," as he always introduced himself, seemed to have no clear purpose and failed to escape, despite repeated attempts, and in his confusion, he even ventured to ask Fanny to dance. Doing her part to serve the family's interests, Franziska did not, for once, give into her usual habits and seek to humiliate Segal. She politely pretended not to have noticed him. Amused, she and her favorite cousin, Else, from the Segal family with two *l*'s, curtsied past him on their way to the ladies' room. There they found Elsa's mother, Dora, bent dramatically over the sink, allegedly suffering from an attack of the gall bladder.

Meanwhile, in the hall, the tailor from Bromberg, Segal with one *l*, had found a purpose. He was trying his hand at witty conversation with the lively half of Fanny's face, which had now taken on the rosy hue of a suckling pig. That boded well for his success. Even Mindel "the sleepwalker" was suddenly transformed, as if someone had set in motion a mysterious inner mechanism. She dispersed charm and wit throughout the room, like an atomizer perfume. She was hardly recognizable. Her presence itself was a surprise, as she had originally planned to stay at home with her problem-child, Martha, who was lying ill in bed at home in Sauermühle. However, she changed her mind, in light of the fact that Martha was always coming down with some mysterious illness just as soon as her parents' attention turned to one of her sisters, and that it was Fränze's bat mitzvah after all, and she also had the potential happiness of her poor daughter, Fanny, to think of—all of which outweighed Martha's real or imagined illness. Besides, one of the maids could take care of her. Mindel decided that she should be precisely where her family's future welfare required her most: in a gray-and-black striped gown with her fake pearls in the banquet hall of the Jewish community of Schwetz, beneath an enormous Star of David made from crinkly silver paper.

Fränze's entry into the adult world was celebrated with a polonaise, a popular Polish processional dance. At the climax of the party, she was hoisted up on a chair that was supported on the shoulders of some of the stronger guests, and for thirty minutes they rocked her back and forth above the heads of the dancers, who were singing and chanting congratulations. Once the waves of exuberance had already passed their peak, Samuel Kohanim clinked his wine glass. Everyone acted surprised, to say the least, when he officially announced the long-awaited engagement of his eldest daughter, Fanny, to the master tailor, Segal with one *l*, from Bromberg. "L'Chaim!" "To Life!"

No one would accuse Franziska of being someone inclined toward serious reflection or melancholy. However, after her bat mitzvah and Fanny's engagement, even she had to engage more intensely with such serious issues as adulthood and the mystery that seemed to surround the relationship between man and woman. She didn't think much of "mushy stuff"—a broad category in which she contemptuously included every emotional state. In this complicated way, she resembled her mother, from whom she had inherited an ability to maintain a certain emotional distance from the world. This trait, combined with her own gift for clairvoyance, helped her grasp the essence of things without the aid of reason, by pure instinct alone, bringing her to conclude: "The whole thing—adulthood, romantic relationships, all of it—is completely and utterly wrong!"

With such a declaration, she was thinking first and foremost of her sister's romantic nonsense. She also considered her parents' counsel that marriage was a serious life commitment, necessary for the continuation of the species and the inheritance of property. Not even kings had the luxury of romantic attachments; they too were bound to obey the necessities of life—just like us! For a Jewish girl, it all boiled down to one question: Should you let your parents choose your husband or do as the Christians had started doing and follow your own heart? Then again, why on earth did you have to get married at all? What was the point? Why did adults laugh so patronizingly about the whole thing and assume that she was an idiot when it came to such matters? When she thought of her parents' marriage, in which two strangers were chained together like a couple of galley slaves, condemned to spend their joyless lives together, she felt sad and sorry for them.

She recalled with horror the fate of Rachel Halevi, the ancestral mother of the Kohanims in West Prussia. When she was barely fifteen, about the same age as Fränze, her parents had married her off to a man thirty years her senior, Baruch Kohanim, to whom she, his second wife, bore twenty children! Eight survived.

Wedded at fifteen
A child each year she bore,
'Til she'd reached twenty-four!

So had it been since 1651. And so had it been just over thirty-three years since her own mother's parents had married her off at just sixteen years old to her father, Samuel Kohanim. As far back as she could remember, her mother had been either pregnant or in childbirth, surrounded by the metallic-sweet smell of blood or the sour scent of milk, often smelling of both at the same time, and when there was no wet nurse, she had one or two babies at her breast. The very thought of those smells turned Franziska's stomach.

Just like any child born and raised in the countryside, she knew about copulation and reproduction, and therefore didn't waste any time thinking about them. She had also noticed that women gave birth more frequently than the cows they kept. Only, unlike the women, the cattle were at least given time to rest in between. These disgusting facts were as plain as day. Yet girls only slightly older than her continued to operate under the delusion that love would make them forget everything and were thus eagerly awaiting their own marital bliss. Such a state of denial could only mean one thing: "Women are totally meshuga!"

Her two older sisters, Elli and Selma, seemed to be more reasonable. Elsbeth, known as Elli, had taken her obsession with sports so far out of the microcosm of her tightly knit Jewish family life that she could practically do whatever she wanted. Elli was hardly ever home, constantly traveling to tournaments and competitions or accepting invitations or money for trying to turn awkward Jewish daughters into equestrian or tennis amazons. She came home to unload her prizes and trophies and to preach to them about the unhealthy Jewish world, which, she said, degenerated Jews, keeping them fearful, small, and weak. But Selma, who was otherwise the exact opposite of Elli in everything, also managed to get her way. She was allowed to take lessons with her father's great cousin, Rabbi Ruben Conitzer in Danzig. She was now trying to get her parents to allow her to study theology at the university in Riga. Selma wanted to become a religious teacher for Jewish girls. It was criminal, she said, how Jews had been neglecting the religious education of girls for centuries and yet women were supposed to be the guardians and keepers of the faith. Unprompted, Selma quoted from scripture in the most minute detail. Her views were not particularly welcome in the synagogues and prayer houses. "What do women have to teach us about religion?" Samuel Kohanim warned his daughter to reign it in. Selma didn't heed his admonition, however; she wanted to save the world, or the Jewish one at any rate. She wrote provocative tracts on the subject in Jewish and non-Jewish newspapers that were radical in one way or another.

Each of these articles signed "S. Kohanim" somehow landed on Samuel Kohanim's desk, causing great distress. The "S." before "Kohanim" could only be understood as Samuel Kohanim. Had the region's "beacon of Reform Judaism" suddenly gone into an Orthodox religious rage and condemned the liberal education of Jewish girls as un-Jewish and harmful? Samuel Kohanim's indignant protest that he was not the author did not help matters. His business partner Zacharias Segall, the Segall with two *l*'s, with whom he ran the furniture factory, told him that people were secretly mocking him. His daughter's insolence could hurt the business. Samuel Kohanim could handle being hated, but he couldn't tolerate being mocked!

For the first time in his life, he was fuming with rage. He called all of his daughters to the salon, red with anger and trembling. He forbade Selma from signing his good name to her "bullshit" and threatened her with immediate marriage and disinheritance. Mindel had only barely managed to dissuade her equally furious and combative daughter from an equally flaming retort. Had she done so, Kohanim might have dropped dead from the shock of it. Selma left the house without saying goodbyes and moved in with her mentor in Danzig. She signed her new articles, "Wanda Vogel."[4]

Franziska didn't spend too much time thinking about what she was going to do with her life, apart from an excellent marriage to a banker or dignitary. As clueless as most people her own age, the only thing she did know was that she was adamantly against everything. As such, she would take pleasure in her private nihilism and do her best to irritate everyone around her until tension reached fever pitch. "Well, wait until the first time she falls in love," the adults would say, gazing at her condescendingly. Did she need any more proof that the whole idea of a "great love" was nothing more than a conspiracy against young girls? If she didn't want to end up like all these adults who were threatening her, she would have to arm herself against love. Love turns the lover into the victim, she concluded with a wisdom beyond her years. And she would never become a victim! If love were to play a part in her life at all, then she would rather be loved than love someone herself.

Her eccentric sister Flora had fallen in love with a spiritualist bookseller named Harry Fisch, during a visit with Selma in Danzig. The big hullaballoo it caused in the family merely confirmed her reservations about this madness called "love." From Warsaw to Berlin, every member of the Kohanim and Beinesh clans disapproved of the bridegroom, feeling justified in their objections to such a truly odd man. They, nonetheless, celebrated the engagement. It may not have been her turn yet, but there were, after all, worse things than a suitor who made his living selling mystical books. The parents agreed that the only thing Flora had going for her was her dowry of ten thousand marks; she would thus never be the most prime attraction on the marriage market. So why be picky? They paid for a modest celebration, stayed for two days, and then departed. One more daughter married, one less thing to worry about.

Not long after Flora's wedding, the second oldest Kohanim daughter, Selma, had secretly married an assistant rabbi in Danzig. It was with mild displeasure that Samuel and Mindel received the marriage announcement printed in silver letters, without an accompanying word of explanation. After the initial shock had worn off, relief prevailed. Fate had freed them from the troublesome task of finding a husband for their daughter, who was as difficult as she was unattractive. They took comfort in the fact that a secret marriage meant that they didn't have to pay a dowry and that there would be no local gossip, since Selma was already living in faraway Danzig. Plus, at least she was marrying a Jew. "Well, so be it," Mindel concluded. Samuel nodded with a sigh and then immersed himself in an article about the latest artificial fertilizers.

In the summer of 1910, two or three events overshadowed Selma's elopement.

For only a few days later, good news eclipsed the last traces of Mindel and Samuel's annoyance. As usual, the dispatch came by telegram courier, who had whizzed over from the village of Osche to the Sauermühle estate on his old, one-horse cart. Max had won a competition in Berlin for promising pianists! He would now be able to study with the famous Professor Busoni.

The sensation more than compensated Samuel for his daughters' strange acts of rebellion and earned him a great deal of respect in the county. Even those residents of Schwetz who had adopted the latest trend in seeing Jews as a separate race, celebrated Max as "a son of our city, on whom our highest hopes rest." It was a matter of honor to prepare a fitting reception for Max's next visit.

Max gave a concert in the Schwetz ballroom and was honored with ovations. As a farewell present, Kohanim gave him a tailor-made suit with tails and patent leather shoes in a suitcase that befit his status. Like a convalescent, Kohanim basked in the glow of his protégé's rising star.

In all the hustle and bustle of saying goodbye, Max secretly pressed a note into Franziska's hand at the station, "So that we can stay in touch." Before Fränze could say anything, Max boarded the train with a face flushed a deep red.

"Imagination is also education!" she exclaimed. Max didn't hear her, though, he was already waving cheerfully from the train window, his color returning to normal. The locomotive jerked with a start as white steam enveloped the train station. Franziska waved thoughtfully after Max.

Watching the steam-engulfed train carrying Max away to Berlin, she realized to her dismay just how boring it would be in Sauermühle without

Max. But before Franziska could get around to tormenting a new male victim, a scandal emerged that stirred up the whole county. Oda von Güldner, the ward of the German-Russian, sugar czar von Steinfeld had run away!

A few weeks after the news broke, Martha received a postcard from Berlin. "Post Restante," Schwetz main post office.

Dearest Martha,

A cat always lands on its feet! I have found a good position with a confectioner who is a like-minded Social Democrat.[5] *Write to Post Restante Post Office Berlin, reference: "cat."*

Yours,

O.

Martha stared dreamily at the bouquet of forget-me-nots on the front of the card and traced the raised embossing of the flower motif with her fingers. She could hardly wait to finally lock herself in the attic to answer Oda in her candlelit hideout.

Dearest Oda,

Finally! A sign of life that you are safe and sound. May God protect you! You have no idea what rumors are circulating about you here. First people said that you had run off with the pastor. Then they said that the pastor helped you escape. Then, and this part is documented, your guardian rode into the Lutheran church on horseback and from atop his horse amidst the pews, whipped the pastor. When the bells rang for vespers, the spooked horse must have run right up to the altar! To top it all off, the confused horse then drank the baptismal font dry! That's what I heard at any rate. Then Pastor Eickelmann and the church councilman Kümmerling took your guardian to court. He had to pay the pastor twenty marks for the disgrace and bruises and then gave the church a new roof, by choice or by force. How the miser must have suffered! Praise be to the Mighty One!

Affectionately yours,

Martha

P.S. It's just as well that your brother Rudolf is far away at the cadet academy and therefore couldn't have known where you were. I think your guardian would have beaten the living daylights out of him otherwise. Another novelty, thanks to what you did: it's not only the usual Jewish gossips who are now eagerly seeking my company. Even the German ones, like widow Mehlich and Mrs. Hundertschön as well as the Polish gossips Pani Lublinska and Kowalska have been courting me in hope of some news about you from me. You'd hardly be surprised, however, to hear that they still will only receive me through the servants' entrance at the back of their homes. At least that's true at Pani Lublinska's. At Kowalska, by contrast, I have to sit on a chair opposite the crucifix and stare at a tortured Jew the whole time, who they think is God. To comfort me, Kowalska serves me pork-fat buns, knowing full well that I'm not allowed to eat it. So rude!

PPS: Something top secret: I have an admirer! But not a word to anyone!!!

Reading the PPS, Oda raised her eyebrows. You had to take Martha's comments with a grain of salt and appreciate them as a mere vision of reality or an idea of what might be. No one knew this better than Oda.

Oda had always thought it unfair how the Lord God had so exhausted himself on Martha's older sister Franziska that all he had left for Martha were the rejects from the ancestral line. Martha was small, chubby, had frizzy, dull grayish brown hair, a color called "dun," that is normally associated with mongrels. From her mother, she had inherited her stone-gray-eyes, but hers were even more closely set, making her look like a mouse when she squinted. Her face was dominated by an overly large, fleshy nose that overshadowed her small, thin-lipped mouth that was filled with bad teeth that always looked like gray moss. Her skin was constantly mottled by rashes, and she suffered from asthma. And the way she wore her hair, in a sort of antiquated pompadour known as a French quif, made her resemble an overgrown chicken with a cockscomb. As if her looks, somewhat misshapen figure, and whiny voice were not bad enough, even worse was Martha's colorful imagination. Martha lied through her teeth.

What was it that inspired Martha to want to invent her very own world? Why couldn't she be satisfied with her life and the world in which she lived with the lumber-industry Jews in Sauermühle? It wasn't so bad, was it? Why did she tell people that she was actually the illegitimate daughter of a Habsburg prince? Everyone had tried to get her to stop, to help her see reason. Nothing worked. She simply could not resist the urge to fantasize. Her tall tales were so absurd that they prevented anything worse from happening. She did not understand references to facts nor the grief that such talk caused her mother.

"What does one have to do with the other?" Martha wondered. "The sky is actually black, and everyone still think it's blue! It depends on how you look at it."

"There's still no way to turn an owl into a nightingale," Mindel argued. All appeals to the love of truth and the eighth commandment fell on deaf ears. Martha fought tooth and nail to defend the rights of the world of fantasy. According to her screwball logic, every person had three lives: the first one you were born into by chance and resided there only temporarily, like a train in a switching yard awaiting its reassembly and eventual departure. From there, you boarded the transit train of vivid dreams, that is, your second life. That dream train, in turn, transported you to the third and final life, the unique one that is truly your own. Such a life had been earned by the dreams and ideas conjured up during the first and second lives. You might say it had been dreamed into reality. As Martha saw it, those who failed to enter the third world, were condemned to remain stuck in the world in-between, in the realm of dreams, or even worse: they remained caught in the putrefying banality of first world.

"Yes, but…?!" Grandmother Beinesch implored her eccentric granddaughter "You shouldn't go around talking about such delusional fantasies!"

Martha still didn't want to hear it.

"Why not?" she raged. "Everyone's waiting for the Messiah and the resurrection of the dead, and they talk about and live by it, acting as if it were a fact, don't they? Can you please tell me what any of that has to do with reality and reason?"

The "yes, but" with which they tried to talk her out of the whole thing by trying to reconcile the normal nonsense of the "here and now" with the even deeper nonsense of the belief in the hereafter, the resurrection at the end of days, gradually drove the whole family crazy. As the head of family, Samuel Kohanim put his foot down: "Where would we end up if everyone took the liberty to imagine a completely new life for themselves, ignoring reality? We'd all end up wearing a spring hat in winter and ready for the madhouse!" He thus forbade all further sophistries about truth and falsehood and the meaning of spring hats in winter and the like—effective immediately. If Martha told any more tall tales, she would be sent to a mental hospital. Forever!

Oda thought back on all this when she read her friend's letter and thus put little stock in the notion that her friend's admirer existed in real life. She was nonetheless curious to see what else Martha could come up with because she enjoyed her stories.

After the ban on all manner of philosophical discussions, the family realized that Martha's delusions could no longer be given free reign. Something had to be done. Inspired by articles in his scientific gazettes, Samuel Kohanim concluded that his third youngest had fallen victim to the latest female ailment: hysteria.

Dr. Rosenzweig, the esteemed neurologist in Bromberg, was an expert in the field of hysteria. Mindel went to see him with Martha while on a visit to the Segals with one *l*. Much to her surprise, she found out that Martha's condition was called *mythomania*, and was a form of hysteria known as *pseudologia fantastica*. It was not a disease for which you should punish someone for having any more than you would someone with mumps or influenza.

"Does that mean it's contagious?" Mindel asked in horror.

"Well," Dr. Rosenzweig chuckled merrily, "it depends on how you react to it."

Martha, meanwhile, after undergoing Dr. Rosenzweig's inspection, was standing behind a screen putting her clothes back on, after which she took a seat on an Ottoman stool covered with Persian pillows.

Scribbling away with his steel-shaft pen on Martha's file, Dr. Rosenzweig added: "As a side note really, you might consider an enema. They won't do any harm, if done only now and again, and a good bowel movement is good for your mental health," the mental health specialist continued, giving Mindel a mischievous wink that caused his monocle to fall from his right eye.

Mindel breathed a sigh of relief. Recently doctors had discovered that hysteria was located in the intestines and uterus. And so, it must be with Martha! All her troubles—her illnesses and her insanity—had their origin in her abdomen. Why hadn't Mindel thought of that before?!

After the visit with Dr. Rosenzweig, Martha's lies flew faster and freer and she had significantly fewer rashes. Progress came at a price, however. The toilet at the Kohanim home was now constantly occupied. To prevent an imminent epidemic of *pseudologia fantastica* in the household, all female members were regularly given enemas and treatments with salt from a Bohemian spa town, Franzensbad. As you might expect, this in no way improved the family's mental health. It did, however, give everyone diarrhea and flatulence, and a major grudge against Martha. Elli and Fränze responded by being even meaner to Martha. Little did they know, however, that their revenge against Martha for the enemas would eventually lead to further harm.

Around this time, one of the Seven Biblical Plagues, the sports-crazy Elli, also known in the village as "the Jewess on horseback," came home one day from one of her rides with some incredible news: "Martha's gotta boyfriend!"

Everyone awaited with bated breath for the punch line of this outlandish idea. But unfortunately, Elli remained quiet. Since she didn't add any further detail, they chalked it up to Elli's typical bluster and quickly forgot her having ever mentioned it.

Dearest Oda,

Congratulations on your marriage to your Reinhold! May God protect and bless you!!! I hope your husband, God willing, bakes you a cake every day. For life won't seem so sweet if you have to look for work as a seamstress. My sister Fanny and her family (she gave birth to twins in Bromberg) may be able to help you out of your troubles. The Segals are moving to Berlin and will soon be opening a high-end tailor shop for men on Friedrichstraße! Perhaps you might find something to do there? Just don't say that I sent you or that we're in touch. As for me, I'm doing well and am happy. It's not only because of love. It's also because "King Cobra" (Fränze) has found a new victim and has thus left me alone for a while now. Sending you hugs, love, and blessings!

Yours truly,
Martha

King Cobra wasn't harassing Martha because she was preoccupied with another matter: she had managed to catch the eye of a young nobleman, Stanislaw Solkowsky, the county hotshot. Because of some shady incident that was only talked about in back rooms and at billiard and gambling tables, Pan Stanislaw had had to take leave of his regiment a few months prior. Since then, he had let the whole world know just how incredibly bored he was to be stuck on his home turf. Apart from gambling, which his family had forbidden him on pain of disinheritance, the only appropriate occupations for a young nobleman were hunting and romances. He might have tried his hand at running the estate. But, alas, he lacked the requisite interest, experience, and intellect. Not to mention the fact that even a Rothschild would have despaired at the state of the count's finances.

Out of sheer boredom, Pan Stanislaw wanted to inspect the vaunted assets of the daughter of his family's former estate manager, Samuel Kohanim. To this end, he planted himself on the balcony of the Elbing confectionery, just as he lounged nonchalantly in the officers' casino. Through the mysterious clouds of smoke coming from his Oriental cigarette, he practiced the brooding gaze with which he intended to captivate Franziska just as soon as she entered the café. To enhance the effect, he pushed a monocle in front of his left eye and sat perched like a hunter on a deer stand, waiting for his unsuspecting prey to appear. When Franziska stepped into the paradise of cakes to consume a Schiller curl, her favorite buttercream-filled pastry, as she always did when she was in Schwetz, she noticed the arrogant snob sitting in the balcony, with the piece of glass covering his herring-colored fisheye, and she smiled. It was a Mona Lisa smile, half mocking, half blissful. Pan Stanislaw, however, mistook it for one inspired by the same charms he had practiced on chambermaids and innkeepers' daughters.

"Well, I'll show him!" thought Fränze with a sneer. So began the torment of Pan Stanislaw just as soon as Franziska had entered the confectioner's shop. For the next four or five weeks, she ignored the fisheye so perfectly that you could practically hear the sounds of his breaking heart. Soon, not a day went by without Pan Stanislaw sending perfumed letters with silly love poems, sweets, or flowers. She shared the sweets, carried the flowers to the cemetery, and tore up the letters, and carelessly tossed them into the estate's dung pile. Burning letters in the stove seemed too cumbersome and conspicuous to her, because the kitchen was always occupied, and even at night the kitchen maid slept there on a cot. The most discreet solution thus seemed to be throwing the shit to the shit! Only she hadn't considered that the maids might pick out the pieces of the torn letters from the muck. So before long, young people in the village mockingly recited the count's love letters to Franziska, with feigned pathos, especially when someone from the count's family was within earshot. Everyone in Schwetz and the village of Osche enjoyed the scandal of a Solkowsky allowing himself to be led by the nose by a Jewish woman. To add insult to injury, "the little count," as the whole world now called him, sent a letter to Samuel Kohanim in which he asked for the hand of his daughter, whom he intended to elevate to the nobility by marrying her. She would have to be baptized first, of course. Enclosed with the letter was a ring of middling value, intended to confirm the seriousness of his intentions. It was clear to Kohanim that the man must not have been in his right mind when he wrote the letter. Only serious intoxication would have excused such a letter. Nevertheless, he was annoyed at the awkward position into which the count had put everyone with this blunder. Samuel had to do something. However, he was at a loss as to how to deal with this affront appropriately. So he simply let the matter slide and hoped that it would resolve itself. If everyone involved wanted to save face, he reasoned, they would have to act as if nothing had happened, preferably without saying a word about it. Fränze decided to help her father out of the precarious situation by sending the following reply to her admirer:

Dear Sir,
I'm sure that many young maidens would feel extremely flattered by such a proposal. However, I must confess that a union between two people of such socially unequal social status would be most unfortunate, since it would involve a union between a member of a noble family, who can trace her nobility back five thousand years to Moses and whose merit is based on religion and wisdom, and an aristocrat of your sort, whose ancestors only very recently rose in rank and honor, most likely through bloodshed on glorious battlefields. This would be true even if the bridegroom were to convert to the Mosaic faith. For this reason, I must gratefully decline your generous offer. In the interest of our families' allegiance, I am relieving my beloved father of the delicate task of responding to you and I hereby return your ring to you. Your intentions were surely honorable, as mine are now. With respect, we wish you a happy future with a bride who is your equal.

Sincerely yours,
Franziska Kohanim
Sauermühle

In the aftermath of Fraziska's letter, relations between the Solkowskys and the Kohanims, which had been good for generations, cooled rather abruptly. Not long thereafter, the family shipped off the "little count" to

Krakow, where he was supposed to pursue some pointless course of study, which, as everyone in Schwetz speculated, most likely consisted of learning about alcohol, whist, and love affairs. The Jews in the district reacted to the whole story with cheers, and a derisive smirk, pleased that one of theirs had put one of their goyish lords in his place. For their part, the German and Polish neighbors found the audacity of someone they deemed a Jewish brat genuinely troubling.

Fränze's special nimbus was becoming more like, a "disaster waiting to happen"! Only a good, quick match as far away from Schwetz and Zempelburg as possible could remedy the situation and prevent the worst, the family said. But Franziska thought otherwise. She was not enthusiastic about a "good, quick match as far away as possible."

Meanwhile, roused by rumors and curiosity, fate made a small effort to alter the course of affairs. By chance, it inspired the busybody Franziska to poke her nose in an unexplored aspect of the small synagogue's rituals, the *mikvah*. Her mother went there once a month to engage in ritual bathing for purification. Fränze had been wondering why Martha had recently been eager to accompany their mother to the bath. Most Jewish daughters wholeheartedly resisted this obligation. What was behind Martha's sudden devotion?

The mikvah in Schwetz was an enclosed, dark, moss-lined hole in which the water was freezing cold and smelled musty even in summer. Sharing this water hole with all the other Jewish women in the district, who perhaps still had fleas jumping out of their wigs, required a good lantern, solid faith, and, not least of all, strong nerves. The Jewish women in the rural area therefore preferred to immerse themselves in the fresh but ice-cold waters of the village mikvah, which drew its water directly from the Schwarzwasser River. Instead of waiting like a good daughter would, on the stone bench in front of the mikvah, Martha suddenly darted under a nearby hedge. There, camouflaged by the green leaves, lurked a pomaded provincial dandy, whispering sweet nothings to Martha. Unfortunately, an elderberry bush blocked Franziska's view. She thus had to be satisfied with merely taking note of the overwhelming scent of his burdock hair oil and of his equally oily conversation. "Martha's got a boyfriend! I can hardly believe it!"

Franziska kept the discovery to herself. She couldn't resist, however, regularly dropping hints to Martha that suggested that she knew her secret. Martha reacted by going into a panic. The severity of her coughing fits betrayed just how close Fränze's comments were to hitting the mark.

From Max in Berlin, there was nothing but the usual reports of his success, along with newspaper clippings and concert programs. The count's son, who had courted Franziska so scandalously, was now in Krakow, and the never-ending parade of upstanding, single Jewish gentlemen were boring her to tears. How else to punctuate the intense boredom of the countryside than to thoroughly investigate Martha's dubious admirer? In exchange for some sweets, she learned from the children in the Jewish quarter of the village that the man's name was Wilhelm Rubin and that he worked as a hewer in a coal mine in Oberhausen. He was staying with relatives and merely "passing through town."

In other words, Mr. Rubin was no gentleman. He mooched off his relatives. "Well, who else would be interested in someone like Martha?" thought Franziska. Should she tell her father, warn him, and cry foul? Should she condescend to rat out her younger sister? Or should she take matters into her own hands and foil this false suitor's plans?

Franziska being Franziska, she decided to handle it herself. She simply had to; otherwise, the terrible boredom would set in again. Therefore, the next time her mother was preparing to go to mikvah, Franziska insisted on accompanying her. "Mom, Martha has already gone with you four times. I've only been once," she said to justify her suggestion. Her mother agreed. Martha would have to stay home and take her prescribed enemas. The fight against her hysteria never seemed more necessary, as Martha howled and made a scene.

It was agreed that Mindel would perform her religious duties at the bath, while Franziska, armed with a pot of chicken soup, would pay a visit to a sick tenant's wife. There was no better excuse for strolling through this part of Osche. It was close to the famous part of the village where Napoleon had suffered a broken axle on his escape from Russia. At night, Polish villagers still secretly laid flowers in memory of their former liberator from the Prussians. That was where the Rubins were said to live. What a horrible place! Franziska thought, wrinkling her nose. She stepped cautiously through the mud and garbage, protecting her fine violet-blue boots. In the village alleyways, unbathed children played with dried, horse droppings that gleamed like gold, while a young man with a flat cap pulled down to his ears and plaid knickerbockers practiced riding his bicycle through the muck without using his hands. With his arms casually folded across his chest, he pedaled and whistled the imperial waltz.

Willy Rubin in the flesh! The difference between Willy Rubin and the count's son was that Willy Rubin not only thought that he was irresistible, he actually was. Apart from his "village beau" hairstyle, Rubin embodied his name, *rubin* meaning "ruby" in German. Like a glistening red jewel, he stood out amidst the coal briquettes of the other Jews in this district. Lively, tall, and quivering with energy, his alert, gray-blue eyes always seemed to be on the lookout for an opportunity, like a fired arrow in search of its target. If someone like him was poking around with someone like Martha, it could only mean one thing: he's a gold digger! "Well, I'll put him in his place," Franziska determined with delight.

She did have to admit, however, that this provincial dandy had a certain *je ne sais quoi*. Despite his *kleedaje* or "get-up," which corresponded to the vulgar taste of the street, there was no mistaking that this Willy Rubin, apart from his athletic, broad-shouldered build, full, thick hair, straight nose, blue-gray eyes, and strikingly light skin, had a typical Jewish face that radiated indestructible health, enterprise, and wit.

Dealing with this provincial dandy promised to be amusing. Besides, it was for the good of the family. It wouldn't be anything spectacular like the story with the silly little count, but it sure beat boredom. Applying a similar logic, she figured that although Willy Rubin may have been a nobody: better a nobody than no one. Plus, she could get one over on Martha, have a good laugh, and act like she was defending the family. No need to be modest!

Fränze was still wrapped in thought about where Martha might have picked up Willy or Willy Martha, when the man she was observing suddenly hit the brakes and then came hurtling toward her. Before she knew it, the man had persuaded her to "take a turn" with him, perched on the bicycle's handlebars. Fränze consented, not merely out of curiosity, but also because she had smelled Jucthen aftershave on him, a radical departure from most men around there, who usually smelled like a mixture of sour sweat and stale tobacco smoke. A certain *je ne sais quoi* indeed!

"So, am I mistaken, or do I have the incredible honor of chauffeuring the legendary Franziska Kohanim?" Wilhelm Rubin whispered with a wry grin and a touch of irony.

"Don't be such an idiot, Mr. Rubin!" she said harshly.

"Oh, did you hear that?! The fräulein already knows my name! Well, to what do I owe this honor?"

"If you do everything you can to attract attention, which isn't difficult in a backwater like Osche, then you shouldn't be surprised if people know who you are! They have no choice!"

At this point, Willy would have liked to have showered Franziska with compliments. His usual schtick. But he instinctively held back, preferring to laugh out loud and show off his magnificent pearly white teeth. Franziska couldn't help but be impressed by his restraint and was therefore all the more eager to demonstrate that he had failed to make a positive impression.

"Well, thank you very much! I can't say that your driving skills are much to my liking! This whole bicycling thing is really more in keeping with the tastes of simpler souls. For goodness sake, just pull over!"

"I cannot do otherwise, ma'am," he wisecracked and, with a skid, brought the bicycle to a hard stop.

Franziska dismounted the handlebars haughtily, smoothing her skirt and hair. Willy Rubin interpreted the gesture as feminine self-consciousness and grinned broadly. This nettled Franziska all the more. Who did he think he was?

Before Willy Rubin could continue his ride, Franziska grabbed the handlebars with both hands, and eyes narrowed, hissed at him, "And one more thing, Sir Gallant! Keep your filthy hands off my sister Martha!"

"Only if I get her caring, older sister as her replacement," he teased, as he fished a cigarette out from behind his ear.

"Replacement for what? You have got some nerve!"

"Well, everyone has their talents!"

"On a bike and in the coal mines, perhaps!"

"Wait and see!"

He looked her firmly in the eye and held the lit match he had struck to light his cigarette in front of her nose. Without flinching or showing any sign of pain, he let the flame burn down to his fingers, where it extinguished itself.

"Schmuck!"

After all the unpleasantness that Franziska had caused the family with the count's son, the family was delighted that the disaster-waiting-to-happen had decided to accompany her sister Fanny and her children to Berlin.

She was supposed to make herself useful there for a while. Perhaps she could find a suitable match in the German capital? After all, Berlin's elite frequented the tailor shop belonging to the Segals with one *l*.

Dear Oda!

The Cobra is out of the house, at last, and I am coming back to life now that my Willy is finally thinking of asking my father for my hand. I am enclosing a photo with this letter, which he had taken in Bromberg on the day of our secret engagement. Wilhelm doesn't come from our social circle, but his father, as far as I know, owns a hat shop in the "first building on the square," across from St. Mary's Church in Königsberg. His parents divorced when Wilhelm was young, and his father's business likely did not have room for him. So he went to the Ruhr, like many other Jews who were driven there by poverty, to seek his fortune. But you don't necessarily find such a thing a thousand meters underground. And because he doesn't want to walk around the village with a heavy rucksack on his back, peddling goods like the other poor devils here, he is considering starting a construction business with his savings. If I could add my dowry, we'd be just fine. His father also plans to contribute something. Please cross your fingers that it all goes well! I'm delighted to hear that Fanny has hired you and that you've even been promoted to head seamstress at the tailor shop. Now you can make a living. Don't be surprised, by the way, if you cross paths with the Cobra in Berlin. She is staying with Fanny for a while and may the good Lord make her stay there as long as possible and preferably never return!

May God protect you!
With love,
your Martha

My Dearest Martha!
Thank you for the wonderful news about you and your Willy. I am keeping my fingers crossed for you and hope that your father is not too strict with him and that your marital bliss can finally begin. There's some news here too.

Regarding the Cobra, to everyone's astonishment, we've hardly seen her at all. She's been out all the time, not returning until the dead of night. Gerson, Fanny's husband, has worried what "disaster waiting to happen" might be expected from Franziska? But the situation has, thankfully, gotten better. Max has been keeping Fränze busy, showing her Berlin's music scene and taking her to various soirees and dinners, where she should finally be able to find a proper suitor. And in case you haven't yet heard: Max played in front of the emperor!!! He'll now have access to the most elite society, which of course the Cobra doesn't want to miss out on. So you can hope that

Fränze won't be coming back to Sauermühle anytime soon and will stay in Berlin for some time.

Your Oda

The bomb dropped on Yom Kippur.

The news arrived by way of an innocent card. Every year Fanny sent the family a card with well wishes for the holiday, listing every one of her sisters by name. This year she did exactly the same as she always did, and so included Franziska's name. A careless mistake? Why would Fanny send a greeting to Sauermühle that included Franziska, if she was, to everyone's great relief, still staying with her in Berlin?

Samuel sent several telegrams to Fanny:

+++ Where is Fränze? +++

Gerson Segal wired back by express telegram:

+++ Fränze left 7 weeks ago +++

Samuel then sent a telegram to Max:

+++ Where is Fränze? +++

Reply from Max:

+++ Puzzling question +++

Since this was a delicate matter for Franziska's reputation, her parents agreed to maintain strict silence for the time being. They did not want to arouse any suspicion that something may be wrong with their daughter. Whenever Mindel got worked up and imagined all manner of terrible scenarios that may have befallen her fourth-born, Samuel would brush it off. "Fränze may be reckless, but she's certainly not stupid. She won't let anything get her down! Everything will be fine."

"But she can't just disappear like that, can she?"

"We'll find out," he snapped back.

Then an idea occurred to him. He looked up the address of the suitcase manufacturer Bruno Dahnke in the Berlin address book. Against her parents' wishes, Franziska's favorite cousin, Else Segall had secretly married the Christian suitcase manufacturer Dahnke in Marienbad. In consequence, the Segalls expelled Else from the family circle with a week-long shive, as would be done for someone who had died. Else was thereafter deemed an outcast and any contact with her taboo. Until then, the whole family, including the reformed Kohanims, had observed the ban on Else and avoided all contact with her.

Of course! That's where she is! Samuel Kohanim was suddenly sure of it. She just didn't have the courage to say that she was with Else! Why hadn't he thought of that right away? Giving everyone the slip by saying goodbye everywhere and then staying somewhere else, with her favorite cousin who has been disowned by the family and declared dead. Only Franziska could be so cunning! How like Franziska!

An express telegram to Else and Bruno Dahnke:
+++ Kindly request information about Franziska's whereabouts +++

Else Dahnke from Chausseestraße 57 in Berlin immediately wired back to Samuel:
+++ Fränze at our place for coffee the day before yesterday +++ Lives with Fanny +++ What happened? +++

Samuel could finally reassure Mindel that nothing had happened to Franziska. Meanwhile, Martha found a way to monopolize the attention of Samuel's better half, as she always did whenever too much attention was being paid to another of her sisters. But this time, Martha was indeed truly suffering. *Vegetative dystonia*, Dr. Rosenzweig confirmed. The real reason for Martha's suffering was that Willy, her secret fiancé, had vanished without a trace. Not only that but her older sister Elli was marching around the house in men's breeches with clanking spurs and a riding crop, shouting whenever she bumped into Martha or heard about the imbroglios in Berlin, "What a mishpocha! Good heavens, what a mishpocha!"

"Where in the hell is that Jezebel?" Samuel asked himself, feeling less afraid than suspicious that his reckless darling was about to commit a great folly in sinful Berlin. Samuel could not go to Berlin just then, as his business partner Zacharias Segall had suffered a heart attack and his new assistant and Shabbas goy, Alwin, a Christian who was to step in when Samuel could not work on the Sabbath, had not been sufficiently trained. He therefore turned to Max, asking him to make inquiries on his behalf and, if all else failed, call the police. He sent the relevant power of attorney by cable to the lawyer and notary Mr. Lachmund, Esq.[6] in Berlin. This delicate assignment came at an inopportune moment for Max.

Having just completed six months of keyboard exercises that Professor Busoni had given him to improve the agility of his more awkward left hand, he now wanted to devote his full attention to rehearsing the Goldberg Variations in order to expand his repertoire. And then there were also the piano concertos for twelve fingers that he had composed, which he had planned to premiere at his next performance.

What's more, although he felt that he owed such a favor to Kohanim, he did not think he was cut out for detective work. He found a solution, however, in the form of the man who lived on the other side of his music room: a police informant. In exchange for taking on the investigation, Max offered the man, a certain Mr. Alois Steinspalter, two free tickets to his concerts and a small fee, an offer which he gladly accepted.

Mr. Steinspalter had two of the most important characteristics for his job. He was so inconspicuous that no one ever remembered him; and he had the instinct of a greyhound on the hunt after it had picked up the scent.

The first thing he did was pay a visit to Franziska's cousin Else Dahnke, née Segall with two l's to ask to see more photographs of the missing Franziska Kohanim and to inquire about her habits, preferences, and to get information about any other people the missing woman might have known in Berlin, apart from her sister, Fanny, and her brother-in-law, Gerson Segal.

He paid a visit to the very pregnant Oda Hanke, née von Güldner, in the back courtyard behind a bakery located at Oderberger Straße 9 in the neighborhood of Prenzlauer Berg. The sole piece of information he obtained from Mrs. Hanke, however, was that Franziska was obsessed with the buttercream-filled, Schiller horns. But that was of no use since Schiller horns could be found anywhere.

He did not reveal to Max how he actually ended up tracking down Franziska; it was his professional secret.

When Max paid him for the information, he thanked him with such exaggerated gratitude that Max wondered whether he had expected more money and was somehow trying to get him to pay more or if he simply enjoyed being privy to other people's misfortunes.

The sun was shining brightly on the Sunday in October, when Max set off to visit Franziska. Armed with a bouquet of asters and a box of sweets, he was in high spirits as he boarded a horse-drawn carriage at Spittelmarkt and handed the coachman a note with the address. With a thick Berlin accent,[7] the man replied.

"You can't be serious! You want me to take you to that den of iniquity?! The Night Jacket Quarter!"[8]

"Yes, I'd like to get there today, if that's at all possible, please!"

"I'll take you as far as the corner of Müller. You're gonna have to walk the rest of the way yourself. I won't drive no one to that place!" the man said shaking his head.

Sparrstraße in Wedding, where Franziska supposedly lived didn't have as bad a reputation as the Scheunenviertel or Mulackstraße with their rent boys and girls-for-hire. But it wasn't much better than the notorious Soldiner Straße. In a part of town like that, a gentleman with a bouquet of flowers looked about as exotic here as a bear balancing on a beach ball.

"What graveyard did you steal those from?" a boy asked. Max turned to look at him: a mostly good-natured face despite its woeful appearance of a split lip, jack-o-lantern smile, and a left eye surrounded by violet-green flesh that he couldn't open more than a crack.

Max silently asked the Almighty to protect his hands, which rested like precious instruments in his custom-made, saffron-colored deerskin gloves—the only luxury he allowed himself.

He couldn't believe that proud Franziska Kohanim could be living in such a place, a lightless hole, surrounded by ramshackle houses and garbage-filled streets, where she would have to share a toilet with some five-dozen people. Such a toilet was, however, one of the only places where a person could get a little privacy. Tenants often used it for sex, going at it until someone kicked at the door because they urgently needed to go to the bathroom. Men were known to ambush girls and women in the toilet, and do God knows what to them once they had gotten them inside.

In the hallway, into which Max now entered in a state of disbelief, it stank of damp lime walls mixed with the scent of rutabagas and pearl barley, which people called "calves' teeth," along with urine, rats, vermin, and Goldgeist insecticide used to combat lice.

The courtyards were overflowing with screaming children who all looked pale and rickety, and had deep circles under their eyes. Their dirt-smeared bodies only rarely encountered soap and water and it had been so long since a comb had touched their hair that it had begun to hang in matted clumps. The more well-groomed children had shaved heads because of the lice, but they too smelled like animals.

From their noses the snot hung like wax from candles, which they coughed up with a loud rattle and then spit out in high arches. They used to hold competitions in the courtyard in which even the scrawnier consumptives took part, seeing who could spit their bloody tuberculosis sputum the farthest. The healthier among them always won, however, wresting the last little bits of oatmeal, the only sweet they could afford there, from the hands of the losers, who protested loudly.

When the snot-nosed children weren't fighting or attacking someone like wild animals, begging or stealing, they were yelling or scribbling obscenities on the walls that would have made even the most hardened of Berlin's beer coachmen blush. In short, these Wedding children were the refuse of their parents, considered by most to be the scum of society. Their progenitors smelled predominately of sweat, menstruation, cheap booze, patchouli, and sperm, and they seemed to consist of stinking, bickering prostitutes, and raucous drunks, who impregnated their daughters or sent them out into the streets to earn enough for a bottle of hooch. "That way you're at least good for something!" Anywhere you looked you saw a young woman with either a swollen belly or a baby in their arms.

Max stopped on the fifth floor. Franziska was supposed to be living there. He didn't recognize the name on the door, however, and he thought for a moment that perhaps in his eagerness to earn some money, his overzealous informant might have been mistaken. He thus opened the door with some trepidation, uncertain as to what he would find.

Dear Mr. Kohanim,

As instructed, I went in search of your dear daughter and was able to locate her whereabouts. I have just paid her a visit.

First of all, I would like to inform you that Franziska is in good health and is staying at the place in question of her own free will, even as her situation is rather precarious. The young lady has recklessly entered into an adventurous misalliance with a certain person named Wilhelm Rubin from Oberhausen, which has not been, if I am permitted to say so, without repercussions. Not wanting to bring shame upon her parents, she has not ventured to come home. I am aware that your daughter will have to face consequences for her ill-considered actions. But I also consider it a blessing that the man who brought your daughter into these circumstances, is at least

Jewish. A complete expulsion, as in the case of Cousin Elsa, would therefore perhaps be too severe a measure.

Although I am in no way entitled to give you an opinion or even advice on this delicate matter, I believe I know how you feel about Franziska. A speedy marriage for your dear daughter could perhaps be the best thing for all concerned. If this Rubin should be so dishonorable as not to want to marry your dear daughter, I would like to offer you, my generous benefactor, myself! I have long admired Franziska, and even in this hour I stand by her and the family to whom I owe everything. Therefore, I offer to take Mr. Rubin's place, and humbly ask for your daughter's hand in marriage.

I hope you will forgive my boldness and regard this as an expression of my unwavering loyalty to the House of Kohanim.

With highest regards,
Maxim Gulkowitsch

Out of tact, Max failed to mention in his letter that the "business" in question, which Willy had always talked about, had turned out to be a small shop in Kreuzberg's Eisenbahnstraße, which essentially consisted of him, two or three alligator wrenches, and a lot of optimism. Willy Rubin called it "under construction" and owing to his incredible efficiency, spent most of working hours sitting in the betting office or at one of Berlin's racetracks, wagering on "show, place, and win." He was allegedly waiting for money to arrive from his father's store in Königsberg. If he did bother coming home, he came armed with him an expensive bottle of wine or champagne, but only rarely with food or money. Franziska was forced to see what she could do. She had never learned a trade, and what she did know how to do, speak French and play the piano, she did not know very well. She had experienced neither fear nor debt, and in her complete naiveté ran straight to the French embassy in Berlin, inquiring about any office clerk or telephone operator positions that required knowledge of French.

Unfortunately, her first encounter with a native French speaker revealed that what Madame Bertha had taught the girls may have sounded like French to her family but was incoherent to anyone actually from France. The one exception being *le mot de Cambronne*. It certainly wasn't French, nor was it Languedoc, which was supposedly spoken in Quebec and to which the blessed Madame Bertha once referred. It was simply gibberish with some French mixed in. The idea that Madame Bertha had spent years teaching them a completely fictitious language that could only be spoken with her alone, was a joke entirely to Franziska's liking.

"So, in the end, that bony ole hag sure got her revenge on us! Someone should build a memorial for Madame Bertha for inventing an entire language!" she laughed.

She had made a real fool of herself at the embassy, she admitted to Max, and should have been chased away in disgrace. "They only let me in the door at all because of my fashionable clothing and good looks," Fränze recalled with a smile. "I wanted to melt into the ground, which was what I deserved, considering all the pranks I used to play on Madame Bertha. God rest her soul! But the secretary didn't kick me out. Feeling sorry for me, or so I thought, he invited me for coffee and cake. My hunger was greater than my shame, so instead of my usual buttercream-filled Schiller curl, I ordered a giant bockwurst with a mountain of potato salad and lots of bread. It had been two days since I had eaten a decent meal, and I had no idea when the next one would be. I ate until I nearly exploded!"

Laughing, Franziska hit the table with both hands. Max looked down at her hands, the beautiful hands that he had always admired so much were no longer angelic and immaculately manicured; they were red and cracked with calluses and broken fingernails. He would have loved to have held those maltreated hands in his own until they healed again.

"But when the fellow tried to fondle my knee under the table, I was so shocked that I drove my fork into the back of his hand. I am a lady, after all! Well, forget about that! French adieu! I had more luck with the piano, thanks to my great master teacher, Max Gulkowitsch!"

She gave Max a heartfelt bow, bending as far as her pregnant belly would allow. Watching her contortions, Max realized with sadness that Franziska had lost her formerly lithe form.

Franziska continued: "I spend my evenings playing at various new movie palaces that need music to accompany the cinematography. In this line of work, you really have to react quickly. When the hero's left foot enters the lower edge of the screen, you have to start playing Strauss's *Sphinx Waltz*. Then his beloved opens her eyes, and you have to quickly switch to a bit of a Venetian boat song. Then comes something from Wallace or a robust mid-section from *Carmen*. The profession is not without its risks, let me tell you! The movie pianist, Istvan Nagy went mad after having to butcher Schubert's *Symphony No. 8* for the fiftieth time. It's always played when the high drama transitions to the tenderness that accompanies pain so intense its almost blissful. Thank God I'm not delicate! Well, I'm no artist either! Thank God! Ha ha ha!"

Franziska paused for a moment so that she could take in Max's horrified expression. She couldn't resist smiling to herself over inspiring such a reaction. "In any case, I'm not starving, but neither does it really fill me up either. And right now, I have no idea how I'm going to pay the midwife or doctor to help with the delivery! I'll cross that bridge when I get to it."

"Yes, and what about your... uh..." Max struggled to let the name escape from his lips, "with *Willy*?" Max asked timidly, staring at Franziska's battered hands. She wasn't even wearing a fake wedding ring, he noted with astonishment.

"Ha!" The question about Willy Rubin made Fränze laugh like she had just heard a good joke. "Oh *him*!" she said, drenched with such contempt that no further explanation was necessary.

"So you don't love him anymore?" he asked hopefully.

"What do you mean, love *him*? Are you out of your mind?! she exclaimed. "That's just what I would need!"

Fränze seemed quite indignant at the very suggestion. She absentmindedly ran both hands over her pregnant belly that was covered by a less-than-clean, dark-blue plaid apron.

"Back then, all I wanted was to get one over on Martha. To steal one of her suitors. But just for fun! And it was pretty funny at first. But I didn't expect that the amusement would turn serious so quickly. I didn't even really like Willy. Not with my heart or my mind. Only my body had completely different ideas and couldn't get enough of the guy! It's true, I was a naïve, stupid goose, so this all serves me right!"

On May 1, 1912, the boy Walter was born in the Berlin district of Wedding. It was snowing. Outside the two windows of the clammy birthing room, workers were protesting, kept in check by mounted policemen with spiked caps and suppressed anger.

They were demanding the utopian eight-hour workday, and the even more utopian fair wage, and the most utopian and eternally absurd of all demands: equal pay for equal work, for men and women.

With blue, frozen hands, some of the workers were beating red-banded cymbals while their comrades played medieval oboes, called shawms. Clouds of cold air puffed out from their open mouths.

On the other side of the fogged-over windows with gauze curtains, the newborn baby Walter shook his clenched little fists at the world and screamed, suggesting healthy lungs.

The "degenerate trash," as Franziska called the people of Wedding, were in a festive mood. "They're only happy because they're going to drink at the pub afterwards," she sneered as the midwife put the baby to her breast.

Meanwhile, Willy Rubin, the father of the beautiful baby boy, was at the betting office.

Max obediently sent a telegraph to his patron in Sauermühle.

+++ Congratulations on the birth of a Kohanim! +++ Name Walter +++ 53 cm tall +++ 7 pounds +++ healthy +++ mother and child well +++

Not until he was filling out the telegraph form and wrote the word "Kohanim" next to the child's name, did it occur to him why Samuel Kohanim was exposing his daughter and family to the disgrace of an illegitimate child. Max himself would like to have married Franziska, even as a "fallen girl," with or without a child, nor was the child's father adverse to the idea. The child would have been known as a "seven-month child," but it would have nonetheless been possible to present a respectable face to the world.

Kohanim had nonetheless rejected the idea outright, leaving Max perplexed. "She must be punished!" his patron had declared. Only with hindsight did Max finally understand that Kohanim had ulterior motives for which Franziska's "punishment" was a mere side-effect. What Kohanim really wanted was the child: a male Kohanim, a progenitor, and heir!

It wasn't long before the "punishment" he had in mind became clear. On behalf of his client, Samuel Kohahim of Sauermühle, a lawyer and notary public, by the name of Mr. Lachmund, Esq. summoned the unwed mother, Franziska Kohanim, to the district court in Wedding. There Franziska was forced to sign a deed of adoption, making her son Walter the legal direct descendant and ward of Samuel Kohanim. Upon reaching six months of age, the infant was to be "transferred" to his household, by police force, if necessary, where the boy would be raised. Since according to the law, Franziska was still under the guardianship of her father, she therefore had now lost all rights to her child.

For his part, Kohanim claimed such measures were necessary to defending the "purity" of the Kohanims' reputation. He would not, he said, tolerate "dissolute relations" in his family. Whether she wanted to or not,

Franziska also had to marry the handsome Willy. Nothing would change Kohanim's mind, neither Fränze's vociferous protests and objections, nor Martha's fit of jealously and consequent overexcited nerves.

Only the main character, handsome Willy, didn't "give a damn." One Kohanim bride was as good as another, especially since the beautiful Fränze hadn't spoken to him for some time and was intent on making his life difficult. He hoped the Fury would soon settle down and accept her fate.

FROM HEROES TO THE PETTY BOURGEOISIE AND OTHER SOURCES OF PSYCHOLOGICAL DAMAGE

It's almost dark in my room in the department of neurology. The blue hour. In the hallway the hospital staff are starting to get dinner underway, as they do every evening at five. I switch on the reading lamp by my bed. That makes the lighting more intimate. Anything to eliminate the glare of the ceiling lamps; they make it look like a train station in here.

My lawyer tells me that I should trust my therapist, Dr. Vogelsang, and that it would be good to share with her every conceivable form of psychological damage I may have experienced in the past. This is for the reason that a woman accused of a crime should not appear too smart.

Today, Dr. Vogelsang wants to know more about my early childhood and parents. That seems pretty harmless, so I open up about my childhood. When I was young my father looked like a mixture of Erich Kästner and the German actor Horst-Günter Marx, only with darker, thinning hair, and gray eyes, and more athletic, like he could have been in the army. He thought the official channels for finding an apartment were too cumbersome. As someone who had been persecuted by the Nazi regime, he did, after all, have a right to one. Still, the bureaucratic hurdles were time-consuming, and the whole process was demeaning because nearly all of the Nazi bureaucrats had held onto their old posts. Even under the new regime, they remained true to their old habits. Even worse, smarting from defeat, they took their revenge on the "victors of history" by harassing and humiliating the formerly persecuted to their heart's content. After several unsuccessful attempts, which nearly turned him into either a beggar or a murderer, he wanted to take matters into his own hands. But after twelve years in incarceration, he didn't want to wait another day for what was due to him. They owed him a life. His best years.

"And the soldiers who were in the war?" my mother shot back. "Don't we owe them something too?"

"It was their own fault! They shot at the wrong people!"

My dad turned his brother, my Uncle Benno, the former Benno Rubin. After becoming a naturalized British citizen, he had adopted the name "Ben Rhodes," and after the war had returned to Berlin as a British officer. Uncle Benno succeeded in quickly getting my dad an apartment that met his requirements.

The only complication was that the apartment of his dreams was located in the Soviet sector of Berlin. To get it, Uncle Benno and my dad needed to call in a liaison officer from the Red Army. In return for three bottles of Scotch whisky and four cartons of Player's Navy Cut cigarettes, the Soviet officer at the Kommandantura in Karlshorst was not only willing to help them, but he even felt flattered that he could do a favor for a British comrade.

"To be able to personally provide a piece of justice that the German authorities are unable or unwilling to do," the Red Army officer explained in astonishingly fluent German, "is perhaps the only good deed I can do in this war!"

As if wanting to apologize immediately for saying such a thing, he jumped up, raised the full whisky glass and toasted Stalin, who was looking down sternly from the wall. As to be expected, more toasts followed, lasting until the early morning hours. My father was an avowed teetotaler; alcohol didn't suit his devotion to sports and fitness. He thus employed his utmost powers of subterfuge to make it appear as if the contents of the glasses went down his throat, and not in the withering office plant nearby. In the gray of dawn two hungover Allied officers, along with my father in the back seat, drove up to the house at Buschstraße 56, tires squealing.

Using a false requisition order, they summarily evicted the current tenants, a family of locally prominent Nazis. They gave them twenty-four hours to pack their things. When the man of the house objected, my father told him with a cold smile: "You're lucky you're not being packed off to Siberia!" That got the message across. After that, the humbled man got to packing his belongings.

A few days later he was found shot dead. Apparently, someone else had a score to settle with the hated Nazi.

At first, my mother didn't want to move into the apartment in Buschstraße. "This doesn't have the Lord's blessing," she said. "The neighbors will certainly remain loyal to the old Nazis and make life difficult for us. Our child shouldn't grow up under such tense circumstances." She was ashamed that my father was behaving so imperiously. For his part, my father found her reaction so strange that he joked about it to his friends: "My wife is so petty bourgeois!" And all my dad's comrades—former camp inmates, Spanish fighters, emigrants, and other anti-fascist heroes—who came in and out of our house would burst out laughing at this.

My mother was deeply offended that my father would crack such jokes at her expense. And because she was inclined to bear grudges, she didn't speak a single word to him for three weeks. They would exchange notes in silence across the table whenever something essential had to be communicated.

Only after my mother learned from the neighborhood that the Nazi family had thrown a Jewish family out of the same apartment did she finally relax about our new home. "Then that is poetic justice!"

She, nonetheless, felt alienated by the ready-made nest that my father had suddenly placed her in. A comfortable two-room apartment with central heating, a bathroom with a bathtub, a kitchen with a gas stove, a large loggia situated in a nice residential neighborhood. A dream for anyone who had grown up in a home without indoor plumbing and an outhouse. The Nazi family had also left all their furniture behind, just as the Jewish family before them had. She felt a bit shy as she set about dusting the dark walnut furniture in the living room: a sideboard, dining table with six chairs, and a dainty hutch, with intricate carvings and curved legs. Chippendale! Nearby was also a Chesterfield leather sofa, two matching armchairs, a table with a top made of fake Delft tiles, and a hand-forged frame with legs as curved as those on the Chippendale furniture, and lastly, a cozy reading lamp in the corner. On the wall hung a rather garish still life with fruit and a dead pheasant in the middle. My mother, who otherwise hated housework, worked with abandon on cleaning the furniture. It was her way of communicating with the objects in order to make them her own. It was probably the only time she had ever cleaned a house like that: completely relaxed and in harmony with herself and the world. An absolute exception to the norm. When it came to housework, my mother usually worked herself up into a complete frenzy, terrorizing the whole family. She even cursed the pot on the stove because she hated cooking most of all. Even when I was hungry, I found it difficult to eat the cursed meal. My father, by contrast, kept the habits he had acquired as a camp inmate, and gobbled down anything edible, whether it tasted good or not. He ate so fast that he had already eaten his serving before we had even put three spoonfuls in our mouths.

"Walter don't scarf your food like that! Nobody is gonna take your food away from you anymore! We have plenty! How is a child going to learn table manners when you're eating like that?"

Even when my father and I wanted to help bring a little peace in our home by pitching in with the housework, my mother wouldn't allow it. We couldn't do anything right. Not only did she dismiss us as useless and clumsy, but she also accused us of merely making dirt, and getting in the way! We would therefore leave the house as early as possible before she undertook the infamous housecleaning Saturdays or the even more dreaded preparation of the roast and cake for Sundays.

My father usually took me to the soccer field. We only ventured home again at dinner time, when two smells would reliably greet us as we stood in the stairwell: floor polish and a freshly baked cake. Added to the mix was the aroma of "good, real coffee beans," which my English uncle regularly sent us from London. "That's what peace smells like!" my father would say. My mother would meanwhile already be lurking at the table, grimacing with disapproval. If we were even a few minutes late, she would leave the room in a huff and slam the door behind her. For the rest of the day, she would retreat to the bedroom, not wanting to be disturbed.

As a little girl, it was completely baffling to me that a person could get so upset and mean for no reason at all. But even then, I intuited that there must have been some past misfortunes behind her explosive anger. But what misfortunes? What pain?

My parents began to argue more frequently, growing fiercer and lasting longer. Before long they were pulling me into their fights. At the kitchen table, they would try to get me to take one side or the other, arguing their case bitterly. I must have been about four years old at the time. Because I didn't have the luxury of a room in which to escape, I took refuge in the bathroom, where I would lock myself in for hours. The three or four smacks I would receive later did nothing to alter my conviction that I had a right to the bathroom and tactical control of the toilet during their fights. If nothing else, I did it to get back at them!

Apart from that, there were two iron rules in our family. First, no one was allowed to know that my father was Jewish. Second, no one was allowed to know that my mother had grown up in a garden colony, which many "respectable" Germans considered to be tantamount to coming from a shanty town.

The official line was that we were descended from Huguenots from southern France. This was to help account for the fact that I had such black hair and dark saucer eyes, and why compared to other kids my age, I was, as they say in northern Germany, so *spillerig*, or scrawny, and overall, always the smallest kid. My parents told me to use the name *Lefèvre*, which was easy to remember because of the name of a well-known carpet store in West Germany. Early on, I learned that lying was necessary to survive. My parents, nonetheless, praised the ideal of honesty and truth all the more highly, probably like lofty goals that could never be attained. My father summed it up as follows: You have to be able to afford honesty; and unfortunately, you can't always afford to be honest.

That made sense to me, but I thought the lie about our Huguenot origins was pretty silly. One look at my mother's face and you saw the face of a Tatar with high cheekbones and slanted, extremely narrow, almond eyes. "Like Brigitte Horney," my father used to say dreamily. That surprised me even more, because the German actress Brigitte Horney that I had seen in a magazine from West Germany, radiated serenity, gentleness, and happiness. My tight-lipped mother, by contrast, emanated severity, brokenness, and a deep, unnamed source of unhappiness. I soon learned that part of her unhappiness came from my jovial, grandmother from Wedding, Fränze. She disapproved of my mother, dismissing her daughter-in-law as a poor, ordinary slut from a slum on the outskirts of the city. A communist *shiksa*! Both parts of the insult weighed heavily on my mother. But shiksa was probably the more unforgivable of the two.

In my father's silent rivalry with his brother for their mother's favor, my father was, as he said, "second best," and therefore always de facto defeated. My Uncle Ben, master of sugar, cigarettes, coffee, tea, cocoa, and chocolate, was resplendent in his smart Royal Air Force uniform and constantly explaining the world situation to us in his wonderfully resonant bass voice, just like his idol Winston Churchill had done. In German and the best accent-free BBC English. What fascinated me most about Uncle Ben were his extremely shiny boots. I had never seen such shiny boots before. Uncle Ben smoked his Player's Navy Cut cigarette with an ivory cigarette holder that had a silver piece to hold the burning cigarette. I thought it was deadly chic. He had married a French-English-Jewish woman from a wealthy family in London, and they already had a son and heir. Once again, my father couldn't keep up with Ben.

My mother wanted me to make up for the deficit of being born a girl by being especially talented. Which was why I had made a beautiful picture for my Grandma Fränze's birthday. It turned out so well that my mother had it framed. I felt proud, presenting the picture to my grandmother. "Oh, how beautiful! You have so much talent, my little girl!" she said cheerfully, patting the top of my head. "It's just a shame that you'll *never* be one of us!"

My father, who was already having a hard time putting up with my uncle's extremely politically conservative views and his hymns to Churchill, turned as pale as a sheet. In her own inimitable way, my jolly grandmother had expressed that I would never belong to the Jewish community, would never be, "one of us," because I didn't have a Jewish mother. Before then my grandmother had accused my mother of being a shiksa; she was now making it clear that meant her daughter was an outcast. My mother took it like a slap in the face. She jumped up from her chair with a scream, grabbed me by the wrist, and before I knew it, she was dragging me out of the apartment in a rage, yelling, "We're not going back into this house! Come on, Walter, let's go!"

But my father stayed and argued bitterly with his mother. In the stairwell, my mother shouted against the closed front door, as if she had lost her mind, "I helped, protected, and hid you while the Nazis were in power, and now my child and I are no longer good enough for you! Stupid, hopefully ignorant pack of Jews! You can all go to hell! All of you!" Sobbing, she ran down the stairs with me. She spent the whole train ride home from Wedding to Pankow howling with rage. I sat helplessly next to her and could only hand her my handkerchiefs because her lace ones were already soaked.

"Were not ever going to Grandma's again?" I asked cautiously.

"Never again!" she sobbed into the wet, crumpled handkerchief. I waited a little and then asked, timidly, "And why not?"

"Oh, you wouldn't understand!"

What I did understand was that I wasn't good enough for my father's family and that this was somehow connected to my mother. I didn't know anything about the Orthodox Jewish rule, the *halacha*, that you can only be considered Jewish if you have a Jewish mother.

That night, I scratched myself until I bled. I suddenly had a case of neurodermatitis. My first thought was: Am I going crazy like my great-aunt Martha?

A FUTURE THAT'S NOT TODAY

Franziska's wedding took place on October 4, 1912, within the tightest family circle possible of about twenty people. "The wedding would be a good opportunity to celebrate Walter's belated circumcision, the *milah*," my penny-pinching great grandmother suggested. "That way we could at least make up for the disgraceful wedding with something honorable!"

Samuel Kohanim was still a little reluctant. However, he finally came around to the idea. To avoid causing a stir in Sauermühle, Osche, or Schwetz with the shameful wedding, the celebrations were moved to Berlin's Luna Park. "At least nobody knows us there!" my grandfather had said.

Franziska's readmission into the bosom of the family was a mixed blessing, to say the least. The family referred to such things as *boje zeachany*. Translated literally from Russian, it means "a benign blessing from God." The Kohanims used the expression ironically to refer to all manner of "benign blessings from God": from the utterly useless to the disgraceful; for "blessings" that did not represent blessings in the literal sense but their opposite; and for which you should respond with a touch of resentment, if not outright anger.

When used in reference to Fränze's return, boje zeachany meant that she would have to inhabit a miserable, inferior position in the family, for which she should be grateful and humble. But Franziska, humble? As with every challenge, she held her head high and settled into the new adverse circumstances without complaint, just as effortlessly as she had adjusted to living amidst "the lumpen proletariat" in Wedding. "Tenue!" as she would say, using a loose adaption of the French *tenir*, "to hold on," to express the idea of having the mettle to endure.

At home, Franziska walked around with the tragic dignity of a fallen queen. Because she was as incapable of self-pity as she was of other sentiments, she let all the adversities of domestic degradation roll off her back, as if she had stretched an electromagnetic membrane around her nimbus. When things got really bad, she drew on a trait inherited from her mother. She pulled inward, becoming as inaccessible as a tortoise retracted in its shell. The catastrophes and changes taking place in the outside world couldn't penetrate her armor. The pride with which Franziska endured her adverse circumstances, impressed the domestic staff and other subordinates in the Kohanim household and in the county. The cook and the Polish maids began to venerate the disgraced former favorite daughter of their ruler as if she were a saint.

They took comfort in her example as how someone might endure anything without ever becoming subordinate; her proud suffering, even expanded the aura of her nimbus.

However, no one knew the real cause of her fall from grace. Franziska had supposedly only followed her heart and secretly married beneath her station. That was the official version, cleverly disseminated by Kohanim himself. It wasn't comme il faut, or model behavior befitting her status, but it could be forgiven. The servants and most important local gossips found this version the most credible. Franziska, who had always been regarded as arrogant, was now widely admired.

"We should all learn a lesson from this!" said Teresa Plienska, the Kashubian cook who spoke on behalf of the entire household staff. Taking Teresa's words to heart, they all sought to protect Franziska against her family's cruelties, by pampering and smothering her with the sort of affection and warmth familiar to those who inhabited the lower strata of society. Franziska, in turn, reevaluated her opinion of the staff. Heretofore she had divided people into distinct categories: ranging from good souls, regular people, lowlifes, rabble, scum, and lowly scum, and had relegated the domestic help to the lower rungs. In gratitude for their kindness, however, she elevated them from "rabble" to "good souls." Even later in life, she thought highly of the "common people," provided that they did not reveal themselves to belong to the "rabble, scum, and lowly scum."

Everyone noticed that the otherwise radiant Franziska was looking rather worn out. Her rosy cheeks had grown pale and sunken, her bright eyes covered in shadow, all of which they attributed to her state of long-suffering. But there was another reason why she appeared to be wasting away. Fertile as her mother, grandmothers, and great-grandmothers, Fränze was already expecting a second child. She was furious about it! Furious at the "scoundrel" Willy, whom she now had to marry, and at herself for being unable to resist him. That was why she was sitting like an alabaster statue in the small ballroom on the lake at Halensee in Berlin, gritting her teeth.

Behind the scenes of the festivities, a tough battle was raging over the marriage contract and the dowry. Fortunately, Franziska was unaware of this because these disputes were purely a matter for men.

The Rubins, Willy's family, were looking to capitalize on their son's forced marriage with a daughter from a wealthy family. Under pressure from his family, Willy was refusing to participate in a proper Jewish wedding unless Kohanim agreed to pay out the entire dowry to him directly, putting it at his disposal. In addition, the groom's father was also claiming that all of the couple's children, including the first-born, Walter, who had been declared Kohanim's ward, should belong to the Rubins. And, if not, then… But Samuel Kohanim was not someone to be told, "if not, then."

Franziska's bridal veil was already being pinned on her in the next room while Samuel was stoically insisting that the dowry be administered by the notary Mr. Lachmund in Berlin "for the benefit of all the children to be born" and "with the sole involvement of the child's mother and the notary." Such an arrangement, however, would mean that Willy and the Rubins would never receive the dowry. The notary also explained that none of this concerned the child Walter, because by law, together with all the deeds, he was already a real Kohanim and therefore beyond discussion. It was a fait accompli. The Rubins raged: "How can you steal a father's firth born?"

Jakov Rubin, Willy's father, who had traveled all the way from distant Königsberg to participate in the wedding, complained that this was an insult and an infringement on the rights of the groom and then made a big to do about the nobility of his hat business, as if the trade in hats was superior to that of wood and furniture. The whole wedding was suddenly on the rocks and threatened to fall through at the last moment. The Rubins countered the Kohanims stubbornness with some of their own, invoking the Jewish tradition of handing over the dowry and marriage contract under the chuppah when the glass was broken. The Rubins bullying the Kohanims? The Ashkenazim the Sephardim? With an "all right!" and a cold smile, Samuel brought the haggling to an end, announcing, "All right! Then let's do it the traditional way!" The Rubins heaved a sigh of relief and looked about the room in triumph. "We'll just have to draw up the papers again," Kohanim said with a sigh, before he moved into the room adjacent, along with the notary and scribe. After emerging, they changed the envelope that had the words, "marriage contract" to a new one with the word, "dowry," into which they inserted a prepared document and sealed it with red wax.

Samuel returned to the wedding party, and held the contract up to Willy's face, who simply shrugged in response. His father, Rubin senior, was still busy whining that he hadn't had a chance to check the document beforehand. But after the rabbi arrived and cut him off with a wave of his hand, Willy's father gave up.

The ceremony then proceeded, as planned. Standing across from Willy beneath the chuppah, Franziska uttered the obligatory "yes!" with such vitriol that it resounded like a slap against the groom's face. Just as soon as the glass had been broken, Willy's father tore open the envelope. Inside he found a document with the first line, "Dowry and marriage contract for Franziska Kohanim are vouched for by Samuel Kohanim and notary public Mr. Lachmund, Esq." Upon reading the words that followed, Rubin senior fainted.

In the document, Kohanim had concealed under a barrage of legal lingo a personal monthly annuity for his daughter Franziska and future grandchildren, which only his daughter Franziska, under the guardianship of Lachmund, could access. Franziska, who up to then had been spared the details of the wrangling over the marriage contract, was shocked and deeply offended, and refused to grant so much as a word or glance at the groom on her left, the man she had been forced to marry. Only now did she realize that from the beginning Willy and the Rubins had only been interested in the dowry, and that Willy had pursued her, the beguiling daughter, for the same reason he had courted the unattractive daughter, Martha. She also understood why her father didn't want to trouble her with the details of the marriage contract. While she resented the ole mishpocha, in hindsight she was also grateful to him for preventing the worst from happening.

"You'll pay for this!" she hissed at her new husband. The handsome Willy, however, played innocent. Through her lorgnette, Mindel scrutinized the deceived cheaters with amusement. Her son-in-law Willy and his brother Georg and their father Jakov Rubin were all impeccably dressed like gentlemen. "That's how we do it in the fashion industry!" Jakov said, fending off their penetrating stares. But Mindel noticed other details. She was amazed by the contrast between his father's elegantly tailored clothing and his ruddy complexion. For a man who worked in the mercantile trade, such sun-parched skin was highly unusual. You could perhaps chalk it up to a passion for horses and hunting, were it a non-Jewish merchant. Or someone who had spent their life at sea, like a captain, might have had such a complexion. The rest of the Rubin clan were as colorful as a swarm of blowflies. The colors of their shoes didn't match those of their pants and their pants clashed with their frock coats, which, in turn, had sleeves that were either too long or too short. The women were all wearing dresses that were either too tight or too loose, garishly bright and out of fashion for over two decades. The Rubins, she concluded, were a pack of gaudy scarecrows! "Russian taste!" quipped the sparsely represented Kohanim clan, exchanging amused furtive glances, and basking in the shared feeling of their infinite social superiority.

After opening the dowry letter, Rubin senior fell ill. On the advice of the hastily summoned doctor, he was told to take to his bed immediately, shielded from any further excitement. Franziska was also suddenly feeling nauseous. "Attitude is everything," Mindel whispered to her repeatedly. "This farce will soon be over!"

Since the members of the Kohanim party only had to attend the bizarre wedding, they all took their leave just as soon as the chuppah ceremony ended. The party for Walter's circumcision that was supposed to be held afterward was canceled. Kohanim sent the dance band home with a generous tip and took his leave. Last as well as least, only the three Rubins remained, sitting at the table and stuffing themselves with cold roast meat while the grumbling staff cleared the tables and loudly pushed the furniture around. The sound of carnival music from the nearby Luna Park and competing organ grinders on the nearby streets wafted through the front door. Several organ grinders and an electric piano were engaged in fierce musical battles.

Samuel had paid for Jakov Rubin's accommodations and doctor while he was in Berlin. However, when he sent requests for repayment, he received no reply. He therefore reached out to some of his contacts to make inquiries about Rubin's business in Königsberg, to which he received the reply, "business is doing marvelously and making its owner "Jacob" Rubin a rich man." Kohanim was perplexed. If his business was doing so well, why wouldn't he pay his bills?

The explanation was as simple as it was preposterous: "Jakov" Rubin from the village of Osche, whose father had fled with his brother from the pogroms in Russia to East Prussia in a mailbag in 1821, happened to share the same name as "Jacob" Rubin from the Seilergasse in Königsberg. Yet no one could claim that Willy's father, and now Franziska's father-in-law was an imposter or fraud. His actually did have the "first hat business on the square": he held out his hat on the market square in front of the synagogue six days a week.

In their coup against the Kohanims, the Rubins, who had only recently settled in the district, had overlooked one tiny but important detail. If they had asked around more carefully, especially the older women, who are the most reliable chroniclers the world over, they would have been forewarned. In the kitchens, pubs, taverns, markets, back rooms, and parlors of Schwetz, Zempelburg, Tuchel, and Bromberg, stories circulated that make it plain that the Kohanims needed neither duels nor plots for revenge nor authorities, like police or judges, to turn to for protection against those who insulted or abused them. They would have said: "The Kohanims stand on the banks of the Vistula and wait until the corpses of their enemies float by!"

Some said that the Kohanims were under divine protection despite the death of their heirs. For others, this very protection from supernatural forces was proof that the Kohanims must be in league with the devil.

Legend had it that this divine protection was not to the liking of the merciful God of the Christians; if such a protection did exist, it was at the hands of the righteous God of the Jews. This was first demonstrated in 1648 when the Cossacks invaded the Kingdom of Poland in a raid and pogrom. On the market square in Lviv, a Cossack on horseback tried to cut down the ancestor of all the Kohanims, Baruch Kohanim. Had it been the Christian God, he probably would have suddenly turned the Cossack into a righteous man, so that he would have ended his days in repentance as a hermit. But the Jewish God chose a different end for the Cossack. Just as he was about to swing his saber, he fell down dead from his horse.

The miracle repeated itself in 1661. The horse trader Jehuda Kohanim's nags had run away. In pursuit of them, he left Zempelburg on Good Friday, an act in violation of the Christian ban on Jews doing so on the Christian holy day. For this sacrilege, one of the Bishop of Kujawy's henchman was charged with delivering the usual punishment: fifty strokes of the cane. Just as the Bishop's lackey was about to strike the first blow, his arm fell limp, paralyzed. Similar incidents were reported in 1708, 1779, and 1825.

"Apparently, God, the Righteous One, is still watching over the Kohanims even in the 20th century," those familiar with the family later murmured. How else could one account for the fact that the handsome Willy Rubin, this promising scion of a dynasty of ethereal existences, imposters, and fortune hunters, who wanted to start a new life at the expense of the Kohanims, suddenly dropped dead at the ripe age of thirty-two years old, in his "little rat shop" at ten o'clock in the morning on June 24, 1913.

Franziska was so grateful to her Lord God for the mercy he had shown her that she returned to synagogue on the Sabbath and tried to live like a good Jew, at least some of the time. She kept it up for a whole three months. Then the desire for Black Forest ham outweighed her new-found piety. To be fair, it should be noted that she only ever craved ham after the Sabbath, when the candlesticks had already been cleared away.

Martha could not accept the mysterious death of her beloved brother-in-law. Even though he had been unfaithful to her, he remained the great love of her life. She was firmly convinced that Franziska must have slipped rat poison into her troublesome husband's morning coffee. A week following his death, Martha thus headed to the office of capital crimes at the police station at Alexanderplatz in Berlin, where she lodged an accusation against Franziska. Even Elli and her favorite cousin, Else, couldn't quite dismiss the terrible suspicion that she might somehow have been involved.

The issue of the alleged murder of her husband divided the family into three camps: the accusers, the defenders, and the skeptics. Regardless of what individual members of the Kohanim family may have thought, Franziska remained under suspicion for the rest of her life as the possible murderer of her husband and even seemed to enjoy a reputation as someone dangerous.

Opinions differed as to whether it was an expression of a guilty conscience, as her vengeful sister Martha claimed, or whether it was just Franziska's extravagant nature that led her to have a colossal gravestone made of fake black marble erected for Wilhelm "Willy" Rubin in the Jewish cemetery in Berlin-Weissensee. She did not, however, attend the funeral of her deceased husband. Nor did she later visit his grave. And to top it all off, she did the worst thing that one Jew could do to another: she left the gravestone without an inscription!

In other words: here rests a nobody. No one shall remember him, not even God himself when it came time to call the names of the dead at the resurrection! The person who rests here had no name and would never rise again!

There was only one instance, later on, in which the dead Willy would even be recalled at all.

BENNO AND BRUNO

On April 7, 1913, Benno was born, the second fruit from the combination of the "disaster waiting to happen" and the "fake ruby."

This time around congratulations only came from Berlin neighbors who hadn't a clue about the child's origins. The mishpocha had remained demonstrably silent. Little Benno was the complete opposite of his older brother. Walter was an exact copy of his father Willy, extremely fair-skinned and athletic like the Rubins. When he was a baby, he had rosy cheeks and looked like a muscley Michelangelo cherub; and unlike any Kohanim, he had a broad Ashkenazi skull. He was also wild and demanding. Little Benno, by contrast, looked like a real Kohanim; he was delicate, had a narrow Sephardic head and a slightly darker complexion. "Benni" was also a quiet child, who from his first moment on Earth, was showered with motherly love.

Carefully protected by his nanny, Fräulein Gerti, Benni grew up on the first floor at Heilandstraße 6 on Nettelbeck Square in Berlin Wedding. Franziska had moved there just as soon as she was able to get her hands on the annuity that her father had granted her. Were it not for this income, she would say, "You might have had to write 'gutter' as place of birth on the birth certificate!" The house at Heilandstraße 6, whose portal was supported on the massive shoulders of two titans, was a mirror reflection of Franziska's attitude toward life.

The area around Leopold and Nettelbeck Squares were home to Berlin's working-class aristocracy. The master craftsmen, foremen, small shopkeepers, employees, and minor civil servants resided in the front of the buildings, facing the street. The skilled workers resided in the first row of the buildings behind them. The wives of these working-class elite didn't need to go to work outside the home and thus enjoyed the social status of housewives, and along with it, an exaggerated sense of propriety, which in their freshly starched aprons, they paraded like a monstrance for all to admire. By the light of kerosene lamps, they decorated their work aprons with elaborate crochet lace. No towel, no tablecloth, no handkerchief was left uncrocheted. The meticulously observed house rules would have been a credit to any military barracks. And nowhere in Berlin were the stairwells more brilliantly polished and the name plates and screens on the apartment doors as shiny as those in Wedding, where they aspired to higher things.

There was a simple reason why Franziska ended up here: a single Jewish woman with a child was looked at askance in the bourgeois neighborhoods of Berlin. People were more tolerant in the northern, working-class district. Plus, Franziska didn't want to deal with people who looked down on her, thinking they were better than she was. To explain herself she used to say, "Better the queen of a minor kingdom than the servant of a great one."

In "Red Wedding," so-called because of all the communist supporters found among the working classes there, Franziska Kohanim could consider herself to be something "better." Bourgeois Berlin could keep its pretense and supposed gentility. She wanted no part of it.

Besides Miss Gerti, who only had to look after Benno, Franziska offered room and board to a woman named Jolanda in exchange for looking after the house. She came from Poznan, Poland and had been recommended by Mindel's relatives.

Franziska was well stocked with furniture from her father's factory and, in addition to the household goods from her trousseau, she had brought the black, unlockable piano from Sauermühle as the crowning glory. The nanny lived in the servants' quarters. Jolanda' realm was the loft above the pantry to which a small, glazed skylight gave the illusion of a small room. There was just enough room for a mattress, three shelves, a wooden chest, and a crucifix on the wall. As a widow with two servants on the second floor, people in the house respectfully addressed Fränze as "madam," although they instinctively wanted to say "miss." Franziska had restored her rank. Even better: at her young age, she could finally do whatever she wanted. What woman of her age could claim such a thing? Franziska therefore held her head very high indeed.

If it had been up to her father, then she would have sold the "little rat shop" with the construction company that she had inherited from Willy right away. But Franziska had other ideas. The year of Willy's death, 1913, was a slow economic one, especially for building contractors in Berlin. The German capital was already plenty full of buildings and didn't need anymore. "Who needs a ramshackle plumbing-installation business without customers and no boss?" her father admonished her.

"That's right, Dad!" Fränze was quick to agree with him. "Right now, it's really not a good time to sell!"

That wasn't what he had meant and so he remained silent, perplexed over why she refused to sell it. What Franziska didn't reveal was the truth. There was only one person who actually needed the "little rat shop," the journeyman Bruno Geißler. It was for his sake that Fränze didn't have the heart to give up the abandoned shop. This Bruno Geißler also happened to be the most unusual plumber she had ever seen. And Franziska had a soft spot for unusual people. Bruno Geißler, who had always called Franziska "meestress," was a grown man, of the prescribed height for the imperial guards, with an imposing imperial beard to match, watery blue eyes and the noble gaze of an eagle. He looked so much like "EssEmm" (a Berlin nickname for "sir majesty"), Kaiser Wilhelm II, that he might have passed for his humbler twin. When he wasn't in his freshly ironed work clothes and leather apron in the workshop, either cutting threads or filing pipes, he was welcoming customers to the store in an impeccably spotless coat, stiff collar and tie, and subtly smelling of cologne. Bruno was surely the only plumber in proletarian Berlin who had perfectly manicured nails. Rumor had it that an unhappy love affair with a milliner had brought him from Dresden to Berlin. Nobody knew why their happiness was so short lived. He never talked about it. Every morning, he strode into the workshop, with a white carnation in his buttonhole and a hat atop his flaxen hair, as solid and as dignified as a Saxon boulder planted in the Mark Brandenburg sand. Bruno was a quiet man, with a sensitive nature, and thus quick to cry. When Franziska was a little harsh with him, tears would drip down his twirled Kaiser Wilhelm beard.

Fränze appreciated that Bruno was, in her words, "a soulful man," and as such she sought to shield him from harm as best she could. He entered the monthly accounts for the business in a black notebook in neat penmanship, like that of an earnest primary school student. From a financial standpoint, they weren't actually that important. Franziska nonetheless found them touching to look at. No matter what figures he had jotted down, they always inspired her to smile to herself over such diligence, suggestive of someone who valued accuracy and honesty.

Her father's increasingly urgent reminders that she should close the business began to get on her nerves. She therefore came up with her own solution to the "little rat shop" problem. She decided she would work for herself and run her own business with Bruno's assistance. She therefore enrolled in a course for aspiring clerks at a business school located at Gesundbrunnen, not far from Wedding. Every day she thanked the Lord that she only had to concentrate on bookkeeping. The other women, who were all looking for a job, had to work on their shorthand and typing skills as quickly as possible and had to put up with a lot of harassment.

After six months, she could arduously record sixty-eight syllables of shorthand per minute, which she was never able to decipher afterwards, type 120 strokes per minute, albeit with countless errors, and had earned an "A" in bookkeeping. And thus concluded Franziska's enrollment in business school. She now felt equipped to take the helm.

"It's in the wrong part of town!" she told Samuel. If there was even the slightest demand in Berlin for plumbing installation, it was perhaps in the northern part of the city, where construction was still going on. But not in the city center, where every inch of ground had already been built up. "No one is going to make a special trip to Berlin-Kreuzberg just to place a building order for projects in Wedding, Reinickendorf, Dalldorf, or Tegel," Franziska declared in an effort to explain the new situation.

When the owner of the "greens-and-things" shop on the ground floor of her apartment building in Wedding was stricken with gout and closed his shop, Franziska took over the space, moving the "little rat shop" from Kreuzberg to Wedding. She used the basement and cellar to store the pipes, sinks, and tubs, reserving the black-and-white tiled space above for the day-to-day business. Chrome faucets, showerheads, and fixtures soon filled the showroom, competing to see which could shine the brightest.

The dernier cri were porcelain washbasins and brass fittings, which she placed in the shop window alongside modern shower fittings of various materials—all polished until they nearly sparkled. No other plumbing installation business did such a thing. The "little rat shop" was now a real shop. Its elegant black-and-silver awnings and signs lent the whole house a sort of festive appearance. Satisfied with what she saw, Franziska caught her reflection in the gleaming façade. She was now the owner. Her eldest sister Fanny asked her why she couldn't be more modest and simply accept her lot in life? Fanny thought that it was too bold for woman to try to run a business on her own, especially considering that the guild license was registered to a master plumber who had never even set foot in the shop but signed everything anyway.

"Oh, Fanny! If you want to be worth something in life, you have to be ambitious! Humility and modesty are virtues best suited to servants!"

MAX AND THE TAILOR, IN AND OUT OF LUCK

In the spring of 1914, Max finally had the breakthrough that he had longed for. "Max Gulkowitsch, a second Alfred-Denis Cortot," Franziska read in Germany's leading national newspaper *Vossische Zeitung*. She couldn't believe it: Max was being compared to one of the world's greatest living pianists. The long article discussed in detail Max's polydactyly, or multi-fingeredness, that statistically only occurred in one in every five hundred thousand people. A surgical "expert" from Prague discussed the pros and cons of an operation to remove his extra fingers, which the pianist had so far refused to undergo. Max was quoted in the paper as saying that he didn't want to miss a single finger, because it was perhaps divine providence that he had been born with six fingers on each hand. Max wanted to remain an original.

Max sent Franziska a postcard from every stop in his tour. She stuck the colorful cards from all over the world behind the mirror in the hall. The last card had come from Rio de Janeiro and showed palm trees, a sugarloaf, a colorful parrot, and the sea. The greetings on the back had been written hastily. Even the usual "kindest regards" had degenerated into a curt, "regards."

"It would be better not to write at all," she said peevishly, as she attached the card to the top of the mirror.

While Max was giving a Tchaikovsky matinée for destitute South American music lovers in the sold-out opera house in Manaus in the middle of the Brazilian bush, two shots were fired in Sarajevo.

Max was stuck in America and now claimed to be Russian despite his German passport. Alongside the article appeared a photo of "Maxim Gulkovich." Looking cosmopolitan and well fed by the "good life" that he seemed to be enjoying, he posed in front of a luxury car, flanked by three adoring fans, American women, who appeared to be as rich as they were beautiful.

The photo bothered Fränze. Max was hers for the taking! Not this Gloria Vanderbilt, Julia de Braganza, and Lydia Katz, who were smiling saucily up at her from the newspaper.

Not long afterwards, the Russian "Maxim" became the American "Max." The German press took it as the final piece of evidence needed to prove that Jews were traitorous. They accused him of betraying his homeland, to which he owed everything. "The only people Max owes anything to are us, my family!" Franziska said indignantly. "Who else, apart from us, has ever done anything for Max? No one and certainly not his fatherland!"

Examining the photo more closely, Franziska noticed that Max looked different, something had changed besides just his citizenship. Fame had refined his ugliness, transforming it into that curious sort of masculine magnetism that only money, grooming, and good food can bring out in otherwise unattractive men.

Furious at her blindness, Fränze sat crying at the kitchen table covered in a blue-and-white checkered wax tablecloth, where green herrings waiting to be prepared sat atop the newspaper with Max's photo. Her tears made the herring even more salty. Even years later, when Franziska saw green herrings, she would think of Max and for that reason banned them from her table. But soon it was no longer a question of being for or against either herring or Max, but a question of hunger.

No one had heard much from Martha for some time. To restore peace in Sauermühle, she had been sent to live with her grandmother Taubine Beinesch in Warsaw. In her Polish familial exile, Martha enjoyed, for the first time in her life, the luxury of undivided attention and love. Like a geranium exposed to the sun, she blossomed. The old familiar nervous ailments rarely occurred anymore, and all talk of Willy had faded away. Taubine Beinesch decided that her milliner Bozena Wrobelska should accompany her granddaughter to Berlin, where she would visit a dressmaker's studio to acquire a new wardrobe.

During her stay in Berlin, she visited Fanny at her elegant dressmaker's atelier. Fanny had to admit: Wrobelska had worked true wonders on Martha. Although she would never be as elegant as her enemy, King Cobra, she nonetheless looked well-groomed and proper. She had grown up to be an attractive young woman. This was partly due to her carefully chosen wardrobe and partly due to her new hairstyle, which showed off the splendor of her voluminous, now strawberry-blond hair. The less beautiful aspects of her appearance retreated into the background. Once she had overcome the initial shock over just how fetching she now looked, she quickly took a liking to the improvement. During long strolls around Berlin, she no longer blushed or felt embarrassed over what was becoming a common occurrence: gentlemen doffing their hats and bowing politely at the very sight of her.

On one such walk, she felt emboldened to head directly to the office of the public prosecutor for capital crimes at the Berlin District Court, to see the assessor Leopold Hirschfeld, Esq. Once there, she felt overcome with a bit of shyness, but she nonetheless pressed forward, inquiring about how she might bring charges against a certain Franziska Rubin, née Kohanim.

"Your honor, a young, healthy, strong man like the deceased Wilhelm Rubin doesn't simply drop dead like that out of nowhere. Things like that don't just happen! It's also really sad when the wife doesn't even show up to the funeral. That tells you everything you need to know! My sister Franziska poisoned her husband. The police don't believe me, and that's why you have to help me, your honor!" Astonishingly, her voice no longer quivered.

"Assessor!" corrected Hirschfeld, smiling indulgently.

"Everywhere I've gone to make my case, I've been told that I'm simply a troublemaker and they have treated me as such. You cannot imagine how humiliating it has all been. Wilhelm, whether he left me for my sister Franziska or not, must get justice!

Hirschfeld listened to Martha with a serious expression.

"If you go to court, you will only get a verdict, my dear fräulein," he explained. "People always expect justice from the courts, but that only exists in heaven. So don't expect too much!"

"That's all right with me, your honor! The most important thing is that my sister Franziska should finally be brought to justice. I owe it to the memory of the dearly departed."

Hirschfeld looked thoughtfully at Martha, then stood up. He rocked back and forth on the balls of his feet a few times, then paced around his large desk. Finally, he leaned, half-sitting, against the desk and stroked her check, like a father would a child, and promised to personally take up the case. Martha floated out of the office as if on a cloud. She had not been this happy since her rendezvous with Willy.

Not even the most hardened pessimists could have imagined in their very worst nightmares the horrors and scarcity that would soon descend upon Europe. And because no one could have conceived of such a thing, no one prepared for it, a fact which only deepened the severity of the crisis when it did come. Thanks to Mindel, however, the Kohanims were spared the worst of the wartime depravities. For no amount of patriotic propaganda could sway her from her steadfast prudence and instinctive fatalism. While they too had to do without certain things, it was her good household management that saw them through. Just as soon as war was declared, she had seen to it that the entire estaţe at Sauermühle, including the house, the barns, and stores, were filled-to-capacity with food.

Throughout the German empire, political leaders wanted to make everyone believe that the war would be a quick little military parade, with the soldiers and officers offering a salute now and again to those on the sidelines. After they had added a bit of gun smoke to freshen up their elegant uniforms, they would return home after no more than three months, with all the African colonies in their back pockets.

Mindel deeply distrusted all the heroic swagger and pipe dreams, and just as soon as news of the declaration of war was announced, she wasted no time before sending out expensive express telegrams in all directions.

+++ Smart people, plan ahead! PROVISIONS!!! Hurry! +++

Against her penny-pinching habits, she used the expensive express telegram with six whole words, where a word with two syllables would have sufficed: "stockpile."

The word was forbidden throughout the Reich as a punishable offense. The secret police snooped everywhere for suspected "defeatists." After sending the express dispatches to all the Kohanim daughters, she sent them express letters with a detailed list and instructions: foodstuffs, wine, oil, schnapps, soaps, fabrics, wool, leather, yarn, sewing needles, buttons, nails, along with counsel about how to store them, and where to find discounts. Only Franziska and Fanny followed her advice. Elli, who had adopted the arrogant worldview of her Prussian husband, cavalry officer, Captain von Strachwitz, and in her mind was already traveling to the Nile, hunting elephants in Kenya, not only ignored her mother's advice, but replied with a letter blazing with indignation.

Beloved mother, beloved father!

At a time when the fatherland is engaged in a bloody struggle with the enemy, it is shameful and unpatriotic to think only of our own private welfare! We should instead give everything to the army and our soldiers, so that victory can be ours!

As for you, dear father, on the basis of a hint from a certain Colonel von Reichenau, a friend of my husband, I urgently recommend that you drop any relations with Max Gulkowisch that you still may have and certainly distance yourself from him in public. He has shown himself to be ungrateful to his fatherland and to his patron. As Jews, we must be especially careful not to fall into a bad light. We should indeed try even harder to prove our unwavering loyalty to our people and our country!

We should also distance ourselves from the count's family. Although for several hundred years, the Solkowskys have, by questionable means, managed to maintain their status as Polish nobles, we all know that they harbor pro-French sentiment and are extremely proud of their Polish patriotism, of which they have never made a secret! I can inform you confidentially that the Solkowskys are at the top of the list of potential spies and traitors and that any contact with them and Max Gulkowitsch is highly dangerous for us.

Therefore, dear father, although we disagree on almost everything, I urge you, in the interest of the family, not to cast my warnings to the wind. With concern and love.

Sincerely,
your daughter Elsbeth

Gerson and Fanny Segal's tailor's atelier on Leipziger Strasse in Berlin was feverishly busy. Scores of officers' uniforms for high-ranking individuals awaited completion. The customers crowded into the shop and were even more impatient and grumpy than usual. It almost seemed as if they couldn't get to the battlefield fast enough to spill their blood on the fields of Normandy and in the vast expanses of Russia. The seamstresses were working twenty-four-hour shifts, going at it until the machines and sewing needles ran hot.

Since the upper echelons were no longer able to call on British tailors to make their made-to-measure coats for their uniforms, those in Berlin turned to Segal for uniforms that would "fit like a glove." Despite all the hustle and bustle, Fanny's husband was ill at ease.

"It's all panic mongering," Gerson grumbled glumly. He was also in a bad mood because the would-be heroes reacted to the request for payment-upon-delivery as if it were high treason and made wild scenes at the Jewish tailor's shop. They told him to wait until victory, which was supposedly imminent. But Fanny's husband refused to budge.

"What does the unpaid tailor gain from the heroism of his customers? Bankruptcy!" Gerson would growl back.

The other thought that gave the Segals with one *l* sleepless nights and which they did not even dare to express publicly: "What if the war drags on? What if the war claims many victims, even among our customers?" Gerson expressed this thought aloud one night when he and Fanny were again finding it impossible to sleep. Fanny immediately sat up in bed, adjusted her nightcap, and then asserted herself for the first time in her life.

"Gerson, I know you don't want to hear this. But we should immediately switch our business to ladies wear and start working for the big department stores."

For a men's tailor who considered himself the crowned prince of his guild, such a suggestion was like asking a devout Catholic to kiss Martin Luther's hand. "Ladies wear?! Over my dead body!" Indignant over the mere suggestion, he turned away from his wife and immediately began to snore.

While only a few men's tailors on Leipziger Strasse and in the clothing district were silently worried about murdered male customers, and what that might mean for business, in proletarian Wedding, they had a more sensitive ear for detecting imperial detachment from reality.

"Ole Bismarck was at least clever enough to attack one country at a time. Our emperor thinks he can take on the whole world at once. There's no way that's gonna turn out well! The fancy people are all sitting pretty at the commander's post, waiting to be served, while down below we're pushing up daisies and our children are going hungry!"

For once, Fränze agreed with the "Red rabble." She saw to it that the cellars in the apartment and the shop, the storage space in the workshop basement, the pantry, the children's room, and the suspended floor beneath the house all buckled under the weight of tinned food, jars with preserves, sacks of rice, flour, sugar, peas, lentils, beans, and smoked and cured meats. Franziska's household would be immune to hunger. She now had only one worry: Bruno.

If she had already lost Max because of this senseless war, then she at least wanted to hold onto Bruno.

"I have to rely on someone. After all, I'm a widow with two small children. We all depend on his work," she complained to the Imperial War Ministry and to the Imperial Enlistment Office. "And do you think that burst pipes will wait until after the war?" she added, providing yet another reason why her journeyman was indispensable.

The authorities, however, were not convinced by the idea that Berlin would drown without Bruno Geißler. More persuasive was the claim that Bruno was completely colorblind and stone-deaf in one ear. Bruno's landlady, a war widow whose husband had died a "hero's death" during the first hostilities of war, thought that Bruno's "ID" (indispensability) was a ruse to get out of military service. As a patriot, she reported him to the authorities and gave him notice to vacate his furnished room. Two snitches soon turned up and interrogated Bruno for a long time. Then three medical examiners were brought in to determine whether Bruno was in fact fit for service or merely faking it. Yet, nothing changed the fact that Bruno was indeed colorblind and deaf in one ear.

To simplify matters, Bruno moved into the apartment behind the workshop at Heilandstrasse 6, where he had to live in close contact with Franziska's stored provisions. Bruno made himself at home among the sacks of potatoes, pickle barrels, noodles, rice, sago, pearl barley, semolina, wheat, rye, matches, sides of bacon and ham, and shelves of preserves from the Osche-Sauermühle.

They hid away Bruno's impeccable suits, jackets, pants, and coats in a discarded wardrobe that his "meestress" had intended to sell to some people in one of the apartments in the back of the building.

His exquisite shaving kit consisting of a badger-hair shaving brush, Solingen razor, a hairbrush and a comb with silver handles that rested atop a marble washstand, alongside an elegant wash bowl and water jug made of fine porcelain that Franziska had brought to Berlin from Sauermühle as part of her dowry. Bruno's basic personal needs were thus taken care of. He was happy. Unbeknownst to her, the lunch that Franziska prepared for Bruno and herself every day in the closed store inspired gossip. The jealous women in the neighborhood were already furious that a cheeky brat in respectable widowhood had all the freedom she needed and could also make a living. They begrudged her the "all-inclusive gentleman" who worked for the "merry widow" and "maybe not only on the first floor, but also in the basement. Ha ha ha!"

"Yeah, well, she'll still get fat like the rest of us!" the women who lived in the apartments in the back of the building and in the side wings, the war widows and "grass widows," whose husbands were away at war, consoled each other with such thoughts. They were filling in for the absent men, working as streetcar conductors, switchmen, letter carriers, grenade turners, welders, and even as iron casters at the blast furnaces for a quarter of the men's wages and on starvation rations.

Franziska's best friend during those difficult years was Charlotte Hörl. "Lotte," as everyone called her, was a droll Berlin Jew with a saucy, quick-witted mouth. She was a good head shorter than Franziska and everything about her had rounded edges. Her thick black hair was as curly as the wooly karakul collar of her winter coat. Nearly all the women envied Lotte's natural curls. Everything else about her was somehow delicate: she had tiny ears, almost children's hands, and shoe size five, which for some odd reason delighted the women even more than the men. Lotte's sparkling, nearly black eyes usually held a mischievous gaze. She started every sentence with a little laugh, even if there was nothing funny to say. She and Franziska's mutual admiration for each other's wit and sharp tongue was the source of their warm friendship. They amused each other so much that the applause and laughter of others only irritated them. You could say that they were infatuated with each other and could hardly go a day without seeing each other. They were bosom buddies, who were constantly chuckling at each other's jokes.

Franziska held her *jour* on Thursdays. People in Wedding didn't know what that was, but they quickly figured out that the door to the apartment remained open all day for anyone and everyone. There you would find piano music, subversive ditties, and, most of all, lots of laughter. None of Franziska's guests left without advice or consolation, provided they didn't overdo it with too much grief.

"There's no laughter here for sad sacks!" she declared, unceremoniously dismissing "hopeless crybabies and whiners." Amidst the activity, Bruno would sit silently in his armchair in the corner with the bay window, happily absorbed in his crossword puzzles. As time went on, small bites that she served on lead-crystal plates became increasingly important. With a plate of carrot cake, she literally shut the mouths of many of her detractors.

Fränze's friend Lotte also had a husband called "Willi." As a foreman Wilhelm Hörl was considered "ID" or indispensable and thus exempt from military service. Lotte's goyish Willi was a staunch supporter of the Social Democrats, a passionate atheist, and the kind of person who would inevitably turn even a harmless conversation about the weather into a lecture about capital and labor. Willi Hörl had a habit of accompanying his speech with energetic fist bumps on the table, causing the cups, glasses, and plates to bounce.

You probably have to talk like that at construction sites, Franziska thought. She refused to be impressed by all the bluster. She could hold her own against "rabble-rousing Willi" and people respected her for it. Few dared to stand up to the supreme master of the Flor & Otis construction sites. Lotte couldn't keep pace with Franziska. She simply adored Willi too much to contest anything he might say. That's why Franziska gave her best friend a gong for her birthday. The gong featured a heavy brass plate that hung from a gold cord and was set in a black frame, suggestive of Far-Eastern origins. "This is so that you can get a word in edgewise!" she said, as she placed it on a coffee table in front of Lotte. Franziska had used the gong back in better times, to summon the servants at Sauermühle. It now had a new purpose. From now on, it would tame the onslaught of words from her best friend's husband.

The gong sat enthroned on the Hörls' living room table and lent the proletarian parlor a festive appearance. Over time, the neighbors could hear the gong more and more frequently, usually followed by laughter, because Willi Hörl was basically very aimable and kindhearted. He simply struggled with his fierce temper. He found the idea of using a gong for something other than intended delightful and wagging his finger at her, he jokingly threatened Franziska for bringing it into his house.

Franziska's fatherless son Benno had taken a liking to the roughneck Hörl. Willi Hörl's biological son, by contrast, was a very quiet, sensitive boy, who hardly even dared to breathe in his father's presence.

The public prosecutor's assessor, Leopold Hirschfeld, had contacted Samuel Kohanim by telephone about what he described as a "delicate mission." It was the third long-distance call ever held from the new telephone in the office at Sauermühle. After telephoning with Samuel, Leopold took a few days off.

He wanted to see the conditions at Sauermühle himself. For professional and private reasons, Martha's bizarre criminal complaint about a murder triggered by an outrageous drama in a good Jewish home had aroused his interest. "For the time being, it will suffice if I pursue this matter unofficially," he decided during Martha's last visit and repeatedly emphasized to Samuel Kohanim the purely personal, unofficial nature of his visit. Kohanim frowned at hearing this. What was this fellow after? Samuel in his straight-shooting manner, decided not to beat around the bush for long. He poured the assessor from Berlin a glass of wine that hadn't been watered down, and said, "It's bad enough that my daughter Franziska has stirred up gossip about my family through her mésalliance. Now a murder investigation and other *embarrassments*," with which Samuel diplomatically hinted at Martha's hysterical *pseudologia fantastica*, "*embarrassments*, Mr. Hirschfield, that unnecessarily drag my family's good name into the mud! Who stands to gain anything from this except the anti-Semites and my competitors?"

Both men quickly agreed on this point. The hopelessness of exhuming the body of a Jewish man from the holy ground of a Jewish cemetery in order to have an autopsy performed required no further discussion.

After a thorough examination of Kohanim's finances, Hirschfeld asked for Martha's hand in marriage. With his voice trembling with emotion, he then described the great personal loss he had experienced not so long ago. Despite investing in costly cures, his first wife Edeltraud had died of tuberculosis two years prior in Switzerland. Childless.

Mindel and Samuel looked at the ground to show sympathy for his grief. They expressed their inner jubilation with the banal sentence: "Well, a man needs order in his life!"

At long last, Martha, of all people, was to be the first to have a proper marriage! With a doctor from an impeccable Jewish family of lawyers and architects! Praise be to the Almighty! Admittedly, you couldn't compare Leopold Hirschfeld with Willy Rubin. The assessor was not a handsome man. He was also more than twenty years older than Martha. Two lifeless eyes resided behind his shiny pince-nez. His bald forehead reached to the back of his head. Nothing else was even worth mentioning, except that he knew how to combine the narrow-minded pedantry of a lawyer with the gutless good nature of an average person. Martha only clung to the seriousness of her fiancé and the signs of a lack of malice, coupled with his comfortable sluggishness, because she no longer had any illusions about her chances on the marriage market. For her too, the prospect of being well provided for was now more important than romance.

Such acceptance might be called maturity, she reassured herself. Or more accurately, resignation. The one had likely dictated the other. Just three months later they held the stately wedding at Sauermühle. In light of the war, it was not a typical grandiose family celebration, but it was nonetheless quite respectable. Fortunately, Martha didn't know that the wedding dress she was wearing had once served as the bridal finery for Franziska's wedding of shame. Frugal Mindel had given it to Wrobelska to alter. By the day of the wedding, it was hardly recognizable. Martha looked like a sumptuous meringue stuffed with meat and garnished with greens. For the feast, they served egg dumpling soup, green eel in dill sauce, salads, and cheese produced at Sauermühle, and Teresa's legendary cherry-cream layer cake. Only a connoisseur of fine wines and champagnes would have noticed the somewhat lower quality being served and thus registered that they were living in hard times. Samuel, however, thought that offering slightly lower-quality libations was more than justified, considering the context of the war.

In an ironic twist of fate, Martha basically had her despised sister Franziska to thank for the fact that she was now the wife of a respected lawyer and would soon live in a lavish villa that belonged to her, thanks to her dowry. The most beautiful thing about Leopold Hirschfeld was easily his feet. Martha could nonetheless be proud of her husband for his very respectable social status.

"Otherwise, Hirschfeld would never have married her," Elli jeered.

"Well, you should know!" laughed her cousin Else. "You with your calvary captain. He may have a noble title, but he's poor as a pauper. Let's not pretend that Captain von Strachwitz married you just for your pretty eyes and trophies!

Elli couldn't think of anything else to criticize, so she just groaned, "What a mishpocha!"

WHEN WE FALL, WE FALL HARD

After the war, all manner of new species appeared on the streets of Berlin. One such creature could be found on the city's main boulevard, the Kurfürstendamm: a dog riding on its master's back. A symbol for the immediate postwar era. The "master" in question was a veteran who had broken his back while serving on the front. Unable to walk, he had outfitted a board with wheels and tucked his useless legs beneath him. And in this position, just inches above the pavement, he begged, the dog atop his back. The emperor meanwhile had given up his throne and was chopping wood in Holland. What no one yet suspected was that Kaiser Wilhelm II was a mere forerunner for the one who was soon to follow. That dark turn would lie ahead in Germany's future. For now, the former emperor was playing woodsman in the House of Doorn in the Netherlands.

Dogs riding their masters. Emperors chopping wood. The world had gone completely and utterly mad!

In the final days of the war in early November 1919, the emperor's soldiers rose up in revolt, refusing orders and declaring revolution. Afraid of their own men, the very same officers who had demanded "bravery unto death" abandoned their posts. When winter descended, the helpless soldiers, abandoned to their fate, wandered home through the vastness of Russia, Poland, East and West Prussia. Devoured by lice and fleas and starving for want of food, they turned to the farmers, begging for food, water, and a bunk in their hay.

While the soldiers scavenged the countryside, their officers had taken refuge in Berlin's salons. Strutting around in boots and spurs polished by their orderlies to shine like mirrors, they acted as if nothing had happened. These military peacocks could hardly fathom the news: the cavalry had been abolished at the end of the war—deemed unsuitable for modern warfare. Not ready to contemplate the changing times, their own failures, and dim-witted hubris, the former elite sat in the officers' messes of Berlin, droning on about betrayal and launching allegations of a "stab-in-the-back." The former cavalry officer, Elli's husband, Captain von Strachwitz was among them, kindling conspiracy theories and looking for scapegoats.

Meanwhile in Berlin, Munich, and Kiel every five minutes someone was shooting a gun into the desolate German air and declaring one revolution or another.

"We're taking over!" trumpeted Willi Hörl, Lotte's husband, confident of victory. "The first thing we'll do is line up all the generals against the wall. That pack of criminals! And we'll put this idiot of an emperor on trial for destroying our beautiful fatherland for absolutely no reason! And the whole bunch of nobles and Junkers as well! If it's up to me, the guillotine is gonna be running hot at Alexanderplatz!"

Unfortunately, the longed-for revolution had to take place without Willi. Concerned about her choleric husband, his wife Lotte had hidden all of his pants. And it simply wasn't possible to fight a battle from the barricades in your underpants. Willi thus squatted in the kitchen without his trousers and could do no more than shout and rave. Lotte trembled but nonetheless stuck to her guns. Striking the gong, she announced, "Even if you beat me to death, Willi, you won't get your pants!" Willi didn't beat Lotte; he would never do such a thing. Instead, he lay on the sofa in his long underpants, grumbling, while the cuckoo called from the clock above him.

Only later did he discover that Lotte and Fränze had hidden his and Bruno's pants at Emmi's house, possibly saving both the men's lives.

For one day in March, nine thousand armed Spartacists confronted at Alexanderplatz around four hundred unarmed, mostly overweight elderly officers, who were plagued by gout and otherwise not particularly good on their feet. At the head of the officers were General von Hoffmann and

Admiral von Tirpitz. The people fell silent. Not a shot was fired. The workers' leaders stared at the generals' uniforms like hypnotized rabbits, suddenly intimidated by the splendor of old power. They could hardly believe that the high lords were talking to them! The officers knew how to twist the situation to their advantage: like the wolf who ate chalk to mask from Red Riding Hood his terrible voice, they craftily masked their true nature, and reminded the insurrectionists that Germans should not shoot Germans. Duped, the would-be usurpers of power gave up their arms without a fight to twenty-five pudgy, gray-bearded officers whose gouty fingers were trembling with fear. The reward for their good faith soon followed.

Small bands of shock troops rounded up around two thousand Spartacists, including many women and children, who, after the canceled revolution, were dutifully making their way home to their workers' quarters in Wedding and Prenzlauer Berg. They took them to the courtyard of the Moabit prison in Wedding.

"The men, women, and children were tied together in groups of twenty-five and shot down with three machine guns. The massacre lasted four hours," reported the only eyewitness, the American reporter Ben Hecht, who had climbed a tree to observe the events in the prison courtyard. Not one of the German newspapers found it worth reporting.

Meanwhile, the whole city lacked nearly everything needed to sustain life. Even the sun looked as if it had spent its nights in prison. Performing the bare minimum, it provided neither light nor heat.

The Kohanim daughters in Berlin didn't notice that a revolution had taken place until the "food parcels," which Mindel used to send from Osche every week, failed to materialize. The shortage of fuel was the most difficult of all. No matter how many sacks of pinecones Walter and Bruno collected in the forests of Berlin, they did not have enough fuel to keep warm. The familiar site of the formerly proud tiled stoves with their gaudy ovens that normally burned hot with coal, suddenly looked like relics of a bygone era. Standing useless and cold in the corners of the room, their oven doors bore no more than an empty grin.

On top of the everyday plagues came the political ones. The Poles and the Germans struggled for power in West Prussia. First, everything in West Prussia was to become Polish. Then there was talk of a Polish "corridor" to the Baltic Sea. The League of Nations intervened. Votes were cast; the majority voted to be a part of Germany. The Jews were to blame, shouted the Polish nationalists. After much back and forth, West

Prussia finally became predominately Polish after all. This left the people in Osche doubly confused.

The Jewish timber baron, Kohanim, had declared his support for Poland and loudly at that. So too had his former rival, Artur Bukofzker, the largest industrialist in the region and head of the Jewish community in Schwetz. Bufkofzker's vote in support of Poland left all sides speechless. Not long before, Bukofzker had been a staunch German nationalist. Loyal to the kaiser, he had succeeded in having the west wall of the Schwetz synagogue decorated with a life-size portrait of Kaiser Wilhelm II. For the liberal Kohanim, this was the straw that broke the camel's back for the Jews.

"Am I supposed to have a goy staring at me during prayer? Even if it's the kaiser he has no business being here in the synagogue!" Samuel Kohanim rebelled against the community leadership and Bukofzker. He even went so far as to file a lawsuit against the Jewish community, which to everyone's astonishment, he won. They had to hide the huge portrait of the kaiser behind a burgundy velvet curtain. Removing the fresco all together was out of the question; it would have been an insult to his majesty.

"You can hide under the curtain and worship your new idol," Kohanim said, mocking his opponents, the German nationalist Jews who were loyal to the kaiser.

The Poles, however, found it suspicious that the two most influential Jewish industrialists in the district had suddenly discovered a love for Poland. They were convinced that it was some sort of very cunning Jewish scheme; they simply hadn't figured out yet what the Jews were up to.

The *Volksdeutsche*, as they called the ethnic Germans, saw the two industrialists' declarations of support for the new Polish state as proof that Jews were "stabbing them in the back," and traitors to the fatherland who cared only about their property! In making such a claim, the Volksdeutsche were ignoring the fact that Jews had been at home in West Prussia for six centuries, working peacefully, long before the Germans arrived and occupied the territory, declaring it their fatherland.

The question on the table for everyone was: "What do we love more, our homeland or the German Reich?"

The most patriotic person in the district was the German-Russian, sugar baron von Steinfeld, whom Samuel had once helped transform from being "Russian" to becoming a part of Osche. No matter how you twisted or turned it, the hostile Germans and Poles agreed on one thing: the Jews were to blame for everything!

In the midst of this political turmoil and social unrest, someone sent an urgent telegram to Berlin, which once again, contrary to custom, consisted of more than three words:

+++ Danger +++ Get Walter to Berlin immediately+++

The Kohanim daughters made the dangerous journey home to no man's land for their parents' golden wedding anniversary. Gangs of robbers and marauding soldiers were wreaking havoc throughout West Prussia.

The journey from Berlin to Osche took three days and nights. When the Kaiser was still in power, it took a mere eight hours. Now, however, the train had to stop at least four or five times for inspections by armed soldiers' councils and committees made up of all manner of commandos. Wearing armbands and carrying loaded guns, unwashed, unshaven, in ragged uniforms, with cigarettes in their mouths, they tried to make themselves important. When Franziska finally arrived at the Osche train station there was not a livery cab in sight.

When she asked, she was told that hired cabs had disappeared some time ago. All the horses had been requisitioned for the cavalry years ago. They were probably all dead on the battlefields, along with their riders, or had ended up in a pot before they could be requisitioned.

Just then the sugar baron's car drove past at full speed, honking its horn and spraying her with mud, clearly intentionally. Fränze was so perplexed that she couldn't even get upset. Her stomach nonetheless tightened a little. Then the young Count Solkowsky appeared. Wearing a new captain's uniform for Józef Piłsudki's Polish army, complete with a square cap and lots of tinsel on his shoulders and chest, he bustled about the station. Was he, of all people, Franziska's salvation?

"Fisheye," as he was called because of his bulging Graves' disease eyes, looked through Franziska as if she were made of glass. Then he gave his men an order: "Search and arrest!"

The soldiers howled and ordered Franziska to undress.

Franziska didn't move. She held her head even higher than usual while one of the soldiers put the barrel of a gun to her temple. As she had once done in the synagogue at her bat mitzvah and during her disgraceful wedding, she took a stance in front of the hateful pack of soldiers. She stared down the once love-struck count who had pursued her so insistently and haplessly, as if to say, "I dare you, you scoundrel!"

Fisheye leaned nonchalantly against the station's restaurant counter, lowered his eyes, and lit an Oriental cigarette. He shot her a wry grin. Suddenly, several shots rang out from afar.

"Well, let her go then. She's already been punished enough!" he shouted in Polish. When the men didn't immediately stop, because they were about to rip her blouse open, he shouted: "That's an order!"

Savoring the situation, he took great pains to put his gloves back on very slowly, removed the cigarette he had been smoking from his mouth and theatrically stubbed it out in front of Franziska, as if he were extinguishing her. He then mounted his horse and galloped off. His troupe followed him on foot. Some of them gave Franziska disappointed looks, as if they were mourning the missed opportunity.

Her clothes in disarray and shaking with rage, Franziska dragged her suitcase out of the station. In front of the building stood the only rental vehicle available in Osche during those horseless times: a large handcart with a team of dogs, two rottweilers. The operator was Georg Rubin, Franziska's former brother-in-law. Out of tact, he didn't inquire about her troubled expression, instead he politely took the heavy suitcase she was carrying and loaded it onto his cart.

"Feel free to sit on the cart. The dogs had six rats each for breakfast. You'll see just how much weight they can pull!" and with that the dogs set off at a brisk gallop toward Sauermühle.

The silent journey through the gloomy forest was accompanied by the sole sound of the panting dogs.

Then her brother-in-law turned to her, and in as careful a manner as possible, tried to reassure her, "The Kohanims can always count on the Rubins. No matter what happened or what may come next."

What's he hinting at? Franziska wondered.

On the hill past the woods, the Kohanim's manor house loomed over the filthy gray landscape by the river. A fine shower of freezing rain, mixed with snow hovered in the air above, like a dirty shroud, almost as if it were trying to hide the house.

Strange, today everything should be lit up and bustling with activity, thought Franziska.

There was a row of mud-encrusted carriages, wagons, and horses wet from the rain, and even a few cars, parked in front of the driveway.

Has Max come? Franziska wondered. But there wasn't a soul to be seen in the yard. Fränze hadn't even thought of her son Walter yet. Suddenly she had the feeling that the house was warning her, "Stay away!"

The tightening that Fränze had begun to feel in her stomach since the assault at the station was now moving towards her heart. She got up carefully from George Rubin's dog-drawn vehicle and silently pressed a coin into her brother-in-law's hand. He was reluctant to accept it. Lost in thought, Franziska scratched the head of the panting dogs and approached the house with trepidation. When the door opened, the now white-haired Grandmother Beinesch, whose head was trembling, ran to meet her and threw her arms around her, sobbing. She mumbled a gibberish mixture of Polish and Yiddish that Franziska couldn't make out. Behind them, Teresa, the Kashubian cook, was bawling. Her pancake-round face was all out of shape from crying.

"You have to be strong now, my child!" Taubine Beinesch implored, sometimes in Polish, sometimes in Yiddish and German, while the uncontrolled trembling of her head of white hair increased to a tremolo.

"What's going on? Is someone sick? Or what is it?"

"Sick?! No, nobody's sick here!" her son, Walter, whom she hadn't seen for a year, shouted angrily. "Grandpa and Grandma have been murdered! By common thieves!"

"By Poles!" someone in the background corrected, their voices filled with hate.

"We don't know yet," hissed another.

Walter approached his mother as if he wanted to throw himself into her arms, but then paused, and embarrassed, turned instead to the banister for support. Conspicuously turning his back to her, he swayed back and forth against the banister.

"What are you talking about?"

Before Franziska could fathom the news, Fanny guided her toward her five other sisters, who had all dressed festively for the planned anniversary celebration. The sisters were doing their best to outdo each other in a fest of sobs. Just then two pale, distraught maids came rushing out of the parents' bedroom with bloody rags and buckets and bowls full of red soapy water and made the sign of the cross with the blood-smeared mops in their hands, uttering, "Oh dear Mary, oh dear Mary and Joseph!"

The relatives, who had come to celebrate the golden wedding anniversary in ceremonial attire, stood out of place like colorful peacocks on a battlefield.

Struggling to retain their composure, everyone had taken a seat in the large drawing room. Teresa had recovered enough to resume her duties. She had coffee and cake served. Tears ran down her cheeks and dripped onto the coffee pot, which she was clutching tightly to her bosom. Something else had mixed in with the grief and disbelief over this act of violence: the smell of pogrom and home distillated liquor was in the air. An ancient, almost forgotten horror. Instinct picked up the scent, but the mind nonetheless refused to believe it, wanting to nip in the bud any thoughts of a pogrom.

Samuel's business partner and Else's father, Zacharias Segall, intercepted Franziska at the door to her parents' bedroom. "Fränze, you really don't want this to be the last glimpse that you have of your parents!"

Utterly lost, Franziska stood staring in the vestibule next to her pale first-born, who was eyeing her suspiciously. Then she did what she always did when others were overwhelmed by their feelings: she turned to stone.

"Tenue!" she whispered to her son. Walter didn't reply, not wanting to embarrass himself in front of his mother who was more legend than reality.

Ascher Nathanson, the rather odd man from Danzig who had married Selma, was the first to regain his bearings. With a leaden face, and eyes fixed on a point somewhere in eternity, he began to recite the prescribed prayers, last heard on the occasion of the crown prince's funeral.

Ascher swayed from side to side like a wind-up doll while the bodies were being prepared for the ceremony.

Meanwhile, Zacharias Segall, took over the secular end of things. "We have to keep our wits about us now!" he said, trying to cheer up the Jews and non-Jews present. "Everything points to a normal robbery-murder!" Coming from him, it sounded as if "normal robbery-murder" was something reassuring.

"That's right! We have to wait for the police investigation. We can't say anything before then," seconded Gerson Segal, Fanny's husband.

Whenever disaster befell the Kohanim-Beinesch-Segal-Segall clan, there were always a few unwavering optimists. "The circumstances of our gathering are different. We simply need to change out of festive attire into our mourning clothes."

The next day at the cemetery, Ascher led Walter, or Kohanim junior, as everyone called him, in bravely reciting the kaddish for his murdered grandparents in a shaky child's voice, thus fulfilling Samuel's most fervent wish. No doves flew up, not even crows. On April 11, 1919, the sun had set behind the black clouds over Schwetz, and on the Kohanims, forever.

The double murder of Samuel and Mindel Kohanim was never solved. When the family made inquiries, they were told rather bluntly and with a cold smile that the Polish authorities had better things to do than to judge the murderers of Jews. Teresa Plienska, the Kohanim's cook stated that she had observed the murder from the attic window of the servants' house: around twenty Polish-speaking men in German military overcoats had entered the manor house and shot Samuel and Mindel in their beds and robbed them of all money and valuables. Later, someone found behind the barn cigarette butts of the English brand "Nelson," the very same kind that the young Count Solkowsky smoked. In the face of such evidence, the police immediately dropped all investigations like a hot potato.

The police closed the file with the note that the witness Pani Plienska could not make any statements that could be used in a court of law because she had not recognized any of the perpetrators.

"That's not true at all! I can describe every single one of them and would recognize everyone!" Teresa protested in German.

"But that might be extremely bad for your health," the policeman advised her. "Especially for you Kashubians! You Kashubians are all traitors and German servants anyway!"

Pan Jerzy Chemienski, Teresa's fiancé, who was a foreman at the Kohanim grain mill, put his finger over his mouth, as if to calm the raging Teresa by encouraging her silence. "What can we do?" he admonished her. "We're servants wherever we are, whether to the Germans, the Jews, or the Poles. So let's keep our mouths shut and think for ourselves."

The two Kashubian servants then exited the room, closing the door behind them loudly, as a sign of their discontent. That left Fränze alone with the new Polish figure of respect. She stood up, "You know," she hissed at the indifferent Polish police commander, "I've learned something important today: home is where you have rights!"

By now Franziska's eldest son was crying loudly. She grabbed his hand, turned her back on the Polish police official, and dragged him home.

For the first time, "home" was Berlin.

From then on, Sauermühle, Osche, and Schwetz in West Prussia were like Salamanca, Venice, and Lemberg.

Places of no return.

THE INTERROGATION

My interrogation is to take place at Schöneberg's Special Commission. The subpoena states, "Division of Crimes Against Humans," third floor, "Human Trafficking and Smuggling Unit." On my way I got lost on the second floor at the "Department of Homicide and Bodily Injury." Walking through the offices is like a trip back in time to the 1960s. The hallways are littered with obsolete and out of commission technology that's waiting around for either redemption or transportation to Berlin's Museum of Technology. Only the desks are new. Ms. Kühnel is sitting next to me. Before the interrogation begins, she vigorously objects to the fact that I was booked at all. She throws out a series of legal references to this or that statute to the confused officers and prevents them from taking my fingerprints and a DNA sample, adding that all of the information that they have already gathered should be deleted from the national database. As a precaution, she threatens to lodge a disciplinary complaint. "The accused has no prior record, and there is not sufficient reasonable suspicion of commercial, criminally organized smuggling to justify such a measure."

The officers sitting in a row on the other side of the table, nod reluctantly.

"As my client has stated, she traveled alone to Istanbul."

An assistant to the chief interrogator holds up a photo.

"Do you know this person?"

"No idea," I say as casually as possible, trying to look nonchalant, innocent, and convincingly clueless.

"Do you notice anything about the photo?" asks the only woman among the officers.

"Well, a woman with dark hair, about my age, I would say," I state for the record.

"And?!"

"Well, she wears her hair almost the same way that I do."

"…Yes, and?!"

"And what?"

"She looks *similar* to you! Anyone with eyes can see that. So similar, in fact, that you are likely to be confused for each other."

"I don't see the resemblance. But then I don't spend the whole day looking in the mirror. Who is she?"

I was ready for this one. My attorney had drilled me. Whenever they put a photo in front of me, I am supposed to ask who the person is, otherwise they will allege that I know the person.

The team of interrogators exchange annoyed looks.

"Please describe, as best as you can remember, the day you left Istanbul."

"Well, I left the hotel around 7:30 a.m. and went jogging in Topkapi Park and then returned exactly forty minutes later. Then I ate breakfast until around 9:30 a.m. and then spent some time studying the guidebook that I had brought with me. Afterward, I hurried down to the thermal baths before they got too full. I stayed there for about forty-five minutes. Then around 11 a.m. I went to the bazaar because I still wanted to find a souvenir.

The chief interrogator smiles at me skeptically.

"So, it's pure coincidence that you were at the bazaar at the same time as your accomplice?"

"I don't have an accomplice. And I really don't know or care about what other people are up to or not at the same time as me. I bought some presents and then around 1 o'clock I took a cab back to the hotel to eat something at a garden restaurant nearby.

"Did someone follow you? Or did you have the feeling that someone had followed you?"

"No!"

"What happened next?"

"Next I used my phone to call a number in Istanbul, and because the person who answered couldn't speak either German or English, the waiter offered to translate for me."

"Yes, that's the number for a construction company. We already knew that from your phone company. What did you want from them? Did you perhaps want to meet your accomplice at the company's construction site? A lot of refugees are housed there, as we have already learned from our Turkish colleagues."

I'm genuinely perplexed and I shake my head.

"I have no idea what you're getting at. I wanted to call a German acquaintance, who has been living in Istanbul for forty years. She had invited me to come over. That was also one of the reasons that I went to Istanbul. But that was the wrong number."

"What's the name of this supposed acquaintance with the wrong number?"

I smile as I open my purse and feel around until I finally fish out my notebook.

"Here is her business card. Have a look for yourself. Her name is Christel Genc."

The chief interrogator inspects the business card on both sides and puts it in the files. My lawyer interjects and asks to photograph the card first, and then to photograph the act of handing over the card to the interrogators.

"What did you do then?"

"I took a cab and got a ride to the address on the business card, but then I realized that my acquaintance didn't live there, and no one seemed to know her."

The interrogators exchange amused looks.

"How did you figure that out?"

"I rang the neighbors' doorbell and showed them Ms. Genc's picture."

I pull two vacation photos out of my notebook and tap the center of the picture. Ms. Kühnel takes another photo of the evidence and its submission to the interrogators.

"So this is Ms. Genc," I continue, pointing to the person in the photo. "At least that is how she introduced herself to all of the ladies in the photo and then handed out this business card. By the way, there was a police station around the corner from this supposed apartment building. I also asked the officers there about Ms. Genc, but I didn't find out anything."

"And then?"

"Then I went to the harbor. I wanted to wash down my anger with a Campari orange. And then the lights went out. I didn't wake up until I was in a hospital in Berlin and didn't know anything at all at first, not even who I was or where I was."

"How did you get to the airport?"

"The German consulate must have arranged it. I have no idea. My memory only started to come back after I was back in Berlin, in the neurology department at the hospital."

"That's a real tall tale you're spinning for us here."

They act amused by the whole thing.

"So, you were at the bazaar at the same time as your accomplice. But of course, you don't know her. Both of your cell phones were connected to the same tower at the same time. Despite a wrong number you set out to meet a mysterious acquaintance who had given you a fake business card? Then you went to the harbor and were served a spiked drink, while your accomplice flew from Istanbul to Berlin, using your ID and your ticket, and thus entered the Federal Republic under a false identify. And we're supposed to believe you?"

Ms. Kühnel raises her hand to stop him:

"Traces of a substance commonly known as 'knockout drops' were found in my client's blood, providing evidence that she was the victim of a drug-facilitated assault, which someone carried out in order to steal her ID and plane ticket. There's nothing, absolutely nothing that justifies charging my client."

"And what was your client looking for on the crypto network?"

An awkward silence, then I take the floor. "As you can see from the documents, I was a journalist. I did some research. Do you know the novel *Deep Web*?

"Should we?" one of the interrogators asks, chuckling with feigned amusement.

"So out of pure literary and professional interest, you were active on a crypto network where drugs, hit men, fake passports, identities, and lots of child pornography can be easily offered and received? And your accomplice just happened to be in the same network? I'll tell you what you were 'researching' there. You were making arrangements for the illegal smuggling of your accomplice to the Federal Republic of Germany!" The chief interrogator leans back, self-satisfied, and crosses his arms across his chest.

My attorney clears her throat emphatically. "Now that's going too far! There's no law against logging onto a crypto network. And for the politically persecuted, such as the accomplice, that is the only way to communicate without fear of repression. However, you have so far failed to provide any evidence that my client was involved in a criminal activity except as victim! You don't even have enough to make a formal charge against my client!"

The chief interrogator throws up his arms in resignation and then jumps up from his chair in frustration. "Okay, we're not getting anywhere for today. Continue to be at our disposal and don't leave the country. You can go for today!"

We have barely left the interrogation room when Ms. Kühnel fires a volley of punishing looks at me. "You really should have told me about the crypto network!"

Outside the police station, a fortress from the Wihelminian era, we decide to get something to eat. "My treat," Ms. Kühnel says, "I can count it as a business lunch. Basically, you're paying for everything, of course."

Below, on the beach of Lake Halen, we are the only two guests. We can talk without having to keep the faucet on. We nonetheless took the precaution of leaving our cell phones in the car. Ms. Kühnel insisted.

"So," I ask eagerly, "what did you find out from Nasi Gohari?"

Ms. Kühnel pushes her sunglasses high up into her hair.

"She stated on record that she bought your ID from a Turkish human smuggler. Everything happened in a hurry because she had to get to the airport right away."

"So, am I out of the woods?"

"Don't count your chickens before they hatch."

LOCAL ANESTHESIA

Servants in gray smocks filled scores of boxes with the files from the Kohanim estate. Amidst the packing and shuffling of papers, sat the executers, Leopold Hirschfeld, Esq., now a judge at the Berlin District Court, and Nathan Weinstock, Esq., a notary in Schwetz. After studying the contents of the files, they declared their deceased client's estate a "total loss." Sic transit gloria mundi! Thus, passes away the glory of the world!

Unmoved by the swirl of activity going on around them, the two lawyers rested in two heavy leather armchairs, like mirror-image Buddhas. As soon as they rose from the chairs, the movers showed up and packed them too. They were silent for a while, savoring the historic moment that they would one day tell their grandchildren about.

Faced with such turmoil, they sought edification in the eternal clarity of jurisprudence and, in defiance of the spirit of the times, they found it "appropriate," even "expedient," to destroy the remaining stocks of port wine that had been anxiously guarded for years. "There's no reason to be stingy when everything is going to hell in a handbasket! Cheers!"

Once everything had been discussed and recorded, they debated until their final round of drinks, the pros and cons of the current theories about who murdered the Kohanims.

Were the men who murdered the Kohanims members of the German military who merely spoke Polish so as to appear Polish? But then why would German robbers, wearing German military fatigues pretend to speak

Polish? Or were they regular Polish soldiers who had disguised themselves in German uniforms? Or were they Polish thieves, pretending to be patriots, who just happened to be wearing German and Polish military coats when they committed the crime? All conjecture! All hearsay! The only evidence remained the butts of Oriental cigarettes, which only one person within miles smoked. The young Solkowsky! But what did that actually prove? Only that he had been at the Kohanims' house and had smoked. But when? It all added up to nothing.

Or should one assume that the Kohanim murders were a pogrom attack, and if so, by which side? Did the crime point more to German or Polish nationalists? Perhaps it really was an ordinary robbery-murder, without any political or ethnic motives? Before Weinstock had allowed the last of the furniture to be loaded up to move to his office in Kamenz, Pomerania, which had remained part of the German Reich, there was just one last sad duty to attend to. Their dispute had meandered without any real momentum through the detritus and quagmires of many suspicions and theories, sometimes this way and sometimes that, and ultimately petered out into the arbitrary "anything is possible." The same was true of the speculations about the upcoming auction of the Kohanims' estate. Weinstock, who was an avowed music lover, saw this mitzvah as the final chord of a symphonic work that Max Gulkowitsch might one day write, an appropriate accompaniment to the downfall of the Kohanim empire.

Kohanim had invested all of his capital in land and forests along the railroad tracks, the Schwarzwasser River and around the factory of the largest Jewish entrepreneur in Schwetz, Artur Bukofzker. It was only now, posthumously, that it became apparent that Kohanim wanted to force his old rival Bukofzker into forming a partnership to build a larger paper factory on the outskirts of Schwetz. Unbeknownst to anyone, over the years Samuel Kohanim had used straw men to buy up the entire area surrounding Bukofzker's factory. For years, he had prepared the coup de grâce of the coup: a groundbreaking new patent for paper production. Zacharias Segall filed a claim to the patent, which, as a former partner, was immediately granted to him without having to wait for the inheritance settlement.

People were amazed at Samuel's bold plan, which would have succeeded were it not for the "stupidest of all wars," as Samuel always referred to it. All because of an Austrian successor to the throne! Were it not for the tense international relations, no one would have bothered to shed so much as a tear for Franz Ferdinand.

Kohanim's plans were all in the past now. Polish rule in the former West Prussia did not bode well for those who had voted to remain with the German Reich. The owners of German and Jewish estates, houses, and farms thus boarded up their homes and fled. Everyone feared repression. The mere idea that the Poles might behave in the same way as the Germans had in the past was reason enough for most Germans to flee to the newly demarcated boundaries of the German empire. Even many Jews who had not voted for Germany were now driven away by the prospect of becoming second-class citizens under Piłsudski's anti-Jewish government. Thus, in 1920, the supply of land exceeded demand a thousand times over.

At the front of the worthless houses, fleeing Germans and Jews were still boarding up the doors and windows, while out of the back, Poles were already hauling out anything that wasn't nailed down. "They can't even annex properly, these Pollacks!" Hirschfeld complained.

In the German-Polish no-man's-land of West Prussia, all hell had broken loose. The new spirit of anarchy and the old one of subservience waltzed in an absurd dance of the dead, as if the Titanic's orchestra were doomed to play the *Dance Macabre* forever.

Infected by the general absurdity, the Kohanim sisters fought vehemently over their inheritance. The sisters who had received their dowry in full now fought with Selma, who had come away empty-handed because of her secret marriage. The designation of eight-year-old Walter as the universal heir made all the sisters furious. Except Franziska. The supposed inheritance consisted almost entirely of air tinged with the smell of wood and glue. All the wealth accumulated over generations had vanished into nothing overnight. The sisters nonetheless continued to make claims and counterclaims against each other, each insisting that they were not interested in money. It was the principle of the thing, they said, which as experience shows is much worse than pure greed. Whereas greed is predictable and makes compromise possible, hurt feelings have no end.

As things stood, all hopes rested on a dubious rumor: the "American" was supposed to be making his way around the area. The legendary American, about whom half of Poland was now fantasizing, was a Pole from Katowice, Jerzy Kowalski. According to rumors, Kowalski had moved to Chicago, where he had become "The Railroad King of America" and now possessed a fortune in American dollars. In the prostrate country, which was no longer allowed to be Germany and could not yet be Poland, the naturalized US citizen was on a shopping spree, acquiring factories, mines, castles, and estates by the dozen, as if they were so many potatoes and carrots being sold for practically nothing at the close of the weekly farmers' market. No one had ever actually seen the legendary American in the flesh. The closest they had come was spotting his spindly secretary, a former Prussian officer cadet stranded in the far reaches of the East but blessed with a diploma in foreign trade and a perfect knowledge of German, Polish, and English. The more fabulous the reports about the empire of the Railroad King from America and his unimaginable purchases became, the more fervently people waited for Mr. Kowalski as if he were the Messiah.

Apart from Zacharias Segall, who had secretly opted for Poland, there were no other solvent prospective buyers for miles around. Segall had already become a Polish citizen and was now taking the opportunity to acquire his former business partner's share in the furniture factory for a pittance. He was even able to make the whole thing look like he was being generous toward the poor relatives of the dead man.

They also pinned their hopes on the former staunch German nationalist Artur Bukofzker, who had suddenly become "Polish" for the sake of his property and his cellulose factory. He finally had the opportunity to acquire at low price the land for the expansion of his factories, which Kohanim had once secretly snatched away from him. But neither Bukofzker nor any of his representatives were to be seen anywhere, leaving everyone completely baffled.

At ten o'clock on the dot, the scheduled time for the auction, a group of men stood on the tracks of the canal railroad, craning their necks. It was typical April weather that day: May 7, 1920. The wind was blowing stray snowflakes. When the sun broke out shortly before the end of the auction, as if to briefly cheer up the hopeful people, the auctioneer knelt on his handkerchief in front of the track. He strained to place his right ear on the canal rail and with an authoritative gesture, he commanded the bystanders to be quiet. Slowly, he raised his right arm and beckoned his assistant over, who then knelt down on an old newspaper and listened to the railroad tracks near Osche, as if the hidden heart of the universe were beating there. Several dignified gentlemen with beards followed his example and also listened intently to the iron of the railroad tracks.

"I hear something!"

"Probably just soldiers on a handcar again," Zacharias Segall warned the optimists.

"No, no, a handcar has a lighter sound, more like something in a rush. That, gentlemen, is definitely a train!" declared one of the bearded men, who then stood up triumphantly.

Sure enough, a cloud of steam billowed in the distance, from which grew a locomotive with two red-painted saloon cars in tow. With loud bells and whistles, the train passed them all at high speed. They looked at the taillights in bewilderment. The first auction item, which only Poles were allowed to purchase, was plot eleven on Lake Schwarzwasser along with a servants' house and corn mill. These items had been removed from the list due to outstanding wages. With this trick, Weinstock sold the family's property to the Kashubian cook for a nominal twenty thousand marks. If everything was lost, then at least it was lost to the most loyal of the loyal. The cook, Teresa, sobbed with emotion and kissed the old gentleman's hands. "…even if I have to carry every penny to Berlin one by one. What a misfortune! No, what a misfortune!"

"Well, one man's misfortune can be another man's good fortune," the notary comforted Samuel and Mindel's daughters, who frowned and shivered like shorn sheep in the cold wind. Then the main crowd was called up. With a cough, the auctioneer caught everyone's attention and knocked imperiously on the makeshift lectern with his metal hammer: "Which of the entitled parties will make a bid for the Sauermühle manor house with a sawmill and two hundred hectares of prime farmland as well as three thousand acres of forest and woodland, including the mill stream and four fishponds? Minimum bid is two hundred and fifty thousand marks!"

When he uttered the sum, there was bitter laughter from the corner where the servants had gathered.

Amidst the questions and uproarious laughter, they again heard the sound of the approaching train. With steam hissing from every pipe, the train came to a stop. Out of it stepped Captain Stanislaw Count Solkowsky in full uniform, with his square Polish military cap on his head and his saber strapped to his hip. He bore not the slightest trace of the limp aristocratic scion from which he had descended. A man had found his destiny.

With the tap of a gloved right hand at the peak of his cap, he gave a casual military salute. Then savoring the stage-ready situation, in Polish he called out proudly, "I offer five thousand-five hundred American dollars!"

Everyone's mouth dropped.

The American's secretary, who now appeared behind the Fisheye, feverishly calculated something on a scrap of paper. He then whispered in the ear of the "Monsieur le Comte," who jutted out his chin and with condescension declared: "Yes, that's more than the minimum bid, and it's exactly the amount Kohanim offered my great-grandfather."

"That's a damn lie!" Franziska shouted, her eyes burning with rage.

The Fisheye reacted with condescension to the interjection and continued unmoved: "No one should be able to say the Solkowskys are skinflints!" He sneered. "After all, *we're* not Jews!" he continued in German, contemptuously throwing several bundles of dollar bills onto the auctioneer's desk.

From the compartment window of the saloon train, a man of about sixty, with bloodshot eyes and a crooked top hat atop his swollen face, his hair a white fuzz beneath, toasted the auctioneers. It was Kowalski, the railroad king himself.

Only much later was it revealed that it was over a game of cards that the young count had also snatched the old hunting lodge and the schnapps factory that had belonged to the German sugar czar von Steinfeld. Some people thought that a lucky streak at the ecarté had given him the old property. Others knew that Solkowsky junior had been boasting for some time about restoring the old ownership. He had gambled with the railroad king. Allegedly with marked cards.

The German nationalist liquor and sugar czar, who had seen the Russian Revolution approaching earlier than anyone else, was surprised this time by the events that followed the world war. After the fiasco of his quasi-expropriation by the Poles, he fled with the remains of his fortune to the Harz Mountains, located safely within the boundaries of the German Reich. There he remained faithful to the production of schnapps, producing "Original Danziger Goldwasser" until the end of his days.

ODA'S PRIVATE REVOLUTION

Oda Hanke, née von Güldner and former ward of the sugar baron, pursued not only world revolution, but also her own private one: she got divorced!

In 1919, Oda Hanke, a communist known to the police, went down in history as the fourth proletarian woman in Berlin who dared to file for divorce from her husband. Reinhold, the "like-minded confectioner" whom the Amazonian Oda had once hastily married to avoid being sent back to the von Steinfeld family, had increasingly given in to drunkenness. One morning he appeared at Segal's payroll office accompanied by a security guard. He insisted that, as head of the family, he be paid his wife's wages. Otherwise, he would forbid her from working. Fanny Segal had no choice but to hand over the pay of her head seamstress. According to Oda, that evening Reinhold Hanke ran his head into a red-hot, cast-iron frying pan that Oda had been holding while preparing mashed potatoes.

Despite Reinhold Hanke's dramatic forehead bandage and red burn scar, the judge granted divorce without fault to Mrs. Oda Hanke, née von Güldner, who was employed by the Segal tailoring company. "The defendant Reinhold Hanke is a notorious drunkard and a depraved subject," the judge ruled. He awarded Oda custody of their children, Hella and Peter. In order to get divorced as quickly as possible, Oda waived all maintenance claims. Firstly, Oda considered maintenance to be counterrevolutionary, and secondly, she would not be able to recover it anyway. The judge also dismissed Reinhold's charges against Oda for assault. Oda had acted in self-defense, he said, regardless of the physical disproportion between the tall, strong Oda and the rather slight, red-haired Reinhold.

Oda's brother Rudolf found it so scandalous for a woman to get a divorce that he told her, "As if being a communist wasn't enough! Now you're also a divorced communist. I've had it! My wife Bertha and I are breaking off all contact with you!"

Leopold Hirschfeld, Martha's husband, did not want to tolerate, even at the very periphery of his circle of acquaintances, a divorced wife and the calamities Oda had suffered at the hands of Reinhold Hanke. Initially, he had had no objections to Martha's meeting her childhood friend, Oda, for she was, after all, of noble birth, something in which Reinhold put a great deal of stock. But even then, he had demanded that Oda only be allowed to visit when he was absent; what's more, her social decline also dictated that she may only enter through the servant's entrance. After a while, Oda's views irritated him to such an extent that he asked Martha not to receive her friend in the house anymore at all, because one must be "considerate."

Leopold found Oda's divorce just as scandalous as the past of his no-less-notorious sister-in-law Franziska Rubin, née Kohanim. Thereafter, he thus forbade Martha from having any further contact with "this person." "That's not out of malice, my dear Martha. It's simply a question of social hygiene," he lectured. Martha responded by immediately darkening the bedroom and sinking into a three-day migraine. When Martha was no longer even allowed to wait for Oda at the Segal's atelier, she sent her letters by post, as she had done in the past.

As a divorcée, Oda couldn't find a place to live. She and the children had to take turns seeking shelter with good-natured colleagues or companions.

Dearest Martha!
I'm quite desperate. No one in Berlin will rent a flat to a divorced woman! A divorcée is too wretched for even the darkest, dampest holes filled with bugs! That's the world we live in! In my distress, I have now decided to rent a plot of land in Rehberge, just outside the city, where Wedding turns into the countryside. I will build an arbor there. I now invest every penny I earn in board and nails. After work, instead of using a needle and thread, I work with a hammer

and saw. A carpenter comrade drew me a plan and comes over on Sunday afternoons with his wife to help be build the arbor. Most of the time, however, he just tears down the boards that I had nailed up the day before. But I'm learning, and by now he's so happy with my carpentry work that he thinks I could start as an apprentice with him. Nevertheless, everything is progressing far too slowly. I want to be finished by August and then finally move into my new "castle" with the children. For the time being, your sister Fanny has kindly taken us in.

I can also get some furniture from Fanny, and if I could get the old wardrobe and the bed with spring bases, comforters, and mattresses from you, my happiness would be complete. Another worry is Hella's legs. Because I was always bent over the sewing machine until the little one was born, her legs are so crooked that she can't walk properly. She crawls on all fours like a weasel. Thanks to the orthopedic splints and the massages that Fanny, the good soul, pays for, Hella's legs are already somewhat straightened. On Sundays, I always sit Hella in the "garden" in the sun and dig her legs into the hot sand. And when I get off the ladder, I massage her legs and renew the hot sand. She always claps her hands and is happy. It obviously does her good. The sun has turned her hair completely white-blond and she herself is as a brown as a raisin. When I celebrate the roofing ceremony, you have to come.

With love,
Oda

Dearest Oda!
I am delighted with your progress and don't know where you get your strength and courage to face life! You can also get things from Elli. Among other things, she will give you a little trolley that you can attach to a bicycle. Then you will no longer need a handcart. She will also send you furniture and household items. You can even count on the help of my sister Fränze. Through Else Dahnke, who also wants to make a big contribution to your household, she will also send you something. But you can probably throw it out straight away, if I know Fränze at all... Can't you ask for help from your brother Rudolf in the Harz Mountains? As a brother, he must stand by you in times of need!

There is also news from the old country. Ole Segall, my father's former partner, wrote. Although he's now been granted Polish citizenship, which can't be said of all Jews, business is so bad that they have switched to bartering: a wardrobe for a pig, a footstool for a half a chicken, and so on. Segall has therefore set up a food trade en masse. How very like him! But he was always the better businessman compared to my father, who was more interested in visualization than accounting.

Speaking of which, I'm sure you remember our old family legend. Well, you won't believe it but Count Solkowsky was struck by lightning while riding from Osche via Sauermühle! What do you say to that?! That's enough to make you dizzy. "That was probably the happiest Sabbath the Jews of Osche have had in a long time," wrote Segall, who still can't forgive the count for using today's worthless mark to calculate the value of our father's land, acquired a hundred or more years ago, just so he could make my father, and Jews in general, look bad.

But I have another worry: my Leopold wants to be baptized! He was told that he could only become president of the court if he and his whole family were Christian! I find that an imposition, especially as this is no longer necessary, as it was in the days of the emperor, and it is now even against the law! It's also against the agreement Leopold made with my father regarding religion. The authorities don't officially require conversion, Leopold says. That's not even possible. But unofficially, when several applicants are vying for a post, they don't appoint a judge of Jewish faith to such a high office. Even for a Catholic, it could be tricky because of the ongoing culture war between Catholics and Protestants, he says. But with the increasing agitation against Jews everywhere, being Jewish has become much worse than being Catholic, don't you agree?

There's no way that I am going to betray my faith! Why should I? I'm not particularly devout, but it's more a question of character than faith. You don't just throw away your origins and change your faith according to fashion or opportunity! But that's for everyone to decide for themselves.

And one more message: I am finally expecting. Out of piety, I therefore visited Willy's grave yesterday. Fränze still hasn't had an inscription put on the gravestone! Apparently, she's at loggerheads with the local authority over the wording, as my cousin Else, who visited us the day before yesterday with her suitcase-business husband, Bruno Dahnke, told me. Bruno brought me a beautiful snakeskin handbag from his factory. I can't accept it of course. Bruno and Leopold get along great. And I really don't know how I should behave towards Else, since she's so chummy with Fränze. I wish you strength and all the best, write soon.

With love,

your loyal friend, Martha

A CROWN PRINCE WITHOUT A KINGDOM

With the death of his grandparents, the crown prince Walter's world came crashing down. Not one of the adults around him gave a single thought to his suffering. They were all preoccupied with their own hardships and catastrophes. Their world had collapsed in one way or another too.

Walter had lost the kingdom that his grandfather had promised him. But he didn't find that tragic; he was too young to mourn the loss of such a thing. What he did find hard, however, was the loss of the grandmother and grandfather that he had idolized. He also missed the house he had grown up in, his room with the dormer window, his nurse, ole Olga, the Schwarzwasser lake in front of the house, where everyone swam with the ducks and fish in summer and skated in winter. He longed for the meadows, fields, and especially the forest that surrounded Sauermühle. But most of all he missed his dog, Hasso, and his pony, Snowflake, which his grandfather had given him for his fifth birthday.

The life he had known had vanished overnight, becoming nothing more than a distant, beautiful dream. Happiness had suddenly been turned to misery by some evil curse. And the evil witch responsible was none other than the woman who called herself his mother. "She is evil. I can't stand her, and she can't stand me either," is how he explained it to the only person who cared about him, Bruno Geissler, the Saxon plumber.

One day, Walter up and left Franziska's household in Berlin. He had almost made it to Bromberg, which was now called, Bydgoszcz, before the Polish police picked him up. The second time he even made it as far as Zempelburg, which was now called Sępólno. He begged Zacharrias Segall to let him stay with him. His father's former business partner would have been happy to take him in, because he liked the boy, but Franziska was against it. The third time Walter ran away, his paternal uncle George Rubin, who, as rumor had it, "probably wanted to ingratiate himself" brought him back to Berlin. That was enough for Franziska, she gave up.

"I simply can't handle the boy, and I don't want him to turn out like his father! It's my responsibility!" she complained to the Jewish orphanage on Breitenstrasse in Berlin Niederbarnim. "He must be taught discipline. Religion too, of course!" Bruno and Else made sure that Walter was at least allowed to come home to Heilandstrasse for Shabbat and weekends.

"Fränze, don't sin against your own flesh and blood!" Bruno had warned her in his strong Saxon-Berlin accent, raising his finger at her in admonition. "And if you really can't put up with him, then the boy can come down to my workshop," Bruno said, rebelling for the first time against Franziska's regime

On the occasion of the next monthly payment that Franziska had to deliver on the first of the month, the head of the orphanage reported indignantly, "The boy is strong, a very good pupil, and one of our best singers. But he is also unruly, completely rebellious, and stubborn! The other day, your son bit the thigh of the porter who was supposed to punish him, nor did he apologize for it afterward! What do you think of that?!"

"That's the father's bad blood. Not to mention, his grandparents spoiled him terribly!" Franziska explained.

During Walter's weekend visits home, Bruno noticed that he stuttered when he got upset. Worried about him, Bruno consulted Franziska's cousin, Else. Thereafter, Else would secretly pick up Walter from the orphanage on Wednesday afternoons and take him to a speech therapist for which she also paid. Afterwards, she would take him out for treats or they would visit Elli in her sports store, Sportshaus Elite, which was a paradise on earth for Walter.

For her part, Elli von Strachwitz, née Kohanim, was immediately smitten by her nephew's enthusiasm for sports, his considerable childlike charm, and his athletic disposition. She would have loved to have taken the little fellow in, as she assured him. But the state of her husband's health, who had returned from the war as an invalid, would not allow it. Moreover, her husband was in a state of anti-Semitic delirium, just like the absent emperor that he idolized so much. There was no way they could have a lively "Jewish rascal" in the house. Elli dealt with this affliction all on her own, refusing to tell anyone about her husband's anti-Semitic turn, not even her family confidante, cousin Else Dahnke.

On Wednesdays, a racing bike awaited Walter at the Sporthaus Elite. He was allowed to ride it in a circle in the courtyard or play with a leather soccer ball and real boxing gloves, "the latest craze from America." The privilege of "Bruno-Shabbats" along with entertaining "Aunts-Wednesdays" and a whole sports store for him alone, helped Walter come to terms with the lost paradise in Osche and the strict regime of the orphanage. And while Walter would never become the king of Sauermühle, he was well on his way to becoming the uncrowned king of the Jewish orphanage in Berlin-Pankow/Lower Barnim. It was his strong sense of justice, eloquent manner of speech, beautiful singing, and access to real leather footballs that propelled him to such star status. Thus, after just two months, he was no longer crying into his pillow at night. He had his mind on other things: politics.

Not that he knew the word for politics yet. But he had nonetheless stumbled onto the topic while pondering how he might be able to use sweets, cookies, chocolate, fruit, and leather balls, along with his gift of eloquence, and the art of singing to help himself and his friends to avert the horrors of the orphanage, the beatings, the despotism of the strong, headbutts, the prick of thousands of needles, group terror, and humiliation. He concluded that he perhaps indeed possessed the means and skills to make life more bearable. Soon, he was putting his talents to use, learning to deal with the bullies by winning their allegiance, putting them off their guard, and, in the end, preventing them from being able to do anything at all. The next step was to help the heroes avoid losing face, and to pick them up from their fall in status and reconcile them with the others. In order for them to remain at peace in the long term, however, the former villains had to rely on him. Walter also discovered that it was important to inspire shared passion for a common goal and to establish new rules to which everyone could agree. In this way he soon established his moral superiority and the preeminence of the common goal over his opponents' tactics of rule by intimidation through violence. That's how you win hearts, the majority, and ultimately the upper hand, Walter thought. The brutal and evil ones who had previously ruled us with terror also needed followers, and that was their weakness!

And his plan actually worked. The weak and strong alike felt liberated from tyranny. Believing in the cause, they followed him willingly and with enthusiasm. The isolated evildoers could do little against the new power of a conspiratorial community; the fear that they had previously had at their disposal was suddenly gone. Their violence was now confronted by the wall of the sworn community against which the ruffians were powerless. If they didn't want to be isolated and despised, they now had to submit to the new rules and play along. Walter then knew how to integrate the former villains with honor, and within eight weeks he had turned things around. The new regime in the orphanage was now run by an elected children's council.

If you didn't want to go under, you had to make the world a better place! The laboratory of life proved to be much more interesting than being a stupid, spoiled, or frightened child who cried for better days. The "ruby priest," as he was called at the orphanage, therefore attributed the pain he felt in his heart now and again to the same cause as the pain he sometimes felt in his shins. It was all just growing pains! No matter how bleak being in an orphanage might be, life lay before him like a precious gift in beautiful wrapping paper. When he grew up, he'd grab it with both hands. The little bit of pain he now felt, was simply a part of it. Only rarely did he think about Hasso or Snowflake just before falling asleep. Everything was only half as bad as it had been before. As a matter of fact, maybe he even preferred this life to his previous one; compared to his new life in Berlin, rural life had lacked challenges and was thus terribly boring.

Bruno Geißler secretly grieved for his "meesstress," who was suddenly forced to live very meagerly after the loss of her father's annuity, so that she once again had to tickle the ivories at movie theaters.

She moved from the grandiose bel étage in the front of the apartment building, where she had lived next door to the owner of the house, Mrs. Melisande Bollin, to a side wing on the fourth floor. Her living quarters now consisted of a cramped, two-room apartment that she shared with Benno. The only remaining luxury was their own indoor toilet. Bruno had chiseled open half the stairwell to lay supply and drainpipes upstairs.

Franziska now lived next door to her closest confidante, Emmi. Four men, using wide leather straps, heaved the black, unlockable piano that she had brought with her from Sauermühle into the new, tight quarters on the upper floor of the front of the building. Due to a lack of space, it remained against the wall in the hallway, narrowing the corridor into a tube with a bottleneck. Any furniture they were not using either went into the attic or to "Red Oda" in the "Joy" garden colony. Bruno, Franziska, and Benno now had to feed themselves and pay the costs of Walter's children's home from Willy Rubin's old place and the evening piano playing in the cinemas.

While Bruno and the apprentice carried out orders and installations, Franziska ran all over Berlin to land new business, collect payments, or wait enthroned behind the counter downstairs in the store for customers to come and see her. Meanwhile, Emmi looked after Benno, who played with her sons in the street.

Walter's inheritance, the dividend payments from the $5,500 American dollars that Lachmund had invested for the boy in American shares, saved Fränze and her sons from the worst. Initially, Franziska had wanted to throw the dollar bills at the Fisheye's feet. No one could talk Franziska out of the idea that her former admirer that she had so cruelly mocked had been involved in her parents' murder.

"That's blood money!" she had argued in the notary's office. "As a Jew, I'm not allowed to accept blood money! You know that for a fact!" she lectured the notary, who was obviously not well versed in religious matters. "Muslims and Christians are allowed to do that, but we Jews are not!"

Lachmund looked at her anxiously, like a mental patient in the throes of an acute attack. "Dear madam! I do not disregard your opinions. Not in the least! But with all due respect, I am duty bound to tell you that it is not your place to decide how the money is spent!" he explained to her and then waited anxiously to see the effect his words had on her. He seemed satisfied with the result, and so he continued, matter-of-factly. "Legally speaking, you have nothing to do with it. This is your son Walter's capital, which I have to manage in accordance with your late father's wishes!"

Previously, Lachmund also had to defend Walter's inheritance against his aunts. "German inheritance law allows you to skip a generation of direct descendants," he had told Selma, who had wanted to file a lawsuit against old Kohanim's will. "The testator knew exactly what he was doing and that can no longer be changed!" Else Dahnke's offer to take in and raise her nephew Walter was also unsuccessful at first. "Walter stays where he is! End of story!" Franziska said.

FIRE AND PICKLED HERRING

Oda had always found her highly acute sense of smell more of a curse than a blessing. No matter how hard she tried, she couldn't overcome her aversion to the smell of poverty and the proletariat; they simply smelled bad. Mostly of sweat, dirt, decay, and illness. She may have felt connected to the working class, body and soul, yet her nose remained stubbornly bourgeois. But on September 13, 1925, at precisely 11:30 p.m., her refined olfactory nerves came to the rescue. For it was her sharp sense of smell that sounded the alarm and caused her to start up from a deep sleep. Smoke! When she opened her eyes, she saw small, bluish flames dancing on the floor around the house as they were just about to ignite the wallpaper on the door. Without thinking, Oda tore her two children from their beds and rushed outside into the garden with them, running back into the burning house to save the most important things: the paperwork and the money. Hella's leg splints were already glowing. Burning roof beams fell towards Oda from above.

Fortunately, she had the presence of mind to pull a wet towel from the washing line over her head before returning to the house. She was thus able to save herself and the last of her possessions by running outside to the screaming children, wearing her improvised protective cloak. In their nightgowns and pajamas, neighbors ran to help, quickly forming a chain to pass buckets of water to put out the flames. However, there was little they could do. It was only when the garden house had almost burnt down to the ground that the fire department and the police were able to make their way through the high sand of the garden colony paths and water the charred boards and planks. The fire chief and the criminal investigation department, who were called to the scene, determined that the fire had been set with the help of accelerants, which the perpetrator had poured around the house to give the sleeping residents no chance to escape. It was almost certainly petroleum. The charge was arson and a dastardly attempt to murder a woman and her sleeping children. The police began to search for Reinhold Hanke, who had been seen the previous evening not far from the scene of the crime.

That very same evening, police arrested the suspect at the pub Zum grünen Anker on Oderberger Straße in the northeastern Berlin neighborhood of Prenzlauer Berg. Reinhold Hanke was drunk, and his clothes stank of petroleum.

Oda and the children found shelter with a work colleague Gerda Kuht in her bungalow way out in the boonies near Lübars.

Oda and the children had escaped the fire barefoot and in pajamas. They had lost everything else. Their neighbors, mostly workers who themselves lived close to the bone, felt for the family and did what they could to help, donating clothes, underwear, shoes, exercise books, and pencils.

Six months later, Reinhold stood before the Second Criminal Chamber in Berlin-Moabit. The defendant had confessed immediately. The judge found him guilty of "attempted murder in a particularly serious case." Citing the elaborate preparation and the particularly insidious nature of the crime, the court rejected the defendant's claim to have acted in the heat of passion and with diminished culpability due to the consumption of alcohol. The court also pointed to the defendant's previous convictions, and the fact that the accused had also planned the death of his two children, which Reinhold denied, sobbing, "I didn't wanna hurt the lil' ones. I just wanted to send Oda a message, that's all. And besides, I was totally plastered!"

On the morning of March 26, 1926, Martha woke up plagued with a strange prophetic restlessness, the sort of which she experienced whenever important events were approaching. She also had heartburn. After reading the morning newspaper with the reports on the previous day's trials, she blamed her restlessness and heartburn on the trial against

Reinhold Hanke and her worries about Oda. Then her husband Leopold returned home. He was in high spirits, which made Martha suspicious. It wasn't only the fact that he had managed to recuse himself for reasons of personal bias from Reinhold Hanke's trial. Something else was afoot.

"Today marks the start of a new life," Leopold announced excitedly, uncorking a bottle of Kellergeister. With exaggerated care, he then maneuvered Martha and her pregnant belly into the comfortable wing chair and then assumed the important expression of a statesman.

"Three things will change our lives from today on, my dear Martha," he began, his chin thrust outward, ready to give a sermon. Martha felt sick to her stomach.

"Firstly, from this day forward we are Christians! To be precise: Protestants! I was baptized exactly one hour ago! But that's not all: Hirschfeld is dead. From now on, we're called Hartmann! And thirdly, from now on, I am the president of the court, Sir President, Leopold Hartmann, Esquire!"

He looked at his wife expectantly, like an artist awaiting applause. On the one hand, Martha was relieved. She had hoped her husband had avoided presiding over the Handke trial for the sake of his own career. To feign the expected joy, she bared her gray teeth and stammered something absentminded that sounded vaguely like well wishes, "Oh, it's perfect for you! Tough man and tough judge!"

As so often happened, Leopold didn't know whether Martha's answer was merely stupid or ironic. He wiped away his irritation with an energetic gesture.

"Court president, Martha, court president!"

She would have loved to have asked whether he had chosen the new name for his new position himself, "nomen est omen," your name is your fate, or whether he had again followed dubious advice, just as he had about the decision to get baptized. Not wanting to appear impolite or sarcastic, as she frequently did, she chose to remain silent and wear an expression that was as neutral as it was impenetrable. Leopold, who was now both Hartmann and the president of the court, seemed only half satisfied with her answer. He furrowed his brow and stared at her as if she were out of her mind. Martha stroked her stomach with a soothing smile and said as casually as she could, "I'll have new nameplates engraved tomorrow."

"Is that all you can think about? New brass plates? Not only am I now a president, but I'm also no longer a Jew!"

"Yes, yes, yes! But do you know what my father, God rest his soul, would have said about that?" Martha intensified her efforts to make a reassuring, playful smile to soften her words.

Leopold pressed his lips tightly together. "Well, what do you think?" Hirschfeld, alias Hartmann, barked, clearly irritated. The quoted wisdom of the Kohanims had been getting on his nerves since their wedding day.

"A baptized Jew remains a Jew, just as a pickled herring remains a herring!"

Leopold tilted his head from his left shoulder to his right, something he normally only did in the courtroom when he was displeased with a plea that had been presented to the court.

"Nonsense! Start getting used to it! From today on our lives will change, completely. We will start to go to church on Sundays and that's that!" It sounded like an order, and it was one.

"But the doctor has said that bed rest is urgent!"

"Oh, you and your illnesses!" groaned Leopold, before adding, "And don't forget: Jews are no longer welcome in our home."

"But Leopold! Let's not get carried away! After all, the house is my house and I'm still Jewish and will remain so!"

"So, you're going against your husband?"

"I am what I am, nothing else! It's just that I am not quite as clever as you!" Martha tried again with humility. And that was not a good sign, as her husband knew. He was surprised that she didn't bring up the passage on religion from the marriage contract.

At this point, Leopold Hirschfeld/Hartmann therefore thought it best to end the conversation for the time being and postpone the Christian conversion of his wife to a later date. He was astonished that his otherwise fanciful wife suddenly insisted on her true origins. He had assumed that she would throw herself into the possibility of a new existence with delight.

An hour later, when the maid was serving a buffet of finger foods, Leopold thought of something else: "Have I told you the latest news about Harry Fisch, your sister Flora's missing husband?" Martha served pickled cucumbers and radishes with the sandwiches and looked at her husband expectantly.

"This Harry Fisch embarked for Brazil as a missionary. For some strange reason, he never arrived there, as his name does not appear on the passenger list from the port of São Paolo. He boarded the ship in

Bremerhaven, but never arrived anywhere! That's crazy. The fellow disappeared into thin air. Or did he end up as fish food? Nobody saw anything, nobody heard anything, nobody knows anything. How strange!"

"What should we write to my sister Flora?"

"That she'll probably have to wait another ten years for the death certificate. But honestly, your whole family is a mess, isn't it?!"

On a hot Sunday in May, shortly before Pentecost, a man as tall as a tree was seen wearing a winter coat of an indefinable color. He wore a coffee-brown felt hat on his somewhat small head. With a set of heavy luggage in his arms, he crossed the tracks of the Berlin Industrial Railway North and set course for the network of paths leading to the garden colonies. Passing the frog orchestra of the "Paddenpfuhl," he headed for the heather path of the foliage garden colony "Kleintierfarm" in Berlin-Lübars. Hither and thither he lugged the heavy suitcases. In that part of town, strangers were not welcome and people thus eyed with suspicion this man who clearly didn't belong there. Every fifty meters he would sit down on one of the suitcases and wipe the sweat from his face with a blue-striped handkerchief with the monogram "RvG," and shook his head, looking helpless, if not forlorn. A man who was painting his picket fence with as much vigor as paint, thought the man looked a bit fishy: "Where ya goin'?" he asked in a thick Berlin accent.

"I'm looking for Heidekrautweg 58, Oda Hanke's house."

"Well, go that way, to the bend on the left, and then you'll see it. She's tarring the roof of her house. You can't miss it!" the painter joked. The door knocker or gong to the garden gate at house number 58 was a piece of railroad track hanging over the gate that gave the otherwise proletarian entrance a Far-Eastern flair. To make himself seen, the man with the suitcases banged the "knocker" against the gate. Just as soon as it hit the gate, a person on the roof turned around; only through the figure's movement did it become recognizable as a woman. She was wearing a hat with the brim cut off, a tattered men's shirt covered in tar stains, men's pants, boots, and gloves, which she took off and shouted at the guest: "Well, I'll be damned!"

The strange visitor turned out to be none other than Oda's brother. They hadn't seen each other since their escape from Osche twelve years prior and had only exchanged nasty letters about Oda's divorce.

"How did *you* get here?"

Oda worked the garden pump, filling an enamel jug full of water and then handed it to him without a glass. Rudolf von Güldner drank almost all of it in one go.

"Please spare me a quiz about the details, just be happy to see me, or don't!"

Only gradually did he recognize Oda. The dark blonde hair that crept out from under her hat, the unmistakable gray-green, slanted Tatar eyes above the typical Slavic-high cheekbones and her Russian saddle nose. She looked just as healthy and worn out as the women in faraway Russia in the "good old days." Although he knew better, when he first set off on the journey from Seesen to Berlin, he couldn't help but silently hope that his sister might have come to her senses by now. But when he saw her, he knew right away that she had obviously become even more stubborn. Sectarians the world over have the same self-righteous, arrogant look, he thought to himself. What was this proletarian cult about anyway? She didn't need that!

"You're traveling with a lot of luggage. You didn't have to lug it here; you could have checked it in at the station."

"No, I couldn't have, because this is all yours."

"Why? What's in there?"

"Your inheritance. Our mother died eight weeks ago. You must have received the telegram. And this," he pointed to the other suitcase, "is your inheritance from what our father left us, or what's left of it. Well, see for yourself!" Then he looked around suspiciously, finally took off his thick coat and opened the shirt that was clinging to his lean body.

"But maybe we shouldn't necessarily unpack everything out here."

Together, they dragged the suitcases into the newly built provisional living quarters. The house still had no floor, Rudolf realized in disbelief.

"I built it all according to the floor plan of Frederick the Great's Sanssouci Palace," Oda explained proudly. Rudolf looked around helplessly in search of similarities with the Potsdam pleasure palace. But from what he could tell the only thing they had in common was that they shared a room with a large window to the right and left of a round building in the middle, which gave the building an absurdly extravagant appearance. Shaking his head, Rudolf handed his sister the keys to the suitcase.

"Don't you want to know how your parents died?"

Oda remained resolutely silent, so he continued. "But you do remember your curses against Mother and Steinfeld, don't you?"

Oda shrugged her shoulders. "That's all water under the bridge!"

"Well, you won't believe it, but your curses came true, down to the last detail. It's eerie really. So I guess you now want to act like you had nothing to do with that?"

Oda pointedly ignored the question.

"Well, you're a strange bird! But I'll tell you anyway. Steinfeld died exactly as you prophesized. He truly couldn't get his fill. Just as you had cursed him, he literally starved to death at a full table: throat cancer! He couldn't swallow any more, a horrible end. You can be proud of that, you witch!"

Rudolf had worked himself into a rage.

"Hmm," Oda grumbled with a scowl.

"And our mother died just as you predicted: abandoned by everyone, completely alone. Satisfied?"

"Well, well!" Oda muttered, feeling embarrassed by the nonsense she used to pull. How did that fit with scientific Marxism-Leninism? Not knowing what to say, she gave her brother a long, disapproving look. "What a bunch of petty-bourgeois nonsense!"

She fiddled energetically with the suitcases until she finally managed to open the locks. Both were filled to the brim with banknotes. In the middle was the family prayer book from 1792, which had always been passed down on her mother's side to the oldest daughter along with the silver tureen with the silver ladle. The rest of the silverware that had once filled two glass-paneled cabinets in the manor house at Ochse had disappeared.

"For God's sake, Rudi, what am I supposed to do with this?" She pointed in bewilderment at the money stuffed into the cases.

"How much is it anyway?"

As if to reassure herself that they were indeed real, she took off her glove covered in tar and stirred the banknotes.

"Because I had to count it myself, I can tell you the amount down to the last kopeck. It's two million two hundred and fifty-five thousand rubles."

Oda's face darkened.

"Two million rubles?! And they begrudged us kids the very air that we breathed and let us starve?

Rudolf nodded thoughtfully. "If only we knew what the money here is worth now?"

"Did you ask?"

"Yeah, I did. But in a one-horse town like Seesen in the Harz Mountains, nobody could tell me anything. Everyone said I should take it to the Prussian State Bank in the capital."

"And what did they say? Come on, don't make me drag everything out of you!"

"First of all, I had to find you. And that wasn't easy. It was hard to get even Fanny Segal to give out your address. It was a big ordeal! Why are you keeping your place of residence such a secret? Are the police looking for you? Or what's going on?"

"That's a long story and none of your business. And just so we understand each other: that money doesn't belong to us!"

"Really? Then who does it belong to?"

"The Soviet Union."

"You've got to be joking! That money was already ours when there was no Soviet Union! For crying out loud!"

"But now there is a Soviet Union, and the money comes from the exploitation of the working masses of Russia, today's Soviet Union!"

Rudolf sighed heavily and turned his eyes heavenwards.

"As far as I'm concerned, you can do whatever you like with *your* money. But tomorrow we're going to the state bank, and first we'll see what they'll even give us for it. We can also have it locked up there in safe straight away."

Rudolf showered in the garden, pouring three cans of water over his head. Then he dozed off on the folding cot next to his snoring sister in her Sanssouci summerhouse.

Like every night, he dreamt of the war, of how he had lain motionless under a mountain of sand. And like every morning, he woke up with a cry of fear.

The next day, Oda and Rudolf packed the suitcases of money onto the bicycle trailer. Oda sat on a sofa cushion on the bike's luggage carrier and let Rudolf bike her to the Dalldorf S-Bahn station. Like everyone else from the garden colonies, they used the train station restroom to get dressed up for the city. They both removed the bike clips from their trousers. Oda traded the scarf that covered her head for a hat and swapped her thick-soled shoes for strappy, lighter ones. Rudolf emerged from the train station restroom in his Sunday best, with a tie, new hat, and polished shoes. They put their overnight case, with the bag containing their country things, and the bicycle in the baggage room. They hurried up the steps of the red-brick building and started the long journey on the S-Bahn into the city, to the Börse Station.

Oda refrained from commenting on his hat and tie. Men in her circles deliberately only wore the open-style *Schillerkragen*, meaning they did not button the top two buttons on their shirt, and instead of a hat, the class-conscious man wore a scarf or shawl and a cap. They looked down on hats and ties as something for leftists and artists. Anyone who wore them was a snob and a bourgeois—something of which no one in the working-class districts would want to be accused. A man, they all agreed, should wear his class pride. However, Rudolf's outfit suited the planned project, Oda thought. Besides, Rudolf did belong to the bourgeoisie.

Rudolf and Oda made their way timidly toward the counter to which they had been directed, intimidated by the colossal marble portal of the State Bank of the German Empire.

A finance man with a starched collar and a clean-shaven face, marked by fencing scars, looked insolently at the two of them with their battered suitcases.

"Good day! We have inherited a considerable amount of money in banknotes," Rudolf said pointing at the suitcases.

The smoothly shaven scarface went slack.

Rudolf responded by fiddling around in his right breast pocket and then presenting an inheritance certificate.

"No one in my hometown in the Harz Mountains could tell me what all this is worth in Reichsmarks. The local bank, the Sparkasse Seesen, suggested that we ask you."

Rudolf then reached into the inside pocket of his left jacket and placed a bundle of banknotes on the counter.

"The rest is in the suitcases there!"

"The rest???" asked the arrogant banker, dumbfounded. With a skeptical look, he held his fingers before him, to fish a bill out of the bundle of money and held it up to the light.

"Well, where did you get *that* from?" His pursed lip curled into a half smile. "Did you rob one of the Romanovs or one of the grand dukes?"

"Yeah, go ahead and say what you're thinking, you… you…!" Oda cried out as if bitten by a viper.

"Don't Oda! Just let it go."

The man didn't react.

"And how much of it do you have... like this... all together?" the banker pointed to the suitcases. Rudolf and Oda looked at each other annoyed at the question.

"Well, all together there's almost five million. I wrote the exact sum down on this piece of paper. The suitcases contain only half that amount. This is my sister's share of the inheritance. There should be about two and a half million," muttered Rudolf.

"The rest of the money is in the baggage room, Oda explained.

"Two and a half million rubles?! In the baggage room?!" the banker shouted, throwing his arms up, half amused, half incredulous. All the bank customers turned to look at them.

Then the bank person waved to his boss, who, with eyes narrowed and lips tight, scurried over with a manner that betrayed a blend of zeal and authority.

"What can I do for you, madame et monsieur?"

With a refined talent for detecting class distinctions, he looked Oda and Rudolf up and down.

"The madame and gentleman have just told me that they have five million of these!"

"What? Five million *tsarist rubles*?"

"Yes, tsarist rubles."

The two bankers dissolved into convulsions of laughter. "I think you have perhaps come with this a bit late," chortled the head banker.

"I don't even want to give this money to you. This money belongs to the Soviet Union," shouted Oda.

The bankers were now squealing with laughter. Just then, a gentleman with a carefully groomed beard and a Panama hat stepped up from behind Rudolf and Oda.

"Pardon me, but I accidentally overheard your conversation," he said with a heavy Russian accent. "If you went to the Soviet embassy with that, they would consider you a counterrevolutionary, madame! And for no reason at all! So don't be foolish and don't get yourself into trouble. Make yourself a nice little fire with it! That's what we did. It warmed us with memories of our former wealth. So long!"

With that, he lifted his Panama hat with a hand covered with precious rings and gave the world the most compassionate smile possible during a time of such political and economic turmoil.

After a brief farewell, Rudolf went straight home from the Friedrichstraße back to the Harz Mountains. The money was no longer worth anything. Without his even noticing it, tears like raindrops ran down his cheeks.

Oda, by contrast, joined in the bankers' laughter and laughed and laughed. After she dragged the suitcases of money back to her summer house, she laughed for three more days and nights until it almost sounded as if she were crying. If she did cry, which is highly unlikely, then it was over the grotesque absurdity of the situation, over the irony of her fate, or because once a certain degree of tragedy and grotesqueness has been reached, you have to laugh, if you don't want to go mad.

When Oda had finished laughing, she resumed her building work. She pasted the tsarist rubles to the walls of her new summer home. After her work was finished, she sat with her children, Hella and Peter, in the middle of their "wealth" of rubles, while wallpaper paste dripped from the walls.

"We need to take a picture of this sight!" said her latest admirer, Julius Bessmer.

There was a photographer in the neighborhood who had a magnesium flash camera. Sporting a wide grin, Oda let herself be photographed with her worthless millions in rubles.

Then she pasted a floral wallpaper over the thousands of tsars' heads and immediately felt better.

Since that day, the area north of Berlin along the Heidekraut railroad has been home to a secret five-million-ruble castle that was once inhabited by quite extraordinary aristocrats.

RUMOR HAS IT

I've been in a slight panic since I found out that the district attorney got wind of the fact that I was using Tor, a network that makes it possible to communicate anonymously. I'll do whatever it takes to figure out how.

Before even going on Tor, I had planned ahead. To make sure that no one could track my computer's IP address, I had quite deliberately chosen an internet café on the outermost edges of Wedding. Ironically, the outermost edges of Wedding are now the new "center" of Berlin. And relying on my outdated West Berlin topography in the "new" Berlin, led me to select an internet café that was located right across from the new headquarters of the Federal Intelligence Service. So many false assumptions! It was like a situational comedy. But even with the help of my green hexagonal-shaped "happy" pills, I still couldn't manage to summon up my usual bursts of laughter.

Big, fat neon letters light up my mind, posing one question: Who or What betrayed me? I'm praying that the internet café I went to still exists. In the age of smartphones, you can never be sure, since most internet cafés have shuttered. Fortunately, the new "center" has remained a little slum, in which businesses like these still have a purpose because the people who live nearby have poor credit and thus can't get internet service.

There's no one there, except for two people: a man who I take to be from somewhere in Africa, who is talking so loudly in a filthy, half-open cubbyhole that I think he must be yelling all the way back home; and a greasy, unkempt, half-asleep clerk sitting behind the counter. Fortunately, this is the very same man who had shown me how to use the computer when I was there before. I'm glad to see him.

"I can't believe you have the nerve to show your face around here," he grumbles in a barely decipherable Berlin accent. Without prompting, he then lets loose. "The boys from across the street closed my shop for two days and carefully checked every computer because you'd been using some websites here that you weren't supposed to."

"But you're allowed to use these websites. You're allowed," I say, cutting him short.

"I don't give a damn! Luckily, I had a copy of your ID. Good thing I'd thought of that."

The bad-tempered man has worked himself up into such a frenzy that his fingers are trembling as he reaches to grab a piece of paper from the shelf behind him.

"Here's the bill! You owe me 560 euro, including taxes, for the trouble! That just about covers the cost of how much business I lost thanks to the hot water you got me into!"

"Send it to my lawyer," I say as arrogantly as I can and then give him the finger. Just then the man yelling halfway across the planet finishes his call. He makes quite a racket as he lumbers out of his booth and pushes himself between me and the crabby manager, who now has to take care of him. I use that as my exit strategy and slip out unnoticed. Outside it's raining cats and dogs. Cars are plowing through deep puddles. Even a taxi without a passenger, comes rushing by like a speedboat. I stand halfway in the street and wave for it to stop. There's nowhere on the street for cabs to stop and pick up passengers. The Federal Intelligence Service across the street has enforced an absolute ban on stopping anywhere. The result: empty stores everywhere. Demolition Berlin, I think, as I get into the car soaking wet. The cab driver watches anxiously as small rivulets of rainwater run from my clothes onto his gray leather upholstery. Without comment, he hands me a fluffy purple towel.

On the way back to the psychiatric hospital, I decide to take a little detour to Berlin-Reinickendorf. To Gotthardddamm. Just because. Every twenty seconds, planes thunder over the houses at a height of thirty meters.

That's why the rents are cheap here. Nasi Gohari, the "co-guilty party," my accomplice, lives at house number 48. I don't know what I want here. We drive slowly past the house. I actually see Nasi on the balcony. She's hanging up laundry and looks in our direction at the exact moment that I look up. We're not allowed to see each other before the trial. Or more accurately, we are not allowed to be seen together. I nod my head in her direction. She recognizes me and nods back.

Nor are we allowed to communicate on Facebook, where we first met. An Australian friend, Pamela Southall from Perth, who doesn't come from Iran, had provided Nasi with a second identity on Facebook. I didn't know that back then. I thought I was exchanging messages with an Australian the whole time.

Nasi and I happened to cross paths on the Internet. I had ranted long and hard in English about a well-known German Green party politician who, normally a strong supporter of women's rights, had dutifully worn a headscarf on a state visit to Iran and even allowed herself to be photographed wearing it.

Nasi, who I was still taking to be Pamela, contacted me with several photos of women on the streets of Tehran without headscarves. She wanted to show me that Iranian women did not let themselves be intimidated so easily and that she despised from the bottom of her heart European politicians who allowed themselves to be forced into wearing a headscarf.

I clicked "like" on her post on Facebook. Still, I wondered how the photos could get past the Iranian censors. As an Australian, she must have taken the photos herself in Tehran and then posted them from a free country. When I wrote on "Pamela's" Facebook page that I was going on vacation in Turkey, near Alanya, the ostensible Pamela from Perth wrote me a message asking whether I wanted to meet up since she would be there at the same time. What a coincidence! I was thrilled by her suggestion. She also wanted to know if I would be traveling alone or with my husband. Unsuspectingly, I told her that I always travel alone so that I can meet interesting new people. Little did I know how interesting this new friend would turn out to be.

At the arranged time, I was sitting in the restaurant in the Old Town that she had recommended, which was full of animated Russians and extremely high-spirited, loud Dutch men and women. I was keeping an eye out for the blonde Australian woman from the Facebook profile picture, when suddenly someone tapped me on the shoulder from behind. She was neither blonde nor Australian! "Surprise!" It was Nasi Gohari, an Iranian woman. I was amazed to discover that we looked incredibly alike. The waiter immediately started joking about the "twin sisters," which I failed to understand and which she, somewhat reluctantly, translated for me. Slowly, it dawned on me that I was a carefully selected target. Any normal person who suspected such a ploy would have stood up and left the restaurant in a huff. But my curiosity got the better of me: What was the story behind all of this? And there was also something else, something inexplicable. I remained rooted to my seat. I wanted to know the whole story, which went as follows:

Nasi Gohari was a doctor in Isfahan and had worked as a woman's rights activist for abused women. For her work, she was imprisoned, raped, and tortured, and was now looking for a way to escape to Europe. She didn't want to trust traffickers. She happened to notice my profile photo on Facebook when she saw my post about Iranian women. She then browsed through all my photos and googled everything she could find about me. That was one or too many things for me to handle and I started thinking: Facebook is usually blocked in Turkey and Google censored.

The whole thing was starting to scare me.

"Yes, but not when you have a US IP address," she informed me. "You can surf quite a lot with it here in the tourist zones."

Evidently, my doubts were written all over my face. I was already desperately looking for excuses, for an elegant exit. I was unsure of how to get away. Nasi apparently guessed my thoughts. With a sad expression, she pushed up her sleeves to reveal deep scars from torture on her arms. "I will spare you my breasts and the rest," she said, pointing at her lap.

I am a woman who knows how to say "no." I do not usually let people blackmail me emotionally. Nevertheless, I sat there, completely calm, took a long sip from my glass of Coca Cola, remaining as impenetrably silent as possible, and listening to my inner turmoil: my father, my mother, my uncle, and both my grandmothers were already vigorously pleading their cases; all my great aunts and all 248 relatives of mine who had died in the Holocaust, whom no one had helped flee and therefore had to die, were now pestering me. "Whoever saves just one life, saves the whole world and is just," says the Torah. And what would I be risking compared to all those who had risked their lives to hide, protect, and help my relatives flee in those dark times?

I told Nasi that I had to think about it first. We rented a boat so that we would not be disturbed or overheard. Bobbing on the waves like two harmless tourists, we hatched a plan for her to delete her fake Pamela Southall identity on Facebook, for us to create a communication platform on the Tor crypto-network, and for me to fly back to Istanbul in three weeks. In Istanbul, a waiter would pass on my ID card and ticket to Nasi, and I would let myself be served a carefully measured Mickey. As a doctor, she knew about such things. After I had arrived at the hospital, she would fly to Germany on my ticket and using my ID, which is not biometric. I would secure my alibi by staying in the hospital and receiving confirmation that I had indeed been drugged. Only then would I return to Berlin on my German passport. She would tell the authorities that she got my ID card from human traffickers, and I would report the theft of my ID card and ticket while I was still in Istanbul.

And that is what we did. We simply had to make sure that the knockout drug wasn't too "medical," to avoid casting suspicion on her, the doctor. That was why we had to get the knockout drops on the black market. Everything was going well, more or less: the drops had turned out to be stronger than we had anticipated.

As the bells on the tower of the reinforced concrete church on Gottharddamm in Reinickendorf begin to ring, my taxi drives on.

Unless you happen to be a narcissist with a desire to bare your soul like an exhibitionist, being forced to tell someone your life story is uncomfortable. Candor and blind trust don't come naturally to me. Whenever possible, I tried to prevent people from peering too deeply into my life. This is related to my hang up about safety, a permanent defect shared by many descendants of persecuted people. I never live at the address where I am officially registered, for example. No government agency should ever have direct access to me, as they had to my father, my grandmother Oda, and the rest of my relatives who were persecuted and killed. My pursuers, no matter who, would have to take detours on which I have installed warning systems. If I get into trouble, I want to always be one step ahead of everybody else. I generally look for safe escape routes in places I do not know. That is why I would never board a cruise ship. They are all death traps. On trains, I stand next to the door. On ferries, my seat is always near the railings, never below deck, in restaurants it's at the door, in airplanes it's in the emergency exit row, or in the safest seats near the tail. Throughout my career as a reporter, I have never reported about someone unless under a pseudonym. My ego and my name, for that matter, was nobody's business and had no place in any reports, nor in the text. In the industry, they say that human-interest stories are something for women's magazines or school newspapers. It now proves lucky that my real name is not known in connection with previous reports on sensitive topics and that my resume does not get in my way, because I now have to convince people that I am a poor, duped victim. My attorney has advised me to expose my most vulnerable side to my psychiatrist, but it goes against my nature. The very thought of it makes me nauseous. The main thing is to establish mitigating circumstances for my case. That is what my defense attorney has impressed upon me: "Feel free to let the tears flow. But don't overdo it either."

I know that already from my work in the editorial office. An old journalist's saying: Anyone who talks and complains too much is not really suffering. I arrange and edit the text of my resume in my head: What do I have to offer? What do I lack? And what has what effect? To buy time, I tell Vogelsang about further episodes from my rich family history.

HURLY-BURLY

The inflation of 1923 “galloped,” as people used to say. It kept the money-printing presses and the women working at a fever pitch. On payday, Friday at noon, Charlotte Hörl stood with her friend Fränze in the drizzling rain outside the Flor & Otis factory gate. Lotte was waiting for her husband Willi. Actually, she was waiting for Willi’s wages. They used to be paid out in bags that resembled envelopes. That no longer sufficed, however. They now needed larger containers. It was thus with a laundry basket full of banknotes, covered with a tarpaulin, that shortly past twelve, Willi swept around the corner at quite a clip.

As head foreman, he enjoyed the privilege of being paid before everyone else. The other workers had to wait for their wages, according to rank. Most of them carried rolled-up sugar or grain bags under their arms to receive their weekly wages. Sometimes those further down the totem pole could be hit hard by misfortune; while waiting to get paid, prices rose and decreased the value of the pay that they still hadn’t received. In the rush to use the money before prices went up yet again, time really was money. There was no time to spare for even a peck on the cheek, let alone to count the money. Meanwhile, stores had begun weighing money in bales. This was faster than counting the bills, and, with a reliable scale, just as exact.

“C’mon girl, get the lead out!” was how Willi greeted Lotte.

Lotte quickly placed the basket with Willi’s pay on the cart. It was filled with tens of billions and trillions, and numbers with so many zeros afterwards that it wouldn’t have been possible to count in groups of threes, even with a pencil in hand. Then she and Fränze trotted off toward the market hall. They ran the length of the street, with Lotte holding the right handlebar and Franziska the left. They stopped every three hundred meters to tighten the tarpaulin over the banknotes and keep watch for the other housewives, who, hot on their heels, were also on their way to the market hall and shops.

With a bag full of banknotes, which Franziska threw over her shoulder, she turned off early at Leopold Square. She was supposed to hurry and pay Lotte's rent before it rose any higher. Lotte relied on Fränze's tough negotiating skills to ward off the landlord's unreasonable demands. Depending on the situation, Fränze's standard lines for opening negotiations were: "You can't pull the wool over my eyes!"; "Who do you think your talking to?!"; and "Do I have the word 'idiot' written across my forehead?!"

Fränze usually didn't need to rush around like this. She got paid daily in the workshop at the current rate and she could also rely on the fixed-rate US dollar bonds from Walter's inheritance. She couldn't necessarily count on the big-hearted Bruno, however, who was completely useless when it came to collecting payments from clients.

Around the same time that Fränze and Lotte were racing against the price of potatoes and carrots, Martha Hartmann, who no longer went by Hirschfeld since her husband Leopold had changed his last name, was trying to purchase a salmon-colored silk blouse at the Tietz department store at Potsdamer Platz. By the time she had made her way from the clothes rack to the register, the price of the blouse had already gone up by ten percent. The world had truly gone mad!

Since the economic crisis Martha's health had improved dramatically. The world's ever-growing madness had had a strangely curative effect on her inner life. By exceeding even her wildest imaginings, reality had outdone her in the competition for the absurd. Thus, the crazier the world became, the more normal Martha did. Put differently, you might say that Martha's mania surrendered in the face of reality's insanity. She thus became reasonable, maybe too reasonable. And even her strange marriage seemed to have had a good effect on her.

Because her fibs paled before the crazy times in which she was living, she was no longer in the mood for spinning tall tales. When, on occasion, she nonetheless felt the urge to bluster rising within her, she went to Huthmacher's confectionary, where she would dish up one of her hair-raising stories to the staff or to an unsuspecting acquaintance. More than once, however, Martha was disappointed to find that the Berliner she was talking to had even more eccentric stories up their sleeve than she did, making her whimsical tales seem almost shamefully boring. Not wanting to embarrass herself by telling uninteresting stories, she gradually stopped.

After the somewhat irksome purchase of the blouse, Martha was suddenly overcome by a craving for a Jewish challah for the Sabbath, which she was no longer allowed to bake at home. She waved at a passing cab and asked for a ride to the historically Jewish, Scheunenviertel neighborhood. Upon arrival, she found herself thrust into the middle of a nightmare. A horde of wild men were looting Jewish stores, beating up their owners, emptying the registers and stealing the goods, and attacking complete strangers who happened to have dark hair and dark eyes, robbing their money, watches, and rings in broad daylight. The policemen looked on with smug grins. Finally, in Grenadierstraße a giant, bearded Jewish butcher with side curls and a yarmulke on his head charged toward the marauders, swinging his meat cleaver, and driving the mob back all the way to Alexanderplatz. A pogrom in the middle of Berlin! In broad daylight! In the twentieth century! In her wildest dreams Martha would never have imagined such a thing. She had the presence of mind to flee into the entrance of a building, where she waited with bated breath until things had calmed down outside. It seemed like an eternity.

While she waited, the last three years of her life flashed before her eyes: her husband Leopold's conversion to Christianity, including his Protestant baptism; the birth of her daughter Susanne, who had been a stranger to her from the beginning; and then the birth of the twins, Siegmund and Siegfried. It took her almost half a year to recover from their birth. She felt nothing, absolutely nothing for the twins. Although she looked after the children just as properly as she did her daughter, she was all too happy when she could leave them in the care of the nanny. From the very beginning, she had the distinct feeling that Susanne, Siegmund, and Siegfried did not belong to her. They were Leopold's children. She was thus all the more anxious not to let her lack of motherly love show. To cover her lack of genuine feeling, she feigned it with exaggerated care and theatricality, smothering the children with food, toys, and kisses.

Oda was the only one in whom she had confided.

"When Susanne died from Spanish flu, I felt nothing at all. Just imagine! As a mother, I'm a monster!"

"Oh well, you can't force love. But if you do your duty, you have nothing to apologize for," said Oda laconically.

Martha now did her duty just as half-heartedly and absentmindedly as her mother Mindel had done years before. Had anyone ever asked if Mindel loved her eighteen children? Is it even possible to love so many children?

Meanwhile, it had grown dark and quiet outside. Martha carefully opened the front door of a building on Grenadierstraße and slipped quietly out of the doorway on tiptoe, and then hurried off in the direction of Chauseestraße to her cousin Else Dahnke. Naturally, Else did not believe a word Martha said.

"Yeah, yeah, yeah, Martha. Okay, that's enough!"

Else's husband Bruno rolled his eyes: "A mass brawl in the Scheunenviertel? So what? One minute they're at each other's throats, the next they're best friends. It happens all the time." They knew what to make of Martha's stories.

The newspapers would also later write that the rumors about an "alleged pogrom" in Berlin's Scheunenviertal were entirely blown out of proportion and unsubstantiated.

Martha was now definitely convinced that the world was crazy, not her! Since that November 1923, Martha knew that reality was more provocative than fiction. Thereafter, she told only the truth, out of protest. But the effect remained the same.

On Wednesday, when Else went to pick up Walter from the orphanage for his usual afternoon outing, he was not there. "No one told you?" an orphanage staff member said and then explained that Bruno had not brought Walter back on Sunday.

Worried, she went straightaway to Fränze's house at Heilandstraße, where Fränze reluctantly informed her that Bruno had taken Walter to the Jewish hospital. Since Friday evening the boy had been holding his head in pain, at first crying and then eventually even screaming.

"That's unusual for him," Fränze said, "He really can take a lot! He never cries. Even when he scrapes up his entire leg after riding his bike at full speed, he doesn't make a sound. He even grins, the rascal!"

Else found Fränze's observations almost humorous: a mixture of her cousin's pride and flair for the dramatic.

At the hospital, the doctors diagnosed it as a severe middle-ear suppuration. They operated on him that same evening.

"He's probably had it for weeks," the doctor scolded, adding that the entire inner ear was in danger. The little patient's skull had to be chiseled open immediately on the petrous bone behind his ear so that the doctors could drain the pus and clean the area surrounding it. If that didn't work, Walter would probably be deaf in one ear, perhaps even lose his sense of balance.

The head physician snapped angrily at Bruno, levying serious accusations against everyone involved, and later even wrote the orphanage a bitter letter, stating "that you would do well to remember!" He also threatened legal action against the orphanage and all those responsible.

Bruno, Fränze, and Aunt Elli all took turns sitting at Walter's sickbed. Walter was clearly enjoying being the center of attention, even as he continued to eye his mother with a degree of mistrust.

For her part, Fränze was feeling the first pangs of conscience over how she had treated Walter. She realized that it was time to end the grudge against Willy, which she had been taking out on Walter who looked so shockingly like him. The boy couldn't help being who he was, and he had earned a genuine chance, Franziska admonished herself. It was still too soon to speak of affection, but maybe compassion and sympathy. For a woman like Franziska, that was a huge concession.

Walter noticed how his mother was warming up to him. He had reservations, but he nonetheless wanted to give her a chance. Sitting by his sickbed, Fränze, Elli, and Bruno talked at length, finally deciding that when he was released from the hospital, Walter wouldn't return to the orphanage. He couldn't return to Fränze's house, however, because it was already too cramped there. So Walter was going to live with Elli instead.

"Would you like to live with Aunt Elli?" Fränze asked him, with as much compassion in her voice as she was able to muster.

"Wow! That would be great!" Walter cried enthusiastically, careful not to move his bandaged head too much.

Before long, the doctors said they were satisfied with how well he was healing and praised "the tough little fellow's courage." For the first time ever, Fränze felt proud of her firstborn.

Meanwhile, Aunt Elli, Elsbeth von Strachwitz, née Kohanim, was clearing out her husband's former bedroom with a zeal born of silent rage. She threw his books and disgraceful anti-Semitic magazines into the coal-burning stoves, distributed a good part of his belongings to the poor, and then sent the rest of them to his parents. Her serious clean-up operation resembled an exorcism. She had filed for divorce the day before Walter's discharge from the hospital.

At first, she wanted to avoid a divorce. She thought it would be possible to live separately. But there was no way around the fact that as long as they were married, she would be responsible for her morphine-addicted husband. "In sickness and in health." Under any other circumstances, she would have endured it, for Elli was loyal by nature. However, her loyalty had ended the day that her husband called her a "Jewish pig." The epithet came after she had caught him trying to steal her wallet from her handbag and grabbed it out of his hands.

Elli never told anyone the real reason for the divorce.

One night after Elli had filed for divorce and purged the apartment of her husband's presence, Walter lay in his new bed in her apartment on Potsdamer Strasse. The room still smelled like fresh paint and the curtains like new fabric. You couldn't get a fresher beginning. In his new bed, Walter lay holding his breath, listening to the chestnuts falling like thunder from the tree onto the tin roof of the shed in the courtyard. Bang! The sixth one hit the roof, making a sound like gunshot. Walter stopped counting, frustrated that he couldn't find any sort of syncopation or rhythm in the way the chestnuts fell one after another. That left him wondering about himself. The whole two weeks that he was in the hospital he had been looking forward to his first night in a real home, and now this!

"This"—he still wasn't sure what to call it—was getting to him. "This," this deafening, silent loneliness which he now felt, was the absence of all his friends from the orphanage. It didn't help that he was sleeping alone in a room for the first time in his life. Even as the crown prince of Sauermühle, he had taken comfort in the sound of good ole Olga snoring away behind the curtains that separated her sleeping space from his.

It was more than that, though. It was also the constant interaction with a woman, without any men present. It was a new experience for him, the way women focused all their attention on men. At first, the endless female care made him happy, but it was becoming increasingly annoying, even bordering on intolerable. Whatever he did, he was accompanied by a pair of female eyes. He always had to explain how he was doing, whether he was comfortable, why he was doing something one way and not another, what he had to say about this or that, why he wore blue with green or red with blue, why he wolfed down his food, or why he decided against putting on a scarf, or wearing a hat, or washing his hands, and so on and so forth.

"Just leave me alone for a while," he begged Aunt Elli, pitifully at first. Later, he remained silent. He did not want to seem ungrateful.

Staying alone in his room made him vomit. "You're just having trouble getting adjusted," declared Aunt Elli, comforting him, but Walter had developed a finely tuned ear at the orphanage for subtle emotional tremors, and in his aunt's voice he could hear her growing disappointment in him. He took it very much to heart. He had failed, he thought, screwed up his luck out of stupidity. But what had he done wrong? Love, so he had learned, was not given to someone, but had to be constantly earned. He had made every effort, so what had he done wrong?

The meals together in the Berlin dining room with the long antique table, the dark walnut sideboard in front of the equally dark wallpaper, which was supposed to resemble imitation walnut paneling, grew increasingly silent. The more silent the meals, the louder Elli slammed the doors behind her. Elli expected something from him, but he had no clue what that might have been.

On the weekends, he was happy, when, as on every Sabbath, he was allowed to "return home" to his mother, or more often to Bruno. There was life there. His room at Aunt Elli's, by contrast, seemed like a burial chamber.

"Could I possibly go back to the orphanage?" he asked, making Bruno tear up.

"Yes, but why would you want that, my boy?" Bruno asked him, startled. "Aren't you doing well at Elli's? Is she treating you badly?"

"No… Everything's fine. Really!"

"Then why do you ask?"

"I can't sleep. I'm so alone."

"That's normal. You'll get used to it."

"But I don't want to get used to being alone! I want to be with you, Benno, and Mom, or go back to the orphanage."

"But you've got it so good at Aunt Elli's. Why, you live like the king of France. You even have your own room, everything a child could wish for! There's not a kid in the whole of Wedding who has their own room, and you're sulking now because you do?"

"Yes, yes, that's all true, but… it all… well… uh…scares me! I'd rather have a room with Benno or with you."

Bruno rubbed his chin thoughtfully. "And what does Benno think?"

"He'd rather be with me too."

"Then Benno should talk to your mother, because if I know her, she can't refuse him anything," Bruno said and winked at Walter conspiratorially.

Two weeks later, Franziska admitted defeat. She vacated the bedroom and from then on slept on the couch in the parlor, even though the grandfather clock made her meshuga. However, a clock without a pendulum and chimes every quarter of an hour made her even more meshuga. A stopped clock reminded her of the deaths at Sauermühle, as did the grandfather clock itself. After a few days, the heirloom ended up downstairs in Bruno's store, where its second-by-second reminder of transience no longer disturbed anyone's sleep. The Westminster chime could strike every fifteen minutes without bothering anyone, since Bruno was as deaf as a dormouse when he slept.

Everyone was worried over how Aunt Elli might react. However, she wasn't the least bit angry that Walter wanted to get away from her paradise. Quite the opposite, in fact. In the brief time that they had lived together, she had realized with increasing panic that she really wasn't fit to be a mother. Secretly, she had to admit to herself that children were completely alien to her and really got on her nerves. When Fränze announced that "a child belongs to its mother after all and blood is thicker than water," Elli was relieved. She was able to take back her hasty decision without losing face. She kissed Walter up, down, and sideways and promised that he could always turn to her, should he need anything at all.

From then on, Elli devoted herself to her latest passion, target shooting. And Walter was decidedly more welcome in her home as a guest, so that the old light-heartedness between nephew and aunt soon returned.

Walter considered it his first victory in the family that he had conquered half of the marital bed, which had previously belonged to Benno alone, and before him, to his father Willy, the "fake semiprecious stone." This made him want to follow up with still more triumphs. Thus, he had set himself the goal of being loved by his mother almost as much as his brother was. Realistically, he assumed that the first place in his mother's heart would be occupied forever by Benno. But he was fine with second place. Walter viewed the battle for his mother's affection the same way he did any sports competition. Second place was not the position of the first loser; it was the position of the second winner. And he wanted to remain a winner, one way or another. You shouldn't be small minded about such matters! That would go against his generous nature.

The just God of the Kohanims apparently agreed that the second oldest Kohanim daughter had chosen her spouse poorly. After marrying her God-fearing husband, Ascher Ben Nathanson, Selma became quickly disillusioned, discovering, unfortunately, that he was exactly what he had always been: an extraordinarily average person without a thought of his own, who was capable only of repeating things he had learned by rote. In short, Ascher proved to be a parrot in human form who babbled Torah verses. Even worse, according to Selma, he lacked any ambition to make a name for himself as a rabbi. In less than six months' time, he was becoming a nuisance. He wasn't even much good for marital fights. He let her deliver long monologues in which she complained relentlessly, while he merely nodded. That made her completely lose it. After devoutly putting up with ten tough years of marriage, Selma thanked the Almighty that he corrected her mistake by taking Ascher to himself with the help of the Spanish flu.

Selma did not mourn for long. She soon married a man her parents would have been delighted with had they been alive—even if his father was ole Kohanim's fiercest adversary. Selma's second husband bore the proud name of Caesar. This Caesar was the son of Artur Bukofzker, the most famous industrialist in Schwetz, who, in 1903, had founded the largest sawmill in West Prussia and who was once Samuel Kohanim's secret role model and rival. Caesar's father, the staunchly German nationalist Artur Bukofzker had been responsible for the larger-than-life portrait of Kaiser Wilhelm II in the synagogue, against which Samuel had successfully campaigned as an offense against his religious devotion. Bukofzker and Kohanim were each other's favorite enemies, who hated each other as fiercely as they fought each other.

When West Prussia became Polish and Bukofzker, who had previously been an extreme German nationalist and loyal to the emperor, suddenly voted for Polish nationhood in order to be allowed to remain on his property and hold onto his factories, Kohanim was finally done with Artur Bukofzker, once and for all. However, the same did not apply to his son Caesar. Even if Polish values and customs now eclipsed Prussian ones, Bukofzker's son was still considered one of the best Jewish matches in northern Poland. Caesar called himself a "man of independent means," which was the most accurate description of his existence. He was the figurehead, the public face of the company, a man without a portfolio whose only responsibility was to represent the factory by dressing impeccably, making titillating conversation, and maintaining a cheerful disposition. Samuel and Mindel Kohanim would have viewed the marriage as Selma finally making the right choice, but at the wrong time—after they were already dead.

The triumphant march of the Spanish flu had also left Caesar Bukofzker a widower. To win over Selma, however, he first had to warm up to the idea of Zionism, which he did. The work of a particularly persuasive Zionist propagandist, none other than Selma, along with his own observation of the increased harassment of Jews, finally convinced him to join the movement. Selma and Caesar were thus married a mere six months after the passing of Selma's first husband. They didn't even observe the year of mourning, an omission which in normal times would have been scandalous. But there were other, rather obvious, reasons for rushing to get married, as evidenced by the birth of the "seven-month baby" Leon.

Selma adapted easily to the vicissitudes that came along with the life of a Zionist activist. She had merely changed the object of her zeal. As for Caesar, his easy life as the son of a factory owner and cheerful figurehead was definitely over.

"The Holy Land doesn't need managers, it needs farmers," Selma stated categorically.

"Well, aren't there any farmers in Palestine?" Caesar wondered.

"Sure, so what? There aren't any Jewish ones."

"Well, wouldn't it be more practical and smarter if everyone did what they do best? If the Palestinians continued farming the land and the Jews took care of God, business, and the rest?"

"That's how we lived here. And what's become of us? We've become a pitiful, degenerate people who've lived in Poland for more than six hundred years and who still cannot speak Polish properly. We're alienated from our own nature! We live in shame and bondage, like in the days of the pharaohs, and like our forefathers, we must return to the promised land and farm our own land! That is the order of the day!"

Caesar might have objected that most Jewish scholars were of the opinion that the Jews may only return to Israel with the Messiah and that returning to the Land of Israel without the Messiah was pure blasphemy. However, religion was not Caesar's strong point. But it was his wife's, so he remained silent, not wanting to embarrass himself. Then he did what he usually did: he smiled in a conciliatory way until Selma seemed satisfied and kept his mouth shut.

However, there was a second, no less important question that was troubling him: How would the Jews get their own country? Did Palestine happen to be completely deserted? This problem did not seem to have been sufficiently clarified. Statements about it were generally vague or hazy, at best, with references to Switzerland, where people from different cultures also lived together in peace.

Contrary to his name, Caesar was good-natured, and something of a joker, who preferred to chat about some funny story or the latest operetta or to think about some witty anecdote he had heard rather than attend to the big questions of life. He thus lightheartedly followed the orders executed by his better half. In deference to her, he took to learning about farming. But he did so in the only way that he knew how: through books. Accordingly, Caesar had devoured several meters of agricultural literature, dutifully writing a summary of each book he read. He then memorized the summaries in order to shine before the strict examination committee which bore the name of Selma.

As part of Caesar's rigorous course of studies, a caterpillar called Pieris brassicae, also known as large white or large cabbage white, was writhing under the magnifying glass five centimeters below Caesar's silk bow tie with the pearl attached. Precisely because it was so hard to imagine that this worm could become a butterfly, he thanked the Almighty for the splendor and diversity of his creatures. Selma could hardly comprehend that Caesar would find a common cabbage white caterpillar so fascinating. She nonetheless thought it advisable to continue to encourage Caesar, who was not accustomed to work of any kind, to make further discoveries about nature. "Then you'll soon know the best way to kill all those caterpillar things."

Like a good schoolboy, Caesar had also done his homework on the topic. "Well, you have to pick them off the cabbage and give them to the chickens to eat. Caterpillars are, in fact, a very nutritious food. Rich in protein. I have therefore already asked myself whether we should perhaps somehow combine the growing of cabbage with the keeping of poultry."

Selma was speechless.

For purely educational reasons, the country girl Selma stopped herself from pointing out that nothing grows where chickens peck. It suddenly became very clear to her that Caesar desperately needed some practical experience with farming.

It was thus a happy coincidence that she was supposed to accompany a group of Zionist teenagers who were preparing for immigration to Israel, known as aliyah, to a training site on a farm southeast of Berlin.

Dearest cousin Else,

Please forgive me for not writing for such a long time. As you know, I am completely absorbed in the whole Zionist movement. It seems that the whole world now wants to return home to the Promised Land. Blessed be the Almighty!

It so happens that we will also be stopping in Berlin on the twentieth of this month with a group on the way to our training farm, Philadelphia, near Beeskow. We will arrive at the Anhalter train station in Berlin at 2:23 p.m. and will have about an hour before we have to board a slow train to Beeskow. Time enough for a cup of coffee or two. You and your husband Bruno are cordially invited to visit us at the Philadelphia in Brandenburg.

If you get the chance, perhaps you could also see if Fränze thinks her boys might be interested in a summer retreat? Some farm work might do them some good. However, don't bring the entire mishpocha with you. At most, perhaps sister Fanny. But I'm sure she would prefer to work herself to death for her husband. Well, God shall protect!

I am awaiting your telegram. Best wishes from Caesar and the kids as well,

Your cousin,
Selma

Not long after, she addressed another letter to Fränze.

My dear sister Franziska!

It's too bad that you couldn't make it out here to Philadelphia with the boys. Perhaps I shouldn't share this with you, but instead of using their train fare, Walter and Benno cycled all the way from Berlin to Philadelphia. They arrived here late in the evening safe and sound, but completely exhausted. Walter, who had probably planned the whole thing, told us that they had cycled without a break or flat tire in three (!) hours, according to schedule, with Walter in front and Benno always behind, probably with clenched teeth. Quite an achievement for a sixteen, or rather a fifteen, year-old boy, seeing as it was almost seventy kilometers. If it's true. So don't give the boys too hard of a time, because otherwise they're so well behaved. Just let it go!

To put your mind at ease: I will personally put them on the train back home to you. The two are a real asset here, and they are bright, too. Instead of falling over backwards with a full pitchfork of hay like the others, they secretly had a farmhand from the neighboring farm show them how to do it properly. Walter probably still remembered from Sauermühle that there's a trick to it, just like mowing with a scythe, which is how the two youngest literally ended up showing the seasoned men how it's done.

Walter's earliest childhood memories must be coming in handy now that they're working in the fields, and this explains why he is so skilled in the stable, as if he has been doing such work his whole life. Everybody is complaining about sore muscles and blisters on their hands except for your two boys. They were smart, as they had bandaged their hands to protect them. You can be really proud of them!

I would love to take them both with me to Palestine right away. Your son Walter exhibits the right morale. When the work starts to slow down, he strikes up a song, and everyone forgets about their tired backs. What a beautiful voice your son has. But I don't need to tell you that, you surely already know.

Walter and Caesar have become bosom buddies. You can rest assured that when I put them on the train to Berlin next week, you will hardly recognize the boys. They are tan and bursting with good health.

With kind regards to you and Bruno—even if we've never met.

Your sister,
Selma

Walter was absolutely enthusiastic about Aunt Selma's second husband, Caesar Bukofzker. Since enthusiastic was Walter's normal emotional state, the word absolutely has to be added to describe an emotional state that in normal people would be a state of euphoria, but which in Walter's case was merely a normal expression of approval.

Walter was particularly impressed by Caesar's statesmanlike eyebrows, which cast a shadow like black-gray cotton balls over his mischievous brown eyes and which he would comically wiggle up and down when he sang his music-hall songs or told his emcee jokes. He was also thrilled by their shared love of childhood places in Schwetz, Osche, and on the Vistula. They could also, without uttering a word, break into resounding laughter about the same things.

Walter's younger brother, Benno, didn't share his enthusiasm for Uncle Caesar. Like a gloomy cloud behind the sunshine, he followed the two happy souls, who after a few minutes always forgot that he was even there because they were completely caught up in outdoing each other with jokes and tricks.

"Uncle Caesar is a windbag! And he's not entirely kosher either," Benno announced coolly when Caesar had to trudge off in the direction of the apiary where Selma had sent him.

"What's your point, Benno?! Since when have we been totally kosher?"

"Come on, you know exactly what I mean! The guy's not clean. There's something wrong with him."

"Just because he's funny and livens things up a bit? Aunt Selma likes Uncle Caesar much better than Uncle Ascher, that dimwit. May God rest his soul."

"Well, maybe, but I've watched him. Haven't you noticed that he sometimes looks at you funny? Sort of from the side?

"What? Looks at me how? You don't think he's gay or something, do you?"

"No, not that exactly. But I've noticed that he sometimes looks at you like, like, like… well, as if he had a guilty conscience. And when Aunt Elli showed up here, he snuck off, and when Aunt Jenny and Uncle Albert were here, he also behaved pretty strangely."

"Baloney!"

"Come on, Walter, believe me! There's something going on here. I'm just saying, keep your eyes open."

"Well, what's this *something* supposed to be, huh? He didn't even know our aunts back then, because he was away at boarding school, and by the time he returned to Schwetz, we were already long gone. Plus, he lived in Danzig. So, tell me why Uncle Caesar might have something

to hide from us? That's crazy! Honestly, Benno! Even Aunt Martha couldn't come up with something like that. Go swim a few laps or something. Maybe it will clear your head!"

"I know what I know," Benno growled defiantly, feeling chastised by his older brother, as he often did. He hunched up his shoulders and dug his hands into his pockets up to his elbows which was only possible because he was wearing Walter's old pants. In a huff, he stalked off toward the lake, furiously kicking small stones into the meadows and bushes along the way. Walter looked up at the unwaveringly blue summer sky above Brandenburg's Philadelphia and shook his head. "What an idiot!"

However, Walter did have to give Benno some credit. He had a knack for picking up the scent on certain things, even if it got on Walter's nerves. When the two brothers argued it usually had to do with Walter's tendency toward chaos and hot-headedness and Benno's toward fussiness and mischievousness. It was hard to imagine that they had descended from the same parents. Not only were their characters so very different, but they didn't have much in common physically either. In Wedding, thin and lanky Benno was known as "Gandhi," whereas the powerhouse Walter was known as "King Kong."

"Apparently, you only feel happy when you can rain on someone else's parade," Walter said angrily whenever Benno came to him with objections and concerns, or when Benno wanted to reign in Walter's enthusiasm for something or the other.

"No one is forcing you to listen to me, Walter. I'm just saying it. But don't go complaining afterwards that I didn't warn you!"

It may have been Benno's whole "keep your eyes peeled" speech or something else that caused it. But whatever it was, after that the whole stay at Philadelphia farm was ruined for Walter. He didn't want to burden himself with mistrust, nor did he wish to contemplate the spiritual depths of Caesar Bukofzker or those of his brother. Even though Bukofzker did his utmost to keep the Palestine euphoria going, he couldn't prevent boredom from beginning to spread throughout the Zionist model farm, especially once the country girls' curiosity about circumcised penises had run its course. Walter started to think about what he was missing out on in Berlin, including the six-day race at the Sportpalast, for which Aunt Elli had promised to get him tickets. How could he have forgotten about that? Without missing a beat, he decided to head out. After filling up his water bottle, he leapt onto his bike, and he was off!

Unburdened by "slowpoke Benno" he wanted to ride nonstop as if he were participating in a competition. The stopwatch that Aunt Elli had given him for his birthday swung like a pendulum around his neck. He stuck it inside his shirt and put his water bottle on the handlebars like any real racing cyclist would do. Then he leaned far forward and began pedaling until his body felt like a well-oiled machine and the only sounds that he could hear were the rhythm of his breathing and the humming of the tires on the asphalt. Nothing gave him a greater sense of happiness—or almost nothing.

Checking the milestone markers along the road against his stopwatch, he noted with satisfaction that he was riding faster than he had ever done before. There was no better place in the world, he thought, than to be astride the seat of a racing bike, alone with himself, the landscape, his bicycle, and the road. Speeding along towards home, he let his thoughts wander, returning to what happened before he and Beno had arrived to stay with Selma.

He wanted to be back home in time for the Sabbath. Before dusk. That was when the 'White Poplar'—as Walter and Benno jokingly called their mother because her chatter and first white hairs reminded them of the rustling tree with shimmery leaves—would be setting the table with candlesticks.

Franziska's way of carrying out the ritual involved a lot of bustling and hurrying back and forth and she usually fumbled about, unable to find the matches. Just recalling the scene, made Walter grin as he cycled down the road. The bathing rituals were probably already in full swing: the kettles already on the stove. As usual, just when Walter and Benno were about to fall asleep at the kitchen table, Fränze would make them climb, one after the other, into the zinc tub that sat enthroned on two kitchen chairs. To get to the tub, they would have to clamber over the kitchen table. Bruno would have already been heating the bath water for an hour in the large kettles on the stove. Then they would scrub each other down with curd soap, and afterwards, drain the bath water into buckets and pour it down the sink. Fränze would take this opportunity to remind Bruno, once again, that they needed to build a bathroom in the pantry, saying: "Yes, the tailor is missing buttons on his shirt; the carpenter's chair has wobbly legs; and here at our place the faucet drips and the bathroom remains a pipe dream!"

Bruno would pretend he hadn't heard anything and engross himself in his crossword puzzles.

Freshly washed, with red faces and wet hair, all the men of the household would then sit at the table and wait until Franziska had finished her rather erratic ritual preparations in order to ceremoniously commence the meal after the berakah or blessing.

"Why don't we go to Palestine too?" Walter asked Fränze every other day. "Every year for Passover we say: "Next year in Jerusalem." But nobody's goin' nowhere! That's baloney, don't you think?"

"Don't talk like a Berliner! And just what do you think we should do in the desert among the camels?"

"Same thing as here. Open a plumber's shop."

"They don't even have water there! Let alone water pipes! Who needs a plumber there?" the White Poplar asked with amusement.

"Now is exactly when they need it!" countered Benno. "If there aren't any water pipes, then you need people to build and lay them. Everyone needs water. It stands to reason!"

"And what about Bruno?"

"Uncle Bruno can become a Jew."

"Just to sweat with us in the desert?" Franziska wanted to burst out laughing and held onto the dining table with both hands. "The summers here are too much for him as it is. Nebbich!"

"Ain't nobody gonna snip me no how, and certainly not on my nobl'st part, not even a rabbi," Bruno grumbled, and went on spooning his soup. "I'm stayin' like I am!"

"And when are you two finally going to get married? Even that dragon Aunt Selma got herself another man and remarried. Why don't you two?"

Bruno and Franziska acted as if they had not heard the question. They continued to eat their chicken soup with relish, as if their fate depended on the solemnity with which they spooned up their soup. The oppressive silence was interrupted only by the sound of spoons scraping against porcelain, until Walter asked once again, as he always did before departing for the Zionist camp: "And why don't you want to go to Israel too, Mom?"

"There are too many Jews there for me," Franziska let slip.

"And what's so bad about that? Not a day goes by here without people working to turn public opinion against us."

"Too many Jews heaped together get on my nerves. So do any situations in which one type of people are heaped together. Put together one sort of people all by themselves and they all go berserk! They get stir crazy or something. It's unhealthy. Really, forget about this Palestine stuff. I'd rather stay where I am. In this hullabaloo. And you? Is being here making you sick or why do you want to leave?"

"I don't wanna go nowhere. I was just asking, ok?! It's no big whoop!"

"Walter, stop talking like a horrible Berliner!"

After he had passed Königs Wusterhausen in record time, lost in thought and wondering what Aunt Elli would say about his new course record, Walter let his mind turn to the serious question of his future. He had been putting it off for a year now. Should he do an apprenticeship or go to secondary school to prepare for college? He had to decide after the summer holidays. Thanks to his US-dollar-based inherited shares, he was one of the few in his school who actually had a choice. Walter's problem was not the school fees, unlike his friend Eddi. Walter knew Eddi from Fränze's apartment building, where he and his family lived in the side wing. Eddi was vastly superior to Walter in arithmetic and geometry and helped Walter with those subjects. Walter returned the favor by helping Eddi write essays and memorize poems. Eddi's father was on state welfare, and Eddi's mother barely managed to make ends meet for the family of five by doing work from home. Day and night she would fill box after box of rolled "holiday firecrackers" with the tiny little toys you find inside. Walter found this so disillusioning that from then on, he hated "holiday firecrackers." Eddi's mother came regularly on the fifteenth of the month to pump Fränze for money.

"Basically, we give Eddi's family ten marks if they always borrow on the fifteenth and bring it back on the first. Then they come back again on the fifteenth and work the pump again," as Benno later explained. Benno knew the particulars because he was the numbers man in the family. That's why already a year before leaving school, Benno's path in life way already laid out like a railroad track. He would do an apprenticeship at a bank with the aim of finding a job as an accountant.

Walter, by contrast, was torn between what his mother wanted and what he wanted. She wanted him to do an apprenticeship as a plumber, so that he could take over his father's business. He wanted to take the university entrance qualification exam and study history and literature or music or theater, or, or…

But even heartfelt desires have their pitfalls. As his mother pointed out, if he went to a secondary school and university, he would be suddenly uprooted from his circle of friends and planted in a strange environment, among the children of civil servants and bourgeois snobs who would despise him.

"Guess why we live in Wedding? Away from all that? I know what I'm talking about. I, for one, don't like it when people try to mess with me and turn up their noses at me. And at a secondary school, they will all mess with you and look at you funny. You can bet your life on that."

"Mom, I can take whatever they dish out."

Franziska gave her son a perplexed look and burst out laughing. "That sounds like something I would say."

If Walter were honest with himself, he would have to admit that he wasn't completely convinced by his own words, especially when he thought about teachers like Mr. Fleischhut, who was known for being especially hard on all of the Jewish students. Besides, said another voice in Walter's head, do I really want to spend at least the next ten years stuck in school and sitting behind desks at a university, eternally dependent on the judgment of authorities like Mr. Fleischhut, instead of being able to take control of my own life in three to four years?

Walter had a hard time with discipline and subordination, even when he was treated fairly, and he was always rubbing people the wrong way with his big mouth. Even in situations in which he least expected it, or thought he was holding back. He couldn't help it; he was always getting out of line. Sports were his favorite thing. After that he also liked reciting poems and performing songs, plays, or parodies. He was especially good at imitating voices and dialects. His favorite subjects were German, geography, and history. But become a teacher? No thank you!

After a short downhill run, he decided to do a quick sprint, remembering how he had performed the Hamlet monologue in the auditorium. The dumbest bullies couldn't help but be moved by it. Even the principal himself had tears welling up behind his glasses, which was all the more surprising, since he didn't really like Walter and thought he was a showoff. But after Walter's performance, he praised him, saying in his husky baritone, "Now you can see the power of words, boys!"

And yet, despite his success playing Hamlet, Walter wasn't sure he wanted to pursue a career in the arts. At Aunt Elli's he had on occasion met artists and he found them rather unappealing and a bit suspect. They were all cowards and foppish schmucks: all show and no substance. Cut from the same cloth as people from the snootiest parts of Berlin, Wilmersdorf and the Bavarian Quarter. Nah, those types of people weren't for him. Too bourgeois! He preferred Wedding and people from Wedding. Even if Wedding knocked you around a bit now and again! That's where he found people just like himself: hearty, warm, trustworthy, and straightforward. So did that mean he would rather do an apprenticeship as a plumber and take over the business?

"Well, you can read books and make music or go to the theater even if you run a plumber's shop. Just as you can still play sports," his mother said.

Yet again he found himself thinking that his mother was perhaps right after all. But what about sports? He had cycled the roughly seventy kilometers from Beeskow to Berlin in about two hours. No small feat.

The noise in the Sportpalast was deafening. A brass band was playing, people were whistling, singing, celebrating, cheering on the racers and themselves.

"Hey pal, I think your mama's callin' ya!" someone yelled in Walter's ear. The guy tugging at his sleeve pointed toward the entrance and the rows of seats. Walter reluctantly tore his eyes from the cyclists, who were chasing each other around the Sportpalast track, and craned his neck in the direction that the guy was pointing. In the back, near the entrance, Elli, who in honor of the day was properly attired in a wide-brimmed hat, was flailing her arms about and signaling to Walter to come down and join her. Walter fought his way through the pulsing crowd of fans who were swaying to the Sportpalast waltz with beer mugs in their hands and whistling through their fingers to the refrain, preferably directly into their neighbor's ear, which everyone found very funny.

"Come on, Walter!" Elli yelled against the background noise. "I want to introduce you to someone important."

Despite having to negotiate the new experience of wearing such a prominent hat, Elli made her way confidently, in an evening dress no less, to the stairs leading down to the exclusive infield around which the track ran. There, in the most expensive seats, the financial elite, Berlin's high society, were cavorting with famous athletes and the event organizers at a most spectacular gala. The glitterati smoked Cuban cigars and let the champagne corks pop to the accompanying sound of screams of delight while the cyclists whizzed past them.

Elli was one of these privileged guests at the six-day race, because the Sporthaus Elite, which was opposite the Sportpalast, belonged as much to the event as a Christmas tree to Christmas.

Walter was supposed to help them pave their way through the crowd. But he didn't know exactly where he was going. Elli subtly nudged him along the right path until they landed in front of a table full of bottles of liquor. From behind the table emerged a man in a tuxedo, in his mid-sixties and heavyset, and with a bright red face that made him look like he might have a stroke at any minute. With his fat hand and equally fat signet ring, he gave Walter a weak handshake.

"This is my nephew, Walter!" Elli peeked out from under her oversized hat brim, which billowed out over the crowd like a sail. The man plucked a rather stale-looking cigar from the corner of his mouth with his reddish, hairy sausage fingers.

"Well, boy, you like it here?" he asked with a gurgly voice, pointing the cigar around as if he owned the whole Sportpalast. "If you're good enough, you can join us here in a few years. You wanna do that?"

He pinched Walter's cheek with his sausage fingers. "I heard a lot 'bout you from your aunt, over here." Walter bowed like a good boy and put on the expected smile of the hopeful young athlete begging for his chance. Aunt Elli acknowledged this with a silent applause in her eyes.

"Next Sunday, when this is all over, the junior cyclists are gonna go on a short ride 'round the Reh Mountains. Near where you live. Your aunt here says that you really got some speed. You can show everyone on Sunday, boy. One of my cyclists has dropped out. It's just a tryout. Don't worry. But, hey, if we got negroes boxin' nowadays, why can't Jews ride bikes, eh?!" He doubled over with laughter and then almost coughed himself to death. "So, I'm countin' on you, kiddo!"

And to emphasize what he had said, he poked Elli in the ribs with his elbow so that she would laugh along with him. Walter was surprised to see that Elli actually joined in, albeit with evident discomfort. In the meantime, Walter had had time to rummage his memory for whom Aunt Elli might be tempted to bend over backwards with such politeness. Then, it dawned on him that it was probably none other than the cycling patron, Paul Peschke, the liquor manufacturer from Wedding, who now stood before him and who took a particular interest in sponsoring the young cycling talent of Wedding.

Before Walter could stammer his "yes, I'd like that," the noise level rose again because the Tietz department store had just donated free beer for the "hayloft," as the nosebleed section of the Sportpalast was called. The director of the department store, wearing a tuxedo and standing to one side behind Paul Peschke, threw his arms up in the air like a prizefighter after winning a point, and the hayloft gratefully sang, "That is the Berliner Air, Air, Air!"[9] accompanied by the orchestra.

Now Walter was whistling along. He would soon have to figure out whether he would want to ride around in circles like a poor lunatic, the way that the cyclists at the six-day-race were doing. But not today.

Franziska was mad at Elli for two whole weeks for planting the seed in her son's head.

"Bike racing! Nebbich! You might as well join the carnival and have your nose smashed in for a sixer. Bruno, why don't you say something?!"

"I got as good as nix to say 'bout it, Fränze! A man's gotta do what a man's gotta do," Bruno bellowed in a surly voice from his armchair, where he was poring over a new crossword puzzle.

"A man maybe, but not a boy! He's still wet behind the ear!"

"Geez, Fränze, let 'im have a bit a fun and ride along with 'em. The boy needs to let off some steam. Better this way than fightin' in the street with them Polacks or brownshirts, or dancing all the time to that negro music that nobody can't stand—Name of a hill near Braunschweig?"

"Elm," answered three voices in unison and rolled their eyes. Bruno's obsession with crossword puzzles had been driving them all crazy for weeks.

After Walter vanished from Philadelphia, there was a week of radio silence between the brothers, after which they came together again by going to local dance events. Should they sign up for the Charleston Shimmy contest at the Fatherland House? They had rehearsed a kind of Laurel-and-Hardy Charleston number, which was funny because of the contrast between Benno, the long and thin "Gandhi," and Walter, the athletic powerhouse "King Kong." Walter always ended the dance number with a back handspring and the splits on the floor, while Benno flapped his long limbs, looking pleased with himself.

They got a big laugh at every event. To their dismay, however, participants under the age of eighteen were not allowed to take part in dance competitions or were only allowed to perform when accompanied by their parents. But that was out of the question. Ever since Walter had been picked up by two policemen "for uncontrolled dancing on the median of Müllerstraße" and charged five marks for "insulting an officer," dancing had been a touchy subject. So the boys could only let loose at private dance events, such as backyard parties or harvest festivals in the northern garden colonies.

It was there at the dance events sponsored by the garden colonies and sports clubs that the two brothers, who were so very different from each other, met the legendary Oda Hanke for the first time, who was now known as Oda von Güldner, with the aristocratic "von" in between and who previously had been referred to as simply "the crazy Red." When Oda wasn't traveling on behalf of the Communist Party, she was serving the betterment of humanity as a paramedic and therefore turned up unexpectedly at all kinds of events.

When the day of the "Wedding Youth Bike Ride" arrived on a Sunday, Walter was the first to show up and report to Paul Peschke's racing team representative.

"Walter Kohanim-Rubin ain't on my list. What kinda name is that supposed to be anyway? One name ain't enough for you? You need two?"

"Mr. Peschke promised me personally that I could come along today. I'm Walter, the nephew of Elli von Strachwitz from Sportshaus Elite."

"You could be the Emperor of China for all I care, fella. If you're not on the list, you don't exist!"

"There are supposed to be ten riders starting for Paul Peschke, right?"

"Yeah, that's right. But like I said, your name ain't among 'em."

"I'm not talking about names. I am talking about numbers, my good man! Mr. Peschke told me at the six-day race that one of the riders had dropped out. So if the tenth doesn't start, I can start. Do you really want to get into trouble with Paul Peschke over such a trifle?"

"Hmmm… Well, have you at least gotta proper bike, you lil' pain in the neck?"

"C'mon, leave him alone now," intervened another man who was proudly sporting an armband that read, "official."

"Ok, wise guy, if the tenth cyclist ain't here in five minutes, you can do it. What's your name again?"

"Walter Kohanim-Rubin."

"That's too complicated."

"Then write 'Walter Rubin.'"

"Ha! He's a Jew to boot?!"

"Yes, but for once that doesn't make the wheels go any faster."

"And a big mouth too! We'll see if you'll be talkin' such a big game later, you Jewish greenhorn. We'll see if you make it to the cobblestone in Rosenthal!"

Walter got his number and positioned himself at the starting line, where he thought there would be the fewest scuffles and his fellow riders wouldn't be sneaky and kick his spokes right at the beginning or try to eliminate the competition by means of employing other dirty tricks. Walter was lucky. After the customary pushing and shoving, which he managed to fight his way through, he got off to a good start, and like the other boys, he made sure not to spring to the head of the pack right away and use up all his energy too early.

"Always ride with the group in front of the field of riders, stay in the slipstream of the rider in front of you, and stick closely to their rear wheel. Pick up the pace two-thirds of the way through the race and then start passing them one by one. Continue to take advantage of the slipstream of the rider in front of you, ride in fourth or fifth position and then, when the finish line is almost in sight: off you go and don't let anyone else past!" Aunt Elli had drummed into him, adding, "But if you finish in the top five, that's good too. To impress Peschke, you absolutely have to be in the top five, remember! The top five!"

Exactly as Aunt Elli had told him, Walter slowly rolled up on the field from behind and saw the many startled eyes as he passed them. To intimidate his competition, he gave them angry looks and made snide remarks—"Hey, you ole geezer! Pretty tired today, eh?"—and then took the lead. On the home stretch, however, he thought he had already secured victory and noticed too late when someone close behind him on his right was sprinting past him and managed to cross the finish line a hand's width before him.

Walter came in second for which he received a silver cardboard laurel wreath and a winner's certificate. He was the only member of Paul Peschke's team in the top five, and his future patron was bursting with pride.

"Well, my boy! It's gonna be fun with you! If you hadn't been nappin' at the end there, you'd a been first. Typical beginner's mistake. Don't worry 'bout it. It's gonna be just fine. It'll all work out when we build you up. Out of sight, kiddo!"

Then he turned to the co-organizers and the astonished spectators: "Here comes the lil' guy from the street who up and takes second! First-rate, ain't it? This fella's gonna be a big name in cyclin'!"

Franziska was speechless in the face of the storm rushing up to greet her and Walter: Oda, wearing her Red Cross cap, with her daughter Hella in tow, and Aunt Elli too. Fränze didn't quite know how to face Martha's best friend Oda, nor how to react to Walter's sporting triumph. And then there was Elli von Strachwitz, coming in at full speed! Fränze braced herself by leaning against the wall of the building behind her.

Elli hugged Walter and danced a funny little victory jig with him. Oda clapped him on the shoulder and then, turning to Franziska, said, "Long time, no see, eh?"

"It's been about fifteen years," she replied slowly.

"And yet we have so much in common!"

"Well, I wouldn't know what that might be," Fränze replied coolly.

Oda broke into laughter, "Allow me to jog your memory—the two of us were the most disreputable girls in our little backwoods town!"

"Yeah, maybe, but I don't see how that connects us," Fränze snapped back, not wanting to be reminded of her youthful indiscretions, especially not in the presence of her sons.

"Well, you can think what you want, but the gossips who used to pick us both to pieces still lump us together as part of the same scandalous lot!" Oda brushed a strand of hair out of her face. "I can see that you are and will always be the same old Fränze, as batty as ever! All the same, you can be proud of your golden boy! Congratulations!"

Franziska was baffled by the situation. What good were cycling triumphs? The whole thing irritated her. Suddenly, she was being greeted by complete strangers with respect or like a family member. Even the neighbors she loathed were breaking character and acting nice. At the butcher's they gave her the best cuts without a fight. Then there was a never-ending stream of this new species: sports club officials. They showed up at her doorstep, turning on the charm and wanting her to sign various contracts or to buy something. The newspaper reporters tried to take pictures of her with Walter. Preferably with the Icarus on the Spree bridge in the background, which she, of course, refused for religious reasons. She sometimes resorted to calling her sister Elli for advice on understanding sports matters. As confusing as it all was, she refused to be deterred. She insisted on calling the shots. "I'm his mother after all!"

For understandable reasons, Walter, the soon-to-be junior champion of Berlin no longer wanted to deal with the hassle of conceited bourgeois snobs and domineering teachers at secondary school. He planned to start an apprenticeship with the master plumber Krüger, who was also a cycling enthusiast. He couldn't do it with Bruno, because Bruno wasn't a master tradesman and, as a journeyman, he was not allowed to train any apprentices. Besides, the license of his rinky-dink shop was made out in the name of his master, Krüger. Walter now had exactly the kind of fool's freedom that every young person could only dream of, and he made ample use of it.

"I can't let my three men walk around in their underpants for my birthday. What would the guests think when they arrived?" Fränze explained to her best friend Lotte, who was standing outside the door at half past seven on May 1st with red carnations and a bar of chocolate for Walter. It was her way of rejecting Lotte's proposition that she employ a similar tactic to the bloodless pant-confiscation coup of 1919. Franziska's sons, who sympathized with the Commune, would be better off keeping their butts behind their mother's stove on revolutionary May 1, 1929. "What was good for the fathers ten years ago is also good for the sons today," Lotte said.

All open-air markets and rallies were strictly forbidden. The police had already been deployed during the night around the working-class districts of Wedding, Prenzlauer Berg, and Neukölln. Benno and Walter, who were already sitting in the kitchen munching on their jam sandwiches and drinking malt coffee, were acting as meek as lambs and assuring their mother that they were "just checking out the situation." Franziska was skeptical but wanted to believe her sons. Lotte, on the other hand, only heard: "We're taking the streets!"

Less than a quarter of an hour later, Lotte's husband Willi, the Social Democrat policeman, was at the door to have a "man-to-man" talk with the boys. It didn't escape Franziska's notice that Walter was on the verge of bursting into an outrage when Benno elbowed him in the side, getting him to simmer down, and then they both started suddenly acting suspiciously innocent. She was sure that they were up to something.

Willi Hörl wanted to give them a way out.

"Why don't you come with me? There are some really interesting people speaking at our May Day party, and at least our party at the SPD has been authorized!"

"That's because if the Social Democrats have their way, the revolution takes place in the assembly hall," Walter teased mockingly.

"Don't waste your breath, trying that out on us, Uncle Willi," Benno jumped in to help his brother.

"Well, what then? What if there's another bloodbath like in 1919, with the machine guns blazing and hundreds of workers ending up dead on the pavement? If the communists march today in celebration of May 1st, then the exact same thing is going to happen again."

"Yeah, because the Social Democrats betrayed the workers!"

"No, because you simply can't support the communists' harebrained way of doing politics. Have you ever noticed that the German communists turn every victory into a defeat, instead of every defeat into a victory, just like Lenin and Trotsky and their cohort? They simply can't seem to pull off anything effectively. Seems to be a disease specific to German revolutionaries!"

Walter and Benno groaned and writhed as if in unbearable agony. They gazed imploringly at the kitchen ceiling, struggling to keep their tempers under control in the presence of their mother.

"Give me your word that you won't march with the communists!" Franziska added. "I don't want to hear anything about participating in Revolutionary May! Nebbich! You stay away from them! Your absolute word of honor! Walter? Benni?"

Walter and Benno exchanged glances and mumbled insincerely, "We'll be careful, we swear."

Just as soon as the front door slammed behind them, Benno and Walter dashed down the stairs, leapt onto their bikes, and headed out to survey the scene. When they ran into Eddi at Nettelbeck Square they bragged that they were out on "party business." Eddi, in turn, told them that the police were swarming around there and on Soldiner Straße and that on the dead-end street, Kösliner Straße, there was a hastily constructed barricade. On the rooftops opposite, the police were already moving into position with machine guns.

"Man, no one will get out of there alive when it starts! Benno, I'm going to race over to party headquarters and let them know what's going on. They have to call it all off! You can get to the other side from Pankstraße via the courtyards and cellars."

When he arrived at the party headquarters, everyone was in celebratory mood. People were already rejoicing over the assumed victories in the street fights going on at Soldiner Straße, and in Neukölln, and Hackescher Markt. Walter realized that as a youngster, no one there was going to take him seriously; there was simply nothing he could do to convince anyone to listen to him. So he rushed back to the Wedding combat zone. Benno was nowhere to be seen. He heard that the cadres had sent Benno to Neukölln. Walter quickly stashed his bike behind a pile of wood in a cellar in Pankstraße, climbed over three courtyard walls, crept and crawled through the cellar labyrinth, which he still knew how to do from his trapper-and-Indian games, until he ended up in the rear building at Kösliner Strasse 8.

The closer he came to the front of the building, the louder the noise and the stronger the smell of petroleum. In the second courtyard, children were pouring the liquid into milk bottles and stuffing rags into the tops, which the older kids then passed onto the barricade and roof, while bullets whizzed around them. The first wounded men were lying on blankets and old mattresses in the first courtyard. Women were squatting down next to them, tearing bed sheets and tablecloths into bandages.

Red Cross flags were visible on both sides of the entrance gate as well as in the courtyard. Crouched beneath the flags at the entrance gate, protected only by a heavy wooden door, was Hella, Oda's little daughter. Terrified, she sat clutching a rag doll. Oda was busy giving commands and tending to the wounded, her rubber apron already covered in blood. When she saw Walter, she couldn't believe her eyes.

"How on earth did you get in here, hot shot?! If there's a safe way out, please take my child to safety. Sooner or later, they're bound to storm the houses. And on the way back, be sure to bring a doctor with surgical instruments and plenty of morphine."

"Well, I'd like to see the doctor who'd dare to come here and jump over three walls."

"There are still comrades!" Oda gave him a punishing look. "Now get out of here!"

Walter took Hella by the hand, who was pale with fear as she sought to fight back her tears. "Well, I hope you're a bit agile and not a wimp too! Besides a leg up, you're also going to need good climbing and jumping skills. And don't be afraid of mice and spiders, young lady, because we're going to have to crawl through some cellars on our stomachs! Do you think you can do that?"

Offended, the little girl replied: "Phooey! Only babies are scared of spiders and mice."

"Well, then nothing can happen to you!"

"And Mommy?"

"The good Lord will watch over her in the meantime."

By May 3, 1929, Oda had worked two days and two nights on duty as a paramedic. By the time her shift ended, Berlin was mourning the loss of 32 dead and 234 wounded.

Walter's seventeenth birthday went down in history as Berlin's Bloody May.

IN THE SHADOW OF HEROES

Today is the last meeting with Dr. Vogelsang. It's a beautiful day. The late autumn sun is falling into my room from a steel-blue sky. Shadows dance against the wall, cast by the few remaining bright yellow leaves of the maple tree growing outside my window. Vogelsang and I sit at the table, directly opposite each other like chess players. The thing between me and "Pamela," I tell her, "first got going when I posted a video on Facebook. Someone had recorded it from inside a car. It showed a beach on the Mediterranean with beach umbrellas. On this idyllic beach were the dead bodies of thirty women, children, and men, lapped by rolling waves.

Fishermen were squatting between the bodies, sorting their catch into containers. It was probably somewhere on the coast of Libya. But even more disturbing than the pictures were the reactions of the Facebook community, who normally went on and on for pages and pages about cute cat videos and debates about the possible closure of West Berlin's main airport. Only four people had reacted to the horrifying pictures! Completely beside myself, I told my Facebook friend Pamela about it. Then she fell silent. Only when I ranted about the Green Party politician in Iran, did she reappear.

"How often are you on the Internet?" asked Dr. Vogelsang.

"A few times a day." I let her wander around for a little while longer on the wrong track of my latent media addiction. Apparently satisfied with my answer, she drops it. However, she still wants to hear more about my childhood.

"What was it like to grow up surrounded by heroes?" she asks me. That's my favorite topic. My role models were all so unattainably capable and virtuous that emulating them successfully seemed completely hopeless. Any ordinary person was doomed to fail. These paragons of virtue, towering above me and putting me to shame, silently demanded that I do the same or even surpass them. I was not allowed to be just an ordinary person.

I was, of course, supposed to be the best student in the whole school and be able to play a musical instrument so masterfully that I could pursue a career as a soloist. I was also expected to earn a doctorate summa cum laude and, last but not least, start an academic career. Preferably a position that entitled me to a state pension, my mother used to say, at which my father would laugh. "My daughter, employed by the state? Don't make me laugh!"

My mother saw me as a professor. It didn't matter what I wanted, I was supposed to make up for everything that had been denied to them through war, persecution, and poverty. "You will be the first in our family to be an academic." Children in other families also bore the weight of such expectations, but I had the added burden of being an only child, a princess, and a rather weak soloist. The only special gift that I possessed went unnoticed for a long time. I had an innate inner compass by which I always knew the cardinal directions immediately and could later tell the time without looking at my watch. I also had a knack for finding the saftest place in the room, usually the place near the door. Easy access to escape routes.

Were it not for me and my mother, my father would have undoubtedly had a remarkable stage career as a singer or actor. But such an unsound life plan was not possible with my mother. It dawned on me early on that I had tied them together against their will, by dint of my mere existence. And I often had the feeling that I was making life even more difficult for them. After my spat with my Grandma Fränze, I suffered from a skin disease. The treatment for it involved putting various ointments on my head and limbs every morning and evening. I also had to take a bath twice a day and wash my head vigorously, giving it a good scrub to dissolve the grease from the pungent ointment in my hair. Despite these exertions and pains, my mother insisted that I have long hair and either long pigtails or a French braid. Every morning and evening, there was a lot of screaming because of the knots in my hair and my mom tugging at it mercilessly until my scalp was completely sore. Braiding my hair in the morning took an extra fifteen minutes, during which I would have loved to have cried. However, out of pride, I stifled my tears. Needless to say, I hated having long hair.

Over the years, I grew into a cute little girl with dark cherry eyes and black hair decorated with white or red bows or woven into an ugly French braid. My mother dressed me up like a little doll who had to show off all her cute dresses, bows, and patent leather shoes. One night shortly before my seventh birthday, I had had enough of the business with my hair. In the gray of the morning dawn, I secretly fished her sacred dressmaker scissors out of the drawer and cut off my hair. In the morning my father looked at me with pity but kept quiet after my mother shot him a look. She then gave me a beating. Only my mother beat me. My father never did. But I preferred spankings to days of cold, punishing silence. After twelve whacks to my bottom with a carpet beater, at least the atmosphere was cleared. Then I could turn the tables and act resentful toward my mother: stubbornly push her away from me and refuse to speak to her. This was my way of showing some remnant of obligatory heroism in order to win at least a scrap of my parents' respect. Whenever my mother beat me, I didn't make a single sound of pain. No tears. No fear. Lips pressed together. Unfortunately, my proud suffering simply provoked my mother to hit me even harder. But I didn't care. Of course, I was always reminded that this was all child's play compared to what my parents had been forced to endure when they were young, which only resulted in making me even more stubborn.

My mother was the stronger of the two parents. I was at her mercy all day long, so I had to take her side if I wanted to get by relatively unscathed. In imperceptible doses, she passed along to me her bitterness towards my father's family, a bitterness that gradually grew from resentment to become out-and-out hatred toward my father. The only person in my father's family that she tolerated was my Grandpa Bruno, who continued to visit us secretly and timidly diverted chocolate, oranges, bananas, and Western newspapers from the small bit of spending money Franziska gave him. So I was constantly torn between feelings of guilt towards my father and childish opportunism, which was calculated according to who provided the greater protection, care, and food. Despite everything, my mother adored me, practically besieging me with her love. And because I was the sole object of her affection, I found it all the more burdensome.

As best I could, I evaded all proof of love, especially since I didn't deserve it. Wasn't I an imposter, who received unwarranted favors? Strangely enough, unlike my father, my mother had no friends or girlfriends at all. It seemed like she set such high standards for friendship that no one could, nor even wanted to, fulfill them. Plus, she expected people to court her favor, while she, in turn, did nothing to maintain relationships or friendships. She found something wrong with everyone. Often, it took merely the suggestion that the person used to be a part of the League of German Girls or the Hitler Youth or had had fun participating in the "Strength Through Joy" program, while she had been living in mortal fear.

I don't know a lonelier person than my mother. And because she was also incapable of doing things on her own, she monopolized my time. I always had to go everywhere with her.

So I began to dream of attending boarding school. I eagerly read a series of books about a group of English schoolchildren for whom attending a boarding school seemed quite normal. My mind was made up. I wanted to go to a boarding school! As far away from my parents as possible, far away from their control and constant arguing. I saw childhood as degrading, a type of bondage from which I wanted to escape as quickly as possible.

Then something frightening happened. For some inexplicable reason, I was suddenly no longer able to progress with handwriting. I was always last, always reading something other than what was in the book or on the blackboard. But it wasn't my eyes that were failing. It was my head! I now lived in constant fear that others might notice that something was wrong with me. So I tried even harder. Where others wrote neatly and fluidly in beautiful handwriting, with notebook pages that looked like paintings, I hacked the pages of the copybook to pieces because my hand would not obey, simply stopped against my will, cramped up, and pressed so hard on the nib that it tore holes in the paper and got stuck. Blotches! Whenever I read something, it was as if I had a loose connection in my head. Memorizing a poem was an agony. I was probably a slow ADD dreamer, but back then I felt like a lonely idiot. For even though I was small, I was agile and determined and thus able to take on anyone who tried to tease me. Even when I was obviously outmatched, I could hold my own because I was usually the better runner and by far the best jumper in my age group at school.

In our house, being a victim was considered even worse than being a failure. I had already learned that at an early age. My father would boast to Jews who had "only" been racially persecuted and not imprisoned for twelve years as a "political" opponent like him, that "I was never a victim, I was only an inferior fighter. I didn't wait for anyone to lead me to the slaughter. Because fighting is always worthwhile, even if only for your own pride!"

This statement must have hit the "apolitical Jews," who had "only" been racially persecuted, like a ton of bricks. It certainly made a deep impression on me. If I was no good at anything else, I at least wanted to gain their respect is some other way, whatever the cost. As an only child without older siblings, that was practically impossible. All the other kids had at least two, three, even four siblings and looked like a real family. Not me. I was always the only one standing alone. An outsider. "But that's good practice!" my father would always say to cheer me up.

TO EACH THEIR OWN

"I don't normally talk to strangers, you know. My mother told me not to. After all, I'm only ten years old. A ten-year-old girl can talk to strangers but only about things like timetables, where to get sandwiches, whether it's raining today, and what movie is showing at the cinema. Harmless stuff. If it's not about stuff like that, then I'm supposed to play dumb and not say anything. I'm not even allowed to keep a diary anymore. There might be something in there that would be bad for us if it fell into other people's hands. But I don't have a dog anymore to tell everything to, so I really do wish I had a diary so that I could write everything down. Today it would say, 'Good Friday 1933 is the worst day of my life. I don't know if the worst is yet to come.'

And thank you, sir, for comforting me when I got on the train earlier and was crying my eyes out. But please don't think that just because you were kind to me, bought me something to drink and three sandwiches, and lent me your handkerchief that I'm going to become trusting all of the sudden. But I am desperate to talk to someone! Earlier, when the police and the two SA men were going through the train, I noticed that you turned very pale. You seemed to be just as scared as I was. They're looking for you, aren't they?

Stupid question. Pardon me! Sometimes I'm still a child. By the way, my name is Hella.

But I can tell someone like you, why I'm sitting here alone on the train and crying. Because I don't know where I'm supposed to go. My mother was arrested today around lunchtime! I had just finished cleaning for Easter and had put a cake in the oven. My mother was sewing the last of the coats that she had been working on. She had to get them ready for delivery on Saturday. My mother sews coats at home. Piecework, if you know what that is. Then suddenly ole Minna came running in. She's not quite right in the head. 'War, war, the soldiers are coming!' she shouted and ran back and forth in front of our fence. We knew right away what had happened: A raid with arrests! Mother immediately tipped out my school bag and put the party flag, the membership card, and papers at the bottom, then the exercise books, the work bag, and the pencil case. Then she sent me off with the satchel on my back, saying, 'If someone asks you, you go to class 4a at the Hindenburg School in Rosenthal with Mrs. Schubert! You forgot a notebook with your teacher and have to pick it up.'

I didn't think that story was all that convincing, but I couldn't think of anything better. She didn't tell me where I should go. The police had already closed one exit and I had to run in the other direction as quickly as possible, acting harmless and not the least bit suspicious. I'm good at pretending, you know. That's what you have to do to live illegally, my mother says. But now I was in a jam: Where was I supposed to go with the flag and the party cards in my bag? Definitely not to anyone in the party. Not even to a close relative. Who isn't politically suspect? Who is the least likely to be associated in any way with my mom? I thought about her best friend, Aunt Martha. But she is Jewish and has her own worries now that her husband, the judge, is no longer allowed to work. And then I suddenly remembered my father.

My parents are divorced. And angry that my mother had left him, my father set fire to our house. After three years in prison, he got out and tried to get in touch with my brother and me. He begged us to please, please forgive him. But my brother Peter said no way and refused to see him. And I don't let myself be so easily duped either. Adults think children are so stupid, like they can all be so easily fooled. But even if I wouldn't see him, I secretly hid the note with his address inside my pencil case. Thank goodness!

He was beside himself with joy when I turned up out of nowhere. I told him straight away that he now had the chance to make up for his mistake back then with deeds instead of words. He listened to me and bricked up all the stuff in his bakery. After that, I wanted to hurry home. My father wanted to take me in the tram, but I said that wasn't possible. It would be best if he weren't seen with me, I told him, for his sake and for mom's safety. He understood and I could see that he was very proud of me.

When I got home, I discovered that my mother had disappeared. Arrested. No one knew where she had been taken. Our house had been completely trashed. My cake was trampled on the kitchen floor. Flour, sugar, salt, rice, milk. All dumped out. All the cushions, all the mattresses, pillows, and feather duvets had been thrown out. Beds were slashed open, feathers scattered everywhere. What a mess! They had even destroyed my schoolbooks and toys. What kind of people would do such a thing? But the worst thing was that the coats my mother had finished sewing and was going to deliver on Saturday were also ruined. That will be deducted from her wages.

Completely upset, I kept walking through the rooms, not knowing what to do next. Then I thought, knowing my mother she kept her wits about her and left me a message somewhere. And she did! In the toilet, on the edge of the newspaper we use as toilet paper, she had hastily written in pencil that I should go to her brother, Uncle Rudolf, in the Harz Mountains. I could borrow money from the neighbor Mrs. Kuth. And Mrs. Kuth went to the station with me and sent an express telegram to Uncle Rudi: Oda arrested +++ Daughter Hella arriving Seesen 1 o'clock! +++.

When I arrived in Seesen shortly after one o'clock, Uncle Rudolf was standing on the platform in his SA uniform with Aunt Bertha. Although no one else was there, they kept looking around to make sure no one saw them with me. Ten minutes later, they put me on the return train back to Berlin. And here I am! But why are you crying? It didn't happen to you, it happened to me. You're going to Prague. Out of Germany.

My mother could perhaps go to Russia. She was born in Moscow and speaks perfect Russian. But there's a catch. Precisely because she speaks Russian and was once a noblewoman, the Soviet Union might not be so good for her either, people told her.

A while back she was supposed to visit the Soviet Union with a party delegation. She was a comrade who had earned such a privilege. But in the end, it didn't happen. Everyone got a visa, except my mother. Probably because of her supposed right-wing activities. In other words, her collaboration with people who were Social Democrats and so on. That's what we conjecture at any rate.

Either way, she had her own opinion on the matter and said that the czarina wasn't the only one that they'd built Potemkin villages for. She later explained to me what a Potemkin village is because I didn't know. But since then, she has listened very carefully to what Russian emigrants have been saying. They're not all reactionaries and bad people, you know? In any case, she lectured me on how religion is the enemy of the people. Only reason and doubt can help us progress. I don't know anyone who believes in God, except for the really religious Catholic woman in our garden colony.

If you believe in your God that's why you leave Germany. That makes sense. But he should at least protect you since you're a good person!

My mother told me that we can't get out of here anymore. We have to stay in Germany and defend ourselves honestly, whether we like it or not. That's how it is for all poor people, she says. Look, the sun is already coming up! Yes, look fast! There, well, I'll be a monkey's uncle! Look up there, up there by the chimney! I can't believe it, there's a red flag flying! A red flag on the highest smokestack in Berlin! Isn't that something? The Nazis will be fuming!

Ha ha ha! Isn't that great!

Well, I'm home now! Thank you for everything and good luck in Prague!"

A HIGHLY TREASONOUS UNDERTAKING

On a fine spring morning, atop Berlin's tallest factory smokestack a red flag flapped gaily in the morning breeze. Red Wedding was sticking its tongue out at Hitler! It was May 2, 1933, the day the Nazis officially outlawed all trade unions. The factory sirens had begun to wail for the early shift to start. The workers were pushing their way through the turnstile, smirking and elbowing each other in the ribs. Berliners don't wear their hearts on their sleeves. So to mask their astonishment, they made bets: How long would it be before one of the brownshirts had the guts to climb up the chimney to tear down the red cloth?

For two days the factory chimney had remained cold. Sunday was the usual day off and that particular Monday, May 1st, was a holiday. Every other day, however, it was scorching hot and impossible to climb. Someone had obviously known that.

To calculate their bets, the workers first tilted their heads far back and then sized up the big clock on the nearby factory building. Speculations about the feasibility, the possible sequence, and the time required to remove the flag were making the rounds. After thirty minutes, the odds were already 1:3 for two hours, 2:1 for four, and 3:1 for five.

A spectacle such as this was very much in keeping with the tastes of the proletarian public. They jeered and howled as they watched the various unsuccessful attempts to climb the red-hot, forty-meter-tall smokestack. First the police and then the fire department made a go of it. But the firetrucks' aerial ladders were far too short and only made the authorities look pathetic for even trying. The "necktie nerds," as the factory workers referred to the white-collar workers, who now hurried past the men in flat caps with angrily pinched faces, drew mild derision from the crowd of onlookers.

This daring display of the red flag couldn't have been carried out in fulfillment of party orders. It was much too populist for that. You could certainly accuse the German Communist Party of many things but humor and being in touch with the common man were not among them. Someone had acted of their own accord. A petty-bourgeois, individualistic, anarchic act, which hovered somewhere above drunken prank and political protest in such a liberating and yet completely useless way that it warmed the hearts of everyone. On the very day that Hitler had banned all the trade unions and occupied their headquarters, one person was whistling at the brown state's power and all the red party lines! Perhaps a whippersnapper? A holy fool from the northeastern suburbs?

Even Martha couldn't fail to notice the curious energy coming from the Berliners that Tuesday morning as she was making her way to the station. Instead of the usual grumpy morning mugs, she saw sparkling eyes, and confident, smiling faces, and even—it was hard to believe—a faint flicker of pride, pride that someone had really shone "them" up today. Maybe everyone wasn't celebrating, but it sure looked like well over half the people she passed were. When was the last time that she had seen such an expression on the haggard faces of ordinary Berliners? Could they perhaps still pluck up their courage? Find resolve? Still cling to the hope that Germany could produce something other than bootlickers and yes-men?

"They still haven't got the flag down! None of the jackboots dares to climb up there. Must be damn hot, and til they shut down the furnace and the smokestack has cooled down, well, that can take a while. But if they don't, it's bye-bye til Sunday! Ha ha ha! In the meantime, look at the Nazis down below! They sure are wearing a groove in the sidewalk, running back and forth, 'cause they can't do a thing! Well, far out! I'll be damned," went the murmurs. "If they catch whoever did it, it's so long and good night!"

Meanwhile, Martha was elsewhere with her thoughts. She was at her wit's end. Ever since Leopold had been summarily dismissed from his post as senior judge of the higher regional court of appeal because of his Jewish ancestry, all he did was sit in the study and stare at the wall for hours on end. "Even a pickled herring remains a herring," chuckled Leopold Hartmann, a.k.a., Hirschfeld, as he mumbled to himself this hackneyed Jewish saying that rejects the idea that you can simply get rid of your Jewishness through baptism and assimilation. After a time, however, he no longer said anything at all. It was clear to Martha that Leopold was in a serious crisis, having a mental breakdown in slow motion. But Leopold brusquely refused the medical assistance that Martha had summoned in the form of the neurologist, Dr. Süverkrüp.

Their twin sons Siegmund and Siegfried had been following Martha for weeks, their faces contorted to permanent scowls. They blamed their mother for the fact they, too, were suddenly Jewish. It was her fault that they were no longer welcome at the swimming club. Just three days ago they had learned that they were full Jews! Full Jews! They couldn't believe it. It had been their dearest wish to become members of the Hitler Youth. Tough as nails and swift as greyhounds. And suddenly they had been declared completely un-Aryan? You couldn't be more German than their very German nationalist father, the former senior judge of the higher regional court of appeal, Leopold Hartmann, Esq.! They were horrified to discover that not only was their mother, Martha Hartmann, Jewish, but their father was too! Their mother was even cheeky enough to continue being a paying member of the Jewish congregation. That was why, the twins agreed, they were suddenly being treated so badly. They gave their father credit for having at least tried to stop being Jewish. They now referred to their mother as "the dirty Jew who stinks up our house." They refused to sit at the table with her in the dining room. They demonstrably grabbed their plates, marched briskly out of the room and ate their meals in their bedrooms.

Leopold no longer reacted to any of this. He simply continued to shovel his food down his throat, as if completely unaware of what was happening around him. When his plate was empty and dessert finished, he rose from the table. Without uttering a single word, he then retreated into the dark realm of his study, slumping into his leather armchair and staring at the wall with the deer antlers.

"Else, something has to be done!" Out of breath, Martha stormed through Else's grand marble entrance, without so much as a greeting, thrust her hat, gloves, and coat into the hands of the curtsying maid.

"Martha, something's always happening with you!" Else said, trying to slow her down. "Granted, usually nothing good! Come in and sit down!"

Else couldn't stand it when visitors blurted out sensitive family matters while still standing in the stairwell. Especially in this current political climate. Deeply annoyed, she assumed a sharper tone than usual when she barked instructions to the maid who had taken Martha's things, adding, "And then please take the coffee and pastries to the green parlor immediately, do you hear? You may then be dismissed. We don't wish to be disturbed, understood?"

Before Martha could launch into her story, Else stopped her by putting a finger to her lips, holding it like that until the maid was out of the room and a few steps down the hallway, and thus out of earshot. "Let me tell you something before you launch in. Yesterday, Elli up and left the country! A few days ago, she managed to sell the sports store for a reasonably good price. She had already moved out of her apartment a week ago and stayed with friends. She's now on a train to Vienna. She's storing her furniture with me, so if you need anything, just let me know. I'll be happy about every chair and every wardrobe I can get rid of."

Else then settled into the green sofa, waiting for Martha to begin her lament. She had good reason to expect such a thing: Martha always had something to complain about when she came to see her, often in the morning. There was nothing you could do but sit back and listen. But instead of a stream of chatter, she heard only silence. Martha, her head turned away from Else, was crying to herself.

"Well, what's the matter? Have you decided to leave the country?"

"Oh, Else. That would at least be a way out. But Leo is completely opposed to the idea of leaving Germany. Not to mention the boys," Martha sobbed and wiped her eyes. "Leo's a lawyer. What could he possibly do somewhere else? Since they showed him the door, it's like he's been chloroformed. He says nothing and just sits there. And my children are Jewish Nazis who hate me! What's going to happen?"

Else and Martha talked for hours and, after a few phone calls, came up with a rescue plan for Martha and the family of the dismissed senior judge of the higher regional court of appeal, Leopold Hartmann, Esq. It was already late in the afternoon by the time that Martha was walking down Chausseestraße, making her way to the Börse station. Her eyes were bleary but her face slightly more at ease.

Hella liked to ride her bike around Berlin. It was the only means of transportation for residents of the Kleintierfarm garden colony and the only way to internalize a map of Berlin. Hella now knew Berlin prisons best of all. When she went to the police station in search of her mother Oda, they couldn't give her any information. Feeling sorry for her, they tried to offer her some help by writing down various addresses on torn-out pieces of paper or on the margins of newspapers. Her older brother Peter was of no help either, because he was also wanted by the police and had to go into hiding. To provide her brother with fresh clothes, food, and mail, she had to meet him in secret at train stations outside the city limits or at night by the back garden fence.

She certainly couldn't expect the neighbors to accompany her on the arduous search for prisons, torture chambers, and other gates of Berlin hell. For now, it was enough that they offered Hella comfort and reassurance; that was enough to help her get through it. "You'll see, in a week your mom will be back like the "Red Hannes" who lives on the main path next to Kaufmann!" Despite such words of comfort, Hella still cried herself to sleep at night.

After a week, Oda was still not back. Other political prisoners had already returned, apparently the authorities had merely wanted to intimate them into submission. Hella didn't know anyone who either could or would help her, leaving her with no other choice than to open the city map herself and find the addresses where her mother might have been taken. With a parcel of laundry attached to the rack and a cake in her bag on the handlebars, she hopped on her bike. Hella got to know all the official prisons with female prisoners as well as the SA's illegal torture dungeons in Berlin, where political prisoners were presumably also being held.

Her schoolmates meanwhile were looking for adventure elsewhere: on trips with the BDM (League of German Girls) or as Hella disdainfully referred to it, "Baby Do Me." Despite such proclamations, she secretly envied them for their smart BDM uniforms and took comfort in the idea that the silly BDM girls didn't have the guts to smuggle a party flag, dangerous papers, and party file cards past the Gestapo in their school folders like she did. But she, on the other hand, didn't sweat it. In fact, Hella found it exciting to be a courier of secret material. She was proud of that. The adults made a big fuss about it, but she outwitted them all—the adults, the police, and the informers.

Since her mother's arrest, Hella, now eleven years old, had been on her own. Only the neighbor and Martha checked in on her from time to time to make sure she had enough money and food. What a big, intelligent girl! At night, no one saw or heard her crying herself to sleep. At a certain point, she forbade herself to think about what could be done to her mother. After recovering from the initial horror over being abandoned and worrying about Oda, she began to feel like a lonely pirate on the high seas: "Only the sky above me," she hummed the song about the thirteenth-century pirate Störtebeker that she had learned at school and shuddered. Was there perhaps something seductive, not merely threatening, in life with so much freedom? She felt a little ashamed that she had even asked such a thing.

Hella finally found her mother at the Columbia Haus, a secret torture prison in Berlin-Templehof that later achieved notoriety. On her visit, Hella was at least allowed to hand over the parcel of clean clothes, soap, cake, and fruit from the garden. Although she had been told by insiders that this was the most horrible place in Berlin, just the mere fact of being able to give her mother these things, gave her a bit of hope. "As long as they accept parcels, everything is fine. It's only bad when you're no longer allowed to do it." On her second visit to the Columbia Haus gate, she was told to wait. "Has something happened?" she asked anxiously. "Has my mother perhaps been transferred to another prison? Can I see her?" No answer.

She was too proud to beg and plead. After an hour of waiting, she was finally allowed to enter. An SA man stood in front of her. He wore oversized boots and had silly, short-cropped hair. Hella eyed him suspiciously, when the man suddenly broke out in a grin. With a silly giggle, he then held his right hand in front of her face and then bent and stretched out his thumb.

"Well, do you recognize me?"

The voice sounded very familiar to her. Good God! "Idiot Kalle," the village idiot from Lübars, who had once nearly hacked off his thumb while chopping wood. In her capacity as a paramedic, Oda had done such a good job of administering first aid to him that the finger had been successfully reattached, which was nothing short of a miracle. Hella suddenly remembered why Kalle had wanted to learn to drill so badly. All the children in Lübars had made fun of him back then. "Idiot Kalle wants to join the SA!"

But the SA didn't want poor Kalle. Not even the Nazis could use someone who was so daft as to confuse left and right. In an effort to teach him the difference, Hella had tied straw to his right arm and hay to his left and alternately commanded "hay" and "straw." Hella eventually grew bored drilling Kalle and decided to focus on catching frogs, which she sold as "weather forecasting frogs" to supplement her allowance. And unfortunately for Kalle, the SA didn't call out "hay" or "straw" when doing foot drills.

"Everything's swell, Hella!" Beaming with joy, SA-Kalle pointed to his moving thumb with the large scar. "I don't get left and right confused no more. You and your mother did a great job helping me back then! A first-rate job!"

"But I don't believe you that you've seen my mother. You're just showing off," replied Hella cheekily. She wanted to pump SA-Kalle for information, hoping he'd take the bait and want to prove her wrong.

He immediately frowned, looking worried, "See her.. See her...! Sure, I saw your mother. Waddya think? She's doing well. Just as someone here can only do well. I ain't the sharpest knife in the drawer, but when someone has helped me once, I'm not gonna leave 'em in the lurch. No matter what. You can ask anyone."

Hella tried to squeeze more out of Kalle, which made him nervous.

"I can't tell you nix but this. I told 'em that your mother is a good nurse, and that's why they've laid off interrogating her. Now she's bandaging the injured and stuff like that. She does a darn good job too. But keep you trap shut. Ain't no one allowed to talk about it."

"Can I see my mom?"

"Again, with the see her, see her, see her?! What is it that you actually have to see? You got nix to see here! Maybe she'll be released soon. Anything can happen with our Führer."

Feeling a tad bit relieved, Hella left the Colombia Haus, walked to her locked bike, and went out into the bright day, pedaling away happily. She wanted to deliver the news right away to Martha, her mother's best friend! Hella stopped at the closest phone booth and dialed the number. No one answered. Then she remembered that Jews were no longer allowed to have telephones. What choice did she have other than to cycle the ten kilometers from Tempelhof to Schmargendorf? She wasn't fazed by the distance. What she didn't want to think about, however, was the roughly twenty-five kilometers from Schmargendorf to Lübars, just as she didn't want to think about whether her chain would come off on the way or whether she would break down with a flat tire. Had the "village idiot" Kalle told her the truth or was he just trying to reassure her? She certainly didn't want to think about that.

Two hours later, Hella turned into the quiet residential block in Schmargendorf. She was looking forward to seeing the relieved expression on Martha's face and to enjoying the lemonade made from real lemons that the Hartmanns always served. It was nothing like the "Prussian lemonade" made from vinegar and sugar that they made at home. Her mother thought lemons were too expensive.

Hella found the shutters down, and even after ringing the doorbell several times, nothing stirred. Hella figured that in this weather they must have gone out to the Havel River or Grunewald Lake. But then she noticed the mailbox stuffed with several days' worth of newspapers. Worried, she rang the neighbors' doorbell. A buxom woman wearing an apron covered in big flowers opened the door. "Well, looks like the Hartmanns have also up and left, just like the Goldsteins from the house on the corner. All of them have been clearing out in the dead of night, most of them going to Switzerland or America!" America sounded like a magic word to Hella. She would also rather be in America.

Disappointed, Hella turned back. Martha's neighbor with the apron didn't look like she would be kind enough to give her a glass of water. So she drank another handful of water from the pump on the corner. It was brown and tasted like rust. She consoled herself that she could buy two pieces of chocolate with the twenty pfennigs that she had saved from the phone call, and then began to make her way home.

"Suum Cuique!" Hella read on the gable of a house. "To each their own." She knew that from her teacher, who had recommended her for a scholarship to an advanced secondary school.

"In the name of the people, the following verdict is reached: The prisoner Walter Kohanim Rubin, born on May 1, 1912, and the brother of the aforementioned, Benno Rubin, born on April 7, 1913, both in Berlin-Wedding, are found guilty of preparing a highly treasonous enterprise, carried out on the premises of the Schering company on the night of April 30 to May 1, 1933. In the main proceeding, the defendant Walter Kohanim-Rubin is found guilty upon the basis of circumstantial evidence of planting a *subversive* red flag on the factory chimney on the night in question with the aim of inciting riots and disturbing the security and peace of the German Reich. As neither of the two defendants made any statements on the matter or the exact course of events, the criminal court finds both defendants equally guilty and thereby sentences them to ten years and four months in prison and hard labor! The defendants' pre-trial detention is credited against the prison term. The defendants shall bear the cost of the proceedings!"

The presiding judge, who had read out the verdict, closed the file, looking pleased with the outcome. An indignant murmur went around the courtroom. In the past, there would have been shouts of "outrageous!" and "class justice!" But in the face of four violent-looking thugs, who were waiting in the courtroom for their chance to swing their truncheons, those in attendance kept such thoughts to themselves. When the work was done, the judge rose to his feet, gathered up the bundles of files and swept out of the courtroom with robes billowing behind him. "Heil Hitler!"

Walter and Benno stood motionless, and merely scowled as they listened to the verdict being read. Looking at Walter though, you could tell that he was champing at the bit and on the verge of launching into an inflammatory speech.

"Keep your trap shut," Benno whispered, putting his hand on his brother's arm. "That's exactly what they're waiting for. So clam it!"

Franziska was sitting in the second row of the gallery next to Bruno and Lotte. She slumped in her seat when they read the sentence. Lotte reached over and patted her hand to comfort her.

"Fränze, the boys are young and healthy, and are sure to get an amnesty soon," Lotte whispered. "Believe me, they won't do ten years."

"Lotte's right. Hitler's not gonna last ten years anyway." Bruno agreed.

"Ten years for such an absurdity, for such a stupid schoolboy prank," Franziska hissed indignantly in the direction of the judge's bench.

"Leave it be, Fränze."

"It's not okay. And I won't leave it be, Bruno!" protested Franziska. "I could never let something like that 'just be.' Never! Do you hear me?!"

The policemen with shiny black shakos on their head looked in their direction.

"Fränze, please don't make a scene. Let's go. Two political prisoners in the family are enough for today," Lotte whispered to her.

Bruno took Franziska's arm and heaved her up from the bench to a standing position. Walter and Benno were now being led out of the courtroom in handcuffs. They quickly exchanged one last glance with their mother and Bruno.

"Take care of Mom," cried Walter to Bruno, who was dragging Fränze and Lotte from the courtroom, past strangers and acquaintances who suddenly wanted to shake Franziska's hand. Bruno was surprised that despite the crackdown on communists, so many people dared to openly show their solidarity. Some furtively raised their fists on the courthouse steps. Agitators perhaps? Several women silently pressed red carnations into Franziska's hands.

"What's that for? This isn't a funeral."

When Bruno and Franziska finally made it home, the entire landing was covered in red carnations.

"That ain't right! Not everyone likes what your two sons have been up to. Not everyone, you hear me?" nagged the apartment-building caretaker. "You gotta clear this all away immediately, you hear? It's a real disgrace! A disgrace!"

"Hey you! Leave the poor woman alone! You hear?!" chimed in neighbors from the second floor.

Greeting cards and post had piled up behind the front door, thrown through the letter slot. Among them was also some hate mail and threats. Before Franziska could discover them and work herself up into a frenzy and start shouting at the walls for hours, Bruno carefully fished out the nasty letters. He tossed them straight into the flames of the kitchen stove, where a pot of coffee that Willi Hörl had put on for everyone was already rattling away. It was probably the first pot of coffee that the head foreman Hörl had ever brewed himself. It was Willi's slightly awkward gesture of solidarity, despite all the political differences between them. His wife's friend had no part in her sons' deed, and her sons' deed had only symbolic character and no practical value. That didn't matter anymore, Willi thought, and snapped his suspenders onto his pants.

"At a time like this, when everything else has failed, we need symbols," Walter had said to him during their last exchange of words about the sense or senselessness of the deed. "The Nazis are currently liquidating the workers' movement. They should see that 'Red Wedding' is alive and kicking."

Willi could only shake his head. Ten years in prison for nothing but symbolism!

"If the communists hadn't divided the workers' movement with their unfounded rumors about the social fascism of the Social Democrats and we had formed a popular front, Hitler would have never come to power," he scolded Walter and Benno both.

"That's too many conjunctives for my taste," Walter had quickly replied, to avoid letting on that Willi was right.

"You mean conditionals," Benno corrected him precociously.

Willi could understand how some people might find such insane deeds uplifting, starving as they were for heroes from among their ranks. The

"Red Berlin" up north had its popular idols, and Franziska was once again honored as the "mother of a hero" as she had been after Walter's sporting victories. Status-conscious Franziska had nothing against such adoration. She was happy to accept her son's populist heroism when it translated into getting the best roast from the sympathetic butcher, and the biggest potatoes and freshest vegetables at the market. Deep down she was convinced that she was entitled to all of it. But the politics confused her. What drove her sons to take such senseless risks without self-interest? That simply flew way over her head. Mother of heroes or no, the family's financial situation had deteriorated even further since the American shares and bonds from Walter's inheritance had vanished into thin air on Black Friday. Now her sons were in prison, and they had nothing left to rely on but the "rinky-dink" plumbing shop. What was she supposed to do? Marry Bruno perhaps?

Without giving it much thought, she sorted all the letters and cards that she had received that day. That's when she found a thick envelope among them with a black border from her sister Fanny as well as another letter with a black border from her cousin Else.

Considering the social status of the deceased, the mourners who gathered at the Berlin Cathedral cemetery on July 12, 1935, were surprisingly few in number. Only around twenty had gathered in the ornate side chapel of the Berlin Cathedral. They all seemed rather lost there. Three coffins stood in front of the altar. The body of an adult was laid out in the middle, flanked to the left and right by two smaller white coffins, children's coffins. No one sat in the front row reserved for the closest family members. Did the once important man really have no relatives? In the second row sat Oda Hanke. Pale and visibly ill, Oda had been released from prison a few days prior. Next to her sat Else and Bruno Dahkne.

"Why don't you sit in the front row? You're a member of the family," Oda asked Else.

"But not directly. We're only relatives by marriage," Else whispered.

The rest of the Jewish relatives stayed away from the funeral service in protest. They did not want to pay their last respects to a convert, suicide victim, and murderer of family members. Apart from Oda, the only person Else Dahnke recognized was Mr. Weinstock, the now-elderly former lawyer for the Kohanims. The family's staff were scattered across the rows. A few of the deceased's former colleagues shifted nervously in the pews, more ashamed than mourning. They were visibly worried about the potential damage that attending the funeral service for their former boss might cause. But they came, nonetheless. They wanted to appear brave for paying their last respects to the departed.

Armed with handkerchiefs, two of the children's teachers had furtively squeezed into the last row. The organ erupted into Handel's "Largo." When the last notes had faded away and the priest had made the sign of the cross, the sermon echoed almost eerily throughout the otherwise empty cathedral.

"Dear relatives and friends of the deceased. We have gathered here today to mourn Leopold Hartmann and his two sons, Siegmund and Siegfried, who after a terrible tragedy have now found eternal peace in God. Let he who is without sin cast the first stone, said our Lord…"

Else didn't want to hear anymore. Together with Martha's sister Fanny Segal, she had been summoned by the police first to her cousin Martha Hartmann's house and then to the morgue to identify the remains. The subsequent police report read as follows:

> *Final protocol on the investigation of the corpses found at Rehwiese 5, in Berlin S/W, on May 28, 1935, 3:35 p.m.*
>
> *The police were called into the abovementioned address at the abovementioned time to investigate the circumstances of the case and for this reason entered the property and house of the Leopold Hartmann family. In the house, the officers, Chief Inspector Wlodarchyk accompanied by Constable Henschke, found four bodies, which were the mortal remains of the Jew, Leopold Hirschfeld, a.k.a., Hartmann, his wife, the Jew Martha Hirschfeld, a.k.a., Hartmann, née Kohanim, as well as the children, the twins Siegmund and Siegfried Hartmann. The bodies were positively identified by the relatives, the Jew Fanny Segal, née Kohanim, sister of the fatally injured wife, and Else Dahnke, née Segall, cousin of the fatally injured wife Martha (see Appendix 1). The bodies showed fatal gunshot wounds to the heads by one bullet each (38 mm). Each individual shot led to immediate death (see Appendix 2). Death occurred around 10 or 11 p.m. on May 27, 1935. Concerning how the crime was committed:*
>
> *No foreign traces were found at the crime scene to suggest the involvement of third parties. The children Siegfried and Siegmund were killed in their beds in the order mentioned above, followed by*

the wife in the shared bedroom (see Appendix 3, Forensic Report on the Trace Evidence). Based on the traces of smoke on the hands and sleeves of the head of the family's robe and the murder weapon, which Leopold Hirschfeld, a.k.a., Hartmann, was found holding in his right hand with his right index finger bent at the trigger of the revolver, sitting at the desk in his study, it is beyond doubt that this was an extended suicide, i.e., the killing of a family by the father, who then killed himself by his own hand.

The suspected motive: forced action due to mental derangement. This suspicion is substantiated by the fact that the above-mentioned officials found in the wife's desk first-class ship passages for July 1, 1935, for the entire family from Bremen to Boston, together with passports with valid entry visas to the United States of America as well as an employment contract from the Boston law firm Shapiro & Feldman together with a work visa for the lawyer Leopold Hirschfeld, a.k.a., Hartmann, issued in the name of Leopold Hirschfeld. This evidence indicates that the Hirschfeld/Hartmann family wanted to leave Germany on July 1, 1935, the date of the ship passages, to build a new life for themselves in the United States of America. This evidence in particular suggests that the crime was committed by the father, Leopold Hirschfeld, a.k.a., Hartmann, in a fit of mental derangement.

Signed by Senior Detective Superintendent Osterholz
Signed by Detective Superintendent Kölling

Appendices:
forensic investigation report, autopsy report, statements of identification by relatives

Three cabs were waiting in front of the Berlin Cathedral to take some of the mourners to the next funeral service. The cars made their way to the Weißensee Jewish cemetery. It was here that Martha would finally be laid to rest next to her beloved Willy Rubin. Willy Rubin's gravestone had been inscribed in the meantime. In golden letters. An act of mercy from his sister-in-law, Fanny Segal, who finally wanted to put an end to the family scandal. On each stone it read: "Rest in peace," in the second person plural.

STALIN IS DEAD!

In the early morning hours of March 6, 1953, I heard the newspaper rattling in the mail slot and then hitting the linoleum floor. I tiptoed through the hallway. I wanted to be quiet. In the living room, I lay down on the Persian rug, spread out the newspaper, and tested my reading skills as I did every morning. "Stalin is dead!" Happy to be able to read such important news, I walked around with the newspaper in my hand and sang: "Stalin is dead! Tralala! Stalin is dead! Tralala!" into my parents' bedroom. I saw their faces blush deep red before rolling apart from each other. I had forgotten to knock, but that day they didn't get mad at me. "Stalin is dead," I crowed into their coitus interruptus. My father snatched the newspaper out of my hand, and I managed to slip under the warm comforter into the gap between them. I kept my cold hands on my father's stomach and my cold feet between my mother's warm thighs. That was perhaps the happiest morning of my childhood: Stalin was dead, and instead of fighting as they usually did, my parents were being peaceful, and warming up each other and me. My father immediately complained about the newspaper photo, which showed people almost theatrically distraught as they gathered around Stalin's corpse. My overly cautious mother promptly warned him not to rejoice so loudly. Because of the neighbors. "They can all kiss my ass!" my father shouted up to the ceiling with a laugh. One-hundred-and-fifty-percent loyal party members from Saxony lived above us. As my mother knew, they were reliable Stasi informants.

That morning my father once again resembled a young version of the German writer, Erich Kästner. He couldn't leave the subject of the photo alone. "You can learn something here, girl!" he said. Then, in a mockingly conspiratorial tone, he continued. "That picture's a lie, of course!" He slapped the paper angrily with the back of his hand. "But they're all really sad, Dad," I protested meekly. "Exactly! That's the power of words! You can put practically anything into people's heads, even against their better judgement and experience, just like these people in the picture! Every single one of them has lost at least one family member in the gulags that Stalin sent them to, but they still act as if the world had ended with Stalin's death. So remember one thing: no fist is as strong, no sword as sharp as the word! Only with the word can you really set the world on fire: Moses, Buddha, Christ, Mohammed, Karl Marx! Compared to them, all other world conquerors like Alexander the Great or Napoleon are incompetent fools. Today they rule the world, tomorrow they are almost totally forgotten. Only the poets live forever! At their core, the founders of religions and ideologies are also just poets," he added.

Skeptical, I looked over at my know-it-all mother.

"Yes, yes! You can really get your mouth scalded on the big word," she grumbled as if on cue.

"All these shitty slogans only hurt the people who believe in them!"

That day she finished her complaining with astonishing speed and even flashed my questioning face a conciliatory smile. "For once, your father is right," she said.

Words, such seemingly harmless little words, were supposed to have such an effect? I was dumbfounded. Equally astonishing was the fact that my mother was in a great mood on the day of Stalin's death, even though it was Friday and once again time to clean the house. Throughout that whole day joy prevailed. No bickering. No arguing. To celebrate, my parents treated themselves to a bottle of Tokay and even let me lick the glasses afterward.

"Everything will be different now," my father trumpeted in high spirits during his second daily shave in the mirror by the kitchen door. "You'll see!"

My mother remained ambiguously silent and, as usual, the edges of her mouth twitched skeptically. But even she couldn't deny that Stalin's death in 1953 heralded an early spring. Gloomy East Berlin seemed less gray. Almost dove gray. People's eyes lit up in a way that I had never seen before.

I also felt lighthearted that March. I had finally managed to be accepted into the boys' club! For some odd reason, only boys lived on our block. If I didn't want to be bored, I had to fit in somehow. A girl, much too short for her age, with black hair and cherry eyes, surrounded by a bunch of blond, course-featured brats who would have done credit to any butcher's shop or farm! They weren't eager to have me around. Not that I had expected anything other than rejection. My only way to shine was with courage and good ideas. I had been able to observe as much from the window.

My test of courage came sooner than expected. Behind the hospital meadow and the sports fields stood huge iron towers for the overhead power lines. The pylons were about forty meters high.

"Are you brave enough to climb up one?"

"Sure, I am. But I'm only gonna do it, if you show you ain't no sissies and you do it too! 'Cause I ain't interested in being around a bunch of sissies," I answered cheekily. They liked that.

So we all climbed up. The boys lost their courage between twenty and twenty-five meters up. I was the only one who climbed all the way to the windswept, swaying peak. I was fine until I got to the top and looked down. That's when I got queasy. It wasn't so much the height as the fire department, which had driven up with flashing blue lights, and the large crowd of people that had gathered there. If I had had the option either to stay up or fly away, I would have stayed or flown. There was a lot of trouble waiting for me down there. As I climbed down, accompanied by the oohs and aahs of the gawkers, I recognized my mother in the crowd.

I almost let go of the last iron strut out of fright. Her slanted eyes looked dark and scary. She took me in her arms, sobbing. The love lasted only a short time. At home, I received the biggest spanking my bottom has ever had to endure. But such suffering was nothing, because it served a higher purpose. My position in the boys' club was now unassailable! My mother soon tired me out with the carpet beater, and my father, who never hit his wife or child, fled the house, as he always did when I was about to be beaten. My proven fearlessness with bravely endured beatings instilled a deep respect in all the children in the street. In recognition of my courage and bravery, I was offered the status of diplomat of the gang. The unspoken implication was that in the future it would be my job to keep them entertained. New pranks, new games, and the temptation to try out the power of words.

There was a bombed-out villa nearby that we liked to play in. I began to spread the rumor that it was haunted. I told them that around midnight little children would walk around with their severed heads under their arms, and that the heads would cry out loudly, calling for their mothers. On some days, around dusk, the ghosts would also be out and about, I said. When the group came to the ruins one late fall around dusk, the wind howled, and strange sounds rang out as the breeze passed through the iron window bars. The boys ran away screaming in horror. I laughed to myself and felt infinitely superior.

A few days later, I told them that you could expel the ghosts by barricading all the windows and doors with stinging nettles. As expected, the boys yanked up all sorts of nettles, which resulted in them breaking out in serious rashes across their hands, arms, and legs.

"Now we have to go through the house in groups of three and sing among the nettles."

However, only Manne, the leader of our gang, and I were willing to do it. The others were all too scared.

"I'm not sure if it will work with only two," I warned.

After Manne and I disappeared through the entrance, I made him swear to secrecy and then confessed to him my dirty trick.

"You made it all up? You were just pulling our leg the whole time?" Manne exclaimed in amazement. Manni and I now shared a secret in common that cemented our leadership. This was probably how religions came into being, I concluded. We sang as we skipped around the ruins and had to keep hard from breaking out in laughter. My parents were perplexed when they heard about my spooky tale and shook their heads. "Yeah, that's pretty much how the world works. But don't you go messing with that stuff anymore. Got that?!" Upset, I simply nodded. What a shame, I thought, and reluctantly promised that I would never do it again.

"Where did the child get the impulse to do such a thing?" my mother wondered.

"Aunt Martha sends her love," my father concluded. "God and the Blessed Mother forbid it!"

I never did figure out how Catholic exhortations ended up in our atheist household.

My mother could obviously read my thoughts and said, "Remember your great-aunt Martha, the baroness of lies! Don't end up like her!"

A few weeks later, on the morning of June 17th, we were woken up when our entire apartment house started shaking and swaying. Glasses in the vitrine were leaping off the glass shelves. The huge crystal trophy that my father had won as the victor in the Berlin road race danced perilously close to the edge of the buffet on which it was perched. I was just barely able to catch it.

"Get away from the window!" my mother shouted as I was about to stick my head between the curtains. Down the street, there was an endless column of Russian tanks. Soldiers peered out the tanks with machine guns at the ready.

Unfortunately, my mother didn't hide my father's pants, the way my grandmother had hid Bruno's. If she had, our lives would certainly have been very different. So, despite all the warnings, after curfew was lifted, my father grabbed his racing bike and rode to the headquarters of Sternradio, his Patenbetrieb.[10] As a former communist cadre, he was in charge of maintaining relations with the radio station and his employer, the police department. In the evening, just before curfew, my father came home. Pale as a sheet, he fell onto the nearest chair and started howling. He screamed like an animal. Never in my life have I ever heard a person scream and cry in such pain. As he explained to my mother, he had taken the side of the workers who had revolted and declared his resignation from the party in a fiery speech in front of several thousand people. "A party that shoots at the workers is no longer my party!"[11] With that, he pulled his party card out of his pocket and theatrically threw it at the feet of important party members sitting at the podium. To the applause of the workers, he left the hall with his head held high. Undefeated in defeat! A grand exit!

At that moment of crisis, my mother revealed what she was made of. She insisted that my father go immediately to St. Joseph's Catholic Hospital to see Dr. Kastner, the Catholic doctor. Dr. Kastner was her former reliable partner in the underground. During the Nazi era, he had allowed her to hide people hiding from the Nazis in the isolation ward. Two hours later, my father was lying in a mental hospital, diagnosed with a "nervous breakdown." As my mother had rightly feared, the doorbell rang the following morning, shortly before six o'clock. I opened it. Two men in dark green leather overcoats, one with a beret without a small tail on top; the other with a mud-colored felt hat pulled down low over his face, wanted to speak to my father.

They entered our apartment on soft crepe-soled shoes, the kind you only saw in the West. My mother shooed me away into the kitchen. There was a short, heated exchange of words in which my mother's voice sounded firm and calm, which reassured me. This was the first visit from the state security henchmen, known as "the Stasi." When they had left without having accomplished anything, my mother said, "Your father won't be going to jail as a political prisoner in Germany a second time! I can promise you that much!"

SAVE YOURSELF, IF YOU CAN!

Walter arrived at Ettersberg hill in August 1937. The air was humid and heavy with anticipation of a storm to break the tension. In the distance, below the gloomy clouds, stood the remains of Goethe's famous beech tree, under which Goethe once loved to rest and under which he wrote to Frau Stein in 1776:

Thou that from the heavens art,
Every pain and sorrow stillest,
And the doubly wretched heart
Doubly with refreshment fillest,
I am weary with contending!
Why this pain and desire?
Peace descending
Come ah, come into my breast!

Walter wished he could walk in Goethe's footsteps here. With Weimar in the valley below, he would lie under Goethe's beech tree, and feel the spirit of the landscape and German classicism. At twilight, they would light the first lamps, and the faint strains of "The Wanderer's Night Song" would waft up the hillside.

Before he could finish setting the scene, a truncheon hit him hard in the back, reminding him that he had not arrived at the most German of places as part of a field trip organized by the Marxist evening school. Neither had the hundreds of others who were being herded up the "Caracho Path" beaten and yelled at by SS officers along the way.

So this is what you call Buchenwald!

He instinctively fell into a jog so that the camp thugs would have a hard time keeping up with him. Then, adjusting his breathing to account for a steady uphill run, he slid into the protective center of the marching column. The best tactical position was always in the middle of the third row from the front, just like at the start of a bicycle race. From there, you could control the front of the field. If necessary, it was always possible to shift to the right or to the left or up to the front as well as to strategically retreat to the rear. What you didn't want to do, however, was run toward the front of the pack. The front is where pure panic prevailed, where you could smell men's fear.

When he caught sight of the horror in his comrades' eyes, Walter Rubin-Kohanim cursed his archenemy, the "bootlicker" Erich Honecker, and not for the first time. Walter and his "comrade" Honecker had spent time in Brandenburg prison together. It was Honecker who had made sure that Walter's name appeared on the list of those inmates assigned to Buchenwald. That scheming taskmaster was always out to get him, whether they were comrades or not. Unfortunately, you couldn't choose your comrades. Once this whole Nazi nightmare was over, Walter would settle the score with this Saarland roofer. The Nazis couldn't last forever!

At a mere twenty-one years old, he was an incurable optimist. As he later realized, this attitude would prove to be of vital importance under the circumstances, especially when combined with the freshness of his youth and his good health that he had steeled to perfection through cycling and ice swimming in winter. He also came to see that his childhood experience in the orphanage prepared him for dealing with hierarchies. In addition to living with enforced discipline, as a child he had also become familiar with the secret rules of the mob. His personal disputes with the bootlicker, Erich Honecker, in the Brandenburg prison aside, from his very first day in captivity, he was able to draw on his secret wealth of experience.

Unlike the other prisoners, he did not plunge into a dark hole of depression, despair and helplessness when faced with the indignity of losing his independence and the humiliation of his powerlessness. He was able to immediately adapt to the new situation. He saw it as a long, hard test he had to pass. He felt up to the challenge and was almost as alert and confident as before a competition.

Then suddenly his group landed in the roll call area. Because he had not been paying attention during the line organization, he found himself back in the dangerous outer row, though fortunately farther back in the group.

An emaciated prisoner with a gaunt face snapped him back to attention. Pushing a wheelbarrow full of boulders, he hissed through his teeth as he rolled past, "King Kong, do you hear me?" he asked, "If they ask your profession, you're a bricklayer! Bricklayer!"

The man, who was clearly not of the right stature for such a heavy cart, wore a red triangle and must therefore have been a comrade. The fact that he knew him by his nickname suggested that he was either a Berliner or knew something about cycling. Less than a half an hour later, Walter, Prisoner No. 3468, was a registered bricklayer in Construction Squad I. After changing into his striped prisoner's uniform with the red and yellow triangles, he climbed into wooden clogs, while his feet adjusted to the unfamiliar feeling of foot wraps instead of socks. He then went in search of the barracks. The sky looked ominous, like a storm was on its way. Down in the valley, lightning was already flashing over Weimar. Thunder rolled in the distance and the wind swept a few noxious gusts uphill. A prisoner in his mid-forties, with a stocky build and an intelligent face, a red triangle on his chest and back, was heading towards Walter, who was still awaiting orders at the door to the orderly room.

"Comrade, tell me, where are the barracks or lodgings?" Walter asked. "Ha! You're a real joker, aren't you?" said the man with the intelligent face above the red triangle, letting out a loud, rumbling laugh. "In the planning stages, my boy, in the planning stages! And you are cordially invited to build your own prison! There are no umbrellas either." Walter stared at him in confusion. "My name is Seifert, head of Construction Brigade I! Everyone here obeys my command, and I only say everything once. Even to you, King Kong! And we need a few reliable, strong guys to break the hegemony of the criminals. Do I need to explain more?"

Walter swallowed and shook his head. He had understood. He would either be Seifert's tool, or he wouldn't be at all.

Just then, raindrops the size of thalers fell from the sky and a tropical thunderstorm descended on Ettersberg. In August 1937, Buchenwald consisted of a sodden area with a few thousand people, ten latrines, and a few backless tents. Thus, unless you had the privilege of being invited by Comrade Seifert into the temporary shelter used to protect sacks of cement, you were immediately soaked to the skin and would remain so. An electric fence surrounded the whole area. Those who couldn't find shelter in the dugouts or the few tents slept in the mud or squatted down soaking wet. Their arms wrapped tightly around their knees, they tucked their heads between their knees for protection, until fever mercifully warmed them.

Walter slowly realized what mazel he had that he, of all possible people, was under Seifert's protection, and that in this place, Seifert was the party. And here the party was the ticket to life!

At that moment, Walter thanked God, on whom he otherwise never wasted a single thought. He had not ever doubted or anything like that but from that moment on, he knew that his stocks had clearly more than doubled.

"Let me tell you something, Berlin Charleston king and bike racing master: I don't tolerate any indiscipline, or any loners either. I know your entire story, my friend!" Seifert shook his finger at him as if he were his great uncle. "And one of our rules is that theft from comrades is punishable by death, same goes for betrayal." "That's no problem for me," Walter declared. "Don't be so cocky! We'll see about that!"

It wasn't long before Walter had a chance to prove himself when the decisive test of power occurred within the camp.

"It's either us or them!" said Comrade Seifert, summing up the situation before explaining his plan to the few initiates, the cadres, and the party fighters.

Walter was considered a "fighter candidate," who still needed to prove himself. What followed was a short summary of how they, as the "spearhead of the working class," would break the regime of terror being run by the criminal kapos, who were using Mafia tactics to rob their non-criminal fellow inmates, in additional to sadistically torturing them and beating them to death for no reason at all. The political prisoners tended to have more education and had thus been given responsibilities in the camp's offices. From their inside positions, they miraculously made the worst leaders and criminal kapos disappear, employing such strategies as producing marching orders to distant outposts and other camps.

Meanwhile, Walter's baptism by fire consisted of cutting a splint on a brake pin. Silently. Undetected. At the right time.

With a "L'Chaim!" Walter released the lock on a fully loaded truck. In complete silence, the wheels of the heavy vehicle started to move. Down in the little valley, the truck full of stones buried the camp's two criminal leaders, whom a "runner' for the political prisoners had deliberately positioned at the right spot underneath the slope. At the party's request. Walter prayed for the men he had to kill, a Psalm that he had not uttered since his childhood in the Jewish orphanage:

We all, like sheep, have gone astray;
each of us has turned to our own way.
And the lord has laid on him
the iniquity of us all.
For he was cut off from the land of the living;
for the transgression of my people he was punished!
Amen![12]

Walter, the atheist, was now also one of God's servants. Here, at Buchenwald, however, God was the party and Seifert its high priest.

The next morning, Walter was solemnly elevated to the rank of combat cadre by Seifert in a small ceremony in which everyone raised their clenched fists. Walter's loss of innocence after successfully liquidating the enemy was sweetened by better food and membership in the camp aristocracy. He was moved from "fighter candidate" to simply "fighter."

When the camp's criminal green corps wished to strike back against the Reds, they stumbled into a trap that Seifert and the comrades had set for them. The green corps gangsters were caught by the SS with concealed weapons. At the morning roll call, the SS executed eight murderers and robbers in front of all the inmates.

There was nobody to mourn them.

As the Buchenwald concentration camp's social structure began to take shape, the Red Brigades became more important, as did the role of the communists in the camp's underground. The SS was satisfied. At last, order and discipline prevailed without them having to make any great effort, the work ran like clockwork. Political prisoners were even responsible for the paperwork. They were left to their own devices. For the time being.

Life at the camp changed abruptly after the SS indiscriminately liquidated a few communists. The following night, "The Internationale" rang out across the camp. The SS went on a rampage. But where they tried to intervene, everyone fell silent, and the singing would flare up again in another part of the camp. And because the song was a signal and a means of binding the resistance, the SS seized the founder and leader of the prisoners' choir "The Zebras," Prisoner No. 3468, Walter Kohanim-Rubin.

With a blow to the teeth with the butt of a rifle, the SS thugs made it clear that this wouldn't be just a chat by the light of a very bright lamp. Walter's lip was split open; the blood was running down in streams. He tested the solidity of his teeth with his tongue. They were intact. Beating him, the SS men drove Walter toward a tree, where they tied his arms behind his back and hung him upside down. People called this common form of torture, "tree hanging," and the pain was indescribable.

"We can do this for days. So come out with it and tell us who's behind the campaign! We know you're deeply involved, so who else?" The SS men had long known that Walter could only name two other prisoners. The contact man before and after him. The conspiratorial structure of the camp's underground organization, an organization in cells of three co-conspirators each, was such that each could betray at most two other co-conspirators. After that, the chain broke. The SS were not often lucky enough to have two tortured prisoners, organized into two subordinate cells, "spill" names or prisoner numbers to reveal an entire cell with a higher-ranking cadre. The fear of being liquidated by their comrades if they betrayed them was even greater than the fear of the SS torture and immediate death.

"Now you can sing, you little robin!"

Walter's torturer spoke with a Bavarian accent. "I'm hearing nothing. Why am I hearing nothing? You red dog, damn watchman!" With that, he once again shoved the butt of his gun into Walter's ribs with full force and then into his genitals. "Sing, birdie, sing!"

Walter took a deep breath and imagined himself far away, sending his soul into an unreachable orbit. He forced his thoughts to seek a foothold in familiar verses:

To be, or not to be, that is the question:
Whether 'tis nobler in the mind to suffer
The slings and arrows of outrageous fortune,
Or to take arms against a sea of troubles
And by opposing end them. To die—to sleep,
No more; and by a sleep to say we end
The heart-ache and the thousand natural shocks...

He didn't know how many more times they hit him. He dreamed of the distant school lesson in the assembly hall when he recited Hamlet's monologue on stage in his shorts and even the hated Mr. Fleischhut couldn't help but be moved.

When his arms finally gave out while hanging from the tree, he passed out. His teeth chattering, he woke up hours later in a bunker, a lightless concrete chamber measuring 1.5 meters square, filled ankle-deep with ice-cold water. During Walter's transport to the bunker Rudi Seifert saw to it that his arms were popped back into place.

In the pitch-black dungeon, you could neither lie down, nor sit, not even prop yourself up diagonally. You could only sit down in the cold water or bend at the waist or crouch in complete darkness with your feet in the water.

The SS man on duty, Harald Sommer, briefly wondered whether he would be better off killing such a "tough nut" as No. 3468 with a revolver. But then he remembered his wife. "The Zebras" were supposed to sing his wife a birthday serenade the following week and No. 3468 was the choir's leader and had already rehearsed the song with them. Sommer didn't want to risk a dissonant serenade as his marriage didn't happen to be going so well just then.

Plus, No. 3468, who had been led out of the dungeon more dead than alive, had something that had become more precious than gold in the camp's daily life: laughter. His parodies of Hans Moser, Theo Lingen, and Hans Albers made everyone laugh. Prisoners and guards alike. It was partly the memory of those parodies that inspired Sommer to put his revolver back in his holster and motion with a jerk of his head to the kapos who were dragging No. 3468 along to "let him go." Walter spent an entire week there, as he later learned when he was in the infirmary. Having passed his second test, he now belonged to the upper cadre.

The daylight hurt his eyes, which were still blinded by darkness. He had to hold his hands up to shield them as he slowly emerged from his dungeon, first sliding on his knees, then staggering step by step. The sun had never felt so wonderful on his skin. He was alive once more. He surrendered himself completely to the intense pleasure of the moment.

"You're a hard dog, 3468! I've got to hand it to you. What's your prescription?" the prisoner who was assigned here as an orderly wanted to know.

His white rubber apron concealed his prison badge. He didn't look like a serious criminal. His eyes were too soft, too sympathetic for that. Of course, he could have been a sympathetic thief or swindler from among the ranks of the Greens. But they were no longer making it into such privileged jobs. Walter guessed that he was a "warm brother" or a biblical scholar. Oddly enough, the communists held the Jehovah's Witnesses in particularly high regard. They considered them upright, and respected that they never stole nor lied.

"Standing on one foot with the best poets and thinkers, you can endure anything," Walter confided to the orderly.

"You got that all in your head?"

"Something like that. It only works if you do it with your head. The trick is that nobody can think two thoughts at the same time! I just kept reciting all the ballads and dramas I had once learned by heart. And if you concentrate hard on the depth and beauty of the language and its meaning, you forget about the pain and the cold. The power of the word is one trick. The other is that you have to keep one foot in motion and keep it warm by massaging it before switching it out when the other one is almost completely numb. That, along with Shakespeare and Schiller, is my prescription!"

The prison orderly peered doubtfully at him over the rim of his nickel glasses. To prevent him from suspecting Walter of harboring any bourgeois musings, Walter immediately mimed the harmless joker that the prisoners took him to be. From Shakespeare he had learned that the safest position among the very powerful was that of the jester. Especially in the darkness, laughter, singing, and whistling were the elixir of life. Besides his Moser, Lingen, and Goebbels numbers, he could imitate almost any German dialect, so that everyone would tell him that he was a born-and-bred Saxon, Silesian, East Prussian, or Hamburger. Thus, to the amusement of everyone present, he could pretend to be a Hessian-babbling compatriot of a homesick security guard from Darmstadt, claiming that they had once lived across the street from each other.

After his first experience with torture, Walter was convinced that the only way you could endure the horror was by turning to the best of humanity, to art. Only by visualizing the best could you maintain your belief in the goodness of humanity. However, he could not tell this to just anyone. Walter had correctly interpreted Rudi Seifert's warning. From the standpoint of social class, he, Walter Kohanim-Rubin, was an "uncertain" element, a border crosser. As such, Walter had to hide every possible extravagance that might lead others to label him as a suspicious bird of paradise, a petty-bourgeois individualist, a leftist anarchist deviant, or a bourgeois intellectual. It was for this reason that Walter used every opportunity to act the part of a pleb in the style of a third-rate Brechtian performance. He went to great lengths to reference the popular and trivial so as not to arouse the suspicions of his comrades.

His life depended on it.

At the very same moment, Franziska was no longer bothered by the state of political affairs. She didn't give a damn about the opinions of experts. Undeterred by all the know-it-alls, Fränze had set her mind on rescuing her sons from prison and camp and helping them to emigrate to America or England. Her "good boys" were Jewish prisoners and notorious communists, convicted of treason in Germany. But someone like Franziska didn't despair. An amnesty was bound to come at some point, and she wanted to be prepared for this wonderful eventuality.

Instead of spending her days playing works by her favorite composer Debussy or socializing with friends over a game of rummy or bridge, she now spent her days at the dining table hammering away at the typewriter that she had secretly schlepped up the four flights of stairs from the store at night. As a Jew, she was no longer allowed to have a typewriter or a radio, and so she would always put the typewriter in the bowl in the washbasin in the kitchen after using it.

Franziska was actively corresponding with the German authorities, several lawyers, the Jewish communities of Berlin, and a dozen other cities in Germany and abroad, with national and international Jewish aid organizations, and with embassies of countries of whose existence she had previously been unaware. To ensure that she didn't miss out on any country where she could beg for a visa for her sons, she had asked if she could borrow the globe from Willi. Franziska now systematically worked through it. She wrote petitions, pleas for mercy, appeals, and letters in which she outright begged. Franziska's purpose in life came to be all manner of correspondence, ranging from regular letters, pneumatic mail, to express letters, registered express letters, and letters sent by messenger, requesting an immediate response. Last but not least, she persistently besieged the antechambers of numerous offices. And where it seemed sensible to do so, she saw to it that notarized letters of recommendation from the world-famous pianist Maxim Gulkowitsch landed onto the desks of the powerful. In short, Franziska embarked on a bureaucratic campaign against the world, and nobody could stop her.

After two dogged years of correspondence with the administrative offices of the half-powerful, she managed to get Benno a passport and a visa for England through a Jewish relief organization. Walter, however, was refused entry to England, leaving him with the last resort of Shanghai, which did not require a visa. When Walter and Benno were released on parole shortly before Christmas in 1937, she thought she had achieved her aim and happily celebrated "Christmukkuh." This strange mixture of Christmas and Hanukkah was for the sake of Bruno, who didn't want to do without his Christmas tree and roast goose, even in Fränze's kingdom.

"You can have your candlestick. I want my tree!" he had said. On the morning of Christmas Day, Fränze was out with her friends Emmi and Lotte to pick up the goose they had preordered from the market hall. Bruno was in the kitchen working on the Christmas tree with an axe to fit it to the wrought-iron tree stand when Benno stuck his head in the door.

"I'm making myself scarce!"

"Waddya mean? Not celebrating with us? We haven't even been together for a long time! You wanna break the Silver Poplar's heart?"

"I don't trust the peace. It's all too regulated. Bruno Dahnke is already downstairs with a car and will drive me straight to Magdeburg so that I don't get caught in some grabber's net in Berlin. From Magdeburg, where no police station knows me, I'll take the train to the Dutch border and then head to England."

Bruno put the axe aside and straightened up with a groan of displeasure. "Your mother ain't gonna like this. And what's Walter up to? Is he 'bout to leave too? You're both gonna up and leave us alone with all this roast beef?"

"Nah, you know Walter. His ship to Shanghai doesn't leave for another eight weeks. That's why he really wants to stick around. If necessary, he'll eat the whole goose alone. After the second national holiday, he has to report to the police station. Well, I for one won't wait around another second and won't report to the police in Germany! Just get out of here quickly before they change their minds! Give this letter to mother!"

Two tears dripped down on Bruno's Kaiser-Wilhelm beard.

On the third day of the Christmas holiday, Walter reported to the relevant police station. They were expecting him.

"Do you have a job yet?" the officer asked him duplicitously.

"Yes! In the Geißler Plumbing Company."

"Papers? Employment book?"

"I don't have these with me. I can bring them tomorrow."

"No employment papers?!"

Walter shook his head.

"Not at the moment. I could…"

With a wave of his hand, the officer dismissed his protest and grinned at him gleefully.

"In accordance with the passing of the Asocial Act of December 14, 1937, you are hereby arrested as an asocial detriment to the German people!"

After three days of freedom, Walter found himself back in the Buchenwald concentration camp, with a new prisoner number: 6982. This time he was no honorable "political prisoner" but was branded as an "asocial prisoner" and made to wear a black triangle. He also had to wear a yellow star, indicating that he was Jewish.

It was already the fall of 1938 when the second oldest Kohanim sister, Selma, and her second husband, Caesar Bukofzker, arrived in Berlin on a train from Danzig, stopping to say goodbye on their way out of Germany. The special train from Danzig via Berlin to Budapest arrived at the Anhalter train station fifty minutes late. Fanny, Franziska, Jenny, and her cousin Else walked excitedly along the platform with bouquets of asters and parcels of cake. Would they even recognize her? Apart from the fact that Selma was meshuga, the only thing they knew was that today they shouldn't look for an Orthodox Jewish woman with her hair parted down the middle; the way Selma used to appear. But what did she look like today?

They didn't have the slightest idea. They hadn't seen their sister for almost twenty years, since the death of their parents. And in an echo of her Orthodox past, Selma still loathed photographs, nor could she send passport photos in a telegram. The only clue that Fanny, Jenny, Franziska, and Else had was that they should search the crowd for a rather domineering woman in her fifties about 5 feet 6 inches tall with close-set eyes. On that day, Selma was responsible for the journey of almost a thousand Jews to the Promised Land.

Fanny, Jenny, and Franziska suspected that their sister Selma was in the front car, which were always the first-class cars on normal passenger trains. Their instincts proved correct: they spotted her at the front, just behind the engine: an imperious-looking woman in a British military coat, surrounded by a crowd of people engaged in a debate with several people. Her hair was pinned up in a bun tucked beneath a beret. She was waving a bundle of papers in front of three railroad officials. An assistant next to her kept a list and called out names. Those who had been called to board the train in Berlin crowded into the already full train.

"Suitcases are no longer accepted, only rucksacks."

Standing next to her was her second husband Caesar, looking rather useless. He was wearing boots, breeches, and a sporty tweed jacket, with a scarf and tie pin and looking ready for a fox hunt on the Scottish moors, not for an adventurous expedition into the deserts of British-occupied Palestine.

"And the three youngsters next to them must be Selma's sons Gabriel, Ariel, and Raphael! What a resemblance they bear to our father, "The Great," marveled Fanny, pausing to catch her breath. Several years older than her sisters and cousin, she found it hard to keep up with them.

As if she had sensed her sisters approaching from behind, Selma suddenly turned around: "Well, well, well! So you've come after all? If you've got your passports with you, you've got a unique opportunity to come with us. Four emigrants have changed their minds!" Then she assumed the forced smile of an overworked person and gave her sisters a quick hug. "What are you still doing here in Germany?" she said reproachfully.

"You can't be serious! We live here and have our families here! And nothing is eaten as hot as it's cooked! Things won't get nearly as bad as they say they will."

"How can you be so blind?!" Selma barked back disdainfully. "How hot is it supposed to get?"

Instead of Fanny, Jenny, Fränze, and Else, four young Berliners, who moved up from "applicants" to "emigrants" got on board, whooping with joy.

"Are you sure the English will let you in?" Else asked timidly.

"Sometimes you can't wait around until you get a handwritten invitation," Selma replied.

In fact, the unsolicited entry into Palestine was indeed the main sticking point of the whole venture. Selma only knew that the way to Palestine had to be paved first, but she could not dwell on such issues right then, especially not with clueless, sheltered Berlin housewives. If the wind blew their hats off their heads, they wouldn't dare to step on the lawn to retrieve their hats, unless the police first issued them a permit.

"All aboard! Please mind the gap! The special train to Constanza via Vienna and Budapest is departing from track four!"

Else, Fanny, Jenny, and Franziska quickly pressed their parcels of food into Selma's hands, said goodbye to Gabriel, Ariel, Raphael, and Caesar, hugged Selma, and whispered blessings into her ear: "*Hatsloche un broche*! Happiness and blessings!" Caesar secretly slipped Franziska a package. "This is for Walter! With that we're even! My father cheated Walter out of a large part of his inheritance a long time ago and I'm not allowed to take the money out anyway. Take it, you'll need travel money soon too!" Before Fränze could reply, Caesar had boarded the train.

Deep in thought, she slipped the bundle into her bag. Caesar waved to her from the window, looking relieved, like a person who had long been weighted down by a debt and was finally able to free himself from it.

The conductor held up the paddle.

"Will we ever see each other again in this life?" Fanny murmured and began to cry. Even Franziska, who had never been particularly attached to Selma, became rather melancholy. Cousin Else was already crying uncontrollably, but only because she always cried at train stations. Jenny was sobbing as if heartbroken into the useless bouquets of asters. The people they were meant for couldn't do anything with them. The days when travelers were happy to receive a flower greeting were long gone. The water that the flowers would have needed would be used as drinking water for the journey.

A whistle blew and the train slowly heaved into motion. The Palestinian settlers began to sing the "Hatikva." They did not sing with the usual sad longing, usually associated with the song. They were singing it defiantly, waving their fists and countless flags with the Star of David.

O while within a Jewish breast,
Beats true a Jewish heart,
And Jewish glances turning East,
To Zion fondly dart;

O then our Hope—it is not dead,
Our ancient Hope and true,
To be a nation free forevermore
Zion and Jerusalem at our core.

The song rang out loudly through the swastika-bedecked train station in the capital of the Reich. "How can the police allow that!" hissed the indignant crowd. “This pack of Jews is also getting impudent! They’d better get the hell out of here.”

Else, Franziska, Jenny, and Fanny felt a wave of filth surging towards them.

“Yes, otherwise we’ll make you!”

The crowd had identified the Jewish farewell passengers on platform four. Suddenly Else, Franziska, Jenny, and Fanny felt as if they were surrounded by wild animals. They looked at them with undisguised hostility, jostled them, tripped Fanny so that she almost fell, and then laughed nastily in her face. No one intervened, reprimanded the bullies or defended them. The train and police officers simply turned away. It reminded Fränze of her experience at the Ochse station in 1919.

“It’s just a mob!” Jenny reassured Fanny in a soubrette tremolo.

“Your word in God’s ear,” uttered Fränze, who was picking up a scent. If something that happened almost twenty years ago in a Polish village was now being repeated in Germany’s imperial capital, then something had changed.

Upon arriving home, Franziska was finally able to open Caesar’s secret package. On top lay a certificate that verified how much ole Bukofzker had taken advantage of the Kohanim family’s time of need after the death of their parents. In the letter, Caesar informed Franziska that with this payment, he wished to settle the debt from the lost inheritance. Gold coins and jewels lay neatly wrapped in tissue paper. “Better than throwing it all down Hitler’s gullet. Use it wisely and save yourselves with it!”

BLOOD MONEY

In June 1956, my mother managed to continue her game of cat and mouse with the Stasi, thanks to her carefully devised plot. A medical commission headed by her former accomplice, Dr. Kastner, who had once given refuge at St. Joseph Hospital to Nazi victims in hiding, certified that my father was suffering from vegetative dystonia and an acute attack of multiple sclerosis. "The patient is in no state to be either interrogated or punished." For the time being, my father was safe from the Stasi. They estimated that this tactic would buy them about six months and figured that the party didn't want to mess with the Catholic Church just then.

The generally volatile political situation also impacted our everyday lives. At home, my mother insisted that I follow very meticulous precautions. Every time the doorbell rang, I had to listen for whether it was our code, long once and short twice. If it wasn't, my job was to shove all the West German newspapers under the sofa and quickly change the dial on the radio from the Radio in the American Sector (Rias) to the East German station, Berliner Rundfunk. After a few days, I managed this with both hands in three seconds: the newspapers with my left hand, the radio setting with my right. I also had to be on my guard at school. One day, our teacher, Mr. Böhnke, duplicitously asked us about the break signals on our radio. A seemingly harmless question for unsuspecting minds. Most of the children innocently whistled the break signals. They were usually those for Western stations. As I listened, I grew suspicious that the question had nothing to do with our knowledge of broader Berlin radio culture. I whistled the signal used by the Berliner Rundfunk. Mr. Böhnke made a note of everything and smiled at me with satisfaction.

For the next lesson, we would normally have had mechanical arts or handicrafts at school. Until recently, these double lessons were intended to be used for religious instruction. Either Catholic or Protestant. My atheist parents thought religious education was essential to completing my general education. "Our entire art and culture are based on Christianity and Judaism. You'd be a complete ignoramus if you didn't know that!" However, since the second grade, religious education in East Berlin was no longer allowed to take place at school, only in parishes or community centers. The school schedule now included handicrafts for girls and mechanical arts for boys. You could therefore only have religious education if you went without learning needlework and handicrafts.

I was completely indifferent to religion as such. I nonetheless found the crucifixion more interesting than cross-stitch. This was for the simple reason that I always relished a good story, and was thus also willing to suffer and sacrifice for the chance to hear strange fairy tales and legends. In this case, that meant making my way by foot on the dreary walk from school to the parsonage and back again. What really swayed me to choose religious instruction over handicrafts, however, was something else. I suspected that there was a reason why the party chose to send us elsewhere for religious instruction. That aroused my defiance. Whereas the other children had to be forced by their parents to attend religion class at the parsonage, I had a completely different attitude: I was cheerful, curious, and eager.

One day, Mr. Böhnke told us that it would be best for us children if we all joined the party's children's organization, the Young Pioneers. The reward would be a day off from school to take a fieldtrip to Ernst Thälmann Park. Soon not a school day went by without him praising the many pleasures of Thälmann Park and the many other rewards that awaited us were we to join. Most students wanted to do it, and in protest against those who did not, the sulking majority organized a riot. Almost every day after school, the "Pioneers" would lay in wait for the "non-Pioneers" and a massive brawl would break out. Fortunately, my street gang came to my aid and together we handed "the lackeys" chin and liver hooks, bruises, and rather large welts.

Since my street gang had sent the state's loyalists packing, we were, for the time being, secure from the threat of further beatings. When I got home, I had a few things to explain: the torn leather strap and iron buckle on my school bag that I had used as a weapon; my new dress now in tatters; the missing red taffeta ribbons I wore in my braids; and my busted lip.

Desperate to achieve "solidarity," Mr. Böhnke visited the parents of the stubborn refuseniks to plead with them individually. "As former communists, you of all people should set a good example with your daughter," he said, appealing to my parents' conscience. My mother replied with a faint smile. "You know, as old communists, we particularly respect the personal freedom and decisions of the individual, including those of our daughter. So it is entirely up to her. You'll have to convince my daughter. We can't help you with that."

After Mr. Böhnke had left, she explained to me that he only went to such lengths because in addition to getting a good political assessment in his cadre file, he would also receive a bonus of 500 marks if his whole class joined the Young Pioneers. In the end, the only holdouts were Herbert, whose parents were Jehovah's Witnesses, and myself.

The day before vacation, Mr. Böhnke made one last attempt to improve his cadre file and his salary. It was up to me and Herbert. It happened to be Herbert's tenth birthday that day, but that didn't make us especially happy because, as Herbert explained to me, Jehovah's Witnesses don't celebrate birthdays. What kind of stupid religion forbids birthday parties? To be polite, I didn't say anything, but inside I was outraged.

Meanwhile, four men in nicer suits with fat party badges on their lapels had spread out in the back of the classroom.

Red blotches of panic appeared on Mr. Böhnke's face. His hands were trembling and palms sweaty. With a sweat-soaked piece of chalk and feigned enthusiasm, he enumerated the many advantages of joining the Young Pioneers on the chalkboard. Aha, a math problem! I thought, as he rendered the advantages as a point system. Then, Mr. Böhnke drew a line under the "equation" and called me up to the board.

"Add up all the advantages that joining the Young Pioneers offers!" he said with a triumphant expression. Expecting approval, he glanced at the back row where the bigwigs were now waiting for my humiliation to serve as an example to the other students.

As I reluctantly trudged toward the blackboard, the blood was already ringing in my ears. A wave of heat surged up from my stomach, a fury and outrage like I had never experienced before. If my hair had not been bound into braids, each strand would have stood straight out from my head. I wondered fleetingly if I should dash out or if I should simply strike through the whole duplicitous equation. Then I had a better idea, something that I thought would make a good joke. In my scraggly child's handwriting, I jotted the answer down beneath the equation: 30 pieces of silver!!! The sum Judas had received for betraying Jesus.

After the three exclamation marks, I placed the chalk on the edge of the board as delicately as if it were a baby bird.

With a feigned expression of innocence, I returned to my seat. I almost curtseyed in mockery but came to my senses first.

Christian Herbert gaped at me, mouth hanging open.

A deep silence settled over the classroom.

After a brief pause, irritated murmuring came from the back. Probably someone explaining the story of Judas and Jesus to the comrades who didn't know the Bible. My classmates were laughing. Mr. Böhnke was whiter than the wall. The delegation of bigwigs left the classroom, sending me evil glares on their way out.

"You can see what a mess religion makes of children," Mr. Böhnke said, trying to save the situation by using socialist logic. By then, however, the delegation of bigwigs had already ridden off in a wave indignation.

The delicious sweetness of triumph trickled through me, just like after a brawl.

I didn't care about anything else.

SECRETS

Hella celebrated her seventeenth birthday at Siemens. She had been conscripted by the state to work as a "runner" or errand girl. It was her first day on the job. How could she celebrate there? She put on her new dress that her mother had sewn for her, as she always did on her birthday, and spent the day at the Siemens plant, working in the equipment construction division. She was introduced to at least one hundred people for whom she was now going to be working. Word spread through one or another departments that it was her birthday—her seventeenth!—which should have been celebrated in some way. But no one did anything. That was fine by Hella. She had an aversion to social gatherings.

Over the course of the next few months, as Hella revealed herself to be a quick learner and reliable, Siemens equipment construction division gradually entrusted her with increasingly demanding tasks. Hella found this large company, which produced such important things for the whole world, very interesting.

She was so engaged with her new position at Siemens that she nearly forgot about the fact that she had had to quit her apprenticeship as a seamstress with the Segals. One day, Fanny Segal approached Hella, telling her that as Jews she and Gerson were no longer allowed to employ and train Aryans. Not long after, the Segals had to hand over the business all together—to an Aryan, of course. To throw it away, in other words.

However, Hella's mother was allowed to continue working there, which she did because with her political past, it would have been difficult for her to find an equivalent new position.

Oda was still the best seamstress in the company, but since her detention, she was no longer in top form. Almost overnight, her hair had turned gray, and her head shook slightly, even though she had been spared the usual tortures that took place there, thanks to Kalle. Instead of undergoing torture herself, she had been forced to care for those who had. Burns of varying degrees, broken bones, knocked out teeth, half-scalped skulls, torn off fingernails and toenails, lesions from electric shocks, dislocated limbs. She also saw those who had been tortured to death, mostly by electric shocks or by drowning in tubs or troughs. Long before bombs fell on Berlin, Oda would wake up screaming at night. She then had to quickly take her heart pills. Hella often thought that seeing the agony of others and tending to the victims' wounds had been the worst possible torture for her mother.

Hella also wasted no time on regret over her last days at school in 1936. It seemed like an eternity since she had been recognized as the best gymnast at her school and thus allowed to take part in the mass gymnastics competition at the opening ceremony of the Olympics that took place at the Olympic Stadium. If Hella thought about her school days at all, it was only with sadness that she had not been allowed to go to an advanced secondary school that would prepare her for university. Her grades were so good that the school authorities even wanted to waive her school fees. Oda, however, had talked her daughter out it. If she didn't join the League of German Girls, Oda said, at some point Hella would have been expelled from school or excluded from taking the pre-college entrance exam. Hella knew she was right. While she came to accept the situation, she couldn't help but think sometimes of her former teacher, Mr. Päzold, with fondness. He had always found ways to help her avoid the roll call under the swastika in the schoolyard, inventing tasks for her to carry out like fetching maps for geography or preparing an experiment in the lab. Thanks to Mr. Päzold, she thus never had to salute the swastika flag.

Gradually, the war came to the Siemens factory. One man after another disappeared from production. The men had to be replaced. The reliable, intelligent Hella thus continued to rise through the ranks until she was practically running the shipping division for machines and equipment. It was a position that only the most trusted person could fulfill, as it dealt with official secret matters related to the Wehrmacht. But no one had vetted

Hella, a seventeen-year-old runner, in regard to her political status. She had been conscripted. Like all employees, before she had started to work, she merely had to present her employment papers alongside her Aryan identity papers. That was all the Siemens people knew about Hella. She had thus managed to work her way up inconspicuously, step by step, making her presence so familiar and indispensable that it was as if she had always been there. Then they simply forgot to put her through the "political screening" process. By that point, the Siemens personnel department had other worries. Hella also never let herself get caught dropping bread into a wastebasket or leaving a warm jacket hanging on a hook for a slave laborer or POW in the factory. She did her work silently and even enjoyed working overtime, such that her supervisors added such terms as "exemplary fellow German" and adjectives like "reliable" and "intelligent" to her file.

During overtime shifts, the offices were empty, and Hella took advantage of the opportunity to throw an occasional bit of sand into the well-oiled armament machine. She manipulated the already signed packing lists, changing addresses so that equipment arrived late for armament schedules or would be delivered, unchecked, to the wrong places in insufficient quantities or with missing parts. Sometimes Siemens even sent out completely empty shipping crates. While ships like the *Tirpitz*, the *Scharnhorst*, and the *Bismarck*, were being loaded up with cargo and outfitted, Hella was often the only one who knew exactly when which ship was in which port, and by what hour, so that the consignments always missed the ships by just a few hours and then had to wander through the ports. This extended the completion of the warships by days, weeks, and months. No sailor suspected it was thanks to an adolescent saboteur in Berlin-Siemensstadt that they were able to enjoy slightly longer lives.

But that was only half of Hella's daily life. The other half involved traveling by bike sixty kilometers from Berlin to Frankfurt Oder with two suitcases on her handlebars, another one on her luggage rack, and a backpack across her shoulders. Her father, Reinhold, knew someone who lived there that he had met when he was an apprentice baker. A Social Democrat, the man ran his own bakery and was thus able to channel off loaves of bread. In the evening, Hella would slip into the bakery and pack up the forty loaves they had agreed upon in advance. She would then spend the night on a cot next to the oven, since there was a ban on baking activities in effect on the weekends. After she had splashed her face with cold water and the baker had filled her thermos with hot malt coffee, she would head back to Berlin early on Sunday morning. Once she reached the city, she would take the suitcases to certain appointed places, usually to train stations located to the north and east of the city, where people with humble luggage would not stand out. Usually, someone was already waiting for her. When she heard the code, "Aunt Lucie is already waiting with the food!" she would hand over the cases of bread. If the contact person scratched his nose with a folded newspaper, the coast was not clear. She would then keep going, hauling the suitcase with her. Frequently, nobody showed up. In those cases, Hella was supposed to leave after a certain amount of time and go to her father's place in Oderberger Straße along with her backpack and suitcases. At least eight to ten people who were hiding from the Nazis were always waiting in Reinhold's apartment, either for food or to be shipped along to somewhere else.

Since the day of the raid and house search when she had smuggled the embroidered flag and the incriminating papers in her schoolbag and entrusted them to her father, they had grown close. Attempted murder or remorse be damned! Her father was the best person she could count on. Nobody took the drunken cretin Reinhold Hanke seriously and after the murder attempt on his wife and children; no one would suspect that he might possibly have any connection to any of them. No one knew about it, least of all her mother Oda. As is often the case with drunkards, Reinhold Hanke's heroism and wretchedness were very closely connected. Reinhold was so weak in character that he simply couldn't say no to anyone. Especially if that someone handed him money or a glass of schnapps in exchange for a place to hide. So Hella met a panopticon of people in hiding and refugees in the cramped bakery. Reinhold crouched helplessly in the middle of the crowd of people who were all yelling at him at the same time. No one knew what to do next. Reinhold howled snot bubbles. "What am I supposed to do? Where am I supposed to send them?"

"Why did you take these people in to begin with?"

"I felt so sorry for them all!" whined Reinhold, embarrassed in front of his strict daughter. If Hella wanted to protect her father, then she had to lead the people to someplace else.

Hella felt just as bad for the Segals, who had to get ready to be picked up and resettled in Riga, Poland. You could guess what that meant! Hella put out her feelers. Her task was to arrange an illegal passage to Sweden for six people. Her brother Peter had smuggled her into the underground group for which she worked as a food procurer and courier. When she anxiously asked Peter about the reliability and origins of their co-conspirators, he could only tell her that in addition to the comrades there were also "unreliable elements," like Social Democrats, independent Liberals and humanists not under suspicion by the state, and devout Christians, who had influential positions and could thus supply them with information and early warnings. Among them were also former Nazi sympathizers who had become disillusioned and were now desperate to do something about the increasing violence and lawlessness. They were late in realizing the truth about the Nazis and in committing to fight them. They therefore wanted to work toward their own salvation and self-respect by helping people who were in danger. Some of them risked their lives to do so. As Hella could work out from the bread rations, there were currently around twenty-three people in the group of conspirators.

One evening news arrived about planned deportations. It came from a reliable source: prostitutes who worked at "Kitty," the Nazis' and Gestapo's favorite brothel on Giesebrechtstraße. The planned "relocations" on Sophienstraße and Oranienburger Straße were being moved forward by three days. Someone had to warn the Segals! Hella herself couldn't do it, as she was known as a former apprentice there. So her brother went instead.

Fanny Segal's blind daughter, Hedwig, was forced to give up her dog Bobby, because Jews were no longer allowed to keep dogs. Since then, she didn't want to leave the house. Where would she go anyway? To the theater, the movies, the swimming pool? No, Jews were no longer even allowed on the streetcar or in the park. During the day, her parents and siblings constantly had errands to run, and she was still too young to go to the workshop for the blind. Hedwig thus sat at the window all day and sometimes into the night, even though she couldn't see anything.

Her lack of eyesight meant that she had a sharpened sense of hearing and could thus hear very well sounds that were coming from outside. A furniture van was apparently pulling up on the opposite side of the street. The gas lanterns were already hissing, so she knew it must be dark already. Why, she wondered, would someone need a moving van at this time of night? She then heard angry commands being shouted and people from the house opposite gathering in the street, clearly frightened and excited about something. She could hear shoes scraping across the pavement and footsteps cautiously going "tap-tap-tap" up wooden steps or a ramp into the van. Why would people other than the movers need to get into a furniture van? Her practiced ears caught the sounds of shuffling feet over a board, harsh orders, soft sighs of despair, here and there a sob from a child or a woman, the placating murmur of a man who had been struck across the back, causing his voice to break, then fail all together. A crying baby in the hallway.

After she told her mother about these strange events, everything erupted into commotion.

"Deportation!" They could not make a decision about what to do next. Gerson Segal, her father, was not back yet.

"Where is he? He should have been here by now."

"We'll go and meet him," decided Fanny, even though it was already past eight o'clock and it was forbidden for Jews to be on the street at that time of night.

They ran in a panic along the deserted, rain-soaked streets that their father was supposed to have taken. Nothing! The streets were deserted. The houses seemed to be cowering. A lone drunk staggered down the street making a lot of noise. They quickly crossed the street. "Let's head back home!" Fanny shouted to her sons, who always ran faster. "Maybe he came from the other direction?"

Hedwig's shoelace broke. Muttering obscenities beneath her breath, Fanny knelt on the pavement in front of her and hastily tied the broken shoelaces together. Meanwhile, the Segal boys had already disappeared around the next corner. Fanny and Hedwig hurried after them. Just as they were about to turn the corner, they saw the furniture van in front of their building! They watched as Gerson Segal and their sons, who could no longer escape by running back in their direction, were herded into the van. Fanny wanted to shout something. But her mouth fell silent in shock. Together with Hedwig, she squeezed into a recess in the wall between the pillars of the main entrance. At that moment, a man whispered close behind her, "Hella sent me."

He yanked Fanny and Hedwig back into the doorway. The door was unlocked. He had probably been waiting for them there.

"I have to see my family," Fanny protested weakly.

"You can still do that if you want!"

"But I have to…" Fanny no longer knew what she had to do.

"My mother, my sister, and I want to help you. Have you ever wondered where and when Jews were deported? Have you ever received good news from deportees?"

"They won't kill us!" Fanny said defiantly and headed for the door with Hedwig.

"But that's exactly what they do in Poland! It's not a rumor. There are witnesses!"

"Oh, my God! I have to warn my husband and sons!"

"We'll take care of that. Right now, we have to get out of here as quickly as possible. Come on, quickly!"

Peter Hanke was the first out of the front gate. He pretended to scan the sky for rain clouds and turned up his collar. When he saw that the street was quiet again, he fetched Fanny and Hedwig.

"Link your arms! We have to look like a family heading home. If the police or any brown-shirted scum get close to us, we have to chatter casually. Just don't fall silent or cry or look scared. It would be best to laugh a little. Do you understand?"

Fanny swallowed her misery. "Where are we going?"

"Hella is waiting for you at the train station, and she's going to take you somewhere safe."

"Peter Hanke left Fanny and Hedwig Segal standing in front of the Friedrichstraße train station and hopped into the last streetcar to Rosenthal.

"All the best!"

Hella was standing up on the train platform.

"Where are the others?"

Fanny lowered her head and began to weep.

"For the love of God, don't even think about crying! Someone will notice us!"

Offhand, Hella could have recited an entire litany of things and behaviors that could inadvertently attract attention. This was because she had become a specialist in inconspicuousness, able to illicit boredom or disinterest in those with whom she came in contact. She was a gray mouse that no one noticed. Invisible. A feat she accomplished by perfecting the art of appearing ordinary. Thus hidden, against a carefully selected background into which she could disappear, no one would remember her. Even if they did, they couldn't say where she had been or if she had been coming or going.

This also applied to her interactions with young men. She was cautious about attention inspired by attraction, as it carried with it too many incalculable factors. That's why she usually nipped in the bud any contact with the opposite sex, dismissing it as too risky. She had, nonetheless, been thinking about a particular young man for a long time. She suspected that he was a potential risk: not to her safety, but to her heart. Her gaze began to grow soft as she thought of him, but she immediately pulled herself together.

"Here are your new identification papers, in case someone asks to check them. You are now Erika Kampmüller from Lankwitz, born on August 14, 1895 in Teltow. Memorize your birth date right now! If you pull out your ID along with this military obituary, the grabbers will usually walk away immediately."

The photo on the ID card was a relatively poor match for her former employer Fanny Segal, which was why Hella ardently hoped that this late in the evening, there would no longer be any checks on the trains.

"One more thing: When we get on board, we will stay standing at the door across the aisle. Hedwig will need to gaze out the window so that no one will see that she's blind. People who stand next to the doors on public transportation attract more attention than people sitting in the compartments."

An ambulance was waiting at the Greifswalder train station. Hella gave the agreed knock. The door opened instantly, and they climbed in. A nun from the Order of the Immaculate Conception of the Virgin Mary was sitting behind the steering wheel. "Praise be to Jesus Christ!"

"Forever and ever, Amen, Venerable Mother!" Hella replied per the proscribed greeting. The nun ordered Fanny and Hedwig to lie down on the stretchers. She handed Hella a nun's habit. Their drive ended at the Catholic St. Joseph Hospital on Gartenstraße in Berlin-Weißensee.

"Praise be to Jesus Christ!" a rotund Alexian Brother said in greeting.

"The Holy Mother, the Holy Spirit, and God's grace be with you! Quarantine station!" the nun replied.

A monk with a childish face and the stature of a wrestler lifted the barrier and let the vehicle pass.

Lotte Hörl, Franziska's best friend, was always the more anxious of the two. But as the detonations grew ever closer even Franziska trembled. The air-raid sirens howled, while searchlights cast a spectral glow across the overcast sky. The stars on their coats prevented Lotte and Fränze entrance into the air-raid shelters. Bombs were already hitting targets on either side of them. A blast wave swept hot ash and dust into their faces, making it impossible to breathe. "We can't stay here out on the street!" lamented Lotte.

"We're not going to! Come on!"

Normally when there was a bomb alert, they were in the Jewish hospital where they had both been working for the past year. While Lotte preferred to hole up in the bunker there, Franziska chose to go outside on fire watch with her helmet, bucket, and shovel, something from which Jews were usually forbidden, as they could signal to the enemy. But who was supposed to stand fire watch in the Jewish hospital if not Jews? Better to croak outside than be buried under a mountain of debris. On the other hand, she realized that her friend Lotte might lose her nerve, so she dragged her into the air-raid bunker at Nettelbeck Square under the S-Bahn. While Lotte would have preferred to crawl into the farthest corner, Franziska remained rooted to the spot near the front door and held Lotte by her sleeve.

"If it goes boom in here too, at least we'll be the first at the door!"

"Jews out!" the air-raid warden shouted at them, trying to force them out.

"Leave the women alone! And close the door!" someone shouted from the dark depths of the air-raid shelter. "You couldn't send a dog out there!"

Lotte flinched and clutched her friend's arm, while Franziska looked the air-raid warden in the face and made her way into the shelter.

"People who are different than everyone else, have to go first! That includes the lot of 'em that got us into this mess in the first place!" harped a woman's voice from the shelter of the bunker's darkness.

"That's right!" yelled a man. "Especially all the Meiers!" [13]

"Who was that?" The air-raid warden turned on his flashlight and shone it through the cellar, looking for the person who had yelled. Laughter spread behind his back.

"You better think hard 'bout what you're gonna do when this nightmare is all over," someone laughed from the darkness.

"The whole air-raid shelter is under arrest!" shouted the air-raid warden into the blackness.

"Well, then best be careful that you make it outta here alive! You pompous brown twit!"

At that moment, a fifty-kilo bomb went off nearby, the bunker swayed, the earth shook, plaster fell from the ceiling. The air-raid warden moved toward the entrance, where Franziska and Lotte were standing. By the light of his flashlight, he wanted to make notes for a report. But his hands were shaking so badly that he had to abandon the effort. Fränze grinned at him disdainfully. Feeling outed as a coward, instead of continuing to struggle to write he tried to assert his authority by staring at the timid

Lotte, who responded by using her scarf to cover up the yellow star on her coat. The worst thing would be if the air-raid warden asked to see her papers. Meanwhile Franziska, emboldened by the defiant mood of the air-raid shelter, looked the man up and down coldly, the corners of her mouth dripping with contempt. He lowered his gaze nervously, looked at his watch, and then pretended to light up cracks in the wall. Lotte breathed a sigh of relief.

Without her friend Fränze, Lotte would have lost heart a long ago. Two weeks ago, Lotte's mother had been taken to Theresienstadt concentration camp, while her son Karlheinz had been sent to the Eastern Front as a half-Jew "worthy of military service." Every time the letter carrier came up the stairs in his heavy shoes, Lotte's heart stopped. Every day she said a silent prayer that he wouldn't push any mail for the Hörl family through the letter slot in their front door. Like everyone, she knew that the death notices had ceased to come via registered mail a while ago; they simply arrived along with the rest of the mail.

Now only the urns containing the ashes of deceased prisoners and their last belongings were sent by registered mail. A few days prior, one of Franziska's closest friends, Emmi, had showed up in tears carrying just such a gruesome package; her son had been executed as a deserter in Plötzensee. The ashes of her executed son had been sent to her in a lunchbox. The package was accompanied by an invoice for forty-nine marks and eighty-five pfennigs for the cremation for which she had to pay upon delivery.

Since then, Lotte's courage to face life had been hanging by a thread. If it hadn't been for her Willi, she would have been deported to Theresienstadt along with her mother. The same would have happened to Fränze if she hadn't been married to "Aryan" Bruno. Lotte had always known that Willi was the sort of man who would do anything to protect his wife. But Fränze's gentle Bruno, who everyone thought was a wimp because he always broke into tears the moment someone raised their voice, had astonished everyone. Such a lamb of a man didn't suddenly become a lion for the sake of Franziska. He stood strong in another way. He became a great sufferer, who miraculously overcame his opponents with his steadfast gentleness. Fortunately, Franziska and Bruno had gotten married in 1934 without a ceremony or a big to do. Had it not been for that, Franziska would have been taken away long ago.

Shortly before they married, the plumbing business had been "Aryanized," with Bruno identified as the sole owner. But that wasn't enough, the state authorities also demanded that he vacate their shared apartment. Their troubles didn't end with marriage, however. For, thereafter, representatives of the Nazi state began to relentlessly badger Bruno to divorce Franziska. During these interrogations, Bruno would always sit there immobile, like a weathered bronze statue of the abdicated Kaiser, and remain silent and serious while fat tears would drip into his Wilhelm II beard.

"German loyalty!"

He refused to let anyone shake his belief in this credo.

Ashamed and shaking their heads, they released him.

"A relic from the old days," sneered one of the civil servants.

The rowdy foreman Willi Hörl, the soft-hearted Bruno Geißler, and the shrewd suitcase manufacturer, Bruno Dahnke, had since started to meet regularly in Chausseestraße to conspire to solve the problem of how they were supposed to protect their wives.

Bruno Dahnke, the suitcase manufacturer, had it the easiest. He simply sent Else on a long uninterrupted journey. Such a thing was possible because she had reported her passport as missing before having to add a "J" and the middle name "Sarah." Since her departure, she had been a permanent guest at a small, nice boarding house in Davos. Whenever Bruno could, he visited her in Switzerland, usually bringing outrageously expensive gifts like fur coats and jewelry.

"The money has to be spent!" was Bruno's motto. For a businessman like him, the fall of the Reichsmark was as predictable as snowfall in winter. Moreover, many people in neutral Sweden and Switzerland, where he also had branches, were buying his suitcases. "In wartime, suitcases are always in great demand the whole year round," he explained to the other Bruno and to Willi. "My production has quadrupled since the war began. But the money has to go!"

Thanks to his money and Else's departure to a safe place, Bruno was able to wait out the storm in peace. Out of solidarity, he provided Willi and Bruno with moral support and on occasion money, when Bruno and Franziska happened to be short. His motto, "The money has to be spent!" made giving and taking all the easier.

In Bruno's study, they hatched a plan for rescuing Lotte and Franziska. They considered the fact that in times of crisis the safest place was always the kitchen and that similarly, the safest place for their Jewish wives would thus be in the eye of the storm: the Jewish hospital. Once installed there, Lotte and Franziska's survival depended on keeping happy both the local Gestapo and the all-powerful Dr. Lustig—the notorious chief physician of the Jewish hospital, the lord over the life and death of his Jewish patients and staff.

To keep them safe from the SS and Gestapo men stationed at the hospital, Lotte and Franziska offered them all manner of bribes. In a city laid to waste by bombs, how much did the lives of two anonymous Jewish women really matter compared to a free supply of cement, windowpanes, pipes, faucets, tiles, suitcases, and bags? And now and again a pretty snakeskin handbag as a birthday present for your wife? Or maybe a briefcase with chrome-plated locks, also available in pigskin, if that is what you prefer? Or perhaps a men's deerskin toiletry bag, an indispensable travel item in these transient times? The officers gladly accepted them all.

As it turned out, bribing SS and Gestapo men was the right strategy for saving the lives of their wives who were in "privileged mixed marriages." But what about the chief physician, Dr. Lustig? Franziska and Lotte's hearts would skip a beat, whenever he performed selections among his staff: he had to deliver a certain number of people to the Gestapo. He gave first priority to the hopeless cases among the patients, the dying, and the terminally ill.

"If you don't spoil things for me, I bet I'll completely forget about you," Dr. Lustig joked one day when he ran into Franziska, who happened to be a carrying a bottle of milk. What he meant was: I've got my eye on both of you, don't get cocky! Franziska's blood froze in her veins, but she forced herself to laugh. Like everyone in the hospital, she knew that Dr. Lustig wanted to be known as a jokester and thus live up to his name, "funny" in German. And for a man in a position of authority like Dr. Lustig, you readily did him small favors like laughing at his bad jokes. But Dr. Lustig also required other favors, more dangerous ones, from the young Jewish nurses. It wasn't merely their morality that was on the line, their very lives hung in the balance. When Dr. Lustig grew bored with his latest conquest, he no longer wanted to set eyes on her. The young women thus paid with their lives for his loss of interest. It was partly pity and partly relief that led Lotte to quip to Franziska, "Luckily, we're over fifty, and no man wants anything more from us."

During the war, Switzerland was an unreal place. Else Dahnke, undergoing the cure for various mysterious and protracted ailments, enjoyed both the hospitality of the local authorities and an excellent cup of coffee to accompany her apple strudel. Both of which would have been impossible in Berlin. Just beyond the Swiss Alpine glow, Europe was falling into ruins.

On the border with Switzerland, the most common cause of death, after natural causes, was suicide. Most of the mass suicides took place on park benches with a view of Lake Constance or the Rhine Falls in Schaffhausen. Those denied entry to this earthly paradise, took in a beautiful view as their final impression before departing from this earth by taking veronal or by picking up a revolver.

Lost in thought, Else gazed at the glacier as it changed colors. The setting sun was slowly turning it red, orange, and gold until the entire mountain of ice seemed to glow. At such moments, Else Dahnke felt acutely aware of the contrast between her life now and her last days in Berlin. Back then, she had taken for granted the joy of small things: friendly greetings, the exquisite taste of fine chocolate, the smell of freshly roasted coffee, and the soft caress of fur on her skin. Humbled and grateful for all the blessings with which she had been bestowed, she wondered: What had she done to deserve such good fortune? She thought about her relatives back home, whose lives may already have been taken or were still in danger. She prayed for all those who were now scattered in all directions. Most of the time, she was able to push aside these thoughts and musings about her refuge in Switzerland and the question of what right she had to live there in the lap of luxury while others did not. She had a concrete task to attend to: countless letters were still waiting to be finished before the evening mail. Here, too, Else remained a unifying force for the family, serving as its the hub of communication. Thanks to her residence in Switzerland, she was the only one who could send and receive mail from anywhere.

Sometimes Else Dahnke also received strange letters, one of which she had to have translated. It came from Italy. A certain Laura Piccolini had written to her in Italian, introducing herself as the sister-in-law of her cousin Elli. Enclosed in her letter was also a photo, which was supposedly of Elli hunting in the mountains with her new husband Ettore. However, the picture lacked the usual trophies or hunted game. Nor was the couple's outfit dignified enough for hunting. They were too brash, Else thought, and their faces too dark and determined for a hunting trip. In fact, they looked like bandits. But what did she know about Italian hunting fashion and customs in Italy? Yet, she couldn't ignore that it seemed like the guns, not the hunters, were the focus of the photograph. Didn't hunting rifles have a double barrel? The unknown Italian woman wanted to tell her something without words. But what? She couldn't make sense of it all, except that the letter writer wanted to prove who she was by sending a photo that could only come from family or a close friend. Or was it a trap? If they were really on a hunting trip, why had Elli not written to me herself instead of her sister-in-law, in Italian, and not from Milan but from Bergamo? To be on the safe side, Else nevertheless dutifully answered with a meaningless thank-you letter and used the Italian name of the guesthouse's doorman, who had also helped her with the translation and even lent Else his unsuspicious Italian name as an alias for her mail.

In the next letter, which the unknown Laura Piccolini sent to her via the porter, she referred to Elli as "our mutual friend." Based on the letter, written as it was in a kind of code, that Elli was on a long mountain trek with her husband through his Italian homeland and making a big catch, which in plain language most likely meant that Elli had joined the Italian partisans and was fighting in the mountains as a sniper against the Germans, making Italian patriots proud. In Italy, their "mutual friend" even had a nickname, a nom de guerre, that the letter writer did not want to mention. Laura Piccolini seemed less interested in reporting on how Elli was faring, what her nom de guerre was, or where she was than in the fact that Elsbeth, the sports-loving Kohanim daughter, was now called Elsa and had become Catholic at the side of her Italian husband, Ettore. Should "Elsa" die, she would experience salvation and go to heaven, Laura Piccolini reported with delight. Through baptism, "our mutual friend" had now become completely and utterly one of their own, a real Italian! Laura's whole family loved "our mutual friend" like their own daughter, and everyone was proud that she was now rendering great services to her new fatherland.

"How many fatherlands does a person need these days?" Else would have liked to have asked the letter writer. Else's conclusion was: Elli had found her calling as a gun-toting woman roaming the mountains with bandits and shooting at German soldiers! How can I write something like that to Fränze in Berlin? The news about her nephew Benno, whom no one had heard from for a long time, was no less delicate. Plus, sitting on her desk were other letters: a thick letter from Shanghai that had been in transit for six months; a thin letter from Palestine that was three months old; a medium-thick envelope from Sweden that was four weeks old; and alongside letters from her Bruno, sat Franziska's hastily scribbled lines. Else considered how she could at least introduce a little order into her correspondence.

She decided to devise a system. At the top of six slips of paper, she wrote in all capital letters: Fränze, Selma, Willi, Elli, Jenny, and Fanny. On each sheet, she jotted down all the family news she wanted to share with the individual addresses so that she would not forget anything. She put a red exclamation mark on the note for her cousin Franziska, which was intended to remind her to be careful about what she wrote.

For Max Gulkowitsch, it was sufficient to merely send a card thanking him for his help and sharing the news that Fränze's son Benno had now joined the army in England and that unfortunately there was no news about his brother Walter in Buchenwald concentration camp, which could also be a good sign. Done!

The easiest letters to write were to Bruno, her beloved husband. Instead of devoting so much time to crafting clever innuendos, she could be direct. This was for the simple reason that she had found a way to get letters to her husband without the Gestapo seeing them first. She sent them with her husband's business partner in Zurich, who then handed them to his representative in Vienna, and who, in turn, sent them to Berlin by courier, along with his own correspondence.

She decided to send Bruno a letter for Fränze along with the one for him. She thus pushed her initial concerns aside and reached for her fountain pen.

My dearest Bruno,

You know how much I miss you, and I hope that you will be able to arrange a visit to Davos soon. Please forgive me if I have kept you waiting for my letter and if this one is shorter than I would have liked. However, I have seven letters to family members all over the world that are waiting to be answered and they are more urgent. I, therefore, hope all the more that your business will soon bring you back to me in the Swiss mountains and that I can pour my heart out to you, in person. How much longer do I have to wait? Please send me a cable via Vienna.

Compared to my cousins and their children, you and I are living the life of Riley, an almost carefree, tranquil existence. No one's too surprised by the latter. My cousin Jenny reports that she lives in Shanghai in the house of a rich Chinese man, where she teaches singing to his wife, a singer of traditional Peking opera. There's no reason to worry about her at the moment. But we should worry about her husband, Alfred Selbiger, who is still faithfully serving the Jewish community in Berlin. Doesn't Alfred want to protect himself? Cousin Selma is being held in Palestine with Caesar and still hopes to be accepted in the Promised Land. Two of her sons, Ariel and Gabriel, were shrewder. The boys simply jumped off the boat and swam the three miles to the shore. Once there, they "went under," which reads a bit funny in this context. Benno, Fränze's youngest, was first detained in Scotland along with hundreds of other Jews who had fled Germany.

They probably wanted to make sure that the emigrated Jews from Germany were not working as a Fifth Column for the German Reich in England. He's now in the Royal Air Force, working with "intelligence," whatever that is. But he still doesn't sound very happy. Benno is probably very lonely, very homesick for Berlin, and very worried about his brother Walter, and the "Silver Poplar" Fränze. Enclosed you will find a birthday card that he sent for Fränze. Can you please make sure she gets it in time?

Now two sad pieces of news: Flora wrote to me that the Nazis had taken away her son, little Hans. The child was probably sent to the East. Her second husband, the Aryan Runge, was only able to save her, since she is his wife. But not the boy apparently, who is a full Jew. She was told that her little boy had died on the "journey" in "an accident." Dead! The child was not even ten years old! How is that possible? Why couldn't her Aryan husband protect the child? You don't transport children alone! Has anyone ever heard of such a thing? What a tragedy! My God, how must Flora feel? Or did the child end up getting in the way of her new husband? Please try to find out more. The whole affair is extremely suspicious and shrouded in mystery.

Even though I have never met him, I am very upset about what happened to little Hans. I hear that the little boy—May the Almighty have mercy on this pure soul!—was a particularly sweet child. It breaks my heart!

Another sad letter has just reached me from Switzerland. I was hoping to finally receive news of our Fanny. You won't believe it. Our dear Fanny is no more! She drowned while fleeing across the Baltic. The fishing boat in which they were trying to cross from Rügen Island to Sweden at night began to sway and Fanny, who couldn't swim, fell overboard. She sank immediately in the ice-cold water. The pain leaves me completely mute. It seems that Hedwig, of all people, the blind baby of the family, is probably the only one from their whole family who was able to save herself. We can only pray for the other Segals in the Riga ghetto. All the letters came back. We both know what that means.

After such sad news, I have to stop for now and will write to you tomorrow.

My beloved husband!

What is my favorite cousin Fränze up to these days? Is she still working at the Jewish Hospital? Do you have to worry about her? Can you and Bruno G., who we all know is no great light, help to protect our Fränze? Does that crazy Jezebel still go to Emmi's to play Chopin études on her old piano, heedless of the Gestapo and brownshirt spies? And does she still have the chutzpah to wear her fur turned inside out under the lining of her coat? Everyone in the whole building knows that Emmi can't play the piano. Risking her neck over a few Chopin études is irresponsible but typical Fränze! Apples don't fall far from the tree, though, when you think about her son Walter and the story about the flag on the chimney. Well, you always thought there were too many crazy people in that family!

So that the letter goes out to you today, I'll close it quickly, kiss you on each cheek, on your forehead and mouth, my beloved husband.

With love,
your Else

P.S. The lawyer from Zurich is sending you the letter that you requested, with which you can convince the authorities in Berlin of our allegedly pending divorce proceedings. That way they will leave you alone for the moment about the "racial shame." I'm sure that, with God's help and a little cunning and trickery, we'll manage to draw out the proceedings until the Nazis finally come to the end of their road. May God protect us!

Hella was in love. The underground had to do without her for a while. But even her greatest love could not exist without the interference of politics. Karel, with whom not only Hella but all women in the Siemens equipment construction division, had fallen in love because he was such a handsome, tall man with a full head of dark hair, shining dark eyes, and fine facial features, was Czech and worked for the company as an interpreter for all Slavic languages and Italian.

There were surely many women who were more beautiful and more cheerful than the serious Hella, but the easy-going Karel, who made all the women's hearts beat faster, was obviously looking for his opposite and fell just as deeply in love with the somewhat dark Hella. A woman who had dedicated her life to conspiratorial work for the underground was just as exotic to a deeply Catholic country bumpkin as the entire city of Berlin, which did everything with as much determination and gravity as Hella. Karel was a Czech foreign worker from the Sudetenland in Berlin voluntarily. The young man wanted to get ahead in life! That meant that Hella didn't have to keep her love secret the way a German who was in love with a forced laborer or prisoner of war would. For her part, Hella wanted to protect his good nature, and so chose to keep the full extent of her dangerous activities secret. She merely told him that she was "helping friends in need" whom she couldn't "leave in the lurch." Karel's joie de vivre irritated and delighted her in equal measure. She saw in him those things that everyone in Germany had long since lost: lightness, cheerfulness, exuberance, craziness, skipping along the straight path, leaping, frivolity, and the inner freedom to ignore everything. That's why Hella loved him. She accepted the fact that it was something of a risk to be in love with such an attractive man; there would also be other women swooning over him. All manner of women idolized him and when they discovered that Hella had captured his heart, they eyed Hella with astonishment, jealousy, and even a touch of derision. No conspiratorial work was possible with such a man at her side, she thought. Much too conspicuous! Much too exposed! The abandon with which she gave herself to him both surprised and pleased him. No fuss or drama about her virginity like he was used to back home with women in the countryside. A woman who took this liberty so matter-of-factly, without developing complexes or feeling guilty or depraved was something new to him. Karel was impressed. He wanted to share his life with such a modern woman. Only with such a woman, he thought, could a modern man also get ahead.

During vacation, he wanted to introduce Hella to his parents in the Sudetenland. Of course, they couldn't live under the same roof unless they were married. Hella would sleep upstairs in the attic with his parents, while he would spend the night with his aunt across the street. That's just the way things were in the countryside. "In the Catholic countryside," Hella added with a hearty laugh.

"You don't always have to laugh at me. I didn't make the rules." Karel was annoyed. She was always teasing him about his old-fashioned views and chivalrous habits. It didn't occur to Hella that it might offend him. She wanted to carry the torch of enlightenment into this backward darkness and thought that everyone should be happy and grateful for it. They weren't. After entering the home of her future in laws, who had a crucifix in every room and a font of holy water at the door, she realized that not everyone would congratulate her for holding such progressive views.

In what sort of primitive society have I fallen into here? The darkest Middle Ages with superstitions, excommunications, exorcisms, confessions, women in headscarves, saying grace before meals, women spouting off about heaven and hell, silence at the dinner table, and church on Sundays? Hella shook her head.

Karel's parents slaughtered a goose to celebrate their son's return. They only very begrudgingly accepted his German fiancée, especially since they rightly suspected that she would not be a virgin when they married.

"You've both come back from Berlin half-starved. Let's have a hearty meal!"

That night Hella threw up and couldn't stop throwing up. The doctor came the next day. Karel's mother hoped it was sign that she was pregnant. Dr. Prohaska, however, rejected the idea and instead ordered "an absolutely fat-free diet, without sugar either!"

"Just like in Berlin!" Hella complained.

"You've been on very limited rations for too long. Your liver is going crazy. You have jaundice."

"Better than being pregnant during wartime," said Hella, sighing with relief.

Two weeks after they returned to Berlin, Karel made a momentous announcement in the canteen during the lunch break:

"Tonight, there's going to be a big, big, big surprise! We're celebrating!" Hella didn't like surprises. Anything she didn't have under her control, she found unsettling. She thus found a way to postpone the surprise until Saturday.

That evening, Karel ceremoniously asked Hella to take a seat at the table. He then pulled some papers out from behind his back. "It's my declaration of German citizenship! Now we can finally get married!"

Karel's announcement was indeed a big surprise, although not the way he had imagined. Hella's face turned ashen.

"Are you insane? Please tell me that none of this is true."

Karel looked at her in confusion. "Hella, darling, I'm a man of honor and I won't tolerate my wife having to live in unholy matrimony with me and our child being born a bastard if I can help it. That's how much your love means to me!"

"Am I supposed to be happy about that? Are you out of your mind? As a German you now have to go off to this idiotic war! Please, you have to reverse this immediately! The war can't last much longer. Then we can get married, for all I care, but not now! And I don't want a child until peacetime. Who would be so crazy as to bring a child into the world during a war?"

"You can't be serious! I'm willing to make any sacrifice for you and you don't want it? That can't be true, can it?"

"I don't want a sacrifice. I also don't want a man who dies for nothing just because he can't wait a few more months and has such an absurd notion of honor."

"So you don't want me?" Karel was deeply offended.

"Not now. Not under these circumstances! Is that so hard to understand?"

"It's too late," Karel said as it slowly began to dawn on him that he had made a huge mistake. "Now you have to take me, Hella!"

On the night before the wedding, Oda woke up screaming, as she often did. This time it wasn't one of her usual nightmares from the Columbia Haus torture cellar. In her dream, Oda saw her son Peter's head flying through the air and rolling toward a milestone with the number 295 on it.

"Our Peter is dead. Hella, your brother Peter has been killed," she screamed through the nocturnal silence of the garden colony.

"Mom, take your drops and try to go back to sleep. You were just having a nightmare!"

"No, Hella. That wasn't a nightmare. It was a telepathic dream!"

Hella returned to her room, but she could still hear her mother, who was now bawling. Between her mother's sobbing and her nervous state over her wedding, now she couldn't sleep either. This didn't bode well for the future.

Beaming with joy, Karel rushed to the registry office. He had a white rose with boxwood green in his buttonhole. When he saw the tear-stained faces of Hella and Oda, her mother, the ground shifted beneath him.

LIBERATION DAY

Two weeks after their wedding, Hella's husband, Karel Papesch, arrived on the front.

"Fortunately, not the Eastern Front," Oda had declared in relief.

"Only the Balkans!" Karel said to comfort Oda and Hella. "Don't forget: I speak Serbo-Croatian, which means that they can make more use of me on the staff than in the trenches."

Hella hoped that Karel's linguistic genius could save him, but she nonetheless had a hard time truly believing it. He was neither a committed German patriot nor a devoted soldier. What sort of outdated, skewed notion of honor was driving him to war? He was sacrificing himself for love! Completely senseless but very romantic and honorable.

She wanted to remember forever every second that she had spent with him.

Some of the Italian partisans had gone to the Istrian peninsula to join Yugoslav partisans who were being led by Josip Broz Tito. The sniper, Elsbeth von Strachwitz, née Kohanim, called "Elli," alias Elsa Marchetti, found her place way out in front. "The Panther," her nom de guerre, had had an especially good day. She was relaxing after shooting three high-ranking enemy officers, exceeding her target. However, she sat upright when she saw through her scope what people in partisan circles called a "gilded invitation": a totally unprotected enemy. An infantry soldier was striding right in front of her rifle as if he were strolling through a city park. He had probably lost his unit. Or had he taken a wrong turn somewhere? He didn't even have his gun with him out here on the front!

He was holding something else instead: flowers! A bouquet! Unbelievable! What kind of odd bird was this? Picking flowers on the battlefield? Such a provocation could also be a decoy, she thought, but the terrain was "clean." The only people around were herself and this dreamer. War tolerates neither sentimentality nor provocation, Elli thought. So, if you're practically begging for it, what else can I do? She cocked her rifle and fired. Her shot hit the romantic infantry soldier right between the eyes. One week later, instead of the typical military letter with one pressed flower, Hella Papesch, née Hanke, received the letter that all women in the Reich feared: the one that contained the phrase, "a hero's death."

"Do you hear what I hear?" whispered Prisoner No. 72769, whose real name was Kurt Milhofer. Prisoner No. 6982, with whom Kurt shared the cot in Jewish Block 22, growled something about shutting his trap.

"Walter, wake up! I think I hear artillery fire. Wake up, man!"

No. 6982 sat up and yawned, his eyes watering. "Might be a storm."

"Storms roll, but this thunder hammers. Typical for the roar of artillery fire. Really far away, but artillery fire! Just listen!"

Walter was suddenly wide awake. "How would someone as inexperienced as you know what artillery fire sounds like?" Walter strained to listen.

"Man, you're right!" He punched his protégé Kurt in the arm. "You're right! I'm going to lose my mind! It's the Yanks! And how do we know that?" Walter asked, pretending to be a strict teacher.

"Zero Hour. I know where you're going with this," Kurt joked.

"I'll go and assess the situation," whispered Walter.

Once outside, he realized that the SS also had sharp ears. The roll call area was already bustling with activity, which didn't bode well. Machine guns and flamethrowers were being assembled. It didn't take much imagination to guess that the SS were getting ready for a bloodbath. Walter, No. 6982, needed to make contact with the resistance group's leadership squad from Jewish Barrack 22; but he couldn't find a way to do so without being noticed. From his hiding place, he watched the SS bark orders at the kapos and barrack elders; their body language confirmed his suspicions. The only question was: Who would go first? The Russians? The Jews? Knowing the Nazis, Walter suspected that the Jewish prisoners would be liquidated shortly before the SS pulled out of Buchenwald. The camp's underground commanders had played out this scenario for a possible liberation day a hundred times. Walter thus knew what he had to do when the signal came to attack and liberate themselves. Yet, there was one important issue. In their many scenarios about what to do in the case of a possible liberation, they had failed to consider that the SS would single out the Jewish prisoners for "special treatment," something which now appeared imminent.

Walter quietly crept back to Kurt. "Just to be on the safe side, take everything with you, preferably under your cap. I don't exactly know what's going on, but if I'm not mistaken, we're all about to meet our maker."

Then came the command from the SS. "Jewish Barracks 22 and 23, line up, all of you!"

SS assault unit leader, Müller, nicknamed "Dog Müller," was visibly nervous, his face frozen in a scowl. He dispensed with the standard harassment and long drills. Instead, he shouted across the roll call area, "Effective immediately, Jewish Blocks 22 and 23 are dissolved! All prisoners from Blocks 22 and 23 are to exit the buildings and immediately march out to the roll call area! Anyone who hasn't lined up in five minutes will be shot!"

Just behind Dog Müller were the barrack elders, standing at attention with their hands at their sides. When they heard the orders "march out" and "line up" they made synchronized movements with their eyes and heads. In code, these signals meant, "Get out of here right now!"

The prisoners ran back to their barracks in a state of distress.

"Make sure you get to the Hungarians!" Walter yelled at Kurt. "They'll have to hold onto you until the Yanks get here!"

Kurt nodded. Kurt's father was Hungarian. In 1939, Kurt had become a Hungarian citizen to protect himself from the Nazis in Germany. Although that strategy hadn't worked, perhaps it would do something for him now. Or at least he hoped it would. Kurt had never even set foot in Hungary; he could manage maybe three or four words in the language, including the words for yes and no, *igen* and *nem*.

If nothing else, Kurt knew he could count on Walter. It was almost the way it had been when they were children together in the Jewish orphanage on Breite Straße in Berlin-Pankow. Walter was eleven years older than Kurt and had always protected Kurt, the little boy with the straw-blond hair.

When Kurt arrived at Buchenwald he had just turned fifteen. Walter took him under his wing again, protected him from the intrusions of his fellow inmates and placed him with Rudi Seifert in his construction detachment. That had saved Kurt's life. But now he had to fend for himself.

Walter grabbed his bundle. When he stepped out of the barracks, he couldn't believe his eyes. Prisoner No. 88973, the best tenor in his choir, the "politically unreliable, bourgeois element" Robert Fischer, who in a former life had been a sawmill owner and bon vivant from Berlin-Schöneberg, was cluelessly strolling with his bundle towards the roll call area for the prepared suicide mission.

"Eighteen!!!" Walter shouted at him.

Prisoner No. 88973 stopped dead in his tracks. "Eighteen" was the ultimate warning cry in the Jewish barracks, derived from the eighteenth Jewish prayer, which stands for the plea for life. When the unsuspecting tenor from Schöneberg had finally made his way through the distraught Jews rushing around from Barracks 22 and 23, Walter snapped at him. "Man, get out here, you dreamer! The SS have flamethrowers with them, and not for lighting cigarettes."

"Where am I supposed to go?" wailed 88973.

"Jump into the latrine if you value your life! No one from the SS will go looking there! Hang on until I come!"

Robert Fischer ran off. Holding his bundle over his head, he made a beeline for the place where he would be safe. With death-defying courage, he then jumped into the latrine, where he then stood buried up to his neck in urine and feces. He lost count of the number of times he had to vomit due to the infernal stench. When his stomach finally settled down and he could look around, he realized that he had company in the latrine pit. At least twenty heads were sticking up out of the camp's collected feces and urine.

"Do you believe in God?" a voice behind him asked. Astonished, Robert turned around.

"Do I believe in God, are you really asking me that here? Do I believe in God? What could be less relevant? What's more important is that God believes in me, buried in all this shit! Because I certainly don't believe in myself anymore!"

"Then let's pray!" said the rabbi from Barrack 23 now standing next to Robert. Wearing a prayer shawl fashioned from a striped blanket meant for horses, the rabbi from Baden began to sway in prayer, amidst the flood of brown feces. For the first time since childhood, Robert Fischer joined in the prayer, along with all the other men with them in the latrine. Together they composed more than a proper *minyan*[14], and thus their prayers would be heard:

Baruch atah adonai, magen Avraham!
Atah gibor l'olam, Adonai
me chayeh metim atah rav l'hoshi'a.
meshiv haRuach umorid
haGeshem morid haTal.

M'chalkel chayim b'chesed
m'chayeh betim b'rachamim rabim
somech nofl'im v'rofe
Cholim
umatir asurim
um'kayem emunato
l'shne afar.

Mi chamocha baal g'vurot
umi dome lach, melech
memit um'chaye umazmiach Y'shu'a.

Mi chamocha, av haRachaman,
socher y'zurav l'Chayim
b'Rachamim.

V'neeman atah le hachayot
metim
Baruch atah Adonai,
m'chaye hametim.

O king, helper, savior, and shield.
Blessed art thou, O lord, the shield of Abraham.
You, O lord, are mighty forever,
You revive the dead, You are mighty to save.
You sustain the living with loving kindness,
revive the dead with great mercy,
support the falling, heal the sick,

free the bound, and
keep your faith to them that sleep in the dust.
Who is like you, lord of the mighty acts,
and who resembles You, O king,
who orders death and restores life, and causes salvation to spring forth?
Who is like you, father of mercy,
who in mercy remembers your creatures unto life?
Blessed art thou, O lord, who revives the dead.
Amen!

Then silence suddenly descended from above them.

As a "fighter" in the Buchenwald resistance group, Walter, Prisoner No. 6982, belonged to the "camp aristocracy." Even after his second imprisonment as a Jew and "asocial," he was able to maintain his status because of his previous merits. As agreed upon ahead of time, when the Jewish blocks were dissolved, he was immediately placed along with the "Aryan" political prisoners in Rudi Seifert's block. Once there, he quickly exchanged his jacket for that of a non-Jewish dead man from the construction commando. And with that, the Jewish prisoner Walter Rubin was officially "exterminated." Wearing the jacket and number of a dead Aryan, Walter lived on.

The resistance commando put a lower priority on rescuing "non-political" Jewish prisoners. Walter thus had to draw on his talents of persuasion to convince the "Red" kapo to give him additional jackets belonging to unregistered Aryan corpses. Only with great reluctance, and because Number 6982 was a "big shot" in the hierarchy and making such a big fuss, that the Aryan comrades handed over the lifesaving jackets and numbers of the unregistered deceased Aryans.

Walter crept back to the latrine, carrying five Aryan jackets and numbers that promised a new life. He gave two of them to the tenor and the rabbi from Baden; and thus, a second chance at life in the block designated for the Dutch and Belgians. Walter distributed the remaining three jackets and numbers at random. He left it up to the three men who received them to figure out themselves where they would end up. That was all he could do.

"When will the Yanks get here?" Various "experts" among the inmates were constantly trying to find out how far away the American soldiers were, what their primary targets would be, and which roads they would probably take for their advance. "What's the wind like?" "How long until we hear something?" They did the math. According to their calculations, the Americans were about thirty to thirty-five kilometers away.

"The Americans certainly know about the Buchenwald concentration camp. But maybe they don't know the most direct route. The inhabitants of Weimar aren't going to tell them that Buchenwald is the top attraction around here and point them in this direction." Everyone nodded.

"What in the hell?! If that's true, then the electricians have got to get to work. Immediately!" the underground commando decided. The electricians were all trade union members and supported the Social Democrats. Thus, relations between them and the communist-led underground commando weren't, to put it very mildly, the best. The communist leaders hoped that their historical tensions could be put aside on a day like this one.

"Can you build a radio?"

"If we get the materials, no problem at all. It could be ready in no time. But the "Red Orchestra" is closed, though, in case you didn't know," the Social Democratic electricians joked. They were the only ones laughing, however, over their allusion to the alleged Soviet spy group that had been summarily executed by the Nazis. The communists replied with scowls. "In this situation, let's remain impartial, shall we?" Seifert scolded the electricians.

"According to our calculations, the Americans should be about thirty kilometers away from us. We have to send them an SOS so that they can find us faster, here behind the mountain, Ettersberg. If they don't come fast enough, the SS will kill us all first. Where's the radio?"

In the meantime, there was no sign of the SS anywhere in sight. The normally airtight control checks were already showing large gaps.

Camp inmates used a radio "obtained" from an abandoned SS barrack and some other materials from the workshop to create a transmitter. On April 9, 1945, they sent an SOS signal with the coordinates of the camp out into the ether.

They received an answer on the morning of April 10th. The US Army announced its advance. The eagerly anticipated Zero Hour was finally at hand!

The underground fighters were given orders and weapons. Walter was to creep up silently from behind the strategically important Watch Tower 4, then storm it, and take the guard captive.

Since receiving his orders, he had gone over them possibly a thousand times. To carry them out, he'd been given an old Mauser pistol of questionable reliability, along with a dagger, and a garotte, the latter for in case he had to kill silently. Walter prayed that when the time came the revolver would fire and hit its mark. He had had only two opportunities to practice with it in the quarry under cover of dynamite explosions. Although he was nervous about his weapons and training, he was nonetheless proud to have been chosen—the only Jew in the entire commando selected to help carry out this dangerous mission for the liberation of the camp. The job might have fallen to someone with more experience on the battlefield. The underground commando had selected Walter for a number of reasons: he had kept a level head and showed ingenuity during other difficult missions; he was hardened by the experience of torture; he was in relatively good physical condition and could climb faster and more nimbly than anyone else in the underground commando; and owing to his rise in rank to the position of "fighter" he received special food rations. Plus, the camp's liberation commando also preferred a German for the mission instead of a Red Army prisoner, since a Soviet prisoner of war would have simply liquidated every single member of the SS, and would also have been difficult to control.

"Too many uncertainties," decided Seifert. "We have to stay in control. Brothers here, comrades there!"

He then got down to brass tacks and straightened his shoulders.

"Comrades, it is the task of the German resistance on German soil to restore civilization and also the honor of Germany," he declared solemnly. "That is why only German comrades have been selected for the liberation commando! The war criminals that we capture will all be brought to justice! We need them alive. That's an order! Only kill in self-defense!"

Walter received his orders. At last, he could restore his own honor!

After Walter's second arrest, the Nazis had labeled him as an "asocial." They then made him wear a black triangle above the yellow star for "Jew." For a long time, he could not get over that. The black triangle was a personal insult against his honor; it ate away at him, transformed him from an honorable red triangle into a worthless nothing, to an asocial, who like ten thousand other Jews was a mere victim to that wave of arrests. But he, Walter Kohanim-Rubin, was no victim! At most, he was a defeated fighter! He was proud of that. Nobody could take that from him. Now he would show everyone! He had lost the first battle against the Nazis, but now he would belong to the victors of history!

Silently, Walter scaled the back of the watchtower with a captured SS dagger between his teeth. The guard at the top of the tower was dozing off. Walter snuck up behind him and held the gun to this temple. Shocked, the guard obediently threw his gun off the tower. "I surrender!" he said calmly and slowly raised his hands.

Walter was almost disappointed; he had imagined the moment of victory to be more grandiose. In the movies, a scene like this in a newsreel would have been accompanied by a triumphant fanfare and a large orchestra with lots of violins and an oboe in the background.

Time stood still for a moment.

"Am I a hero or just a guy who did what had to be done?" he wondered.

It went against Walter's nature to play the hero. A melancholy tremor wafted through him. Why didn't he feel triumphant and overpowered with joy? Maybe heroes no longer existed! Only a profound weariness and sorrow remained.

And, yet here he was! He had made it! Twelve years in prison!

In the Brandenburg Prison from 1933 to 1937, a short break in which he was amnestied, and then a second imprisonment around the Christmas holidays in 1937.

All told, eight years at Buchenwald!

He had made it!

From the age of twenty-one, in 1933, to age of thirty-two, in 1945. He would celebrate his thirty-third birthday on May 1st as a free man! And what a celebration it was going to be! Today, April 11, 1945, he had been born for a second time! But where was the jubilation? The time of his imprisonment flashed before his eyes: the communist resistance hero Ernst Thälmann's execution and the party's secret memorial service in the camp; the three men, the criminals, whom he had killed in the camp on the orders of the resistance commando and who had haunted his nightmares ever since—a nightly terror against which he was powerless. The agony of torture also crept into his sleep. He would have to live with that forever. His role as resident jester of the powerful, whether they were called Seifert or belonged to the SS, was, by contrast, something to laugh about. He could still clearly recall how he had negotiated three eggs, sugar, and two lemons from the troop's cook in exchange for an exclusive parody of Goebbels, so that the seriously ill young boy, Kurt, in Jewish Block 23, would survive and one day become either a cobbler, a bookseller, or a Nobel Prize winner. He remembered how tens of thousands of prisoners had jerked off all night long when Zarah Leander sang over the loudspeaker. Most of all, he remembered the endless passionate debates about different ways to prepare food. Should rhubarb-porridge be flavored with cinnamon or vanilla? What was the best way to season roast goose? Using sage or marjoram? There was also the debate about whether the ping-pong-sized strawberries in the SS commandant's garden were so large because he fertilized the strawberry beds with ashes from the crematorium. He recalled how during his first winter there, he sought to protect himself from frostbite and lung infection by padding his prisoner uniform with thick layers of newspaper until he could hardly move. He would never forget the nights he had spent with his old Jewish family stories, which he had to keep telling to Kurt and the comrades: the story of his ancestor Zippora Orenstein, who after the Cossack pogrom in the seventeenth century had been carried off to the Ukrainian steppe, where she bore two children to her tormentor. However, by serving her kidnapper copious amounts of homemade schnapps, Zippora managed to flee the steppe and return to Poland, carrying her two children in a horse's saddlebags.

It was because of the legendary Zippora that he had been determined to survive. His fellow prisoners hung on his every word when he told them how after her successful escape, Zippora had to marry ole Chaim Orenstein because of the disgrace of giving birth to two Cossack bastards. Later ole Chaim ran away with his business partner's money in order to follow the false Messiah Shabbatai Zwi from Hamburg to Jerusalem in a salt barrel; the story about why his mother's family, the Kohanims had three horses in their coat of arms, because as horse traders they had saved a Polish count from his marauding bodyguards on their way to the horse market and the peasants had mistaken the Kohanim horses for the king's cavalry, whereupon the Jewish horse trader Kohanim was appointed steward of the Polish count's estate out of gratitude. It was only when recounting all these family legends that he realized what a rare treasure he possessed: his Jewish heritage, which up to then he had always looked down upon.

Walter smiled at the thought of how his Jewish comrades in the camp always teased him for revealing his country roots by plucking dandelions, cress, and sorrel everywhere in summer and by eating elderberries straight from the bush. "There goes Walter eating grass again!" Walter looked back on the establishment and success of his camp choir "The Zebras," his pride and joy, and the camp's theater and cabaret group, which he had set up and run with his buddy Friedrich Kahle. He remembered all the effort it had taken to shore up comrades who wanted to give up and were on their way to becoming "Muslims," camp jargon for those who were tired of life and wanted to surrender to their fate. His whole life he would react with fear when he saw a doctor, remembering how doctors in the camps used the infirm to carry out experiments. You couldn't shake something like that. The mental anguish caused by the horrible gray of the camp was no less awful. It was the gray of death, as if all the colors of life had been executed at the same time and only the red of blood were permitted. It all played in his head like a movie in fast motion.

And now it was all over.

Ah, well, heroism! Perhaps it's no more than an antiquated myth? Something from the past? He collected his racing thoughts and forced himself back to the present.

"You will all be put on trial!" Walter barked at the prisoner. He wasn't even thinking about the guillotine on Alexanderplatz, which he and Kurt had fantasized about before falling sleep, wondering what they would do if they took power one day and tried all the war criminals. They had argued fiercely about whether Hitler, Himmler, and their ilk should be imprisoned for life, because that would make them suffer more, and about whether death was perhaps too lenient a punishment that would also turn them into martyrs.

Once he had made his way with the guard from the tower back to the ground, Walter cuffed the thug's arms behind his back.

"I have a wife and children," the man protested.

"Shut the hell up! Otherwise, I'll shoot you for real, you rat! Because I don't have a wife and children! And you know why, you stupid asshole! Come with me!"

Holding his gun at the ready, he collected his prisoner's weapon and led him kicking and screaming to the roll-call site. The other prisoners looked at them with awe, then backed away timidly, silently opening a path for them. Other arrested guards and SS henchmen were herded together behind Walter, who continued to push his prisoner forward. Suddenly, after his fellow prisoners had recovered from their initial astonishment, stones began to fly at him and the prisoners. The mob wanted to pounce on the overpowered SS men and guards. A lynch mob mentality was beginning to form.

Walter fired two warning shots into the air with the confiscated rifle of the arrested guard. "From now on, law and order will prevail again in Germany! No lynch law! No lynch law! Otherwise, we're no better than those bastards!" he shouted at the murderous mob.

The angry crowd wanted revenge and Walter's talk about morality as the cornerstone of a new beginning, didn't make much of an impression. But the gun did. So the lynch mob, composed of men who had been his comrades just a moment ago, backed away shyly at first. But they again grew aggressive, forcing the liberation commando to surround the SS men and the guards to protect them. The liberators now pointed their weapons at their fellow prisoners, who were hurling vile insults at them. Walter and the others from the commando who had formed a circle around their former guards were attacked with stones and bare hands. They fired warning shots into the air again. They would not be able to hold the furious mob at bay much longer.

"Where are the Americans?" Walter wondered impatiently. The hatred he saw in the faces of the camp inmates was something he had only seen in a fascist mob. Just then the loudspeakers crackled: "Comrades! We are free!"

With that, the camp gates sprang open and an American jeep carrying four armed military police soldiers drove into the compound. The hand on the camp clock stopped at 3:16 p.m. It was April 11, 1945. The Zero Hour for Buchenwald. The mob backed away in disbelief. Then wild jubilation broke out everywhere.

It was over! Even the most enraged among them sank to their knees in tears, threw themselves on the ground, and kissed the dirt. Others hugged each other, or simply stood frozen to the spot. The American MPs took command of the captured SS men and camp guards. In good Prussian manner, the resistance commander Seifert and the senior camp resident reported to the MPs by clicking their heels together and standing at attention. With cigarettes dangling from their lips, the GIs casually propped their machine guns against their hips and gazed in amazement and disbelief at the two prisoners standing before them, ready to report to duty.

After this grotesque image of two colliding worlds had been eternally seared into his memory, Walter let his gaze wander, a habit he had developed in prison to protect himself. His eyes stopped at the clothing dispensary. He could hardly believe his eyes. Wearing a baggy pinstripe suit with a white shirt, an impeccably knotted tie, shoes polished to their highest gleam, and a Homburg hat, No. 92574, the Jewish prisoner with whom he had run the theater group, stepped out into the sun and squinted. The sun had finally pushed its way through the clouds on this cool April 11th. Equally anxious and curious, it wanted to grant this sublime day some additional splendor, albeit belatedly.

Prisoner No. 92574 must have felt Walter's eyes on him, because he suddenly turned to face him. With a grin, he strolled toward him. Walter shouldered the carbine and stuck his gun in his belt.

With a laugh, No. 92574 approached him.

"Until the war is over, around six?!" Walter asked with a grin.

"Yes, until the war is over, around six at the Leipzig Volkstheater, Walter!"

No. 92574 saluted by raising two fingers to his hat brim.

Dumbfounded, Walter looked his theater chum up and down. Though a little worse for wear, in front of him stood the actor Friedrich Kahle from Leipzig, a gentleman with sunken features, a close shave, and an extremely baggy suit.

Brecht would have cast a man just like him as Mack the Knife, Walter thought, as he shook his head with a chuckle. "You'll never make a good prole, Fritz!"

"You won't either, Walter! Don't even try! And one last piece of advice: steer clear of politics! You're too much of a romantic for that!" They embraced each other briefly.

"Don't forget you can find me at the Leipzig Volkstheater, Walter!" Kahle flicked an invisible bit of dust from his lapel. "If you're wise, you'll head that way as soon as this circus is over."

Unperturbed by the unfolding fracas between the American soldiers, the captured SS men, and the prisoners-turned-lynch mob, Kahle straightened his hat and the knot in his tie. Then he sauntered out of the camp as if he were merely making his way from a café to a rehearsal. The sun sent a beam of light after him, like a tracking spotlight across a stage.

What an exit, Walter thought. Heroism, the grotesque, and the ordinary are sometimes remarkably close to each other!

Friedrich Kahle brushed his left hand lightly across the gate inscription: "To Each Their Own!"

Farewell to the horror.

Then he walked out through the gate and into the future.

The last day of school before summer vacation happened to be the day after the scandal over my refusal to join the Young Pioneers. The students all received report cards. Mine was very good, apart from one glaring inaccuracy. Across the top was written, "Student joined the Young Pioneers on July 11, 1956." As it turned out, my joining had been a foregone conclusion, whether I wanted to or not! Dejected, I slowly made my way home. I didn't really want to bother my parents with the silly issue about the Pioneers. They had bigger worries. Plus, I knew that my mother would react by chastising me and carrying on about the trouble I had caused. Frowning, I showed them my report card. I sputtered out the story about what had happened the day before school got out. My mother grabbed her head, then unleashed the anticipated torrent.

"God knows we have enough political trouble. Can't you just shut up for a change?! Do you always have to add your own two cents' worth? And cause such a scene like that!"

The word "scene" made my father's jaw drop.

"Did you ever join the League of German Girls?! No, you didn't! Come on, Hella! Don't you see? Apples don't fall far from the tree! The little girl is our daughter. We brought her up like that! It's not her fault. Besides, she's right, those party functionaries are to blame for not leaving kids alone! First the interrogation over the radio station signal and now an organized coercion of one child in front of the whole class to try to force her to join the Pioneers!"

“That’s right!” she said, turning to me. “You couldn’t possibly miss a chance to make a big scene with lots of applause! Is that what’s important to you?!” my mother shouted back. “How did I screw up and end up with two such childish people!”

My father refused to let that go. Over the next two hours, my parents fought and yelled at each other. I sat between them, feeling guilty and helpless, waiting to see who would win. This time my father had the more persuasive arguments. And he was on my side! My mother had to admit defeat. To escape her resentment, I immediately locked myself in the bathroom.

Furious, my father put my report card in his jacket pocket, quickly attached his pant clamps, slammed the front door, and cycled to school on his racing bike. My father kicked up a ruckus in the principal’s office, insisting that my report card be changed immediately. An hour later, he returned with the corrected report, which he threw down reproachfully on my mother’s desk.

Apart from these misfortunes, summer vacation promised to be never-ending, scorching hot, and full of adventures, excursions, and swimming. From morning to night, I frolicked around Oranke Lake with friends from the neighborhood. This summer was the first time that us “mere mortals” were allowed to go to the lake, and we took it over! Up to then, the lake had been fenced off and reserved for party functionaries and their families. They all lived secret lives in a boarded-up city, with six-foot high fences, guarded gates, and armed watchtowers. If they did leave the compound, it was in limousines with chauffeurs at the wheel and lace curtains across the windows. That summer, me and the other kids liked to dare each other to such subversive activities as pelting their limousines with rotten tomatoes or eggs or distracting the guards so that we could invade the compound. When we did manage to breach the security, we would climb the fence and make off with enormous quantities of cherries from the trees that grew there. After filling several shopping bags with stolen goodies, we would retreat to the lake, whelping cries of triumph.

However, one day, we headed off to the lake to go swimming, only to discover that we weren’t allowed to enter. The lake had been closed off again. They were looking for a drowning victim. Half an hour later, the fire department pulled a man in only his underwear out of the lake. It was the first dead body that we children had ever seen, and that made it extremely interesting. The dead man was about forty years old. His body was as pale as wax and his face had a bluish tinge to it. His tongue hung out of his mouth, while his dark hair was plastered to his forehead. The helm of a ship was tattooed to his upper right arm.

"Drunk, probably had a heart attack," a fireman guessed.

The doctor and paramedic exchanged noticeably oblique glances but said nothing. We children could already understand that much: something was not right with the man's death. Robbed of our joy in swimming, we made up for it by continuing to mill about and theorize about what might have taken place. Just before noon, we departed.

When I got back home, there was a wild commotion in the apartment corridor. I could just make out my father as he chased two men down the staircase with a poker. The men who were running away were the same Stasi men who had woken us up a previous Sunday at six o'clock in the morning.

"You dogs! You were in the Hitler Youth not all that long ago, and you of all people want to tell me what socialism is all about?! How about you go take a sniff in that place where I spent twelve years producing shit for socialism and the New Germany!"

One of the men, with fear in his eyes and a scratch on his forehead, almost ran into me. My father had hit the other man on the back of his head. He was bleeding profusely.

My father slumped against the kitchen door, breathing heavily.

After he calmed down, he exclaimed: "Do you know what they wanted from me? It's unbelievable! They wanted to blackmail me, to make me spy on my former camp comrades who have been successful since then, such as my old friends Seifert and the Axes! In return, they offered to wipe out the incident on June 17th from my file!"

My mother's jaw dropped. Then she pulled herself together and resumed command. "Go, go! We have to be fast now! Pack up! Only the essentials. Our papers and one change of clothes!"

My parents started to frantically rummage around in all the closets. They stashed various papers underneath the false bottom of a small shopping bag; others they stuck under their clothing.

We'll be in the West today, I silently rejoiced. Finally, this dreary, oppressive life would end! I yanked out my small child's suitcase and hurried over to my toy cupboard.

My mother admonished me sharply. "No conspicuous luggage, and definitely no suitcases! No briefcases either. We have to look like a completely ordinary family on our way to visit relatives. And remember:

don't ever get attached to material things! The most important things in life are in our heads and our hearts. Everything else can be replaced."

With a pouty expression, I shoved my suitcase back under the bed. I calmly packed my report cards, my poetry album, my three favorite books, and my teddy bear into my school bag. I topped all this with my new coat. A pity about my pretty new ball! It would not fit in my satchel. "And what about my bike?"

"It stays here! You can have a new one in the West!"

I wasn't sure I believed that. Even my father seemed to be struggling to say goodbye to his racing bike. He ground his teeth as he stood in front of his trophies and his bicycle. He finally shrugged and turned his back on them.

Sentimentality is a luxury!

As my parents frantically gathered up the most important items, I sat down at the kitchen table and wrote two notes. On the first piece of paper, I scribbled, "This bike is the property of Harald Jandte," and I attached the note to my bicycle's luggage rack. Harald was my protégé in the neighborhood pack. He had a speech impediment, and anyone who dared to tease or mimic Harald had to answer to me. On the second piece of paper, I wrote Manne's name. Manne was my best friend and the leader of our gang. I wanted him to have my father's racing bike, which he had long eyed wistfully. After I had attached this note to my father's bicycle, I was ready to go. A strange headiness swept over me. Excitement over our new life! Just to be safe, my mother sent my father down to the streetcar shelter in case the Stasi men or the police returned before we could get away.

Then she made a decision. "No, we won't cross the border until early this evening! The informers will have to talk things through with their supervisors first. They won't be back before tomorrow morning!"

We waited ages until the sun began to set. In the meantime, we listened closely for any suspicious sounds: for cars that might stop in front of our building, for telltale footsteps in the stairwell or down in the courtyard. A bird settling on the flower box? Or was it someone at the door?

"That's just our nerves," my mother explained. She considered suppertime the ideal time for us to cross the border at Wollankstraße. "People get hungry, and they let their guard down! Besides, that's when they change the guards. They'll be wrapped up in their own affairs."

At the last moment, my mother grabbed the bouquet out of the vase and wrapped its damp stems in newspaper. Not a Western newspaper! It had to be the East German *Neues Deutschland*! I was supposed to carry the flowers with the East German paper title and the wet stems. I thought the East German newspaper was silly, but my mother did not wish to run even the slightest of risks.

"If anyone asks you, today is Aunt Else's birthday, and we're going to see her at her home in Rankestraße. And always smile sweetly!"

The prospect of living with Aunt Else in her huge eight-room apartment on Kurfürstendamm made our flight all the more attractive for me. I was looking forward to bubblegum, long-lasting lollipops, and real Coca Cola in tapered bottles with pretty letters, to the elegance of chrome trim, to the glowing West German colors, and to the scent of coffee roasters, and oranges. I was longing to have suppers, which Aunt Else called the "evening repast," and thought it very chic that even sandwiches were eaten with knives and forks at my aunt's home. Nor were the meals served on oilcloth. And the bread didn't come to the table on awful, pig-shaped sandwich boards. We ate on actual plates that sat on a damask tablecloth, accompanied by candlesticks and cloth napkins in napkin rings bearing engraved names. At Aunt Else's, even I had my own silver napkin ring with my name on it! For me, this was the West in "widescreen format," just like "Sissi," Soraya, white crepe-shoe soles, HB, Frauengold tonic, Mickey Mouse, Donald Duck, *Stern*, *Quick*, *Heim*, *World*, and jazz. Finally, out of the narrow gray, East German ugliness. No more listening and pretending! No more flag-raisings in the schoolyard on Monday mornings, no more marching around with flags, no more metal collecting, no more hoisting of flags on the balcony because otherwise the section representative would show up at our door! No Stasi visits on Sundays shortly before six in the morning. No more radio signal quizzes. No more Young Pioneers.

All that would be over for good!

The moment I said goodbye, I instantly forgot Weißensee and East Berlin, as if they had never existed. Friends? I'd find new ones! In less than an hour, I would be in the world I was meant to be in!

It would be wild and adventurous. For someone who had managed to survive this long in East Germany, this would be a piece of cake!

At the very last moment, my mother tied one of the despised wide, red taffeta ribbons in my hair. Luckily, I didn't have to put on the dumb white dress with the petticoat, only my second-best dress with the hem with red handiwork. Wearing our best, with me in my white nylon dress, would attract too much attention, my mother warned. Our inconspicuousness was almost exaggerated and kitschy, I thought, when I caught sight of us together in the hallway wardrobe mirror and evaluated our clothing: schoolbag, jaunty bow, dumb red patent-leather shoes, teddy bear in one hand, bouquet wrapped in *Neues Deutschland* in the other. My mother, the silent grand master of disguise, was finally satisfied and praised me for not bawling. She smiled at me affectionately and confidently. She was proud of me! And she even said as much!

That was the moment I knew that everything would be all right, regardless of what happened. I reached for her hand, full of confidence. In the building passageway, she soundlessly closed the apartment door and placed the keys under the mat. Without turning on the light in the stairwell, we tiptoed down the stairs in our socks, as quiet as mice, with our shoes in hand, then out of the building and away.

Vanished!

Berlin-Weißensee was now just another place of no return.

AN ENDING WITH AND WITHOUT FEAR

In early May 1945, the rocket launchers north of Berlin fell silent. All the girls in the garden colonies in northern Berlin seemed to have had only one destination: Oda's house.

Oda was ready. She started by unearthing the communist party flag from 1923 and nailing it to the wall in her mini palace in the garden colony. For many years, it had laid buried in a box beneath a manure pile, wrapped in a protective oil cloth. Now it was hanging prominently in the "vestibule" of her home, a combination of foyer, hallway, and living room. The flag was highly visible. You could even see it from outside, directly through the window. After hanging the flag, Oda styled her now white-gray hair, fastening it with three combs. Then she took a seat beneath the flag; leaning on a walking stick, she gently lowered herself into place. All that stood between her, and the front door was the dining room table. In the two rooms behind the vestibule where she was seated, stood fifty girls and young women. Packed tightly together like herrings, they hardly dared to breath.

Oda sat there like a monument: solid and protective. She waited.

When she heard the first soldiers' boots on the path out front, she stiffened her spine and lit a fire in her eyes. The door flew open with a crash and two Red Army soldiers stood in the doorway, rifles at the ready.

"You're supposed to remove your cap and take off your boots inside a proper home!" she snarled in Russian.

The two soldiers were so taken aback that they tore their caps off their heads and mumbled, "Excuse us, little mother!" and closed the door cautiously. Oda heard a troop of soldiers gathering around the house and the sound of them saluting at attention to someone. Orders were being shouted in this and that direction.

The door opened again, this time very carefully. An officer stuck his head into the vestibule, carefully brushed off his boots, took off his cap with a polite smile, and greeted Oda politely.

"Mother, how did you get here?"

"With love, young man, not with war!"

"I would have liked that better too."

Then he turned to examine the flag, looking at it in amazement. He ran his fingers reverently over the embroidered letters and the clumsily painted portraits of Karl Marx, Friedrich Engels, and Lenin.

"Tell me, is the flag real? Is it really from 1923?"

"Yes, as real as me, the old local chairperson of the German Communist Party of Germany! And this is a proper communist home! We've protected the flag with our lives all these years!"

To drive home her words, she set her old membership card from 1921 on the table.

"That can't be! All the communists in Germany are dead."

"Then young man, you're talking to a ghost!"

"May you live a hundred years, little mother!"

He donned his army cap, saluted Oda respectfully, marched out of the house, and barked some orders outside.

Once everything was quiet again, Hella was the first to venture forward into the vestibule where her mother was sitting beneath the flag. She found Oda sitting upright. Very pale. Frozen in time, she had breathed her last.

Else Dahnke only knew the famous pianist from the newspapers. The fact that he wished to give a big charity concert for the surviving Jews of Berlin was a big sensation. "A Jewish concert in Berlin of all places!" Since most of the concert halls had been destroyed, the momentous occasion was to take place in the radio station's broadcasting hall and would be transmitted throughout all of Germany. Franziska, who had been invited to attend in person with a special guest ticket, did not want anyone to notice that she was nervous, which was why she was nagging Bruno, the way she always did. Next to Bruno stood Walter and his fiancée Hella Hanke, with whom he had become reacquainted at his new job with the police department.

"Well, I'm glad that I don't have to crawl on my stomach under walls this time to shake your hand," Hella joked when she met the new political commissar on the day he came to Potsdam to check out his new office. Seifert, his former concentration camp comrade, was now head of police in Berlin. In recognition of his loyalty, he had appointed Walter as a "political commissar" in Brandenburg. Puzzled, Walter studied the young woman with the Tatar eyes closely. "Do I know you?"

"Don't you remember? The little girl from the street fights in Wedding, back in 1929?"

It suddenly came back to Walter. "Well, you don't say! Apparently, little girls in street fights turn into pretty women who end up working for the records department for the Potsdam police! Who would've thought?! And how is your mother doing?"

Hella answered by pointing to her mourning band.

"There's definitely too much mourning going on in this country. We have to change that!"

From the moment of that chance encounter in the police department in Potsdam, the two became inseparable.

Franziska was less than thrilled. "You should have a young Jewish girlfriend."

"Why, Mother? Why?"

Fränze had no answer for this. Annoyed, she pressed her lips together.

"She's such an ordinary girl, nothing special! And marriage to her won't bring you anything! She's even poorer than we are. If you can imagine such a thing!" Franziska lamented. "She grew up in a garden colony!" She shook her head. "At least Benno found a Jewish wife with money in London. And they already have a son! Take him as your example!"

Else had forbidden her cousin Fränze from spoiling the evening and the time with Hella with her careless remarks and infamously sharp tongue. "We've been friends forever, but that could change!" she warned Franziska, hoping to prevent any potential dramas. Else also reminded her friend that the two of them also had non-Jewish husbands. "Why shouldn't Walter have a non-Jewish wife?"

"But, Else, our situation is completely different! Children of a Jewish woman always remain Jewish. But not the children of a *shiksha*. You know that!" By then, Franziska had become even stricter than the Jewish congregation in Berlin. Else impatiently waved aside Franziska's additional commentary.

After an interminably long wait, the famous maestro finally appeared. The crowd responded with oohs and aahs, and then applause. Max Gulkowitsch looked around, searching in the crowd. Then he made his way toward the representative of Berlin's Jewish congregation. He stopped, made a bit of small talk, and then continued his search for someone. Slightly puzzled, the now corpulent Max gripped a wilted yellow rose in his six-fingered hand.

Else wanted to go to him and draw his attention to Franziska.

"Leave it, Else…" Franziska said.

"But we made an extra effort to be here…"

"You made the extra effort. I didn't! If the famous Max Gulkowitsch can no longer recognize Franziska Kohanim, then it's not meant to be! Am I a schmuck or something? This no-name maestro shouldn't be putting on such airs! Everything he is, is because of us. Gimme a break, Mr. Big Shot! At least I know where I belong! Come on, Bruno, let's go!"

She rushed out into the street. Bruno trailed behind her, carrying both of their coats.

"Always this Jewish agitation, Fränze!"

They barely made it to the streetcar. On the platform, Bruno helped her into her coat, which she now wrapped tightly around her. When they had finally taken their seats, Franziska stared at the window shrouded in vapor. Shivering, she turned up the Persian collar of her new coat. Bruno struggled to pull the fare out of his pocket. The conductor put the coins into his gleaming fare-collection box, which hung across his chest and jangled when he had to make change. Once the conductor had moved up to join the driver, Bruno finally asked, clearly irritated, "What's this all about?"

Franziska didn't answer. She continued to gaze silently out into the dark night beyond the window. With her index finger, she wrote something onto the fogged windowpane. "German loyalty!"

Two tears dripped down onto Bruno's gray Kaiser Wilhelm beard. He then leaned his head against hers, and they drove on through the cold Berlin night. Past the ruins that beckoned to them like ghosts. Home.

THE APPOINTMENT

Ms. Seraphina Kühnel, my defense attorney, arrives at the hearing in an extremely bad mood. Two photographers scurry down the corridor towards us and take pictures.

"Are you the woman with the knockout drops?" one of them wants to know.

A well-known German court reporter is sitting in the courtroom with a few colleagues, talking shop. The story is potentially newsworthy. A women's activist and torture victim from Iran and a former journalist from Berlin.

"Do you know them?" Ms. Kühnel asks.

I shrug. I am feeling relieved.

Impatient, my lawyer is drumming her impeccably manicured fingernails against the file folder labeled, "The Federal Republic of Germany v. Kohanim-Rubin." She alternates between tugging at her lawyer's robe and fiddling with her phone. Looking at the label on the file, I can't help but think of my father's trial, "The German Empire v. Kohanim-Rubin," and the preparation of a treasonous enterprise because of a red flag on a factory chimney. Is this a hereditary thing? To be sued by the state? I imagine my ancestors looking down from the heavens on the last of their clan and judging me, asking whether I am worthy to be a part of my family's rebellious tradition and show the requisite "Tenue!"

Ms. Kühnel snaps me out of my daydream. "A new judge is hearing the case now."

"Is that good or bad?"

"Neither!"

She returns to beating out a rhythm on the file covers. Judging by the syncopation, it must be jazz.

On the other side of the courtroom sits my co-defendant Nasi Gohari next to her youthful public defender, his inexperience showing in his eyes. People are taking photos, wanting interviews. Nasi Gohari shouts, "No comment!" three times. The press leaves her alone and then gets ready for the doors to open, lining up outside the door like competitors at the start of a race, their press passes hanging down over their stomachs.

Finally, a bailiff opens one side of the double doors, permitting only the public prosecutor and the defense attorneys to enter. Everyone else must wait outside. Nasi Gohari and I exchange questioning glances. Is that a good or bad sign? Is there a deal?

The press is annoyed. Everyone reaches for their phones. Then the door suddenly swings open again and the officer calls the next case.

Adjourned?!

My defense lawyer sails towards me with flushed cheeks and flashing eyes. She is quicker than her elegant shoes would suggest.

"The case against you has been dropped."

She pauses for effect, waiting for applause. I respond accordingly, forming my mouth into an "oh" and opening my eyes wide with admiration. She throws her head back and announces, with pride, "The judge didn't have enough evidence against you to open proceedings for human smuggling. The case against the co-defendant will be heard in a new trial. Congratulations!"

My eyes scan the sky through the window in the corridor. Is my father sitting up there with bicycle clips on the bottom of his pant legs, holding his thumbs up in approval?

"Some people are born lucky; we weren't," I hear my father whisper. "But people who can make their own luck in the face of misfortune are the luckiest of all. That's our sort of luck: the luck of those who find a way!"

ACKNOWLEDGEMENTS

Rolf Kralovitz,
Kurt Milhofer,
Juliet Pressler,
John Richter,
Dr. Hermann Simon,
Dr. Andreas Nachama,
Dr. Iris Hauth,
Krista Maria Schädlich,
Angelica Benedict,
Ulla Bennstein-Wechselberg,
Heidi von Plato,
Gudrun Küsel,
Matthias Dieffenbach,
Heimat Museum Wedding,
Professor George Sava,
Sheraton Miramar Resort, El Gouna, Red Sea.

ENDNOTES: ON TRANSLATION AND YIDDISH VOCABULARY

1 In re geographic terms and place names; To maintain a little bit of the flavor of the setting, I followed the example of other translators of books set in the historic German Reich and Berlin, leaving streets as *Straße* with the house number after, the way it would appear in German. With the exception of the iconic, *Potsdamer Platz*, I did, however, translate *Platz* as *square*, as I thought this would aid readers in imagining the type of space being referred to. In the Eastern part of the former German Reich, today's Poland, I stuck to the German version for cities that later took on Polish names, since the characters would have known the places as such. An exception is the river *Vistula* for which I kept its modern, Polish name, even though *Weichsel* was how Germans used to refer to it.

2 A corruption of the Hebrew *Kazim Elim Bochen*, meaning "the sole commander of the tribe."

3 The original German title of Marcia Zuckermann's Jewish-German family saga, *Mischpoche*, refers to a Jewish family or clan, and thus may extend to include distant relatives or a social unit. The term comes from the word *mishpokhe* in Yiddish (*mishpāḥāh* in Hebrew) and first appeared in the mid-19th century, not long before the beginning of Zuckermann's family saga. *Mishpokhe* is usually transliterated into English in one of three ways: *mishpachah*, *mishpoke*, or *mishpocha*. For the title, and for the occasions when the word appears in the novel, I chose the latter, for the reason that the intuitive pronunciation of *mishpocha* by a native American English speaker would most closely replicate the pronunciation of both *mishpokhe* in Yiddish and *Mischpoche* in German.

4 Selma's chosen nom de plume "Wanda Vogel" is an untranslatable pun. The German word *Wandervogel* refers to a migratory bird as well as someone who likes to travel. Although Selma surely had the former in mind, it is nonetheless worth noting that most German readers would likely know that Wandervogel was also the name adopted by a German youth movement that emerged in 1896 that many consider a forerunner to the Nazi youth.

5 In general, I avoided political party acronyms. Thus, I chose to employ the phrase *Social Democrats* to refer to the Social Democratic Party of Germany, instead of the German acronym SPD. When it came *communists* and *communism*, I maintained the lower case, unless it was a specific reference to the *Communist Party*.

6 In the German original, lawyers invariably use the title Dr. before their last names, which historically was common practice throughout Central Europe. However, to avoid confusing Anglo-American readers, who would likely associate the title with medical professionals, I excluded them all together. To impart a sense of the character's prestige and elevated social status, I inserted *Esq*. after their last names.

7 Strictly speaking, *Berlinisch* is not a dialect. Berliners nonetheless have a distinctive and colorful manner of speech that plays an important role in certain scenes in *Mishpocha* and that, consequently, introduces some challenges for the translator. Its origins are murky, but the most important strands of influence include: Saxon, Low German, French, Yiddish, and working-class culture. Berliners have a particular way of pronouncing German and sprinkle their conversation with phrases that originate from other cultures. They are also known for employing an irreverent manner of speech—not to mention humor—and a host of creative coinages.

Germans know it when they hear it and Zuckermann tried to convey its distinctiveness by accurately representing its pronunciation. Some of the most obvious verbal ticks include dropping beginning or ending sounds (*habe* becomes *hab'*) and pronouncing "g" as "j" (*gut* becomes *jut*), "ch" as "k" (*ich* becomes *ick*), or "ei" as "ee" (*kein* becomes *keen*).

To help me navigate the translation of Berlin speech, I looked to Michael Hoffman's translation of *Every Man Dies Alone* by Hans Fallada (2010) and Niall Sellar's translation of *Babylon Berlin* by Volker Kutscher (2018). I followed their lead in choosing only to represent the pronunciation sparingly, instead simply adding cues to the reader like, "she said in heavy Berlin accent." In cases where it was more integral to an exchange, such as when Franziska chides Walter not to speak Berlinisch, I drew on American working-class and urban slang from roughly the 1920s–1940s to help capture the spirit of the Berlin manner of speaking.

8 "Night Jacket Quarter" was a term used in cities in northern Germany, including Hamburg and Lübeck, to refer to a part of town synonymous with night life, prostitutes, and gangs.

9 "That's the Berliner Air, Air, Air!" is an English translation of *Berliner Luft*, which has several meanings. Beginning in the late 19th century it referred to a particular dessert made from custard vanilla cream and topped with raspberry sauce, and in 1904 it was the name of a hit song "*Berliner Luft*" or "*Das ist die Berliner Luft*" (That's the Berlin Air). During the Cold War, the phrase was often used to describe the feeling of freedom and excitement associated with Berlin.

10 A *Patenbetrieb* was system particular to the GDR in which two institutions were linked, with one acting as the mentor or sponsor (*Paten*) for the other. A mineworkers' brigade, for instance, might sponsor a nearby school, cultivating ties and participating in joint activities.

11 A reference to the East German Uprising, June 16-17, 1953. After the Communist Party-led East German state announced that it would be raising the heavily subsidized price of meat and introduce more stringent productivity quotas, East German workers protested, demanding not only a return to the original prices and quotas, but also for the Soviet tanks to withdraw from Berlin. The East German authorities responded by turning to the Soviets for help putting down the uprising with a joint military force, resulting in the deaths of fifty-five people and the arrest of roughly 15,000 more.

12 Isaiah 53:6, 8, 12. Described as the servant of God, who will be exalted, this person is identified in the introduction to Isaiah 53.

13 When announcing the state of total war, Göring had declared that he wanted to be called "Meier" if an enemy aircraft ever reached Germany.

14 A quorum of ten men who represent the ten tribes of Israel for the prescribed prayers in the synagogue.

www.ingramcontent.com/pod-product-compliance
Lightning Source LLC
Chambersburg PA
CBHW010451310726
48979CB00013B/2154/J

* 9 7 8 1 6 8 5 7 7 0 1 7 4 *